"LORD RAGNAR, MAY I ASK YOU A QUESTION?"

"If you'd like."

"Do you not like me?"

Unsure where this might be going, Ragnar simply stated, "I thought our relationship was decided two years ago, princess."

"But that was such a long time ago. There's no reason for us not to be friends now."

"Friends? You and I?"

She stroked her claw along his shoulder, down his chest, her talons scraping against the scar her tail had left. Part of Ragnar wanted to break every talon she had out of pure spite. Yet another, weaker, part of him wanted to close his eyes and moan.

"I know what you're thinking," she said, her talons now concentrating on that scar. "That I'm too good for you. And, of course among some circles, you'd absolutely right. But I'm a very progressive royal and I don't let little things like unimpressive bloodlines and barbaric tendencies stop me from having the friends I want."

"That's very big of you."

"I've always thought so." She pressed her claw to his chest, the damn scar under it angrily throbbing to life. "I've always thought it's more important to have friends you can trust," she murmured, "than friends who are merely your equal in every other way that matters."

No. He couldn't do it. He couldn't keep talking to this vapid, insipid female. No matter how much his body longed for her . . .

More by G.A. Aiken

Dragon Actually

About a Dragon

What a Dragon Should Know

Published by Zebra Books

LAST DRAGON STANDING

G.A. AIKEN

ZEBRA BOOKS
KENSINGTON PUBLISHING CORP.
http://www.kensingtonbooks.com

ZEBRA BOOKS are published by

Kensington Publishing Corp.
119 West 40th Street
New York, NY 10018

All Kensington titles, imprints and distributed lines are available at special quantity discounts for bulk purchases for sales promotion, premiums, fund-raising, educational or institutional use.

Special book excerpts or customized printings can also be created to fit specific needs. For details, write or phone the office of the Kensington Special Sales Manager: Kensington Publishing Corp., 119 West 40th Street, New York, NY 10018. Attn. Special Sales Department. Phone: 1-800-221-2647.

Zebra and the Z logo Reg. U.S. Pat. & TM Off.

ISBN-13: 978-1-4201-0888-0
ISBN-10: 1-4201-0888-3

First Printing: September 2010
10 9 8 7 6 5 4 3 2 1

Printed in the United States of America

To Kate Duffy

Prologue

"The queen knows we have her daughter?"

Ragnar the Cunning of the Olgeirsson Horde nodded at his brother Vigholf's question.

"And she told you to do what you want with her?"

Again, he nodded.

Vigholf shook his head. "I don't understand."

And neither did Ragnar. He didn't understand any mother—royal or low-born—who seemed to have so little concern for her own offspring. Even one as annoying and devious as the royal pain in the ass currently plotting away in the cave behind them.

Wearing nothing but a gown two sizes too large for her human frame, shackles, and a Magickally infused collar that prevented her from shifting to her natural She-dragon form, Princess Keita of the House of Gwalchmai fab Gwyar had managed to enrapture nearly every male on this venture without doing much more than being a rather dim-witted beauty. She giggled, she teased, she tormented. To be quite honest, Ragnar had hoped the royal's mother would demand her return this very evening so that he could be rid of the brat before she turned blood relation against blood relation. But the last thing Queen Rhiannon had said about her daughter would stay with him for a very long time: "Keep her. Let her go. Makes me no never mind."

Ragnar could never imagine his own mother saying those words about him or any of his brothers and one sister. Although he *could* imagine his father Olgeir, Dragonlord of the Olgeirsson Horde, saying it.

"Well," one of his cousins said, getting to his feet. They'd all remained in their human forms because it was easier to hide from the Fire Breathers that way while on Southland territory. "If they don't want her, we'll keep her then."

Ragnar looked at his brother, and Vigholf quickly lowered his head to hide his laughter. He'd warned Vigholf this would happen if they spent another moment with that viperous female. "We're not keeping her."

"Why the hells not?"

Ragnar thought about throttling the young pup, but decided against it. "Because we don't do that anymore."

"But if her own mum said—"

"If you want a female, boy, you'll have to do it like everyone else—charm her, seduce her, get her to fall in love with you."

Ragnar's cousins glanced back and forth between them before one asked, "And how do we do that then?"

Vigholf's laugh exploded out of him, and Ragnar headed back into the cave, grumbling all the way.

He was exhausted, worn down, and had much more work to do before he left this overly heated land and the last thing he intended to deal with was the idiotic questions of his idiotic kin.

This had all started so simply a few days ago. News of his father having caught the foolish Southland royal on Northland territory had reached Ragnar, and with the help of his brother, he'd moved quickly. He'd planned on sneaking back into his one-time home with the help of his mother, but while on his way she'd urgently contacted him through the lines of Magick and told him that the royal had managed to escape.

He'd caught the princess not far from his father's mountain base and used the underground tunnels to bring her back to her homelands. From there, he'd planned to negotiate an alliance with the Southland Dragon Queen that would allow him to take over the Olgeirsson Horde and, should all go well, the Northland territories. Unifying the Hordes would be his first step—keeping them unified his next.

But the queen had surprised him. Not only had she known from the beginning that Ragnar had her daughter, she'd known that Olgeir had had her daughter before—and she'd done absolutely nothing about it.

Times like this he was grateful the gods had blessed him with his mother, although he did wish that the gods had given her a mate more deserving of her beauty and wisdom than Olgeir the Wastrel.

Ragnar walked down the long cavern until he reached the alcove where they'd placed the princess. He stopped right outside, his teeth gritting as he watched the oldest of his cousins, Meinhard, hold a chalice of wine up to the royal's lips. Her dark brown eyes focused solely on the big male, Princess Keita sipped from the cup, her small fingers lying over Meinhard's big ones. When she'd had enough, she leaned back, her tongue swiping her bottom lip, then her top.

He could hear his cousin growling from here, and Ragnar had no patience for it.

"Out," Ragnar ordered, walking in to the alcove.

Not remotely as intimidated by him as the younger dragons, Meinhard slowly stood tall and said, "I think I'll stay."

Ragnar knew his kin had yet to accept him as their leader. With his father still alive and well, Olgeir's grip tight over the Horde, it wasn't surprising. But Meinhard, like the others, would have to learn that Ragnar brooked no disobedience.

Flicking his wrist and muttering a small chant, Ragnar sent his cousin sailing out of the alcove, the wine cup flying across the stone floor.

"You *bastard*!" Meinhard yelled from outside the cavern.

Ignoring him, Ragnar stepped up to the royal. He could see what had his kin so tantalized, even though it was only her petite human form they'd seen since they'd caught her escaping his father's clutches. All that dark red hair reaching to her knees, perfectly etched cheekbones, a small nose with a light spattering of freckles across the bridge, and those amazingly full lips. But for Ragnar it was those dark brown eyes that held him in thrall. They were endless, a fathomless dark pit any male could get lost in. Too bad Ragnar had no intention of being any male—no matter how much he might wish he was at the moment.

"Well?" she asked, her voice low. "What do you intend to do with me, my lord?"

Ragnar didn't answer right away, his mind too busy turning, wondering what the pair of them could do together with nothing more than a mattress and a week's supply of food and water. So she yawned, using it as an excuse to lift her shackled hands over her head and stretch her entire body in one long, sinuous line. Then she smiled. The most seductive of smiles that Ragnar had ever seen. He almost hated her for that smile alone.

Ragnar waved his hand, and the shackles fell away, one of them slamming against the top of the royal's head.

"Ow! You barbaric oaf!"

He almost laughed because there she was. The true spoiled royal, and the reason it had been necessary to shackle her in the first place. She'd tried running away several times during their journey, and Ragnar had gotten fed up with it. She had nowhere to go so far underground, so all she'd managed to do was delay them.

Ragnar turned from her and headed toward the exit. He was hungry and longed for sleep. He had a meeting with the queen in a few hours, and he needed at least a little rest.

"Wait."

He stopped, sighed, and faced her. "What?"

She stood, pointed at the collar around her throat. "What about this?"

"It will fall off once you're clear of this place and my kin." The last thing he needed was for her to turn into her natural form here, now, sending his kin into new feats of stupidity once they got a good look at her tail. "Now go."

"That's it? But . . . what did you get for me?"

"Get for you?"

"From my kin? How much gold?" She lifted her chin. "I'm sure I was worth quite a lot, but that won't protect you from my brothers when they find out what you did to me."

"I rescued you."

"I rescued *myself*. But nice try."

Did she really think his father would have let her go? Did she really think Olgeir wouldn't have caught her before she got off Horde territory? And Ragnar's father did things the Old Way when challenged. Princess Keita would have lost at least one wing and been handed over to the most brutish of Ragnar's kin as retribution for her escape. In the end, she would have ended up just like Ragnar's mother. The only difference being that Ragnar's mother was the epitome of class and breeding and a good mind. Princess Keita, however, was everything royals were rumored to be. Weak, silly, and a waste of Ragnar's time and energy. No matter how gorgeous or enticing.

"Call it what you like," he told her. "But either way, you can go."

"Just like that?"

"Yes. Just like that."

She went up on her toes, trying to peer around his shoulders. "Is there no one here to escort me?"

"No." He would offer one of his cousins, but that would be a bad idea right now.

The royal studied him for several long moments until she

slammed her hands on her hips. "What did that old cow give you to release me? And don't lie, barbarian. I always know when I'm being lied to."

She didn't want him to lie, he wouldn't. "She gave me nothing."

"So no alliance?" She shook her head as if she pitied him. "You idiot."

Ragnar blinked. "Pardon?"

"How could you be so stupid? Were you rude to her? Was that it? Gods, you really are as oafish as your father, aren't you?"

There were no other words she could have said to cause more damage than those.

Completely oblivious, she raised her hands and said, "Don't panic. I'm sure I can fix it. I'll talk to my father. I'm sure I can convince him to—"

"No, no, my lady. You misunderstand." And Ragnar couldn't help smiling a little. "Your mother made no offer for you, but the alliance will still move forward. I meet her in a few hours to discuss details."

Her arms fell to her sides. "The alliance is still in play?"

"Oh yes. The queen didn't seem interested in you at all, though. Perhaps if I'd taken your sister instead. Morfyd the . . . White? Yes? Perhaps then things would have played out differently. But, as it is, you've had no effect whatsoever on the proceedings."

The royal stared at him, her beautiful mouth opening and closing several times. Ragnar felt as if he'd struck her—and was appalled by it. Immediately he went toward her to soothe, terrified he'd see tears, and he didn't know how to handle tears. But the royal didn't cry . . . she screamed. She screamed like something that had crawled out of a demon pit.

"*That vicious cunty whore!*"

Shocked, Ragnar took a step back and watched the royal pace, her arms waving dramatically over her head, while she called her own mother all sorts of vile names that even the worst pirates would never use.

His kin charged into the cavern, concerned something had happened to their delicate little princess, all of them halting by Ragnar's side.

"I'd kill the bitch myself if I actually thought she'd *stay dead*! But demons live forever." She faced them. "*Don't they?*"

All but Ragnar nodded at her insane bellowing, and when she swung her arms wildly at them, screaming, "All of you— *out of my way*!" they all did as she bade.

She stormed out, but returned a moment later, her rage seemingly—and disturbingly—gone as she asked Ragnar, "You enjoyed telling me that—about my mother. Didn't you?"

"Yes," he replied. "I guess I did." How could he not enjoy it, seeing as it allowed him to reveal the royal's true nature to his kin? Now they'd see the dim-witted princess for what she really was: a cursing, snarling, spoiled royal with the most amazing ass ever created by the gods—*No, wait. What?*

"Good," she told him. "Enjoy that feeling while you can, Lord Ragnar."

"Why? What do you think you can do to me?" And when Meinhard punched him in the back for his rudeness, Ragnar totally ignored the pain.

She smiled—his kin sighing around him—and reached up with one hand, fingers stroking Ragnar's jaw, his neck, trailing down to a spot on his chest. When she was done, she stepped back, gave a small bow of her head. "My lords."

Then she daintily lifted the hem of her skirt so it didn't drag on the ground, and left them all standing there, gazing after her.

"That, lads," Meinhard sighed after she'd gone, "is a fine lady and should be treated as such."

And several hours later, after his father had been killed

by human females, an alliance was in place with the Fire
Breathers, and Ragnar was busy trying to staunch the exces-
sive flow of blood caused by a vengeful princess, he'd remember exactly how big a lot of idiots he'd been cursed with
as kin!

Chapter One

Two years later . . .

Was he supposed to be dead?

Keita the Red Viper Dragon of Despair and Death—Keita the Viper, for short—leaned in a little closer and sniffed the male human lying prone in his bed.

He definitely smelled dead. And she could hear no heartbeat, nor the sound of blood rushing through tiny little human veins. All things she could easily do when a living being was anywhere within a one hundred–foot radius of her.

But this human, the Outerplains Baron Lord Bampour that once was, was not supposed to be dead. Not yet. Not until she'd actually killed him.

Letting out a breath, Keita stood straight and placed her hands on her hips. She wore a gown given to her by the late Baron Lord, made of the finest silks gold coin could buy. She also had on the bracelet he'd given her, a thick gold bangle, and the matching necklace. She hadn't asked for these things, but, as happened with most needy males, he'd happily given them to her. She knew why, too. In the hopes that she'd give him a lusty ride and enthusiastic cries of ecstasy . . . blah, blah, blah.

Males were all the same. A few compliments, a sweet smile, a little teasing, and Keita would be inundated with goods she'd never asked for and didn't necessarily want. She didn't mind, though. If males wanted to give her things, why should she stop them? What irritated her, though, what had always irritated her, was the belief some men had that a few gifts would somehow gain them access to her bed. They didn't. In fact, Keita chose her bedmates as carefully as she chose the accessories for a particular gown. Males on a whole were far too irritating for her to ever think of letting those who brought nothing but gifts, and little else, into her life.

As she explained to a friend once, "I'll take their gifts, but that doesn't mean I'll take their cocks."

So she'd taken the Baron Lord's gifts. Happily, for unlike some, he had excellent taste. She'd also put up with him for the last three weeks. Him and his son. She'd bedded neither and had had no intention of doing so. Mostly because she had no desire to, but also because Keita had come here with a purpose. For Bampour had crossed a line that made him a danger to those Keita loved. Too bad, though, someone had beaten her to the task. Especially since she was ever so good at taking care of such things.

Debating whether she should get rid of the body herself, she heard it. An extra heartbeat in the room that did not belong to the late Baron Lord since his heart had already stopped beating.

Keita looked over her shoulder, eyes narrowing on a dark corner. That's when the human came rushing out. She wore only a sheet, blond hair loose around her shoulders, small blade slashing wildly.

Keita grabbed the woman's wrist and twisted, putting her on her knees. She thought about breaking that wrist just because the little bitch had come dangerously close to cutting

Keita's precious face, but the banging on the door quickly pulled that option from the table.

"Open this door!"

Keita looked down at the woman. She could snap her neck and be gone, but it didn't seem right when the blond had only done what needed to be done anyway.

"It's your lucky day, wench," she said over the continued banging.

Keita released the human and ran to the largest of the windows. She pushed it open. It was small but would do. "Ren!" she called out.

"I'm here."

"Hold on then!"

The woman watched Keita rush back to her. "What are you going to—eeeh!"

Keita swung the human up into her arms, spun on her heel for a little momentum, and flung the female through the open window. Poor thing squealed until strong arms outside that window caught her.

"Got her!"

"Take her. Go."

"What about—"

"Go!"

"Break it open!" someone yelled from the other side of the door.

A second later, the door flew open and guards marched in. The Baron Lord's aide walked in behind the guards. He looked Keita over, his lip curling in disgust. They hadn't liked each other from the beginning. Then he focused on the bed. He walked over quickly and pressed his fingers to the Baron Lord's throat. "Get the Baron Lord's son," he ordered one guard. When the guard ran off, the aide paced in front of Keita.

"I know how this looks—" she began.

"*Silence!*"

Her arms crossed in front of her chest, Keita told him, "Well, you don't have to be rude about it!"

Good day, my little thunderstorm!

Ragnar the Cunning of the Olgeirsson Horde sighed loudly and said without thought, "Do not call me those pet names, insolent female."

"What?"

Shit, piss, and death. He'd forgotten he wasn't alone. No. He was in an extremely long meeting with the representatives of the other Hordes he and his kin hadn't crushed beneath their claws. An important meeting since the war of the last two years was nearly behind them and a time of peace was—he hoped—sometime in their future.

Then again, if the other Hordes all thought he was mad, the peace he hoped for could easily slip away.

I'm not going away, a singsong voice said in his head. She always said these things in that singsong voice. It irritated him beyond all reason, and Ragnar was all about reason.

Knowing she truly would not go away, Ragnar lifted off his haunches and said, "If you all will excuse me, Vigholf will keep things going until my return."

Vigholf, one side of his mouth raised in a grin, nodded and returned his attention to the representatives. Vigholf knew who drove his brother insane, and he found it amusing. "She never calls to me," he'd whined more than once, forcing Ragnar to lob a boulder at his sibling's head. Most of the time, though, Vigholf moved out of the way fast enough to avoid any real damage.

Ragnar walked through the Olgeirsson stronghold, which had been passed down from generation to generation for thousands of years, from dragonlord to dragonlord. Yet it was rarely handed over like someone passing the cream. Instead it was usually taken. It would have been taken from Ragnar's father as Olgeir the Wastrel had taken it from his father, but Ragnar never had the chance. His father, so determined to bring his son to heel, had stupidly followed him into the Southlands and had fallen to the swords of human females. Although Ragnar had not allowed the truth of that to spread past the Southland borders. Going against his innate sense of pride, Ragnar had claimed that kill as his own. Not because he wanted to, but because it was necessary. To be the son of a dragonlord who couldn't fight off two women was to come from a weak bloodline, something Ragnar and his siblings simply could not afford if he hoped to calm the unrest his father had been stirring up for centuries by being a right bastard.

Through caverns and alcoves he moved, trying his best to ignore the humming inside his head. Yes. She was humming. In his head. He hated humming in general. It was one of those annoying habits many had that, to Ragnar, only proved their weakness. People couldn't stand the silence, the quiet, so they hummed. But this female . . . she hummed because she knew it annoyed him. She *enjoyed* that it annoyed him.

"I'd have been better off selling my soul to demons from the underworld than this wench."

What was that? I didn't hear you clearly, my raging tsunami.

Gods, and the nicknames. He hated nicknames almost as much as he hated humming.

Honestly, Ragnar had met some brutal females over the last two and a half centuries of his existence, but none quite like this one. None who seemed as heartless as the Northlands were cold. But she'd served a purpose these last two years. A purpose that he could not now ignore because she wore at his brain the way sand wore at his scales.

Ragnar walked out onto one of the mountain plateaus. Brutal winds from the nearby ocean brought ice and snow across his field of vision and nearly froze his claws to the ground beneath him. Few of his kin knew why he came out here, where it was icy cold whether summer or winter, spring or fall. But his kin couldn't feel the Magick that came up through this sacred space. Only he and those who studied the Magickal arts knew the true worth of a place like this, a worth that made risking the freezing winds and ice quite rational.

Ragnar closed his eyes and raised his left front claw. He called to the gods who watched over him and his Horde, who endowed him with powers that few of his kind were lucky enough to ever have. The Horde dragons, like all North-landers, were about war and strength and battle skills. They also believed that Magick was for the old females who lived alone in caves or small houses talking to their gods, or for males not worthy of picking up a sword or a warhammer. Magick was definitely not for dragonlords who hoped to eventually rule not only one Horde but many. Perhaps all. But Ragnar never bothered to fool himself on how far he could go among his own kind. His time as Dragonlord Chief of all the Hordes would not last long. He knew that, understood it, and already had plans to transition the title and most of the power to his brother. Vigholf didn't know that, though. Not yet. Why bother him with the little details?

And although not being Dragonlord Chief until his last breath was something that should bother Ragnar, it didn't. He'd known from early on that his life would never be simple. If he'd chosen one path or the other, either warrior or mage, his kin would be fine with that. Yet he'd chosen both paths. Ragnar simply couldn't imagine not getting up early in the morning, at the coldest part of the day in the Northlands, and training hard with his favorite sword and ax. He also could not imagine not going to the ocean when the moon was at its fullest, and offering up a sacrifice of his blood to the gods. All of these things were a part of him; he refused to choose one over the other.

Yet raw ambition had never been Ragnar's goal. To see how far he could go in the shortest amount of time. What an empty, useless goal. Instead, he simply wanted more for his people. For the Horde dragons who populated the mighty Northland Mountains he wanted more than the hard life they'd all endured for so many eons. Yet that didn't mean they needed to be as ridiculously lazy as the Southland dragons; or constantly dazzled by their own brilliance like the East-landers; or superior to all beings that had or ever would live, like the Iron dragons of the west; or purposely cut off and removed from everything outside their own territories like the Sand dragons. In other words, Ragnar wanted more for his kind than merely a higher level of being annoying.

The brutal winds faded away, and the warmth of the two suns beat down upon Ragnar's head. He opened his eyes and saw her. She stood by a tree, picking the ripe fruit with her tail and watching him.

"Hello, my cheery squall," she said, smiling. So many fangs for a dragoness not yet that old. All bright white and twinkling like stars in the sky.

Ragnar dipped his head and said, "Queen Rhiannon. You summoned me."

"I did, Dragonlord. I did." She pulled a fruit down and tossed it to him. Ragnar caught it, marveling at the feel of it in his claw. Gods, now this was power. She'd not only created a space for them to meet between worlds, but a space where everything felt real and *was* real. The grass beneath his claws, the light wind blowing against his neck, the crows and hawks playing in the trees. Ragnar could never create something like this. He wasn't powerful enough. But he hoped to be. One day.

"So you are finally Dragonlord Chief of the Hordes."

"At the moment."

"Gods. Are there already those trying to take it from you? Do you Lightnings not rest?"

"It's not that someone's trying to take my title away. Instead, when the time is right, I plan to hand it to my brother."

Her white head cocked to the side, her white horns glinting in the sunlight. "You'd give up your power?"

"I'd do what is best for my people, lady."

She let out a little laugh, her white claw covering her snout. "You are just so damn adorable."

"It wasn't me, you fool," Keita continued to argue. "I didn't kill the old bastard. And you can't prove otherwise."

"Really?" The aide stopped in front of her and caught hold of her hand. He turned it, palm up, and peeled back the sleeve of her gown. "And what's this then, my lady?" He snatched the vial she'd tied to her wrist and uncorked it. He sniffed. "Kitto Bloom." He held up the vial. "Three drops of this on the tongue and your victim would be dead in seconds."

"Very true. But there'd be much more blood and some suffering. Look at him. He clearly didn't suffer. So it couldn't have been the Kitto Bloom, which means it wasn't me!" She smiled, proud of her logic.

"Right," the aide said.

"Right," Keita said, her grin growing wider.

The aide motioned to the guards. "Take this murdering bitch to the dungeons."

"Dungeons? But I already explained that it wasn't me. This is a complete injustice!"

Two guards grabbed her arms and pulled her out of the room.

"You'll regret this, servant!"

They took her down the backstairs and through the kitchens. With more guards falling in behind them, they all took another set of stairs down into the bowels of the Baron Lord's fortress.

They took Keita to a large cell filled with at least ten men.

"See how you like spending your time with these blokes, you murdering whore!"

They shoved her inside and slammed the cell door behind her.

"But it wasn't me!" she yelled, which they completely ignored. "Well . . . aren't you at least going to give me something to eat? I haven't had first meal yet. I'm starving!"

Laughing at her, the guards locked the gate, and one of the men ordered an enormous dog with a spiked collar, "Watch her, boy. If she sticks an arm out, tear it off." The guards laughed more and walked off.

Annoyed and truly starving, Keita stamped her bare foot and crossed her arms over her chest. "This isn't fair. You should at least feed your prisoners."

Hoping the guards would return with some food, she faced the other prisoners.

"I can assure you I've murdered no one. Today," she told them. "Nor am I a whore. Unless, of course, you're talking to my sister. But she doesn't count because she's an uptight prissy tail."

One of the prisoners, a very large, swarthy fellow, slowly stood. Keita watched him, but after about three steps in her direction, he stopped, swallowed, and backed up again.

Not surprising, really. Keita had found over the years that predators knew predators. And smart predators knew when they were in the presence of something much more dangerous than they could ever hope to be.

Already bored beyond all reckoning, Keita again faced the front of the cell. She knew she could shift to her natural form and escape this dungeon. True, she was small compared to many She-dragons, but her true form would still go through at least the kitchen and servants quarters above and possibly the floor above that. Plus she'd destroy at least three of the walls around her and many humans. Not only the bastards who'd put her here, but possibly the sweet servant girl who combed her hair at night, the old baker who always made sure to set aside treats for her, and the house maid who kept her laughing with all sorts of castle gossip. Killing them would be unfair in

Keita's estimation, since their only mistake would be that they were merely in the wrong place at the wrong time.

No, Keita didn't like that idea at all. So she'd wait. She had talked herself out of worse situations—she'd do it again.

So Keita stared through all those bars hoping to see the guards returning with something to eat. When they didn't, she rested her hands on two of the bars and that's when the guard dog right outside her cell leaped at her, snarling and snapping at her hands.

She immediately pulled away and watched the crazed beast attack the bars again for good measure.

Keita smiled and said, "Why . . . hello there, you yummy-looking little thing you."

"Do you hope to convince me, my little rain droplet, that you'd give up your power? We both know that sometimes it's what's behind the throne that is the true power. But tell me, my adorable lightning strike, does your brother know he'll be your puppet? Or is he big and dim-witted like your father?"

"Is there a reason you summoned me, Queen Rhiannon?"

"Oooh. Terse. I must have struck a barbarian nerve."

"Your Majesty . . ."

She held up a white claw. "Aye. There is a reason I've summoned you. I have need of a favor. Two favors, in fact."

"And they are?"

"Well, one is my son."

"Your son?"

"Yes. My youngest?"

Ragnar stared at her.

"He's been with you for two years? So he could learn the illustrious warrior ways of the Lightnings?"

Ragnar still stared.

"He's very tall? Very wide . . . very blue?"

"Oh. Right." *The idiot.* Well . . . he wasn't exactly an idiot.

Just young. Very young. Offspring in the Northlands grew up fast, usually heading into battle before they were fifty winters. But the Southlanders babied their offspring and often those spoiled creatures weren't ready for much until a century or more passed. The queen's youngest had that issue. But because he was Southland royalty and the fact that Ragnar's cousin Meinhard looked out for him, the warriors left him alone. Yet that, and the fact that the young dragon was very good at quickly and efficiently clearing out trees with his bare claws, was all that kept that idiot safe from daily sound beatings. Like Ragnar, the queen's son liked to read, but he also liked to daydream and eat. By the gods, could that dragon eat. When they had to have additional cattle shipped in, Ragnar felt it was strictly due to that damn royal. And when he wasn't eating, reading, or daydreaming, the Blue spent the rest of his time trying to sneak off so he could indulge his ridiculous whims with the tavern girls in the human towns below. He spent a lot of his time in the human towns.

Yet Ragnar never cared about any of this. Not really. For the royal had served a purpose. He represented the goodwill and alliance of the Southland Queen during a time of war among the Hordes. So Ragnar, Vigholf, and Meinhard made it their business to ensure the young royal was kept alive and mostly intact.

"Well," the queen went on, "I want him to come home for a family feast that will take place in the next two weeks."

That would work. If the royal went home, perhaps he'd never return. He was no longer needed, and it would be one less thing for Ragnar to worry about.

"Of course. He has my permission to go."

"Excellent! And when will you two leave?"

Ragnar frowned, his instincts warning him of a trap. "Pardon?"

"You're coming with him." Did it ever occur to these royals to *ask* rather than order? No. Probably not.

"My lady, if you are fearing for his safety, my best warriors will be—"

"You, Dragonlord. *You* will accompany my son back to the Southland."

"And why would *I* do that?"

"Simple. Because it would be a grave mistake for you *not* to bring my son back here."

"I was hoping we were beyond threats, Queen Rhiannon."

She came toward him then, moving in until there was only a tail-tip length between them. She dropped several more pieces of fruit at Ragnar's claws before reaching out and pressing her own claw against the side of his jaw, her talons caressing him there. Amazing. He was still on that freezing plateau and she was thousands of leagues away in her court, but it was easy to forget all that when he could actually feel her touch against his scales.

"We *are* beyond threats, dear boy. We are. That's why you must do this. Leave today, tonight—and bring my son. He'll be a good excuse of why you have to be here."

"An excuse?"

"Trust me, Ragnar."

It was true, Queen Rhiannon could be luring him into a trap. She could have her Dragonwarriors waiting for him as soon as he crossed into Southland territories. She could do a lot of things. And yet . . . he didn't think she'd bother.

"As you wish."

It was brief, but he saw the relief that washed over her features before she dredged up that false smile, created specifically to hide any truth she might reveal.

"Excellent. I can't wait to see my son. I've missed him so." She backed up until she could turn without hitting Ragnar with her tail and walked back to her tree.

"You said there was another favor."

"Oh, aye. There's a witch who lives in the Woods of Desolation in the Outerplains. A dragoness, but she lives as human."

"Yes. I know her."

"Of course you do. So does my son Gwenvael. And my youngest daughter." She looked over her shoulder at him. "You remember my daughter, don't you, my lord? Keita?"

Ragnar worked hard not to sneer. "Yes. I remember Keita." Keita the Brat. Keita the Nightmare. Keita the Late Night Fantasy when he'd had too much to drink.

How was he expected to forget her? He was a dragon, not a saint.

"Of course you do. She's so beautiful it's hard for males to ever forget her. Perhaps, if you're lucky enough, she'll be attending the feast and you two can become reacquainted."

"I doubt I'll have time to stay for the feast, lady. Although I appreciate the offer."

"I understand." The queen watched him for a moment longer before pointing at him with one of her talons. "Do you need some ointment for that, my little rolling thunder?"

Confused, Ragnar looked down and realized he was scratching his chest again. Right on the scar that cut through his thick purple scales. The same one that spoiled royal had given him two years ago when she'd snuck up on him and stabbed him with her tail. Even after he'd rescued her useless life.

Ragnar snatched his claw back.

"No. Thank you."

"Nasty scar. Some take forever to heal."

"The witch in the woods, lady?"

"Oh, yes, yes. Be ever so kind and bring her to me. Alive."

"Why?"

"Well, she is my sister and traitor to my throne, so if anyone should take her head, it should be me. Don't you agree?"

Gods. Esyld. She wanted Esyld. A powerful witch and excellent healer, Esyld had been a part of the Outerplains as long as Ragnar could remember. And, unlike many others, he'd known for years who she was. The sister of Queen Rhiannon who'd fled the Southlands when her sister came into power. For that reason alone, and no other from what he'd been able to tell, Esyld the Beautiful had become Esyld the Traitor among those loyal to the queen.

"Or you can leave her there, Your Majesty," he suggested. "She's causing you no harm."

"My, my, you do seem to know my sister well." She chuckled. "But you'll bring her to me."

"And if I don't?"

"Simple. I'll unleash my mate's crazed relatives on her like a pack of ravening wolves on a wounded deer. Would you prefer that?"

"When we spoke two years ago, you knew where your sister was. But you choose now to capture her. Why?"

"Because you never know . . . some attractive young thinker of a dragon may be able to save her useless life. But only if she makes it to me alive. And my mate's kin will ensure that she *never* makes it to me alive. They do so loathe traitors."

"And you're so sure she's a traitor?"

Her grin was cruel. "I don't have to be sure. I'm queen. Now"—she tossed him another fruit with her tail before again focusing on her tree—"good travels, my light drizzle. I do look forward to seeing you again in person. Oh!" She held up a talon, her gaze focusing far off before she sighed, shook her head, muttered to herself something like, "That girl," and then said to Ragnar, "And one other thing . . ."

"Yes?"

"Do you know a Lord Bamp . . . something? In the Outerplains?"

"Bampour?" She shrugged at this question. "Yes, I know him." A very unpleasant bastard that Ragnar had only mild dealings with over the years. "What about him?"

"I wouldn't fly *over* his territory. You might be better off walking through it."

He normally would avoid the town and the Baron Lord's lands altogether, but it was easiest to get to the forest where Esyld the Wise lived from there. "Why?"

"Must you question everything, my perky little downpour?"

"As a matter of fact—"

All the beauty around Ragnar shimmered, and the spell ended, taking the suns, the grass, the trees, and the unstable monarch with it.

"—yes!"

He was back on his plateau, the ripe fruit the queen had tossed at him resting by his claws. Gods. That female.

Letting out a breath, Ragnar picked up a piece of fruit and held it between his talons.

But . . . such power.

Yet before he could sit and ponder how she managed to do something so amazing, that damn itching started again!

Throwing down the fruit, Ragnar scratched at the healed wound on this chest. Healed it might be, but the itching. Gods, the itching! Some days it drove him mad. Especially when he had his armor on. And nothing he'd tried in the last two years had done much to stop it. He'd tried ointments, spells, creams . . . everything! Some days he could barely think because of the damn itching. And sometimes he forgot about the wound altogether for days, even months. But now that the damn queen had pointed it out . . .

Roaring in annoyance, Ragnar shifted to human, dropped to one knee, and scratched at the human flesh for all he was worth. Short of ripping his scales off—something he was loath to do—this was the only way to really scratch the damn thing properly. In fact, his human fingers scratching against his chest felt so good, he didn't even notice the freezing cold or that he was no longer alone.

"Uh . . . brother?"

Ragnar's hand stopped on his chest, but he didn't turn around. "What?"

"The others are wondering if you're returning. Or should I leave you to keep . . . touching yourself? And where did that fruit come from?"

"I am not touching—" Ragnar stopped his reply. Honestly, why bother? "Who can take over for us for the next few weeks?"

"Us?"

"You, me, and Meinhard." Their cousin was a mighty fighter and always good backup in any situation. Plus, he was loyal—and loyalty meant all to Ragnar.

"Uncle Askel. He's back from the Ice Land borders, and he'll keep this rabble in line."

"Good. We leave in two hours."

"Leave for where?"

"The Southlands. And we're bringing the royal. So you best fetch him."

"I'll take care of it."

Ragnar nodded and stared out over his cold and brutal Northland home. He wished he could ignore the Dragon Queen's orders, but something told him that would be a very foolish thing to do. He was never foolish. He didn't have that luxury. So he'd return to the Southlands and risk not only his safety among the lazy Fire Breathers, but also meeting up with the one dragoness he hoped never to see again.

And as Ragnar thought of the cruel viper, his hand reached for the itchy scar on his chest once more. He stopped in mid-reach, though, when he realized he was still not alone.

"Something else, brother?" Ragnar asked.

"Well . . . are you going to eat all that fruit or just leave it out here to freeze into useless lumps?"

Ragnar swept up the fruit with both hands and pitched

them, one after the other, at his brother's big, fat, scale-covered forehead.

When he'd driven Vigholf back inside, Ragnar again faced the mountains he called home while his brother complained, "You could have just *handed* them to me, Ragnar!"

He was Lord Bampour now. He ruled this land. Of course, there would have to be an appropriate period of mourning, but then, once that was done, he'd take everything in hand.

But first, before he'd bother worrying about all that, he'd see his father's killer up close.

His men had left her alone with some of the worst scum that could be found on his father's . . . no, *his* lands. Not long enough to kill her, but long enough to make her realize that the days before her execution would be the worst of her life. She deserved it, of course. One, because she'd killed his father. And two, because the little whore had turned him down flat when he'd asked her to his bed. Even after he'd given her those lovely earrings.

Aye. Her last days on this earth would make her regret that decision. He'd make sure of it.

Following behind his men, Lord Bampour walked into the farthest part of the dungeon. His men had stopped a few feet away from that bitch's cell and didn't move.

Filled with anticipation, he impatiently pushed past them. The little whore had her back to them, and he called out, "Well, my lady—"

Startled, she spun around, her eyes wide, her mouth still chewing, a long tail hanging from her lips.

Lord Bampour and his men looked at the spot where the vicious mongrel they kept to keep these scum in line used to sit. His long chain was still there, the last ring pulled open. As one, Bampour and his men returned their gazes to the woman. Still chewing, she held up one finger, asking them to wait.

His men took a step back, but Bampour examined the cell. A leather collar, torn open, lay at her dainty bare feet. And the other murderers, rapists, and thieves who shared the cell with her were backed into one corner. Eyes wide, all of them shaking in terror, they pushed against each other—one of them even trying to claw his way out of the cell using his bare hands.

Bampour looked at her again. She sucked the tail into her mouth like a wet noodle and swallowed. "Let me explain—" she began.

Bampour shook his head. "Move back," he ordered his men.

"Wait. I didn't kill your father. It wasn't me."

"Move back!" he ordered again.

"And no one would feed me. And the dog . . . how many more years could he have had? I'm sure that"—she gave a delicate cough—"this is a misunderstanding that we"—another cough—"can easily clear up. If you just let me explain—"

She stopped talking, pressed her hand to her stomach, coughed . . . coughed again, then retched.

A good-sized skull, perfectly cleaned as if washed in acid, long fangs locked together, extended jaw and nose suggesting a snout where a wet nose once was, flew out of the woman's mouth, hit the ground, and bounced across the floor several times before landing in front of the closed cell door.

The silence that followed was almost physically painful, and Bampour watched as small white teeth nibbled gently on a plump bottom lip until the woman finally said, "I can explain that too. . . ."

Bampour didn't give her a chance. He screamed. Gods in the heaven, he screamed like a woman and ran. He ran, his men right beside him, the scum they'd left behind yelling for mercy, begging to be released from their cell.

Bampour and his men didn't stop running until they'd made it around the corner and back to the jailer's desk. With several guards pointing their pikes at the door they'd just come through, Bampour tried to catch his breath and think.

"What do we do, my lord?" his father's old aide asked him.

"What do you think we do? We have a battalion of my soldiers guard this dungeon, and when the executioner arrives, we kill that bitch. Understand?"

"Aye, my lord."

Getting back his breath as well as his reason, Bampour began to relax, the entire dungeon again quiet.

Then that voice that, only a few days ago, he'd thought so alluring, called out, "And how attached to that dog could you have truly been? I mean . . . *honestly*?"

That was around the time Bampour pissed himself, but he felt no shame. He knew his men would always understand.

Chapter Two

General Addolgar walked through the camp set up outside the Western Mountains. For more than two years now, he, his sister Ghleanna, and the human troops and Dragonwarriors they led had been trying to tamp down the barbarian tribes raiding the towns around this area. And, until a few months ago, Addolgar would have said they were winning the fight. But something, something had changed.

He walked into his sister's tent. Ghleanna sat at her desk, a mug of ale within arm's reach but untouched—a rare thing for his sister—and her eyes focused across the room.

"Sister."

"What is it, Addolgar?"

He stood in front of her, not wanting to tell her his news but knowing he couldn't avoid it. "The unit I sent out. To that small village outside of Tristram. They just got back."

"And?"

Addolgar shook his head.

Her eyes closed, and she let out a breath. "Damn."

"I know."

"They killed everyone?"

"Aye. Everyone." Even the children. "You still think it's the barbarians, sister?"

"I don't know. But if it's not, then who?"

Addolgar placed a coin on her desk. Found under one of the bodies in the village, its markings distinct, it spoke of enemies all the Southland dragons hoped they'd never hear from again. Ghleanna barely glanced at it. "You can't seriously think they'd dare."

"We'd be fools to ignore this. We should send word and what we've found so far to Garbhán Isle."

"Little soon for that kind of panic, isn't it?"

"That's not panic, sister. That's prudent planning. Especially since you know as well as I do that"—he retrieved the coin and held it up for her to see—"they do like their misdirection. For all we know, these raids, these murders . . . could be just the beginning."

Ghleanna stared up at him. "You, brother, are like a bright ray of sunshine in my life," she told him flatly.

"And your happiness is my whole reason to live. Honestly. My concern keeps me up at night. Can't you tell?"

Because they left the Northlands quickly and the wind was with them, they arrived in the Outerplains early afternoon.

Still that was hours—gods, so many hours—of nonstop talk from one big, blue, idiot dragon. How old was he again? Eighty-nine? Ninety? Gods, it was time for him to grow up! Or shut up. Preferably both. Meinhard, who'd watched over the hatchling for the last two years to make sure he didn't get himself accidentally killed during a battle, had become quite adept at tuning him out. And Vigholf seemed to enjoy how much he was annoying Ragnar, so he goaded the big bastard. If he stopped talking for five minutes, Vigholf would give him something else to go on about. And on he went. He only shut up when he ate or slept. Otherwise it was a never-ending stream of thought.

As the Dragon Queen had suggested, they'd stopped

outside the town that belonged to Lord Bampour, and Ragnar sent Meinhard to investigate the surrounding area. When he returned, he said, "The queen may be right. We best walk it, cousin."

"Why?"

"They've got more weapons and troops than I've seen in a long time manning the fortress walls. Weapons that can kill from a distance."

Ragnar frowned. "Do you think they're expecting us?"

"No. Their weapons are pointed toward the inside of the town. But if they see us flying over . . ."

Ragnar agreed, glad the queen had warned him. "Good point. We'll walk it."

So they changed into chain-mail shirts and leggings, leather boots, and surcoats that bore the coat of arms for The Reinholdt—a little something Ragnar had taken from the human warlord on his many trips into that territory; something he'd never mentioned to the warlord's daughter—and the four males pulled on capes with hoods that could be pulled low over their heads so as to hide their purple and, in the Southlander's case, blue hair. Once they were ready, they headed into town. To Ragnar's surprise, it wasn't as busy as it usually was. Middle of the day and everything seemed to be closed down.

"Where is everyone?" Vigholf asked.

"I don't know."

Yet as Meinhard had said, there were troops manning the towers and fortress walls, but none of them even noticed Ragnar or his party. Unusual. If their defenses were so heightened, he'd have thought they'd definitely stop and interrogate four large armed males.

The Blue pointed to a street that led all the way across town. "I hear people down there."

As useless as he found the royal, he did have the best hearing of anyone Ragnar had known.

Vigholf stared down the street. "Should we go around?"

Ragnar's first thought was a definite yes, but . . .

"Let's go see what's going on. Be watchful. If the situation looks unstable, we leave. Quick and quiet."

"What if they need our help?"

The three Northlanders turned and stared at the royal.

"If who needs our help?" Ragnar asked. "The humans?"

"Aye."

"Why would we help them?" Ragnar had always considered himself quite benevolent for not simply crushing humans like ants when the mood struck him. And although he had to admit that some humans did serve a purpose, they didn't serve enough of a purpose to get him to involve himself in some town drama.

"It may be a bad situation," the Blue argued. "We can't just . . . leave. What if women and children are involved?"

Not about to spend one precious second of his life dealing with this, Ragnar said, "Meinhard."

Meinhard quickly stepped up to the royal. "Remember what we talked about before we left?"

"Aye, but—"

"And remember what you promised?"

"But I'm only saying that—"

"Remember?"

The Blue let out a sigh that made Ragnar contemplate slapping him . . . just to make him cry. "Aye. I remember."

"Then do as you promised." Meinhard patted his shoulder. "That's a good lad."

Ragnar headed down the street. As they got farther and farther along, they began to see more people. The biggest crowd was near the Baron Lord's four-story castle.

"An execution," Vigholf murmured behind him. "That explains it."

"Good," Ragnar said and pointed to another street shooting

off from the main one. "We'll cut around that way and head out. By the time they're done, we're through and out."

Ragnar headed off, his kin and the royal following. But he kept one ear open for what was going on at the execution. Sometimes, if it was a popular local being executed, the occasional uprising might start and those could turn ugly fast. He'd prefer not to get caught in the middle of something like that. Especially with the royal do-gooder bringing up the rear.

They were nearing the corner where they would turn onto the next street when Ragnar heard whoever was running the execution say, "Do you have any last words?"

He picked up his pace, knowing that those last words could really get a riot moving along.

"Good people—" He heard the words ring out over the yard and street, and Ragnar stumbled to a stop, his chest—which hadn't bothered him since he'd last spoken to the Dragon Queen—beginning to itch again.

His brother and cousin stopped short next to him.

"What is it?" Vigholf asked.

Ragnar ignored him and looked over at the royal with them. The Blue had stopped too, and when he saw that Ragnar's gaze had locked on him, he cringed.

Stepping around his brother, Ragnar looked up at the executioner's block. A fresh noose swung in the cool afternoon air, and a black-masked bull of a man stood at the ready to do his job.

And there, at the front of the block, wearing more chains than seemed necessary for someone these humans should at least *think* was also human, and with two units' worth of men aiming pikes at her, stood one royal who didn't know how *not* to find trouble.

With her long dark red hair blowing in the same direction as the noose behind her, and dirt on her cheeks, nose, and blue gown, she held her shackled hands out, her big brown eyes imploring as she said again, "Good people. I beg you

to see the injustice you are doing here. The unfairness. For I
am innocent!"

Hardly.

"What is she doing here?" Vigholf asked, his gaze fastened
on the executioner's block.

"Performing," was Ragnar's only answer. Because that was
the only explanation. She was a dragoness for the gods' sake!
She could blast the entire town to embers without even shifting to her natural form, and yet she'd let them put her up there
for execution!

What exactly is wrong *with these Southland royals?*

Keita clasped her hands together and looked up into the
skies above, making sure to angle her head so the crowd
could see the tears glistening in her eyes.

"I assure all you good people that I had nothing to do with
Lord Bampour's tragic death. For I—"

"Is this going to take much longer?"

Keita snapped her mouth shut and glared into the audience
at her feet. She looked past all those unnecessary guards, focusing on the male who had interrupted her eloquent soliloquy.

"Sorry," he said, the hood of his cloak covering his handsome face. "Go on."

"Thank you," she snipped.

Keita let out a breath, looked up at the sky again, and
asked, "Where was I?"

"You had nothing to do with Lord Bampour's tragic death,"
that familiar voice offered.

"Thank you." She cleared her throat. "I am not the one who
has done this horrible deed. I am an innocent! And I beg all
of you"—she brought her gaze down and opened her arms as
much as the thick chain between her shackles would allow—
"to save me from this horrid fate that I do not . . ." Keita's
words faded away, and she leaned forward a bit, trying to see

beyond the crowd of men and pikes in front of her. After a moment, she asked, "Éibhear?"

Her baby brother, towering over the entire crowd, waved at her and, grinning, Keita waved back. Making sure not to hit herself in the face with that stupid chain. "Éibhear!" she cheered. "What are you doing here?"

"Just passing through," he called back. "You all right?"

"Oh, I'm fine," she answered honestly. "Are you going to stay for the execution?"

"I guess I better so we can bring your body back to Mum."

"Don't take me to her. She'll just spit on my corpse and dance around it. And being trapped in the afterlife, I won't be able to beat her within an inch of her miserable existence. But tell Daddy I said hi." Keita clasped her hands together again and said, "Now, where was I?"

She heard her traveling companion clear his throat, and when she glanced over at him, he pointed to something that had pushed past all the townspeople and guards and now was right in front of the block she stood upon.

She examined the male. She could smell the lightning that came from within him, knew he was a Northlander. The blue hood of his cloak probably hid purple hair—common among the Lightnings. But his human face was surprisingly handsome for a barbarian. Sharp cheekbones, delicious-looking full lips, a strong jaw, and a once-battered nose that kept him from looking too perfect. But it was his eyes that made her think she might know him from somewhere. They were blue with shots of silver, like tiny bolts of lightning. They were as beautiful as anything she'd seen, and Keita felt sure that if she'd fucked this one, she would have remembered. She tried to be very good about that sort of thing—especially if she fucked the one-time enemies of her people, since that sort of thing brought all sorts of problems.

She pointed at him. "Don't I know you?"

"What do you think you're doing?" he asked, rather than answering her.

"I'm about to be wrongly executed for something I didn't do."

"And yet something tells me you did do it. Now get your ass down here."

"Get my . . ." Keita slammed her hands onto her hips, the chain nearly not allowing it. Although she refused to believe her hips were that wide.

"You need to go away before I get angry," Keita told him.

"I've seen you angry. I wasn't impressed. Tell me, princess, did you hit at them with your tiny little fists or use that tail to ward them off?"

When Keita's skin began to itch and the overwhelming desire to kill everything within a league of her rage flowed from her pores like honey, she knew *exactly* who this arrogant, lightning-breathing, worthless scum of a whore bastard was! "You! I should have finished you when I had the chance, warlord," Keita told him.

"Should haves. I bet your entire life is filled with should haves."

"Only where you're concerned. Because I *should have* torn your feeble barbarian heart from your weak chest and I *should have* danced around you in a veritable orgy of blood and pain and suffering that would have called the dark gods to me so they could make me their *reigning queen*!"

"Keita?" her traveling companion called out lightly.

"*What?*"

When he didn't answer, she lifted her gaze from the dragon in front of her. The entire crowd now watched her in horror.

"I could be wrong," her friend said, "but I'm thinking the 'good people, I have been wrongly accused' speech isn't going to work at the moment."

And whose fault was that? The Lightning's fault, that's who!

"Finish it!" Lord Bampour yelled from the safety of the gate walls, his men scrambling to get him to safety.

The executioner grabbed Keita by the shoulders, yanking her back. The guards on the ground tried to force the Lightning back with the now screaming-for-her-blood townsfolk.

"Well, you've left me no choice," Keita told the audience watching her.

"Keita, no!" Éibhear cried out. Typical of her baby brother. What would he have her do instead? Let these peasants hang her, a royal, like meat? Was that what he wanted?

The executioner reached for the noose, and Keita sucked air into her lungs. But guards were tossed aside, and Ragnar the Bastard, as she liked to call him when she thought of him at all, jumped onto the block and caught hold of the front of her dress. "Oy!" she gasped. "Watch the dress!" Ignoring her, as he always seemed to do, Ragnar hauled her forward and over his shoulder.

"Put me down!" she ordered.

"Quiet!" the bastard snarled, already moving away from the block. "Just the sound of your voice irritates me."

Keita raised her head and saw the Baron Lord's guards charging forward. "Kill him!" she ordered them, causing them all to stop and stare at her. Humans. Although she found most of them quite entertaining, they could be a little on the slow side.

Using her chained hands, she gestured at the bastard who was walking off with her over his shoulder like a sack of grain. "Kill. Him," she said again. "Now!"

Finally, swords were pulled, and the villagers made a run for it. The fight was on, but all Keita could do was sit there on this idiot's shoulder, hoping the human soldiers could finish what she hadn't two years before.

"Keita!" She heard the urgency and warning in her friend's voice and looked back at the block she'd been dragged from.

The executioner, who'd stopped by her cell last night and promised to fuck her corpse when he was done stretching her neck—she sensed he had no interest in her while she was still moving . . . and warm—was off the block and heading toward her. With the barbarian busy fighting the guards in front of him, he had no clue the executioner was coming.

She saw the man smile under the black mask that covered everything to his nose, his hands stretching out for her throat. One good twist of her human neck and she'd be done. It was the risk they all took when they shifted to human—they were a little easier to kill. But there were some abilities Keita still had access to, no matter her form. So when she felt those big fingers against her neck, she unleashed the line of flame she'd been holding on to and turned the executioner into ash.

Of course, she also demolished the wooden executioner's block behind him and set fire to several other nearby buildings, but that couldn't be helped. Yet around her, everything froze, all eyes on her and Ragnar.

And in that moment, all Keita could think was, *Ooops.*

Ragnar stopped, his eyes briefly closing in pure irritation. "Tell me you didn't do what I think you just did."

"It's not like I had other options. I'm still chained!"

"You have to be the dumbest—"

"It's not my fault!"

He sensed that would be her eternal mantra, which explained why he was already sick of hearing it.

"Kill them, you fools!" someone commanded from the tower gates.

Ragnar let out an annoyed sigh. "Thank you very much, princess. You just made this harder and probably upset that overly sensitive brother of yours."

Rather than being concerned about their lives or anything else he'd said, the spoiled royal demanded, "Did . . . did you just call me princess or prince-*ass*?"

"Does it matter?"

Vigholf and Meinhard had their shields at the ready, their

swords drawn. The Blue, however, stood between the dragons and the humans, his hands raised. "Wait, wait! This isn't necessary. We can all work this out!"

The body Ragnar held shook.

"Are you laughing?"

"Isn't he cute? Two years away with blood-thirsty brutes and he's still as adorable as the day he was hatched. I was, in point of fact, the first face he ever saw when he hatched his way out of his shell. My mother had told me to tell her when it was happening, but I didn't want to. I wanted him all to my—"

"Shut up."

"Did you just tell me to shut up?"

"Yes."

"You rude, self-centered, egotistical—"

That was when Ragnar tossed her off his shoulder.

Vigholf blinked. "What the hell are you doing?"

"We're leaving her. Finish the execution!" he called out. "She's all yours."

"We're not leaving my sister!" the Blue protested.

"Then you can stay and be executed right along with her. I, however, am leaving."

"How could you?" the princess wailed from her place on the ground. "To leave me here to die! Like an animal in the street! Will no one care for me?"

"Shut up."

"Oy!" The Blue shoved him. "That's my sister you're speaking to!"

"Do that again, boy, and I'll make you more like your sister than you'd like."

From his crouched, battle-ready position, Meinhard asked, "Is this really the time for this argument?"

Vigholf pushed his shield forward to ward off the weapons aimed at him. "What do you want us to do, brother?"

The soldiers were getting bolder, starting to prod with their pikes, pushing at Vigholf's and Meinhard's shields.

True, there were many things they could do in this situation to save more than not, but Ragnar wasn't in the mood to bother.

"Kill them all," Ragnar ordered.

"Or we can run," the Blue threw in desperately, still trying to save the humans.

"Run? Away?" Vigholf shook his head, disgusted.

"If you try to harm anyone"—the Blue swallowed—"you'll force me to defend them."

Ragnar, unable to help himself, snorted at that "threat."

The Blue frowned. "Now what does that mean?"

The ground beneath their feet rumbled, and Ragnar looked down, watching dirt and stone pop up as something moved under them.

The commanding officers of the guards ordered their men back as the ground in front of Ragnar and his kin exploded around them, and something he'd only read about in books burst into the open air.

"What," Vigholf demanded without backing down, "in all the battle-fucks is that thing?"

Unlike Ragnar, Vigholf didn't read many books. So to see something that was as long as Ragnar was in dragon form, but not as wide, gold scales glistening in the two suns and a mane of black and gold fur trailing from the top of its head down its spine to its tail did nothing but confuse him. Plus the creature had no horns but antlers; no talons but fur-covered striped claws like Ragnar had seen on big jungle cats. It had fewer fangs and more chewing teeth than either the Horde dragons or the Fire Breathers; and no wings, yet it floated on the air as easily as any winged dragon could. In other words, a being that would not only horrify Vigholf with its oddness but Meinhard as well.

Yet it wasn't something that unusual, if Ragnar remembered his readings correctly. It was simply an Eastland dragon.

Circling over them without any wings, the foreigner

unleashed flame. What was strange was that although the flame covered everything within a hundred feet, no one was harmed.

Ragnar raised his hand and ran it through the flame. He felt no heat, no pain. And yet it wasn't an illusion. He felt the strength of the flame blowing against his hand. Strange. Just . . . strange. No wings, no sharpened tail, and no bite to his flame. *What a weak kitten, this dragon.*

The flames stopped, and they were now all alone, the streets completely deserted.

The foreigner shifted while he still hovered in the air, and, with a shocking amount of skill, his human form floated to the ground, bare feet lightly landing on the cobble-stoned street. The Eastlander paused a moment to shake out his straight black hair, the tips appearing as if dipped in gold.

"Everyone all right?" he asked.

"Ren! Thank the gods!" the princess cried out, making Ragnar snarl, just a little. "You've come to rescue me!"

Laughing, the foreigner walked over to her.

"Honestly, Keita," the Eastlander lightly chastised. "Your lack of subtlety with flame is something you have to work on."

He removed the metal cuffs, and the princess rubbed her wrists.

"I was in fear for my life and trapped by Lord Low-Brow over there." She shrugged. "I just . . . reacted."

"Liar."

"Oh, whatever. The important question is did you like my speech?"

He helped her to her feet. "A little wordy. The looking up at the sky with the tear-filled eyes was a nice touch, though."

"I thought so. I'll have to use that again."

The rest of her chains hit the ground, and the foreigner walked around the group and retrieved his clothes a few feet away.

While Vigholf and Meinhard watched the foreigner closely,

their weapons still drawn, Ragnar focused on the princess. She glared first. He glared in return. There might have also been some sneering. Then she suddenly charged past him and into the arms of the big blue ox standing behind him.

"Keita!"

Her baby brother lifted Keita into his arms and swung her around. Keita marveled at how much he'd grown. At this point, he might be even bigger than their father . . . and grandfather. He was massive! And that was as human. She couldn't wait to see what he looked like when he shifted.

Keita wrapped her arms around her brother's neck and squeezed him tight. "I'm so happy to see you, Éibhear!"

"And I you. Has it been two years?"

"Oh, yes." She kissed his cheek and hugged him again. "Too long! Now put me down. I want to get a good look at you."

He placed her on the ground, and Keita stepped back. Actually, she took several steps back so she could see *all* of him.

"By the gods of mayhem, Éibhear. Look at the size of you!"

"It's not that bad," he said self-consciously. "I haven't grown any in a few months."

She didn't know how to tell him he probably wasn't done growing yet, so she decided not to tell him at all. He'd figure it out when he needed new leggings.

"You look as handsome as ever," she told him instead, enjoying his shy smile. Ahh, she'd missed him so. The youngest of her siblings, Éibhear was the one she mothered. Some days she couldn't do enough for him, and she enjoyed being that way because he never took it for granted. Fearghus and Briec, her oldest siblings, were the classic big brothers. Always protective and caring, they watched out for her when they could. And then there was Gwenvael. She was closest to Gwenvael in age and in temperament. Gwenvael was more like a best friend than a brother; the two of them getting into lots of trouble as they'd matured in their mother's court. But that was more than a century ago and times had changed.

Just like the size of Éibhear's neck. *Gods! Look at that thing.*

"So what brings you here, brother?"

"Can we have this discussion some other time?" asked that voice. That voice she'd worked for several days—maybe even a whole week!—to get out of her head. That voice that made her want to tear its owner's face off with her talons—preferably while singing something jaunty.

"You can go," she told *that voice* without looking at that voice's owner. "But as you can see, I'm in the middle of a conversation."

"We need to move out. Now."

He spoke to her like one of his barbarian Dragonwarriors. Without a bit of reverence for the fact that she was of royal blood and, more importantly, not afraid to tear his face off while singing something jaunty!

Keita, feeling particularly difficult this day, pointedly ignored the rude bastard, but then she heard another voice.

"Please, my lady. We should leave before those human soldiers manage to find their manhood and return."

Ahhh. The brother. She remembered the brother. And the cousin. She'd forgotten they'd been standing right there beside her for several minutes.

Two years ago, Keita had easily charmed the two barbarians and their younger kin while they'd traveled from the Northlands to the South. Only the barbarian bastard had managed to ignore her. Something that bothered her much more than it should have.

Curling her lips into an appropriate—and quite seductive—smile, Keita turned and faced the other two Lightnings.

"By the gods," she said, her hands to her chest. "It *is* you!" She quickly recalled their names and tried to place which was which. Not easy when they both looked quite similar. Both had purple hair braided into a single plait that reached to the middle of their backs, both were wide of shoulder and long of height, both had scars. So, how did she tell them apart before . . . ?

"Vigholf!" She hugged the one with the grey eyes and the brutal scar across his jaw. "Meinhard!" She then hugged the one with the green eyes and the brutal scar that cut from his hairline to below his eye. "How wonderful it is to see you both again."

She grabbed a hand from each and held them tightly. "I hope you've both been doing wonderfully."

"We have, my lady, thank you," Vigholf said. He'd always been the more confident one when it came to speaking. Meinhard always looked cornered when she asked him a direct question, before muttering a response. Although she'd found in time that Meinhard said much with his eyes without speaking a word. A lovely trait—rare with most males.

"And I see you've been taking excellent care of my brother. Thank you both for that. I don't know what I'd do if something horrible happened to him."

"Meinhard's my mentor," Éibhear filled in.

"And I know my brother's learned so much from you, dear Meinhard." She gave her most dazzling smile, and poor Meinhard appeared ready to crumple at her feet.

That's before the rude one stepped between them, prying her hands from his kin.

"And what do you think you're doing?" she asked him.

"Moving this along."

"Well, if you'd bothered to ask me nicely—oh!" she gasped when he again lifted her up and tossed her over his shoulder like so much trash. "How dare you!"

"Move out!" he ordered.

"Are you going to let him do this?" she demanded of Ren. For many, many years they'd been traveling companions and dearest friends. He made her laugh the way Gwenvael always did but, unlike her dear brother, Ren was much more reliable. Gwenvael was a lot of things, but unfortunately, she could never call him reliable.

"He seems quite determined," Ren explained, his lips curled into a small smile. "Can't you just relax until he's done?"

"I want you never again to ask *that* question of any female for as long as you live, Ren of the Chosen!" she ordered.

Yet with no one willing to help her, Keita was forced to settle down and wait this out. Although she did use every opportunity to bring up her foot so she kicked Ragnar the Bastard in the nose with her heel.

If nothing else, she did find that quite entertaining.

Chapter Three

Fearghus the Destroyer, First Born to the Dragon Queen, Heir to the Dragon Queen's Throne, Consort to Annwyl the Bloody, Father to the Demon Twins of Dark Plains, and suspicious, jealous male of Queen Annwyl's court sat on the stairs leading to the Great Hall of his mate's castle and watched Annwyl walk from behind one of the guard houses. Behind her trailed the two dogs given to her by her chief battle lord, Dagmar Reinholdt. Fearghus didn't mind the two dogs, though they did make him hungry. But Annwyl adored the beasts nearly as much as she adored her horse and Fearghus wasn't in the mood to fight with her if she found him using one of the dog's leg bones to remove the other bits from between Fearghus's fangs.

Eyes narrowing, Fearghus studied his mate. Although Annwyl had always trained hard since he'd met her, she'd been training even harder since a few months after their twins had been born. He knew what drove her, too. Fear. Not fear for herself, but fear for the safety of their twins. Fear that she couldn't protect them. He didn't know why she'd think that. She'd slaughtered an entire herd of Minotaur to protect their babes. But she seemed to think worse than Minotaurs was heading their way. That whatever this worse thing was, it—or they—was coming after the babes.

And maybe she was right. Although not quite two winters old, the twins were feared by many. Demons, abominations, unholy—all words used to describe the amazing creatures upstairs with their latest nanny. A position they couldn't seem to keep filled for long periods of time. He'd known his offspring would be different. But not this different. Not this dangerous. And gods, for something so small, they were dangerous.

Picking sticks off the ground, Annwyl held them out for her dogs and then played tug with the beasts until they reached the Great Hall steps.

"Oy. Wench," Fearghus said by way of greeting.

Annwyl looked up at him with those green eyes that still made his heart stumble a bit in his chest.

"Oy. Knight."

"Where you've been?"

"Training."

He could see that. Her body was covered in sweat, fresh bruises, and new nicks and cuts.

"Training with . . . ?"

She shrugged, glanced down at her dogs, which were still fighting her for the sticks. "A few of the men."

And he knew she lied.

"How did it go?" he asked, rather than accuse her of something he couldn't yet prove.

"It went well." He could see the truth in that. She was getting stronger every day. More powerful. Her muscles were well-defined, and her body bore no fat. Her own men feared her strength, which was why he knew she hadn't been training with them. And his kin feared her as well. Dragons known for fighting anyone at any time gave Fearghus's mate the widest berth possible when she searched for a sparring partner. But someone was helping her. Someone she wouldn't tell him about.

"Brastias and Dagmar are looking for you," he said

"Oh." Annwyl blinked a few times and said, "I should check on the babes first, though, eh? I'll track down Brastias and Dagmar later."

There'd been a time when Annwyl would track down Brastias first. She'd search out fights, battles, wars, anything that hinted at a little bloodshed. But that had been before the twins. Now, she avoided her army's general and her chief battle lord as if they brought news of the latest fashions from town. The twins, however, were merely the excuse the queen used to avoid what was closing in around her.

Yet how much longer did she think she could continue to do that? She was queen, one of the most powerful queens in a millennium, and there were many who relied on her. True, she could be like some monarchs—his mother included— who sent out troops and supplies while staying safely in their fortress homes. That, however, was not Annwyl. That would never be Annwyl. And watching her live like this was tearing him apart.

Annwyl made a strange clicking sound with her tongue, and the dogs released their sticks and charged up the stairs and into the Great Hall. Annwyl followed behind them, stopping beside Fearghus.

"You all right?" she asked.

"I'm fine." *Paranoid, distrustful, and worried about you— but fine.*

Annwyl crouched beside him. She looked tired, dark circles under her eyes. She hadn't been sleeping well for months, often leaving their bed before the two suns rose. It might be her dreams that drove her from their bed, for when she did sleep, she tossed and turned; Fearghus's presence beside her not easing her as it usually did.

Annwyl leaned in, waiting until Fearghus turned his face toward her so she could kiss him. Her lips were soft and sweet, her tongue wicked and ruthless, her mouth warm and delicious. He knew he shouldn't be so paranoid about what she was up to when she was off training, but he couldn't help it. Something was going on with her and she wouldn't tell him. She used to tell him everything.

She pulled back with a soft sigh. "I'll see you later then?" And he heard the hopeful note in her tone.

"You need a bath," he told her, his gaze moving over the courtyard. "I can scrub your back, if you'd like."

"I never can reach it," she murmured, her fingers trailing to his neck and across his shoulders. Fearghus closed his eyes at the feel of her hand on his bare skin and through his chain-mail shirt. Of course, those fingers felt even better against his scales and wings. "So your help will be much appreciated."

Then she was gone, into the Great Hall and up the stairs to see their twins.

And Fearghus was left alone a little longer to brood and wonder what the hell was going on with his mate.

Bare feet walked across ice; naked bodies knelt in the snow, uncaring of the violent snow and ice storm swirling around them while heads bowed in honor of the god before them. This was not all their number, merely those who would lead this mission. For their strength was not in their number, but in their power. In their rage. In their willingness to kill without question, without regret, without thought.

Because of what they were willing to do, all in the name of their gods, they were the most feared in the Ice Lands. The most despised. But none of them cared about the outsiders. Not when they had their weapons in their hands and spells on their lips.

Go, the harsh winds roared around them, for this god would not speak directly to them. Not like the others. Instead, the Ice Land winds would give them their mission. The hard-packed snow and ice would enhance their strength and power for the long journey ahead. And the two suns would lead them to death or glory.

Go! the winds ordered again. Then, the screeching winds whispered, *Annwyl.*

Chapter Four

"I have to admit I'm a bit surprised, Lord Ragnar. I thought you would have killed all those humans."

Ragnar gulped several mouthfuls of water from his flask. They'd traveled deep into the thick forests of Outerplains, not stopping until they found a freshwater lake.

"And I thought you wouldn't allow yourself to be executed. Guess we were both wrong."

The royal rolled brown eyes. "Of course I wouldn't allow myself to be executed."

"Then what were you doing exactly?"

She shrugged and, without asking, took his flask from him rather than filling her own from the lake as he'd done. "Seeing if I could talk them out of it."

"Why?"

She shrugged. "Why not?" She studied his flask before using a bit of her gown to wipe the mouth of it. He didn't know which annoyed him more. The fact that she took his flask, the fact that she wiped it first before using it, or the fact that the gown she used was absolutely filthy.

"It's all a game to you, isn't it?" he asked.

After taking several gulps of water, she gave him that smile. She had many smiles, most of them as contrived as she was. But this one, where the left side of her mouth went up just a tad higher than the right and her eyes looked up at him through those thick lashes—this one was the true Keita. His brother and cousin refused to see this Keita.

"Why were they trying to execute you anyway, Keita?" the Blue asked his sister.

She handed the flask back to Ragnar. "They believed I'd killed Lord Bampour."

"Oh, Keita," the Blue whined. "You didn't."

"Actually, I didn't." When her brother raised a dark blue brow, she insisted, "I didn't!"

"Then why did they charge you?" Ragnar asked.

"They found me in his room."

"With the body?"

"Yes. But it wasn't me." Why did Ragnar feel there was a "this time" missing from that declaration?

"What were you doing in his room?"

She stared at Ragnar a moment, then replied, "Wishing him a good morning?"

"Is that an answer, princess, or a question?"

"Och!" She threw up her hands. "Does it matter? I didn't kill him." She pouted a little, her nose scrunching up—it looked vaguely adorable. "They wouldn't even listen to me. Just kept insisting that I had to have done it, simply because they found me alone in his room, the body still warm, and carrying a vial of poison."

The males all stared at her, but when no one else asked, Ragnar knew he must. "And why were you carrying a vial of poison?"

"What does that have to do with anything?"

"I'm fairly certain . . . quite a bit."

"No. It doesn't. Because the point is—the vial was still full, which meant it hadn't been used, which means I didn't kill Bampour."

Ragnar was willing to play along. "If you didn't kill him . . . who did?"

"Some naked blond girl who was in his room when I got there."

"I see. And what happened to her?"

"I threw her out the window."

"Of course you did."

"Don't worry," the foreigner tossed in. "I caught her and set her gently down."

"See?" the female said.

"See what?"

"I rescued her. Saved her life. And yet they wanted to execute *me*. How is that fair?"

Ragnar nodded. "Let's pretend you're not lying."

"What?"

"I'm not sure why you would rescue a murderess."

"Well, she was only doing the rest of the world a favor."

"I see."

"He was not a nice person."

"Uh-huh."

"He had to die!"

"And why is that? Did he not give you enough . . . things?"

"Oh, but he did." She touched the necklace around her throat. "He gave me this." She touched the bracelet on her wrist. "And this." She touched the earrings. "And these . . . oh, wait. No. He didn't. That son of his did. Shame the little blonde didn't get a chance to deal with that one too."

Ragnar gestured to the jewelry. "I'm surprised they let you keep all that."

"I don't think they'd planned to. But after I ate the dog, they refused to come near me except to put on the chains."

"Keita!" the Blue blurted out while the foreigner laughed.

"I was hungry! I hadn't had first meal, they wouldn't give me anything to eat, and . . . and that dog tried to bite me! It was very close to self-defense!"

"Somehow I doubt that."

"You," she said to Ragnar, "can just be quiet."

"All right, all right, all right," the Blue cut in. "Let's forget all that. The important thing is, you're safe." The princess smiled at that until her brother added, "And you can travel with us back to Garbhán Isle."

"Oh."

Ragnar leaned back against a tree, his arms crossed over his chest, and watched Her Royal Majesty try to work her way out of this. Because he knew, just by the look of panic in her eyes, she was desperately trying to work her way out of this.

"Garbhán Isle. That's an option." She glanced at her foreign friend, but he didn't seem to be in the mood to help her either. "And . . . why don't I meet you there? At some point."

"Meet us there? Why can't you come back now?" her brother asked.

"I have something to do?"

"Is that a question or an answer?" Ragnar asked again, and the glare he received would have lacerated a lesser male.

"But what about the feast?"

"Feast?" She shrugged. "There's always a feast, Éibhear. Our family does love a feast."

"But it's to celebrate the twins' birthday. I mean, I missed the first one because I was in the heat of battle—"

Ragnar briefly but quickly moved his gaze to the ground after he heard Vigholf snort.

"—so I can't miss this one. But I guess since you did go to the first one, I could explain it away to the family."

Perhaps Ragnar was watching her too closely, but the way her face became perfectly blank, her brown eyes wide as if she was afraid the truth could be read there, had him asking, "Why don't you tell us about that first feast, my lady? All the details. Down to the last dessert."

"I don't really—"

"Oh, come on. You must remember something. And I've

always wondered what a Southland celebration is like. For instance, what was the human queen's gown like?"

"Gown? I doubt she wore—"

"Doubt?" Ragnar asked. "Don't you know?"

Gods. Did she just hiss at me? Yes! I think she just hissed at me!

"You didn't go?" the Blue asked.

"Éibhear, I was quite busy. I didn't have time."

The Blue's eyes narrowed, and he studied his sister for a long, painful moment. "When was the last time you were home?"

"The Southlands are my home, Éibhear. And I'm always—"

"Don't play with me, Keita. When was the last time you were at Garbhán Isle or Devenallt Mountain?"

"When you look at how long we live, time is such a transient thing."

Ragnar began to have an uneasy feeling, clearly remembering the look on the princess's face when he'd released her. Not when she'd stabbed him with her tail—although that moment was etched into his memory until his last breath—but before that. When he'd told her the queen had offered nothing for her daughter's safe return. True, royal anger eventually took over everything, but before that, he'd seen pain on her face. Acute pain.

Having grown up with a father who enjoyed picking his other sons over "that weak, strange one" for important Horde business, Ragnar knew how much a careless action from a parent could hurt their offspring. He'd realized later that the queen had said such things because she'd known, as only a true witch could know, that Ragnar would never harm her daughter. He'd never drag Keita off against her will. Not after what had happened to his own mother. Not after watching her trapped in a life she'd never wanted with only one wing and a dragon mate she detested. Ragnar had grown up under his mother's avid protection, his father deciding early on that he loathed the hatchling who spent most of his days in books and learning. She'd watched over Ragnar, raised him to think and reason while teaching him the Magickal arts and, finding a caring soul in Meinhard's father, had asked the warrior to train her son without Olgeir's knowledge. Ragnar owed his mother so much and was grateful to her for the very air he breathed, because without her, he wasn't sure he'd have survived into his twentieth winter.

And although Ragnar used to think about going off by himself and living the life of a hermit dragon deep in the mountains near the Ice Lands, his mother's words always stopped him. "You can't live alone in this world, my son. You need your family. And one day, they will realize how much they need you."

As always with his mother's wisdom, her words were true for him, but they were even truer for Princess Keita. She adored her kin and had talked about them incessantly when they were bringing her back to the Southlands. Mostly, she spoke of what her brothers would do to him when they got their claws on him, but Ragnar knew love when he heard it.

So the thought that Keita had cut herself off from her kin all this time because of that last discussion did not sit well with Ragnar at all.

Even now, she was still trying to wiggle out of returning to Dark Plains with them, and the Blue seemed to be buying into her half-truths. The boy simply didn't know how to ask a direct question, which was a problem since his sister seemed quiet adept at sidestepping anything but direct questions.

So Ragnar asked the direct question himself, knowing he'd make her angry and not much caring since this would all be over soon enough, and he'd never see her again anyway. "Have you even seen your niece and nephew, Princess Keita?"

Grateful she had no real Magickal skills that could kill him at a distance, Ragnar met her glare and held it.

As he realized the truth, the Blue's giant human head nearly exploded. "*You haven't seen the twins?*"

"Éibhear—"

"*At all?*"

"You're being un—"

"What about Talaith's daughter? Have you not seen her either?"

The fight seemed to go out of her, her hatred for Ragnar alone, Keita stated, "I was planning to see them soon—when I have time."

"You have time now."

"Actually, I don't."

"Make some."

"And if I don't want to come home?"

"What does what you want have to do with family?"

"Oh, well, when you put it like that—"

"Good!"

"I was actually being sarcas—"

"Because I'd hate to drag you back there by your hair."

"—tic," she finished.

"So we're all settled then?"

She let out a long, weary sigh. "It would seem so."

"Good." He suddenly walked off into the woods. "I'll be right back."

Dark brown eyes seared Ragnar where he stood; then she marched off in the opposite direction from her brother.

Ragnar caught Vigholf's attention and motioned for him to check the area. Meinhard went about getting more water for their trip, leaving Ragnar and the foreigner.

He faced the Eastlander, completely unclear on the relationship this strange-looking dragon had with the royal.

The foreigner's smile was small when he said, "I'm not sure she'll ever forgive you for that, Northlander." His smile widened a little bit when he added, "But perhaps that's what you're hoping for."

Appearing to be following after the princess, the Eastlander stopped in front of Ragnar and pointed at him, asking, "Do you need some ointment for that?"

Ragnar curled his fingers in and pulled his hand away from his chest and that damn scar he'd been scratching— again! "No."

The foreigner shrugged. "As you like."

As he'd like? Somehow Ragnar doubted he'd have what he'd like for at least the next few days.

"Keita, wait."

"Go away, Ren. Let me seethe in peace." Keita spotted a squirrel not far from her and opened her mouth to unleash a line of flame. But a hand covered her mouth and her friend shook his head.

"Must you take your anger out on that poor squirrel?"

She slapped his hand off. "I'd take it out on you, but you'd only enjoy it. And what's the good of that when I want to make something miserable?"

"Your suffering doesn't give you the right to make others suffer."

Keita rolled her eyes. "You with your deep philosophical ramblings."

"You like my deep philosophical ramblings."

"Not when they interfere with my ridiculous rages. It's extremely hard to flounce away with any dignity when you're so busy rationalizing."

"No one can flounce anywhere with dignity. It's a law."

Keita pressed her lips together to keep from laughing. This was why she adored Ren. Because no matter the situation, no matter how annoying or brutal or horrible things might be, he always made her laugh.

He put his arm around her shoulders. "My dearest, loveliest Keita."

"I like when you add the 'loveliest' part."

"You are the loveliest."

"Adore. You."

"So what's really bothering you, my friend?"

"Can't you tell?"

"Is it the current width of your brother's neck?"

"No. Although that is disconcerting." She leaned her head back, and looked up at her friend. "I'd like to know why those Lightnings are taking my brother back to Dark Plains."

"To ensure he gets home safely, I'd assume."

"Well, of course, as a royal he'd need an escort. I'm not questioning that. But Ragnar the Cunning? Current Dragonlord Chief? *And* his second in command, Vigholf? Meinhard and a few of their warriors would have ensured the same thing."

"I see your point. Your mother then?"

"Most likely, which makes me nervous. Mother doesn't call on foreign dragons for no reason."

"Think Éibhear will know the answer?"

Keita smiled and petted Ren's cheek. "That's so cute you'd think that."

Ren laughed. "Not one for questioning the obvious, is our Éibhear?"

"Hardly. He still thinks the best of everyone." Keita stepped away from Ren and smoothed her dress down. "I'll need to find out the answer myself. And since I'm forced to endure that bastard barbarian's presence until we get back to Devenallt Mountain, I might as well get what information I can."

Ren brushed his finger against Keita's cheek, his teasing gone. "Are you all right, luv? Seeing him again?"

It had been Ren that Keita initially ran to when she'd left Ragnar the Cunning alone and bleeding in the forests outside Garbhán Isle. It had been Ren who listened to her rage until the cave walls around them shook. And it had been Ren who suggested that Keita go to Anubail Mountain to get some much-needed training in the fine art of fighting while human—the fact that *that* situation didn't turn out well at all was, of course, not Ren's fault. But that had been two years ago, and to be honest, Keita had sort of . . . well . . .

"You forgot about him, didn't you?" Ren demanded.

"I had other things on my mind."

"How do you do that? How do you just . . . let it go?"

Keita lifted her hands and dropped them. "What can I say? I'm much too beautiful and benevolent to hold grudges. Besides"—she took her friend's arm—"isn't being mad at a Northlander like being mad at a stampeding bull or a rabbit that keeps breeding or a startled bear that mauls?"

Ren gazed down at her. "Are you actually comparing a fellow dragon to dumb, mindless animals?"

Keita's grin was wide as they headed back to the Northlanders. "Why yes, Ren. Yes, I am. And that's what makes me so lovely—because I accept them *despite* their faults."

"By the gods of thunder, Keita—you *are* giving."

"I know!"

Chapter Five

Several hours later they landed in a dense forest in the Outerplains. An area Keita knew quite well. Too well. It was the place her aunt had chosen to live quietly and anonymously the last few centuries. The aunt her mother and court still considered a traitor.

Feeling a tinge of panic, she glanced at Ren, who could only shrug.

"Are we camping here for the night?" she asked the warlord while her baby brother went off in search of something warm and bloody for them all to eat. And, for the first time since they'd taken off from outside Bampour's lands, Ragnar spoke to her. "Not unless we have to."

"We're just taking a break here then?"

"Yes."

She waited for something more, but he ignored her after that, and began whispering to his brother. When he was done, Ragnar walked off, and Keita did not like the direction the Lightning went in.

Keita brushed up against Ren, appearing impossibly playful, her tail tugging with his. But as she giggled and teased, she leaned in and whispered, "Do you see where he's headed?"

"Aye. I do."

"I'll kill him. You take care of the other two." She started to follow after Ragnar, but Ren pulled her back.

"Are we still forced to have this conversation?"

"What would you suggest then, Duke No-Kill?"

"You *delay* King Big Head. I'll take care of the rest."

"Fine."

Ren kissed her cheek and backed away from her. He moved around until he caught the attention of the other two Lightnings. It wasn't hard—they'd been watching Ren with something very close to fear since they'd first seen him. At least, as much fear as any Northlander was willing to show. All they knew was that Ren was different; and clearly different made them nervous.

While they watched, Ren leaned up against a small hill—and vanished.

"What the bloody—"

Knowing the Lightnings would spend ages searching for him, Keita followed after Ragnar.

Dagmar Reinholdt, also known as The Beast among her Northland kinsmen, went to the kennels to do a midday check on all the dogs. Her latest batch of puppies were doing well, and the men she'd handpicked to train and work the dogs during battle were better than she'd hoped.

Always thinking ahead, Dagmar planned to be prepared with strong battle dogs for the Southland Queen and her troops.

She ensured they had been fed, that all were looking healthy, and that they all had fresh water in their runs. Once she'd done all that, she walked down the line, speaking to each animal while noting any changes and thinking about their training.

But as she reached the last cage, the barking dogs, always so chatty when she was around, suddenly fell silent, and

Dagmar felt the hairs on the back of her neck rise up the slightest bit.

"I wish you wouldn't do that," she said after a moment.

"Do what?"

She faced the god behind her. Many gods enjoyed visiting her now, no matter how annoying Dagmar found their presence or how inane their conversation, but Eirianwen, human god and consort to dragon father god, Rhydderch Hael, liked to call Dagmar her "friend." Which was strange since Dagmar still didn't worship any god. They were simply too annoying to be worshipped. "Do not sneak up on me."

"I'm a god, Dagmar. I don't sneak up on anyone. It's not my fault I can simply appear wherever I'd like."

Dagmar's head tilted to the side. "Where's your arm?"

Eir examined her left shoulder. "Oh. Right. Lost it in a fight." She shrugged with her right shoulder. "It'll grow back."

"How nice for you."

Not the most pleasant thing to see before luncheon. Of course, it could be worse. A few months back, the god had shown up missing half her head. After Dagmar finished retching, though, they had a very nice conversation.

"So how goes it?" Eir asked.

"Well enough."

"And your queen?"

Dagmar knew the sneaky cow wasn't here merely to check up on her. "She's fine."

"Liar."

"But you already knew that about me."

"Excellent point." Eir walked over, a trail of shit and blood and mud left in her wake. She must have come right off a battlefield somewhere by the looks of her. "I thought I made it clear to you, my friend, that your queen needs to toughen up."

Annoyed the god had the nerve to say that, Dagmar replied, "If she were any tougher, she'd be nothing but muscles, eyes, and a sword."

"I don't mean physically, and you know it."

"She's doing the best she can. You can't actually blame her for worrying about her children. Not after what your consort did."

"Don't blame him."

"Why not? This is his fault."

"You still haven't forgiven him, have you?"

"After throwing me to Minotaurs? You must be joking."

"You humans take everything so damn personally."

"When I'm thrown to Minotaurs—you're right."

"Fine. Be that way." The door behind Dagmar opened, and Eir walked out, brushing past her.

Dagmar watched her and finally asked, "And where's Nannulf?" She couldn't think of a time that she'd seen the goddess without her loyal wolf-god companion.

"Off taking care of something."

Crossing her arms over her chest, Dagmar scowled. She didn't like the sound of that whatsoever.

Ragnar tromped through the trees toward Esyld's house. He hated doing this. He hated being the one to bring her back to Dark Plains. But he already had a plan.

Initially, he'd thought of telling Esyld to run and then reporting to Rhiannon that she wasn't at her house. Yet he had a feeling the queen would never believe it and he still didn't think the Horde was ready to get on her bad side. Plus, there was the risk that Esyld wouldn't run. She had that air about her. As if she was determined to stand her ground. He admired that about her.

So his next option wasn't perfect but better than nothing. He'd offer to argue her case before Rhiannon and the Southland Elders. He knew a bit of Fire Breather law, and with a good friend's help—at least he hoped they were still friends—

Ragnar felt certain he could build a solid case that would protect Esyld.

Yes, it seemed the most fair and logical thing to do, and all he needed was for Esyld not to worry. Not easy, he was sure, but he would do everything he could to keep her safe. Because if Rhiannon really did want her sister dead, she would have sent her mate's kin to retrieve Esyld rather than him.

Confident in his decision, Ragnar tromped on.

Near the clearing that led to Esyld's house, Ragnar stopped. He had been walking for little more than ten minutes, but still . . .

Turning his head, Ragnar looked over his shoulder. She sat in the middle of his back on her rump, her tail and wings hanging over one side, her crossed back legs over the other. She used a metal file to sharpen her talons—and she hummed.

How long has she been back there?

Ragnar had always prided himself on the sharpness of his senses. Hearing a rabbit's twitching nose a mile away, spotting a hawk twenty miles above, or scenting fresh cattle a hundred miles off. But how could he not know that a spoiled royal was using him like a beast of burden? How could he not hear that gods-damn humming?

He geared up to shake her off, but she asked, "Where are we going?"

"I have some business to take care of."

"Business? Out here? By yourself?" She lifted her claw and blew on her talons.

"I was coming right back."

"Yes, but you might be in danger. I could help."

Right. Of course you could. "It would be better if you return to my brothers."

She slid off his back, her tail taking an enormously long time to slide up and over him as she walked around.

"Lord Ragnar, may I ask you a question?"

"If you'd like."

"Do you not like me?"

Unsure where this might be going, Ragnar simply stated, "I thought our relationship was decided two years ago, princess."

"But that was such a long time ago. There's no reason for us not to be friends now."

"Friends? You and I?"

She stroked her claw along his shoulder, down his chest, her talons scraping against the scar her tail had left. Part of Ragnar wanted to break every talon she had out of pure spite. Yet another, weaker, part of him wanted to close his eyes and moan.

"I know what you're thinking," she said, her talons now concentrating on that scar. "That I'm too good for you. And, of course among some circles, you'd be absolutely right. But I'm a very progressive royal and I don't let little things like unimpressive bloodlines and barbaric tendencies stop me from having the friends I want."

"That's very big of you."

"I've always thought so." She pressed her claw to his chest, the damn scar under it angrily throbbing to life. "I've always thought it's more important to have friends you can trust," she murmured, "than friends who are merely your equal in every other way that matters."

No. He couldn't do it. He couldn't keep talking to this vapid, insipid female. No matter how much his body longed for her—and gods, was his cock screaming at him right now—it was beyond his capabilities as a dragon and a Northlander to put up with this female. And not only that . . . what in all holy hells did she think she was doing with her tail?

Ragnar slammed his back claw down on the princess's tail before it slid any farther where it should not be.

"Ow!" She yanked her tail back and moved away from him.

"Sorry. Was that your tail? I thought it was a snake." He

caught hold of her arm and pulled her around. "Now if you'll go back to my brothers—"

"Get your claws off me, peasant!"

"—I promise I won't be long and we can discuss all your progressive views on peasants and royalty to your heart's content." He shoved her in the direction of his kin. "Now go, princess, before I'm forced to get—"

The crazed princess attached herself to his head and held on, cutting off his next words and making him sigh a little.

"What are you doing?"

"Obviously I'm beating you into submission!"

"Are you not the least bit embarrassed by this display?"

"Not as embarrassed as you'll be when I'm done with you."

Ragnar caught hold of her wing, pulled the royal off, and tossed her away.

She rolled and squealed, but quickly scrambled to her claws. She crouched in what appeared to be a poorly planned attack.

"Princess Keita, I wouldn't—"

She charged him and again wrapped herself around his head.

Honestly, he didn't have time for this. And it especially didn't help that she smelled rather nice for a female who'd been trapped in a dungeon for who knew how long with human males.

He caught hold of her again, prepared to fling her as far away as necessary, but a voice beside them said, "She's not there." Ragnar recognized the voice of the foreigner.

Keita's head came up. "What do you mean she's not there?"

"She's not there."

While this vapid female had kept Ragnar distracted, the foreigner had gotten around them. Realizing he'd been duped, Ragnar yanked the princess off and slammed her to the ground.

"Och!" she yelped. "You rude bastard!"

Ragnar ignored her and raised his claw to the foreigner, unleashing a powerful blast of wind that would shove him back into the tree behind him and let him understand Ragnar was not to be toyed with. But other than the fur on his head getting blown back, the foreign dragon did nothing but stare at him.

Having witnessed the grass, leaves, and trees moving from the energy he'd unleashed, Ragnar glanced down at his claw and back up to the princess's traveling companion.

"Oh," the foreigner replied, sounding almost lazy with boredom. "Was I supposed to fall back, arms flailing, from that? Sorry. I'll keep that in mind for next time."

The princess giggled at that until Ragnar silenced her with one glare. It wasn't being laughed at that bothered him; it was the power he *didn't* sense coming off this dragon. A power Ragnar now knew the foreigner must have because he managed to hide it from him. Did the princess have any idea? And, for that matter, why would a mage this strong waste his time with someone so insipid? So useless? So pretty? Wait. He meant so stupid. Not pretty. *Where did pretty come from?*

The foreigner walked around him, helping the still-outraged princess to her claws.

"Are you all right?"

"I am *not* all right," she complained. "That barbarian assaulted me, and in the process, I scraped my ass on some rocks." She tried to see the damage but only managed to turn herself in a circle.

"Your aunt's gone, Keita. Has been for some time, I'd wager."

"That's impossible." She stopped trying to see her ass and opted for rubbing it instead. "Esyld never leaves her house except to go into town."

"That you know of. It's not like you see her every day."

A moment of regret passed, her shoulders slumping a little, but then those brown eyes locked on Ragnar. "What do you want with my aunt, warlord?"

"That's a question for your mother. She's the one who sent me here."

For a painful moment, Ragnar felt as if he'd hit the princess, she appeared so stricken. He would have said nothing if he'd known his words would cause such a reaction.

"My mother? My mother sent you here? To kill my aunt?"

"I'm not an assassin, lady. I was merely to pick up your aunt and return her and your brother to Queen Rhiannon. What your mother does from there, I have no idea."

"And you agreed?"

"It was either me or your father's kin. I assumed she'd be safer with me."

The Eastlander glanced at her. "He does have a point, Keita."

Keita headed down to her aunt's home, shifting to her human form while walking, and pushed open the door to the house. She searched for some sign of either her aunt or where she might have gone. She did a quick sweep of the room and then went through the back door to the garden.

"I told you she's not here, luv."

"Then where is she, Ren?"

"I don't know, but she's been gone for a bit."

"How do you know?"

"There's a fine layer of dust over everything—and her overall presence has begun to fade from this place."

Keeping her back to Ren and pressing her hand to her stomach, Keita asked, "Is she dead?"

"I don't know. But if she is, she didn't die here."

Ren's instincts were never wrong, and he never lied to Keita. If someone had killed her aunt, he'd know and tell her.

"Was she taken?"

"I don't sense that. It's clean here. Like she just left."

Keita faced him. "And went where?"

"I don't know, but nothing says anything is wrong either."

"Except my mother knowing Esyld's here."

"Your mother knows lots of things. I doubt she acts on a fifth of them."

"But this is Esyld the Traitor."

"Whom the queen sent a Lightning to retrieve."

"Perhaps she was hoping Esyld wouldn't survive the trip."

"Then she would have sent your father's kin, whose loyalty is unquestionable—but whose honor is a little shaky."

"You think I'm worrying over nothing, don't you?"

"You rarely worry, my friend. So when you do worry, it's never over nothing. But I'm not sure what we can do at this point."

"Track her down?"

"So your mother will definitely know where she is?"

He was right. As always.

"What do you suggest I do?"

"Go home." When she sneered, he added, "You'll never find out what your mother is up to if you don't."

"And you think she'll tell me?"

"Doubtful. But your brothers will, if they know. Their mates. Your friends in court. Don't act like you don't know how to get information, my dear Lady Keita."

Now smiling, Keita went up on her toes and draped her arms around Ren's neck. "Why, my dear friend, are you suggesting I *spy* on my mother's court?"

"I'm aghast you'd even suggest such a thing."

They laughed together until Ren gestured to the door. "Let's be off. The sooner we get back to Devenallt Mountain, the sooner we can be rid of your brother's barbarian guard unit."

The thought of that had Keita practically sprinting for the door.

As she stepped into Esyld's house, she stopped in the doorway and studied the barbarian. He stood in the middle of her aunt's house, naked—except for that travel bag he kept with him at all times—looking incredibly delicious in his extremely large and muscular human form and awfully innocent. Too innocent.

"What are you doing?" she asked him.

"Nothing."

Slowly the Lightning's gaze locked on hers, and for what felt like a lifetime, they stared at each other. He was lying—she knew he was lying—but she had no proof.

"Ready to go?" Ren asked.

"Yes," she finally replied. "I'm ready."

Ren walked out, the barbarian behind him, and, letting out a breath, Keita followed. But she stopped halfway through the house, her eyes quickly scanning the room. She felt that something was missing, but whether it was missing when they all first walked in or only after the Lightning had been alone in Esyld's house, Keita didn't know.

Unable to pinpoint anything she could accuse the warlord of—and terribly annoyed by that—she walked out and shifted back to her natural form. In silence, they returned to the others, only to find the two remaining barbarians punching at the rock wall where Ren had disappeared.

Ren turned away, his shoulders shaking, while Ragnar watched his kin, trying to figure out what they were doing. Keita raised her brows at her brother but Éibhear could only manage a helpless shrug.

And gods, she had at least several more days of this. Only the dread of seeing her mother outweighed being trapped with such distinct stupidity.

Chapter Six

They camped near the coast late that night. They stopped at a location that not only had the sea at their back but a river cutting through the land and a small lake nearby.

Vigholf and Meinhard went off to scout the area, ensuring they would all be safe for the next few hours, while the Blue gathered firewood and continued talking. Mostly to himself.

"You're exhausted," the foreigner said.

The comment was not directed at him, but Ragnar still looked over his shoulder and watched the Eastland dragon stroke his claw along the princess's cheek. For the life of him, Ragnar didn't understand the relationship these two had. Together? Not together? What?

"I am," she said, stifling a yawn. "I tried to sleep in that horrid dungeon, but all that soft sobbing and begging the gods for help . . . honestly, how many times can a man chant, 'Save me from the beast, dear gods in heaven, I repent all my ills if you'll only save me from the beast' before he stops? It's not as if I had any intention of eating him. At least that dog had been bathed recently." Her snout wrinkled a bit. "I can't just eat *anything*, you know."

"Excellent point."

"But I must admit, I am hungry."

"I'll get us something!" the Blue offered, dropping the extra wood near a pit fire he'd already started with a blast of flame. He'd been in an intolerably good mood since his sister agreed to return with them.

Keita clapped her claws together. "Would you?" she asked so sweetly it made Ragnar's back fangs ache. "I saw something with antlers over there." She pointed, and her brother charged off.

Realizing that left him alone with the princess and her . . . whatever he was, Ragnar headed off toward the nearby beach. He had no desire or patience for more ridiculous conversation. Because wasn't hearing the couple's discussion about whether eating the tail of a dog was proper etiquette or not more than one dragon should be forced to take?

Ragnar walked to the sand's edge and let the waves roll back and forth over his claws while he gazed off. When he felt calm and part of the earth, Ragnar closed his eyes and released his mind.

He searched the lines of Magick that kept all those who used such power connected. There were those who were so powerful, like the Dragon Queen, they could block at will the weaker witches and mages from ever sensing their presence. But Ragnar had strong skills and, due to the blessings and sacrifices of his mother, much power. He used his skills to skirt around Rhiannon so she could not sense him. Not easy because she was awake at this hour and calling power to her.

Once he successfully avoided the queen, Ragnar took his time and searched for Esyld. As Rhiannon had, it was through these lines that Ragnar had first discovered the queen's sister, but this night there was nothing. He hated the thought that something had happened to Esyld. Hated even more that she might be doing something that would have her head removed right along with her front and back legs and her wings. These were dangerous times, and keeping out of trouble should be a task for everyone, but especially those who lived alone in the Outerplains, because the reigning Southland Dragon Queen thought of them as her enemy.

After some fruitless searching, Ragnar accepted the fact he wouldn't find Esyld. At least not right now.

Disappointed, he released the energy that surrounded him back to the sea and opened his eyes. That's when he saw the claw waving in front of his snout.

He closed his eyes again and asked, "What are you doing?"

"Oh. You're back."

"I never left."

"Yes, but you weren't quite here either."

Ragnar opened his eyes. "Is there something you want, princess?"

"I have questions."

"Can they not wait? It's been a long day, and I'm tired."

"Of course, you're right. We can talk in the morning."

Ragnar watched her walk off, but he sensed she wouldn't sleep if he didn't answer her questions. Since they had some hard traveling coming up—none of which he planned to do with her relaxing on his back, filing her talons—he asked, "Is this about Esyld?"

She stopped, her tail scratching patterns in the sand. "If it is?"

"Then perhaps you can ask your questions quickly."

She looked at him over her shoulder. "How did you know about my aunt?"

Ragnar's eyes nearly crossed. Why did he continue to expect more from her? But at least she seemed loyal to her aunt. Esyld would need friends when she was brought back to Dark Plains. Because Ragnar had no doubt that the queen would not give up until she found her sister. "Let me be clearer, princess. Ask your questions quickly and try not to make them inane."

"Fine." Keita returned to his side. "Have you fucked her?"

Ragnar cringed. "I see we're sticking with inane."

"Not if you've fucked her. Then you're betraying your lover."

"She is not my lover."

"Now?"

"Ever."

The princess sat back on her haunches, eyes narrowing. "Why did my mother choose you?"

"I don't know."

"What has she planned for my aunt?"

"No idea."

"What *do* you know?"

"A vast number of things. But what your mother is thinking is not one of them."

An agitated talon tapped on the sand.

"Why didn't you tell your mother you knew where your aunt was?" he asked.

"Because other than fleeing for her life after my mother choked the life from my grandmother—an escape most would consider wise—my aunt has done nothing to earn or keep the title of traitor."

"Are you sure?"

"What does that mean?"

Ragnar lifted up the traveling bag that lay beside him and placed it in front of her. "Look inside."

Using her tail, Keita gingerly opened the bag and lowered her head to peek inside.

Ragnar might normally be insulted by such actions, but he knew the truth. "Could you be more obvious about having brothers?"

"Among my kin, if you open a bag without checking first, you might find yourself suddenly face-to-face with a poisonous sea snake—and you know how much their bites sting."

When nothing slithered or leaped out of the bag, she picked it up with her front claws and dug inside.

"I don't think you have enough parchment in here. And

yes, that's sarcasm." She paused, pulling a robe out of his bag. "A monk? Really?"

"An innocent nobleman's daughter?" he asked in return. "Really?"

"Point made, warlord." She shoved the robe back in the bag and continued to dig. "Ooooh, shiny."

Ragnar watched the royal closely as she pulled the necklace out from the bottom of the bag and held it up. Her gaze moved from the necklace to Ragnar. "When you're alone do you also wear a matching gown and pretty pink slippers to go with this?"

"It was in your aunt's house. Over her bed."

"Are the Northland dragons truly *that* poor you must steal a She-dragon's lone piece of jewelry?"

"Do you not recognize the style?"

She studied the piece and finally shrugged. "I've seen this style, as you call it, in every market in every town in—"

"Copies. Badly and cheaply made. This, however, is not." He took hold of the necklace and turned it over. "It's signed by the creator. Fucinus."

"I'm not familiar with his work."

"Not surprising. His only shop is in the heart of the Quintilian Sovereigns."

The royal blinked. "So?"

Ragnar handed the necklace back to her. "When was the last time you were in the Sovereigns, princess? Has your mother an alliance with the iron dragons that I am not aware of?"

"Are you suggesting . . . Esyld couldn't have . . . she wouldn't . . . she can't be that . . ." Keita's talons wrapped tight around the necklace. "You can't show this to my mother."

"Do you understand the risk you take if I don't tell her?"

"I always know the risks I take when dealing with my mother."

"And yet you'd keep this from her? Perhaps the only clue we have?"

"A clue perhaps. But my mother will take one look at this and leap, headlong, to a conclusion. That's what she does, and by the gods she does it well."

"But protecting Esyld now—"

"I didn't say I would protect her. I simply want real proof. This necklace could have been smuggled out of the Sovereigns. It wouldn't be the first or the last. Esyld could have found it, bought it. It could have been given to her. All these things are possibilities but once my mother sees this, the chance to explore all that will be gone. So I'm saying again, you can't show this to my mother."

To Ragnar's surprise, he didn't doubt her words, or her conviction. He did, however, wonder at the why of it. Did she love her aunt so much? Or hate her mother even more?

"And what if Esyld has betrayed you?"

"Betraying me is one thing, my lord. Betraying my mother, another." Keita stepped closer. "But if I find out Esyld has betrayed the throne . . . then she will have a problem that even I will be unable to get her out of."

"Isn't the throne your mother?"

"No. My mother is the queen. But the throne belongs to her subjects. To betray the throne is to betray us all."

"And if Esyld has done that . . . ?"

"Then she forfeits her life."

Ragnar frowned. "It would be that easy for you?"

"Of course not. But the throne must be protected." She studied the necklace held in the middle of her claw. "It is beautiful work."

"It is. Have you ever been to the Sovereigns?"

Keita laughed. "Why would I do something so completely insane as that?"

"You were in the Northlands during my father's time. I'd say that was pretty insane. Perhaps I don't see the difference."

"You don't. To get caught in the Northlands may mean a forced mating, which may not be pleasant, Lord Ragnar, but at least one is still alive. To get caught in the Sovereigns, however, means a crucifixion. And a crucifixion means I'll be dead. Not much one can do when dead, now is there? Besides"—she crinkled her nose again—"I've heard crucifixions are not quick deaths, especially for dragons."

"They're not." Ragnar again faced the vast sea before him. "There's lots of screaming and bleeding and a cheering crowd. It's extremely unpleasant."

She leaned around and peered at him. "You've seen one."

"I've seen lots of things."

"I mean you've seen one in the Sovereigns."

"I have."

"Why would you risk going there? I heard the Irons loathe the Lightnings."

"They do, but it's hard to fight an enemy you've never seen."

"I'd heard they loathe you, but I hadn't heard they'd become your enemies."

"I don't know they are, but I've been hearing for years that the Sovereigns are readying for war."

The princess snorted and looked out over the sea, shaking her head. "My Lord Ragnar, the Sovereigns are *always* readying for war. So I wouldn't feel too special." She looked over at him and, with a small smile, said, "From what I understand, they'll kill just about anybody."

"Gods, Ren. The Sovereigns? If she's had any dealings with them, I won't be able to help her. No one will."

Ren of the Chosen Dynasty watched his friend and traveling companion stare off across the small lake they'd been relaxing in while they waited for Éibhear to finish cooking the meat he'd brought back.

"Before you begin panicking—"

"I do not panic."

"—let's see what we can find out first. We'll be passing Fenella in the next two days anyway. We'll stop there for a bit. I know someone who can appraise the necklace for us, and I'd trust him quicker than that slack-jawed barbarian."

Keita chuckled a little. "And I can visit Gorlas. If anyone knows anything—"

"It'll be Gorlas," Ren agreed, knowing their old friend and mentor's reach wasn't confined to the Southlands. That elf had connections *everywhere* and knowledge about *everyone*. He prided himself on that. "But I want you to stop worrying about your aunt for now. There's nothing we can do at the moment."

"I guess."

Not willing to let Keita obsess over what she couldn't control, a little-known curse of hers, Ren removed the wine cup from her hand and placed it on the hard-packed dirt beside them. He motioned to his hair and turned away from her.

"My hair needs a good scrubbing, not your whining."

"I'm not a servant, Eastlander."

"But no one does it quite as well as you, my dear, old, sweet friend." He looked over his shoulder at her and fluttered his eyes.

"You're pathetic," she reminded him even while she rested on her knees and proceeded to scrub his hair clean of all the dirt and grime.

"'Tis true, but I've learned to accept my weakness. You should as well."

He sighed luxuriously and let his head fall back a little more. "I guess I should warn you that when we get back to Dark Plains, we may have to deal with your cousin."

"You'll have to be more specific than that, I'm afraid. If there's a feast at Garbhán Isle, there will be many cousins I'll have to deal with."

Ren laughed. "Good point, but I was specifically speaking of, um, Elestren."

"Oh."

Ren was sure that Keita's last few days at the Dragonwarrior training mountain, Anubail, were still firmly etched in her often fleeting memory. What a bad suggestion that had been on his part. A few months of unarmed combat training were all she really needed, and she only needed that to help her get over how helpless she'd felt while in the hands of the Northlanders. What he hadn't counted on was that green-scaled cousin of hers. For not only was Keita no better in a fistfight now than she had been then, but last either of them had heard, even Keita's father—Bercelak the Great himself—could not manage to get the ban lifted that prevented Keita from ever returning to Anubail Mountain.

"I still say that was not my fault," Keita went on. She'd been arguing this same point since the day he'd come for her at her father's urgent request. Still bleeding from a head wound and nursing a broken forearm, Keita kept saying what she was saying now. "What happened to her was an accident . . . self-defense even, and she has no one to blame but herself. Besides, how many times should I apologize? The fact that I, a descendant of the royal bloodline, apologized at all, should be enough. But ignoring that I not only apologized multiple times but also sent that whiny viper some very decorative and fashionable eye patches to cover that gaping wound where her eye was! In my mind that should be more than enough. Don't you agree?"

Ren clenched his jaw, but the snort slipped past his best defenses and he began laughing. Keita's arms dropped over his shoulders, her cheek pressed against his, and she joined him. Both laughing until they cried—and until they knew they were no longer alone.

The Northland dragonlord stood a few feet away, in his dragon form, scowling at them. Ren knew the Lightning was confused. He didn't understand their relationship, and Ren found that delightful. He had the feeling this dragon was not remotely used to feeling confused.

"Do you want something, warlord?" Keita asked, wiping tears from her eyes.

"There's food," he said. Then, pointing at them, he asked, "Are you two . . . what I mean is . . . are you . . ." He stopped and briefly shut his eyes. "Forget it," he said. And they watched him head back to camp.

Holding Keita's arms, Ren looked at her. "My, my, you do have his cock in a knot, don't you?"

Keita frowned. "You think?"

"Can't you tell?"

"He glares at me mostly. And talks to me as if I'm the stupidest female he's ever met. I don't think he likes me."

"I can't argue that point with you, my friend. But that doesn't mean he doesn't lust after you." And it immediately struck him how he could distract his friend for a bit until they found out more information on her aunt. "Although . . . I doubt you could get him."

"Oh, I could get him."

"Really?"

"You're all alike, Ren. Leading with your cocks, the head on your shoulders following stupidly behind."

"How much, Princess Brag-a-Lot? Since you're so sure."

"Come now. That's the easiest bet ever when a male's involved."

"That dragon is no ordinary male. His high opinion of himself doesn't allow for any fun or unnecessary fucking. He has important things to do. With important dragons, which you're not. In his estimation, of course. Not mine."

Laughing, Keita said, "Well, let's see. . . ." She tapped her chin and gazed up at the sky. "How about that gold chair you have?"

"You mean my ancient throne? It took me months to dig

that up from the bowels of my cave, and it weighs at least a thousand pounds."

"I'm not paying for shipping."

"And what do I get if you lose?"

"Which will not happen, but . . ." She pursed her lips in thought. "How about that Magick-infused sword thing you wanted?"

"The Sword of Mallolwch?" She shrugged. "You lying cow! You told me you lost it."

"No. I said, 'It's around here somewhere . . . I think. Maybe.'"

"You are the most deceitful—" Ren's headed lifted, his nostrils flaring. "Smell that?" he asked.

Keita lifted her nose and sniffed before inhaling deeply. "Éibhear's cooked meat," she sighed.

"Éibhear's cooked meat," he repeated.

Together they scrambled out of the water, shoving each other, first in human form, then in dragon, trying to be the first to get to the delicious feast they were sure Éibhear had created.

Chapter Seven

Swords were strapped to backs or around waists. Battle axes and bows were tied to saddles. Beasts that resembled horses, but with curled horns and red eyes, pawed the ice-covered ground, anxious to be on their way. Pets that traveled by their sides were summoned with a whistle or a howl. Them that were once men were taken from cages and leashed collars placed around their necks. They'd lead the way like eager dogs, running on all fours, their wills long ago broken when they'd challenged those they never thought they'd have to fear.

A never-ending ice storm railed, but it didn't matter to the likes of them. For they were on a mission given to them by one of their mighty gods. They worshipped a few but were respected by all. Because when they was given a task, nothing, absolutely nothing, stopped them from seeing it through.

Their beasts mounted, their loyal pets at their sides, them that were men running nearly on all fours, the gates to their Ice Land fortress opened and they, like demons from the underworld, were unleashed onto an unsuspecting land. And they would follow the edicts of their gods even if it meant death to any and all who got in their way.

* * *

With the sound of mighty hooves pounding against rock-hard ice still ringing in her ears, Keita awoke to find Ragnar the Cunning staring down at her.

She squeaked in surprise and called out, "Evil rises from the pit to destroy me!" He frowned, but it seemed more out of confusion than rage, and Keita turned and buried her head against the scale-covered chest behind her. Ren stroked her back with fur-covered claws, and said, "Now, now, little one. It's nothing to fear. Just a scary North Dragon with plans to destroy all that you love."

She shuddered and whispered loud enough for all to hear, "He frightens me. Make him go away."

"Shoo!" Ren said, forcing Keita to bury her snout deeper into his chest to prevent the burst of laughter bubbling up her throat. "Shoo!"

"We leave in five minutes."

"We'll be ready," Ren promised.

When the Lightning had stomped off, barking orders at his kin, Ren snorted a laugh, and Keita giggled into his chest.

"Would you two cut it out?" Éibhear chastised, busy cleaning up the campsite. "You're being intolerable."

Keita rolled onto her back and frowned at her talons when she realized one had a crack at the tip. "Who? Us?"

"Yes. You. This could only be worse if Gwenvael were here."

Both Keita and Ren sighed. "Ahhh, Gwenvael," she said.

"Good times," Ren added.

"Aye. That they were. The three of us together, causing mayhem wherever we went." Keita sat up, one forearm draped over her knee. "He's not really mated, is he?"

"He is. And she's amazing," Éibhear said.

Keita glanced at Ren, gave him a little wink. Éibhear was at the stage where *everyone* was amazing or interesting or beautiful. Of course, Keita had grown out of that stage less than a year after hatching and, if she had been told correctly, her eldest brothers, Fearghus and Briec, never went through that stage at all. So perhaps Éibhear was making up for all of them. Except, of course, Morfyd. Perfect, untainted, *loving* Morfyd.

"She's ever so smart. Extremely smart."

"Reads a lot, does she?" Ren asked, prompting Keita to elbow him in the ribs.

"She does. But it's not just that. She's insanely logical. Not like you at all, Keita."

Ren, who'd been sitting up, fell back laughing while Keita threw her claws up.

"I'll have you know I'm extremely logical."

Scattering the bones left over from their dinner the previous eve so that the local predators could use what they hadn't, Éibhear shook his head and stated, "I can assure you that Dagmar Reinholdt would never have ended up on the wrong side of an execution."

"Are you still harping on that?" Keita demanded.

"You could have gotten out of there at any time, but you always have to play your little games."

"You're bloody amazing. If I'd allowed myself to be executed, you'd have been angry. But if I'd burned down the town, you'd have been angrier." Keita got up, making sure to slap Ren's face several times with her tail since he was still laughing. "I can never win with you!"

Éibhear stared at her over his shoulder. "You wouldn't have been in that situation in the first place if you hadn't killed the man."

"What part of 'It wasn't me' are you not grasping?"

Her baby brother tipped his head to the side, and Keita bared her fangs before yelling, "It *wasn't* me!"

Éibhear pointed a talon. "But did you plan to kill him?"

"What does that have to do with anything?"

"I'm sorry," Ragnar cut in. "But exactly what kind of answer is that?"

Keita glared over at him. Gods he was big. Completely blocking out the two suns with that big body and even bigger head! And all that purple. What an annoying, strange color! "And at what point did you feel you were invited into this conversation, cretin?"

"Keita!" Éibhear snapped and immediately stood by the Lightning. "That was rude. Apologize!"

Keita was about to tell Éibhear what he could do with his bloody apologies when Ren whispered in her ear, "Have you already forgotten our wager, my friend?"

Dammit. She had forgotten. But that, like most things, was not her fault. It was early, and she hadn't eaten yet. "Besides, we do have to put up with all of them for a few more days. It couldn't hurt to be nice," Ren added softly.

Knowing her friend was right, Keita loosely waved her claws in the air. "Gods! I am sorry, Lord Ragnar. As you can see, I'm not a morning dragon, and I get a bit snappy before first meal. My sincerest apologies."

"We're all that way," Meinhard muttered while he packed up his travel bag.

"No worries," Vigholf tossed in.

"I can and always have been able to speak for myself," Ragnar said, his gaze still on Keita.

"Well, you do forgive me, don't you, my lord?" She walked up to him, her tail swinging out behind her until she was close enough that the tip could move up his chest. "It would be awful if you were still angry with me."

Ragnar stared at her tail while his brother and cousin stood up straight, their attention locked on her . . . which was about the time her brother grabbed her tail and dragged her into the forest.

"We'll be right back," he said, pulling her a good distance away, ignoring all the trees and brush they knocked down or completely destroyed in the process.

"Éibhear, you little shit! Let me go!" He did, by flinging her tail away from him, her body naturally following.

"What are you up to?"

"I don't know what you're talking about."

"Don't lie to me, Keita." He leaned in, pointed a talon at her. "You and Ren together is rarely a good thing for outsiders. So I ask again, what are you up to?"

Keita stood, using her front claws to brush the forest dirt off her scales. "I am up to nothing, little brother."

"Don't give me that. You just better not be playing games again."

"What games?"

"Keita—"

"Oh, what, little brother? You've been off for two years and you think you can order *me* around like Fearghus and Briec?"

Éibhear blinked. "They order you around?"

"They've tried. They've failed. Trust me when I say you will fare no better."

"Look." He caught hold of her shoulder and pulled her a little farther away, lowering his voice. "I understand you have much to hate this dragon for. He kidnapped you, held you hostage, and tried to negotiate with Mum for you."

Keita shrugged. "I'm over that."

Éibhear released her. "What do you mean you're over that? How can you be over that?"

"Because I am. Unlike the rest of my kin, I don't hold grudges. I never have. They're boring. You know how—"

"Yes!" he cut in. "I know how you hate being bored."

"Then you don't have to worry I'm out for vengeance. He never physically harmed me. His brother and cousin were very kind given the situation. So . . . I'm over it, and want nothing but the best for all involved."

"Aw, Keita." Éibhear buried his face into his claws. "You're trying to bed him, aren't you?"

"I don't know what you're talking—"

His head snapped up, silver eyes glaring. "Keita."

"It's for a throne! And what do you care who or what Ren and I wager on?"

"Because I remember well how ugly things can get when you two start this. And I want you both to stop it right now."

"I take orders from no one, brother, but especially not you. Besides. I really want that throne." She turned to walk away, but Éibhear placed his back claw on her tail.

"Dammit! Why do you all attack my tail?"

"Because it's the most dangerous part of you. And I can't believe you and Ren are wagering on who you can get into bed. Aren't you too old for that?"

"Not when it involves a throne!"

Snarling, her brother said, "Now listen to me. When the feast ends, I want to go back with Lord Ragnar and the others. Don't ruin this for me."

"Go back? To the Northlands? Whatever for?"

"I'm learning a lot. I'll never be as good as Briec or Fearghus if I stay here."

"I notice you left Gwenvael off that list."

"I guess he has his moments. When he's not whining."

Keita leaned in and whispered, "You're not becoming like the Northlanders, are you?"

"What do you mean?"

"You don't want to find a mate and lop her wings off or anything, do you?"

"They don't do that anymore." Keita smirked, and her brother said adamantly, "They don't!"

"As long as you're not getting any strange ideas. Or, you know, trying to avoid anyone in particular by returning to the Northlands."

"I'm not avoiding anyone."

"Uh-huh. Not even cute, tall nieces who aren't actually blood relations?"

"We're not having this conversation—again."

"Cute, tall nieces who aren't actually blood relations, but have the most adorable smile known to man or the gods?"

"*Can we just go?*" he bellowed, storming past her.

"No, no, brother. I guess I was wrong. You're clearly not *avoiding* anyone."

Ragnar was waiting to leave, the two suns rising higher as it grew later. He had a talon tapping when the siblings returned. The big blue royal stomping along like a cranky child and his sister running up behind him, yelling, "Just admit it! Just admit how you feel!"

The Blue picked up his travel bag. "Let it go, Keita."

"Just admit it! You'll feel better."

"Shut. Up."

"Make me." She went up on her back legs and brought her front claws up, curling them into fists. "Let's go. Right here. Right now. You're not so big and tough that I can't still take you."

Vigholf leaned in and whispered to Ragnar. "She has no idea the truth of that."

Meinhard slammed his back claw into Vigholf.

"Ow!"

With the elegance of a wounded animal, the princess danced around her brother. "Come on. Take your best shot, little brother."

"I'm not hitting you."

She ducked; she weaved. And all of it quite badly.

Vigholf sighed. "This is what happens when you let females think they can fight like the males."

"I hear their human queen is good," Meinhard remarked.

"She's not half bad," the Eastland dragon stated. "Although I have heard she is no friend of the Minotaur."

Vigholf snorted. "Our Aunt Freida, with her one arm and

missing foot, would be good too, with five thousand legions at her back."

"No, Keita!" the Blue yelped. "Not the tickling! Stop it!"

"Think we should rescue the royal from his sister?" Meinhard asked Ragnar.

"If we hope to leave before the end of time . . ."

Briec the Mighty, second oldest in the House of Gwalchmai fab Gwyar, fourth in line to the throne of the White Dragon Queen now that his eldest brother had bred his demon spawn twins, Shield Hero of the Dragon Wars, Former Lord Defender of the Dragon Queen's Throne, Benevolent Ruler of the fair Talaith's heart, and proud father of two amazing daughters who were perfect merely because they were *his* daughters, located his eldest brother in the war room.

Fearghus stood behind the large table, an extensive map open in front of him. Brastias, General of Queen Annwyl's armies, to his left, and Dagmar Reinholdt, the only female capable of tolerating his younger brother, Gwenvael, on his right. A small group of Annwyl's elite guard stood around the table.

Fearghus looked up from the map. "What is it, Briec?"

"I just heard from Éibhear. He's heading home."

"Good." Fearghus returned his focus to the map.

"And Keita's with him."

"Yes!"

Fearghus's head came up again, and both he and Briec looked over at several of the soldiers who were grinning and slapping each other on the back. When Briec made black smoke come out of his nostrils, they looked away and stopped smiling.

Briec stepped farther into the room. "What's this?" he asked, pointing at the map.

"Dagmar heard from Ghleanna—" Fearghus began.

"Izzy?" Briec immediately asked.

"She's fine, brother. Ease yourself."

Briec's eldest, Iseabail, a soldier with Annwyl's army, had been out with his Aunt Ghleanna's troops for nearly two years now. And although he was not Izzy's father by blood, he worried for her every day. Blood or not, Izzy was his daughter. She would always be his daughter.

"Then what is it?" Briec asked.

"More problems in the west. Entire towns destroyed near the Aricia Mountains."

"I thought the army had a handle on the barbarians in the west."

"The ones near the Western Mountains, yes, but we haven't even moved past them yet."

"Still? How hard is it to drive barbarian cretins back to the mud huts from which they came?" He glanced at Dagmar. "No offense."

Cold grey eyes shielded by small circles of glass looked up from the map. "Since my mud-hut-living, barbarian, cretin people are not from the west . . . none taken."

"We're getting calls for assistance from the western kings," Brastias explained.

Briec didn't see the problem. "So send another legion."

"I don't like it," Fearghus grumbled.

"You don't like anything."

"Not you, of course, but I lie and tell our mother I do." Fearghus looked at Dagmar. "Have you heard anything?"

"What makes you think that I—" A room filled with males snorting in disbelief cut the Northlander off. "I wanted to get more information," she admitted.

"More information on what?"

"Possible problems coming from beyond the Aricia Mountains."

"Beyond?" Frowning, Briec studied the map. "The only thing beyond the Aricia Mountains is . . ."

The room grew silent, and Dagmar raised her hands, palms out. "Let me get more information before we jump to any conclusions."

"A problem coming from that far west," Brastias murmured, "cannot be ignored by Annwyl."

"She's not ignoring anything." And Briec could hear the snap in Fearghus's voice. "Far from it."

"What part of 'Let me get more information before we jump to any conclusions' were all of you not clear on?" Dagmar asked.

"Fine. Get the information. Then Annwyl can decide what she wants to do."

It wasn't that the human warriors said anything, they didn't. It was their silence that spoke volumes.

"What?" Fearghus asked. "What is it?"

"If Annwyl plans to hole up here for the next sixteen years, Fearghus, you're going to have to find another to lead our men into war. *If*," Brastias added, glancing at Dagmar, "war is coming."

"Isn't that your job, general?"

"My job is to lead the troops into battle. But Annwyl's our queen. She has to lead us into war."

Fearghus let out a great sigh. "And she can only do that by leaving her children?"

"No. But she can't keep avoiding war either. Trying to patch up problems with a troop here, a legion there isn't doing anyone any favors. It's just pulling her army apart."

Briec watched his brother. Fearghus knew the general was right, but that didn't make the situation easier for him.

Catching Brastias's attention, Briec suggested, "You may want to warn Morfyd that Keita's coming home."

"Warn her?"

"Trust me, general. Warn her." Then Briec gave a small jerk of his head toward the door. Brastias nodded and left with his men.

Once the door closed behind them, Briec dropped into a chair across from his brother, propping his feet up on the table. "All right, what don't I know?"

Fearghus muttered something, but rather than get the dragon to repeat himself—always a chore since Fearghus was a born mutterer—Briec focused on Dagmar.

"Annwyl has become reluctant to make decisions that might thrust us into war," Dagmar said.

"I've seen your female, brother. She looks ready for war to me."

"She's torn," Fearghus admitted. "She's ready to stomp out whatever is terrorizing the territories past the Western Mountains, but she's terrified to leave the children."

"Why? They won't be alone. They'll have us. The Cadwaladr Clan. She couldn't ask for better or stronger protection than that."

"I can't explain it, Briec. She's not talking to me. I just know that to get her any farther than my cave these days has become near impossible."

"And," Dagmar added, "to discuss problems that might be occurring outside Garbhán Isle is also a challenge." Dagmar walked around the table and leaned against it, her arms crossing over her chest. "It's hard to convince her the children will be safe without her for a little while when we can't even keep a nanny for longer than a moon or two."

"Wait. What happened to the last one?" Briec asked.

Dagmar shook her head, and Fearghus let out a long sigh before facing the wall behind him.

Briec grimaced. "Oh." Thankfully, Briec had no problems like this with his younger daughter. His girl was sweet beyond imagining—something she must have gotten from him, since there was no way she could have inherited that trait from her mother. So he had no worries when he left her alone with anyone. All that worried him was what weight she possibly carried on those tiny shoulders. He'd never seen someone so young look so serious—all the time. She never smiled. Ever. She simply gazed at all around her with those eyes that anyone could get lost in. He had heard a few say that when she stared at them, it was as if she were staring into their souls.

To be honest, Briec thought she was.

But none of that helped his brother now. Because a paranoid, well-trained, ready-for-anything Annwyl with no war or battle to head off to was nothing but a volcano waiting to explode. Everyone at Garbhán Isle knew it—and that's what had everyone so on edge.

"I'm sure we'll figure out something. Maybe Keita can help. When she gets here."

Fearghus sniffed. "Two years and no word from her. And she'll come back like none of it happened."

"You know how Keita is. She blocked us all, even Éibhear."

"Yes, but it's not like she's Gwenvael."

"Because we actually care if she's dead or alive?"

"Exactly."

"You two do know I'm right here?" Dagmar asked.

"It's not whether we know you're here or not," Briec explained. "It's whether we *care* that you're here or not. And, I'm sure to your surprise, tiny crushable human, we actually don't. Care, that is."

Dagmar adjusted her spectacles. "Actually what surprises me is that Talaith has not killed you in your sleep yet."

Briec grinned while Fearghus laughed. "Aye. It amazes her as well."

Chapter Eight

They were still in the Outerplains when they took their first break in the afternoon. It should have been only a quick break of thirty minutes or less, but the princess shifted to human and put on a dress, which was strange enough. Then she dug into Ragnar's bag and threw his chain-mail leggings and shirt at him. "Get dressed," she ordered.

"Why?"

"Don't question—just do." She grinned and walked off. Ragnar kept on eating the dried meat from his bag until Vigholf shoved him with his shoulder. "Go on then."

"Go on where?"

"Wherever she's going. Don't be an idiot."

"I've got more important—"

Now Meinhard shoved his other shoulder. "Go. We'll be here when you get back."

"We need to leave."

"Would an extra half hour really kill you, brother?" Vigholf motioned toward the royal, smiling. "Go. She's waiting."

Knowing this was a waste of time but sure his kin wouldn't let it go until he'd followed after the female like a needy puppy, Ragnar shifted to human and pulled on his leggings and shirt. He also added a sword strapped to his back, several daggers in his boots, and a hooded cape to hide his hair. Once dressed, he set off after Her Highness and found her leaning against a tree less than a half mile away.

"Took you long enough," she complained, then latched onto his arm and started off.

"Where are we going?"

"You'll see. It's not far." She glanced up at him. "You look so tense. All that stress can't be good for you."

"I always look tense; it doesn't mean I am."

"But you have such a handsome face. Why waste it scowling all the time?"

Ragnar stopped, the princess stopping with him since she was holding on to him. "What are you up to?"

"I'm taking you for a walk."

"Why?"

"You don't want to walk with me?"

He didn't answer, and she said, "I'll make it easy for you." She slipped her small hand into his, their fingers interlacing. "Now you can't get away," she murmured, and he realized that she was right.

They reached the clearing Keita had caught sight of when they were flying over the area, and she grinned up at the warlord. He, however, was busy rolling his eyes and looking as if he wanted to wish himself a million miles away.

"Oh, come on. A few minutes. What could it hurt?"

"I am in no mood for a fair, princess."

"I still hear prince-ass, but no bother." She tugged on his arm again, not stopping until he began to walk with her.

"I adore fairs," Keita told him as they got closer. A juggler jumped in front of them, tossing several clubs in the air. "They're so much fun!"

"And I can tell we're getting closer to the Southlands."

"Don't you have fairs in the North?"

"No."

"You should. A fair is a wonderful thing for humans. They don't get enough entertainment in my estimation."

"You're quite the human lover."

"I wasn't always," she admitted. "I could sometimes be quite cruel. Especially to the men. And I nearly destroyed an entire village once. I don't even think I was seventy-five winters yet."

"Why?"

"The leader of their village wanted to use me as a protector by chaining me. And not in a fun way, either, but like some guard dog. Me! A dragoness of the royal bloodline. I made my point, though, and received a spiffy new name to go along with it. I doubt that the few humans left alive—mostly women and children—ever tried that again with some other dragon."

"Most likely not."

"But I realized later they were simply trying to protect their village, their people. It's not any more or less than we do; it was just handled badly by those in charge. Over time, I began to realize it's sometimes all about leadership and who rules. A bad ruler can put the most kind and wonderful people into a very horrible situation they don't know how to get out of."

"Is that why you didn't destroy Bampour's fortress?"

She nodded. "Why make all those people suffer because of their bad ruler?" Keita winked at the juggler, and they walked around and headed to the stalls selling everything from food to clothes to weapons. "These days, with most humans, I'm more like my grandfather, Ailean the Beautiful."

"I thought his name was Ailean the Wicked."

"To some. To me he was Ailean the Beautiful. He adored me. And like him, I love to spend my time as human, among humans. I find them so amusing and cute."

"You mean like baby ducks?" he asked, unable to keep the sarcasm from his voice.

Keita grinned. "Exactly like baby ducks!" She stopped at an iron smith and looked over his wares. "These are nice weapons."

"If you say so."

When she saw the smith glare, Keita quickly pulled the Northlander away. "Could you at least pretend to be pleasant? No use insulting the man's goods while he's standing right there."

"Should I lie to him?"

"Aye! You should. Would it kill you to do so?"

"If I tried to pretend those weak weapons he'd created could protect me in a true fight—yes."

Keita stopped and looked up at the warlord. "Are you always like this?"

"As a matter of fact . . . no." He returned her gaze. "It seems to be *you*."

The royal dropped his arm and flounced away, only to return a few moments later. "You know, I'm *trying* to be nice."

"I know. I just don't know why."

"I'm always nice. I'm known for my niceness."

"You mean when you're not trying to kill people."

She pointed at her chest. "*I* did not kill him."

"But you were going to."

She let out a breath and glanced around. No one was paying them much attention, so she stepped closer and said, "I tell you this in confidence."

"As you like."

"Bampour had sent an assassin to kill my brother's children in their cribs. Because he believes they're evil."

"Are they?"

"Of course not!"

"How would you know? You haven't been home."

"Och!" She stormed off. "I don't know why I bother talking to you."

He didn't know either, but there was something about annoying the royal he did find enjoyable. He knew it wasn't a very honorable thing to do, but he simply couldn't help himself.

Ragnar caught up with her while she stood at a dressmaker's stall.

"What do you want?" she snapped while she examined the already-made gowns.

"I didn't mean to anger you."

"Is that supposed to be an apology?"

"No," he admitted. "It's not."

"You are the most . . . frustrating male."

"So I've been told."

She pulled a dress off one of the wooden racks and placed it against her body. "What do you think?"

"We both know you look beautiful in anything. Will you force me to remind you of that fact constantly?"

"Would it kill you to simply say it?" She placed the gown back on the rack and continued to search. "Do you have a mate, warlord?"

"No."

"Does this surprise you? Because it doesn't surprise me."

"You don't have a mate either."

"I don't want a mate. Clinging, grasping males who feel the need to brand you in some ancient ritual that allows them to feel superior while ruining my beautiful human skin." She held up her right arm and stroked it with her left hand. "Look at this skin. This is gorgeous. And I've managed to maintain it for quite a long time with very little effort. I'm not about to allow some pathetic male to ruin it so he can crow to his friends afterward."

"Well, you've managed to turn eons of ancient and

powerful mystical rituals to dragons everywhere into an 'I hate males' diatribe that somehow centers around you."

"I don't hate males." She picked up another gown, scrunched her nose a bit, and quickly put it back. "On the whole, I adore them."

"How can you say you adore them?"

"But I do. For short periods of time. Then again, I adore children for short periods of time and rainstorms for short periods of time and hot, sunny days—for short periods of time. But anything that goes on and on for ages just gets on my nerves."

"Good to know."

"So what do you look for in a female?" she asked, and Ragnar frowned a bit.

"Pardon?"

"What do you look for in a bed partner? Tall? Fat? Long tail? Short tail? Wide hips? Narrow hips?"

He held his hand up. "All right . . . stop." He didn't like where this conversation was going. "I don't look for anything in females."

"Ohhh." She gazed at the dress in her hands, then said, "Well, I hope you're not interested in Ren then, because that's not his sort of thing." She looked off and added, "I don't think."

"I'm not looking for *that* either."

"You don't have to sound so judgmental."

"I'm not. I just don't know why you're asking all these questions."

"And I don't know why you won't just answer."

"Fine. I'm looking for someone nice and sweet who I won't have to sleep with one eye open to ensure I see the next morning."

"Good luck finding that among She-dragons," she murmured.

"What was that?" Ragnar asked, even though he'd heard just fine.

"Nothing." She put another gown back and headed away from the stall. Growling, Ragnar followed.

Éibhear walked up to his small group and quickly realized that it was even smaller than when he'd left. He'd only been gone for a short time. "Where did everyone go?"

In answer, the only two remaining, Vigholf and Meinhard, grunted in reply. It was something Éibhear had been forced to get used to during his time in the Northlands. By nature, none of the Lightnings was a very talkative lot. Unless they were drinking, but that only happened at night, and to be honest, Éibhear couldn't drink every night as most of the Northerners could. Not if he wanted to be up for training by the next suns-rise.

Yet Éibhear had spent enough time around the Lightnings to know his first mistake. He waited until the Lightnings paused shoveling food into their mouths, and then he asked, "Where's my sister?"

"Off with Ragnar," Meinhard replied.

"Did Ren go with them?"

"Nah. He's over there somewhere."

Shit. Working hard not to panic, he asked, "Do you know where Keita and Ragnar went?"

"Nah."

"Do you know when they'll be back?"

Vigholf chewed his food and studied Éibhear. "You questioning my brother's honor when he's with your sister?"

Éibhear shook his head. "Oh, no, no. Not at all." Éibhear scratched his head with the tip of his tail. "My sister, however, doesn't really have any honor. So that might be a problem."

The two males looked up at him, staring. Appearing faintly disgusted. "Don't misunderstand," Éibhear tried to explain. "My sister is a lovely dragoness. Truly, she is. But, I fear, she may try to . . . well . . ."

"Try to what, lad? Spit it out."

"She may try to use him"—he whispered the next word—"sexually."

The Lightnings looked at each other, and then Meinhard said to Éibhear, "I wouldn't worry about that if I were you, lad."

"You don't understand." Éibhear stepped closer. "My sister has a way about her. . . . Males become attached. Maniacally attached. After just one night with her. Sometimes just one hour. And that could be . . . bad. If my father has to get involved."

"But I think they just went for a walk," Vigholf said, looking torn between laughter and confusion.

"Right. Just walking. Maybe we could go look for them."

"Look, lad," Meinhard said, sounding tired, "I don't see the problem here. They're both adult dragons who went for a walk. And what happens on that walk is their business."

"Right. I'm just a little concerned about inter-territorial relations."

"You're concerned about what?" Vigholf asked.

"Our alliance."

"You think that's at risk?"

"I know how this works. Something happens between them; Lord Ragnar becomes attached. Keita, however, does not. He pushes the issue. Keita gets our father, brothers, and cousins to push back, and before anyone knows it . . . war."

"From a walk?"

Meinhard waved Éibhear's concerns away. "You're assuming your sister wants Ragnar."

"Well, now that a wager's involved . . ." The words had slipped out before Éibhear could stop them, and he knew immediately he'd said too much. With a nod, "I'll go look for Ren."

He started to walk off, but both Lightnings were on either side of him, big arms looping around his neck, holding him in place.

"Now be a good lad," Meinhard said, grinning. "And tell us all about this wager."

Keita happily headed to one of the jewelry stalls. Gods, she loved jewelry!

"So why did you feel the need to handle the Bampour thing yourself?" Ragnar asked her.

"I was in town." When he frowned at her reply, she held up a necklace. "What do you think?"

"I think it looks expensive."

"A cheap one, I see." She sighed, putting the necklace back.

"We call it thrifty in the Northlands."

Disgusted by that word—no dragon should be cheap or "thrifty"—Keita asked, "So when you're ready to mate, will you kidnap a female?"

"We don't do that anymore."

"Your father did it to me."

"And he's dead now. Times have changed."

"Good." She moved to another stall, this one filled with crystal jewelry. "Many of my female cousins will be in attendance at the feast, I'm sure, and I don't need you and your kin trying to take off with them."

When the Northlander snorted, she stopped and faced him. "What's so funny?"

"That you'd think we'd take off with a Cadwaladr female."

"And why wouldn't you?" When he raised a brow, she admitted, "All right, a few of them might be a wee bit . . . burly. But they have good hearts and are loyal to a fault."

"So I've heard."

"Look, not everyone can be as beautiful as me—and I refuse to be attached, so you best go for what you can get."

"How is it possible for you to be this arrogant?"

Keita laughed. "And I thought you'd met my family."

* * *

While she devoured a turkey leg he'd been forced to buy for her—she'd already been eating it when she pointed out that she had no coin on her—they made their way back to the rest of their travel party.

She continued to talk while they walked along, and Ragnar couldn't help but watch her human body move. Her dress was loose around her—and new. He had no idea where she'd gotten it from, considering the last gown he'd seen her in had been the dirty one she was wearing when he'd rescued her. He decided not to ask, since he didn't want to know, and instead focused on the fact that although she made sure to get a new dress, she was still barefoot. He simply didn't know why. Nor did he know why he was so fascinated by her feet . . . and those legs . . . and whatever else she had under that dress.

Yet before Ragnar could really bring himself to worry about his obsession with the royal's lack of footwear, he stopped and replayed in his head what she'd just told him moments before until he was forced to ask for clarification. "You tore out your cousin's eye?"

"I didn't *tear* it out." She licked the juice from her turkey leg off the fingers of her free hand. "I yanked it out with the tip of my tail."

When his mouth dropped open, she quickly explained, "It was self-defense."

"Isn't that the same excuse you used about the guard dog you ate?"

"Perhaps. But with Elestren, it really was self-defense. She hit me with a warhammer. In the head and arm. And let me tell you, she put some force behind it."

"Why? What did you do?"

Now her mouth dropped open. "*I* didn't do anything."

"Keita—"

"I didn't! For once. Unless she's still holding that time I called her a fat-ass against me. But that was years ago."

They began walking again. "Anyway, she came at me again with that bloody hammer after she'd already broken my forearm and bashed my head in, and I panicked and used my tail . . . which apparently one is not supposed to do during training."

"Training for what?"

"To fight. So the next time the likes of you and your father try to kidnap me—"

Ragnar again stopped walking, his hands curling into fists. "Don't ever put me in the same category with my father," he told her plain.

Eyes wide, she said, "I didn't mean—"

"And I rescued you. And when you were safe in your territory, I let you go. With both your wings still in place. I can assure you that Olgeir the Wastrel would have done none of that."

"All right."

Ragnar knew he'd snapped at her, but he couldn't help himself. Yet he felt like a right bastard when all she did in return was hold up what was left of the turkey leg and ask, "Do you want the rest?"

He should apologize to her, but he wouldn't. Not when she dared compare him to his father. "Well . . . since I paid for it." He took the leg out of her hand and tore off what remained of the meat before sucking out the marrow. When he was done, he handed her what was left—about three inches of hollow bone.

She held it up, her gaze moving from it to him. Several times.

When she said nothing, he did. "Let's get back. We've got many miles to go before we can stop for the night."

They began walking again, and Keita, after tossing aside

that piece of bone, asked, "Tell me, Lord Ragnar—do you want me?"

"Like the air I breathe."

They both stopped walking again, the royal's eyes wide as she looked up at him.

"But that's why I have to stay away from you, isn't it?" he asked.

Her shocked expression faded, and that smile—the one he was certain no one else but him saw—slid into place. "Only if you're one of the clingy ones," she admitted. "I do so hate clingy."

She nibbled on her bottom lip, her gaze examining him from his head to his feet and back. She giggled. "And gods, I do so hope you're not one of the clingy ones."

Her smile now wide, she headed back to their traveling party. "Come along, warlord, we've got many miles to go before we can stop for the night."

And for the first time in nearly a century, Ragnar felt completely out of his depth.

Chapter Nine

They made good time to where they'd rest for the night despite their brief break at the fair, and were up and moving before the two suns rose the next day. By mid-afternoon, they finally landed a league outside the Southland border city of Fenella at the request of the Eastland dragon. It was supposed to be a short break, one for food and water, but then Her Majesty was walking off with her Eastland companion—as human. In another new gown. *Where is she getting these clothes from?*

"Where's your sister going?" Ragnar asked the Blue.

"I don't know."

"Did you think to ask?"

"No."

"Aren't you concerned?"

"No."

Ragnar's claws itched to wrap around the royal's throat, but that would be a waste of a perfectly good tree-clearer. "Get us food."

"All right!" the Blue said happily, and headed off to raid the herd of sheep they'd passed on their way here.

"Could he annoy you more?" Vigholf asked with a chuckle.

"I don't think that's possible."

"You're too hard on him. He's a pup. We were like that once. Well . . . maybe not you, but I was. So was Meinhard. He'll grow out of it."

Meinhard cracked his neck, the sound echoing around the glen. "You going after her then?"

"She has her little foreign lap dog with her—what does she need me for?"

"Someone sounds bitter. And you've been a bitter bastard ever since you've returned with her from the fair. Why? What happened?"

"Nothing." And that was the absolute truth of it. Nothing had happened when they returned. Instead, the royal had spent the rest of the previous eve talking to her foreign ally, which was fine with Ragnar. He didn't have time for the royal and her games. "And I'm not bitter. I'm wary. As you both should be. Don't let that beautiful smile and swishing tail fool you."

"You are such a tail dragon," Vigholf said.

"I'm trying to give you some advice, brother."

"And don't forget her beautiful smile, Vigholf. I don't re-member either of us mentioning a *beautiful* smile," Meinhard chimed in.

Frustrated, Ragnar demanded, "What are you two talking about?"

Vigholf patted Ragnar's shoulder. "We understand, brother. Really we do. All of us get to a point where we start thinking about settling down."

"Settling down? With *her*?" That wouldn't happen. And not simply because she saw becoming someone's mate as some form of excruciating bondage either. As Ragnar had tossed and turned last night, unable to sleep with the dragoness that close to him, he'd realized what a mistake any involvement with her would be. Why? Because she was up to something. He knew it. Her brother knew it. That Eastlander definitely knew it. The only ones who seemed oblivious were his own damn kin.

"But you said yourself, brother, that she has that swishing tail."

"And that beautiful smile with those perfectly aligned fangs."

"I said nothing about her fangs."

"But they are perfectly aligned, and I'm sure that's important to you."

Fed up, Ragnar grabbed his bag and headed toward the city, shifting as he went.

"You're not leaving us, are you, cousin?"

"If you're going into the city, you may want to have a healer look at that chest of yours, brother. All that scratching you've been doing lately can't be good," Vigholf said.

"It might be scale-fungus," Meinhard added.

"And your pretty princess with the beautiful smile and alluring tail won't like that much."

"'Cause it spreads, it does!"

"Aww, now, Ragnar! That's rather a rude gesture!"

Ren parted from Keita as soon as they were in the center of the small city of Fenella, which boasted some of the top universities, mage schools, and witch's guilds in all the Southlands. It was here that the paths of both Ren and Keita had shifted dramatically more than a century ago. And where they always returned when they needed answers.

And the gods knew, they needed answers and quickly.

Ren handed the necklace the Northlander had found in Esyld's house over to the jeweler. An old human who knew his craft very well. And while the human did his work, Ren sat back and let his mind drift, letting his energy reach out around the city to make sure all was well. He smiled a little when he saw that Keita had found their old trainer. An elf named Gorlas. Ren himself had never been a fan of the elves. Yes, they had a way with the trees and land, much as Ren's people did, but gods, they could be superior-acting bastards. To most of them, dragons were nothing more than giant lizards that needed to be brought to heel. How Keita managed to find one of the few elves who respected almost all creatures equally amazed Ren. Although if there was one being who could find the exception to any rule, it was his Keita.

Knowing she was safe, Ren explored more, only to ram right into a protective barrier. From his spot inside the jeweler's store, he felt around that barrier. It was a relatively small one and was moving, meaning that it protected an individual rather than a building or one of the many secret guilds that existed here. Still, he hadn't met many who could keep *him* out. Keita's mother and sister were two, but they were both white Dragonwitches. Their kind's power legendary, even in his home country.

Using more of his power, he caused a rip in the barrier and pulled it open enough for his essence to look in. A monk? A monk managed to keep Ren of the Chosen out?

But then that monk slowly turned his head and looked right at what he shouldn't be able to see. He looked at Ren with blue eyes as cold as the mountains this dragon came from.

It seemed Ren wasn't the only one using Magick to hide the true level of his power, and he'd only managed to think, *The Northlander*, before the Lightning raised his hand and, with a flick of his fingers, sent Ren's essence slamming back into his body.

Ren jerked forward, his chest bending over his knees while he gasped for breath, the jeweler watching him but not making a move to help.

"Keita," Ren gasped out, "is not going to be happy when she finds out that prick followed us."

Then he laughed, because it had been a long time since anyone, much less a barbarian, had managed to surprise him.

* * *

Keita had been searching Fenella's largest bookstore for nearly twenty minutes for her old friend and mentor Gorlas, and was moments from giving up. Perhaps he'd gone out for a bit.

Remembering her one year at the university here, Keita smiled. She came as human, her mother sending her off in the hope that her youngest daughter might have some skill other than seducing a few of the Elders' sons and grandsons. Although Keita had a wonderful time that year, she didn't attend many classes—except for the one with that very attractive professor. Of course, when she was caught bent over that professor's desk, her robes tossed over her head . . . well, that had been the end of that, hadn't it?

But that had been, what? Seventy-five years ago? Give or take a few years. And that very attractive professor had died nearly twenty years back from old age.

It was Keita's little secret, but that's what she adored about the humans. In short time, they left this world for the next, and new ones came along quickly to replace them—unlike the dragons that Keita had bedded, who, half a century later were still writing her long missives of their undying love and what great fathers they'd make for her offspring, blah, blah, blah. She wasn't ashamed to admit, when her past dragon lovers became a little too insistent, she had no problems unleashing her brothers or father on them. At least then they only lost a wing or a foot. She herself couldn't promise to be so kind. Keita never liked being pushed.

Deciding to try the first floor again, Keita returned to the stairs to head back down until she heard a bang followed by a "Gods-dammit!"

Keita walked over to the front desk and went behind it but found no one there. Then she studied the round tables that were usually filled each night with local students, and that's when she heard a sneeze. She crouched down on the floor, looking under the tables.

"What are you doing?" she asked.

The elf under the table, surrounded by books and wiping his nose with a handkerchief, looked up. "Keita?"

"Are you comfortable under there, my lord?"

"Keita!" The elf tried to stand, slammed his head, and sat back down.

"Oh, Gorlas! My heart of hearts. Are you all right?" Laughing, she crawled under several tables to get to him. He pouted, and she pulled his head to her breast and petted the spot where he'd slammed it. Rumor was Gorlas was nearly a thousand years old, but he looked only to be thirty-five or so. "Your poor head. I don't know how it handles the abuse."

"It's not only dragons with hard heads, my dear Keita. We elves are known for them." He pulled back and studied her. "What are you doing here?"

"Looking for information."

"About?"

"My aunt. Esyld."

"Oh. Of course." Gorlas rubbed his sore head. "Found out about her lover then, did you?" And when Keita only stared at him, his smile faded, and he said, "Or . . . perhaps not."

"Brother Ragnar!"

"Brother Simon." Ragnar allowed the human monk to hug him. "It's been a long time, brother."

"It has. It has." Simon pulled back and frowned. "Good gods, man, you haven't changed in forty years."

"A blessing from our patron gods, brother. They've been kind to me."

"I see that." Simon shook his head and offered Ragnar a seat in his den.

Ragnar, worried the weak wood chair wouldn't be able to

hold his human frame, sat down gingerly. He currently wore the robes of the Order of the Knowledge. A well-known and powerful Northland order whose members rarely left their precious Spikenhammer Library. And since Brother Simon's Order of the Shining Suns rarely traveled farther than Fenella's city borders, Ragnar always felt safe presenting himself as a Knowledge member. He'd found throughout his more than two centuries that traveling as a monk was often the safest way to get around. Thieves and brigands rarely challenged him or those who traveled with him, because monks were notoriously poor and all about their gods and being pious.

"So what brings you here, brother?" Simon asked, lifting a decanter of wine.

"No thank you, brother. And I'm actually only passing through. But I did have a question and I knew you were the one who could answer it. If that's all right with you, of course."

"Of course indeed, brother!"

Forty years and, except for physically, Simon had not changed. He enjoyed being the source of all knowledge so much that he never thought too much about whom he told things to. He just liked that he'd been asked.

"I'm wondering about a bookstore."

Simon picked up his chalice of wine and chuckled. "You'll have to be more specific than that, brother. Fenella has many bookstores."

"An extremely large one. Over on Saxton Street."

"Ah, yes. Owned by an elf, I believe."

"An elf?" Ragnar tried to emulate the sense of surprise he'd felt earlier when he'd seen an elf with his arm around Keita's shoulders, the pair of them heading to the back of the store. First Ragnar at the fair, now this elf. Honestly, was there any male that She-dragon *didn't* make it her business to seduce? "In the city?"

"There are no problems with elves here in Fenella. Gorlas

is his name, and he's a nice enough chap. One of the few bookstore owners who allows our young brothers to spend hours browsing without making them buy anything."

"And is there anything else?"

Simon frowned a bit. "Anything else?"

"Well, when I went in there, I had a"—Ragnar looked up at the ceiling as if trying to get the answer from one of his gods, always nice for dramatic effect when dealing with monks—"*sense* of something. Something beneath the surface."

Simon pursed his lips. "Well . . . there are always rumors."

"Oh? What kind of rumors?"

"I'm sure it's nothing."

"I'm sure."

"And you know I don't like to spread rumor or gossip."

"Of course not, brother. And I only ask because I sense the gods are trying to tell me something. I'm just not sure what. But I knew if there was one person who could help . . . it was Brother Simon."

"Oh. Well." It was sad, really. How the monk couldn't resist the compliment. Which was why Ragnar used the man for information, but never returned the favor. At least not with any information that could do any real damage.

Simon leaned forward, and Ragnar did the same. "There have been rumors."

"Yes?"

"That *that* particular bookstore is a cover for—"

"An orgy den? A prostitution ring? A sex-slave commune?"

Simon blinked. "Uh . . . no."

Feeling foolish, Ragnar explained, "Sorry. Again, it was that *sense* I got."

"I understand, but it's nothing that interesting, I'm afraid, brother. Actually, the rumors I've heard are almost silly, but . . . I have heard it said that the bookstore is a cover, or a front, you might say . . . for a guild."

"A thief's guild?" Ragnar asked bluntly, thinking of Keita's constantly growing wardrobe.

"No, no. A spy guild."

Ragnar sat up straight, his chair making noises that suggested it wouldn't last much longer, but Ragnar didn't care. He was too blindsided by Brother Simon's words. "A spy guild?"

"Aye. But as I said, it's just a rumor."

Just a rumor indeed. Yet a rumor that Princess Keita would easily believe. And he knew why, too. Because she probably liked the idea of bedding spies. Spies who could use her to find out information about the courts of the two queens. He wanted to ask, "Could she be so stupid not to see that?" But then he already had the answer to that question, didn't he? She *was* too stupid to see that.

Ragnar did, however, wonder how far Keita would go to keep her bed filled with "spies." Would she simply provide information to her lovers or actually search information out? What had she already told? Was Esyld suffering now because her niece had become bed acquaintances with those who would harm her? Ragnar really didn't know.

Although he did realize that he longed for the days when he didn't have to deal with the royal Fire Breathers.

Gorlas watched one of his favorite beings pace restlessly around his private office. He clearly remembered when Keita had first wandered into his store. She'd been a bored student then, but with one look, Gorlas knew that sitting at a desk all day, listening to boring old professors give lectures, wasn't the life for this beauty. Within a few days, the only classes she attended were his. Along with her Eastland friend, Ren of the Chosen. Both of them beautiful, smart, and devious. And considering the path Keita truly wanted to take, it was a perfect match for all of them.

Too bad she continued to forget the most important thing he'd always tried to teach her—her mother was not to be fucked with. Something Keita refused to believe. And now . . . now she was here.

"What the fuck was Esyld thinking?" Keita demanded. "She couldn't keep her lovers in the Outerplains? She had to come *here* to meet them?"

"Calm down."

"I will *not* calm down! Has she lost her mind? Has old age set in early? She's going to get *both* of us killed!"

"Keita—"

She rested her hands on her hips. "Where?" Keita demanded. "Where was she meeting him? Here? In a rented chateau? At the queen's favorite human pub? Where was this dumb female settling in to meet her lover so that everyone who reports to my mother could see her clearly? Where, Gorlas?"

"She was staying at Castle Moor."

Keita gasped, reached back for her chair, and dropped into it. "No! You must be wrong."

"That's where she was sighted by my people. More than once."

"My aunt was at Castle Moor?"

"I'd assumed you'd sent her there. It's the one safe place I know when one wants to be discreet."

"But . . ." she said, still dazed. "Castle Moor? *My* aunt?"

Smirking, Gorlas relaxed back in his chair. "I must say I'm a little surprised by the tone, Keita. Coming from you, I mean."

"It would surprise no one that *I* have been to Castle Moor . . . several times. Or that I'm on a first-name basis with your oddly alluring fellow elf, Athol. But Esyld is not me."

"It is a smart choice." Castle Moor was far removed from Southland politics and the notice of either the Dragon Queen or her human counterpart, the Mad Queen of Garbhán Isle.

For enough coin, anyone looking to have some private time with a lover or lovers could find it at Castle Moor. And Athol, lord of the manor, was well known for keeping his mouth shut. Gorlas only knew who came and went because he made it his business to know, and he didn't spread around what he heard.

"I guess that's true," Keita said "Do you think she's there now?"

"It's possible, but I haven't exactly been monitoring your aunt." Perhaps he should have, but he'd never thought the dragoness would be so foolish as to get caught. Now Gorlas wished he'd contacted Keita and told her what he knew, but he thought her aunt simply had desires that needed to be filled. He knew it must be hard to live all alone in the Outerplains with nothing but your herbs, spells, and forest animals to keep you company.

"I'll need to go there. See if I can find her."

"How long has it been since you were there last?"

"Ages. Think Athol will mind?"

"Extremely doubtful. He was always quite fond of you."

"That's good. Because if my mother finds out about all this, I may have to hide in Castle Moor myself."

"Will that be such a hardship, my lady?"

"At the moment . . . yes. Besides, you know I don't like being trapped anywhere." Keita rested her elbow on the table, her chin in her palm.

"What else, Keita?" he pushed. He knew she wasn't telling him everything.

"There is the slightest chance . . . that Esyld's lover is a Sovereign."

Gorlas's heart plummeted. "Oh . . . Keita."

"I know," she sighed. "Because this all couldn't just be bad, my dear friend. It had to be *very bad*!"

* * *

Keita had just turned a corner, heading toward the city gates, when Ren fell into step beside her.

"Well?" she asked, her mind turning.

"The Northlander was right about the necklace. Designed and created by Fucinus himself, most likely."

Keita stopped walking and stamped her foot. "Fuck me!" she snarled.

A man walking by with his friends turned toward her and said, "Is that an offer, luv?"

Without taking her gaze off Ren, Keita reached out and grabbed hold of the man's balls through his trousers. She let heat sear him while she said to Ren, "We have a problem."

The man began to scream, but Keita didn't even notice or care. She had more important things on her mind.

Ren slapped her hand off the man's damaged groin and yanked her down the road until they were well away from the man and his friends. "Must you take it out on some poor sod because—"

"Because I may have trusted a traitor?" she filled in for him. "And who else would I take it out on?" she asked. "Clearly not myself!"

Ren stopped and released her. "I forgot who I'm dealing with. So what's our problem?"

"Apparently Esyld has been coming into Southland territories for months."

"Oh, shit."

"Exactly. She's been going to Castle Moor."

The friends stared at each other a moment and then said in unison, "Moor, Moor, Moor."

They laughed until Keita said, "It's not funny."

"No, no. Not funny." Ren rested his hands on his hips. "Although, it is Esyld . . . so that's a little funny."

"She was going to meet a lover."

"Esyld had a lover? A Sovereign?"

"All Gorlas could tell me was that he wasn't a local."

"So what do you want to do?"

"We have to stop at Athol's before we head home."

A shiny black brow peaked. "Do we really have time for that, Keita?"

"I can assure you, I only go there to get my questions answered. My orgy days have *long* been over."

"Huh. I don't think I've ever heard you say that before."

"I can give you lots of reasons why." She took Ren's arm in her own, and they slowly headed toward the city gates. "But honestly, my friend, orgies are simply too much work."

Chapter Ten

Although Meinhard slept under a tree, he still knew what was going on around him at all times. It was a skill he'd been forced to develop since the first day his mother had placed him among his brothers, freshly hatched and vulnerable. More than two centuries later, he still had the skill. So he knew the moment his cousin returned even before he sent the Blue off to get them something for their dinner.

And by the time Meinhard sat up, yawning and scratching his belly, his cousin had told him something that, twenty minutes later, still sounded ridiculous.

"You're telling us she's fucking spies?"

"Yes."

Meinhard simply didn't understand his cousin. Here before him was a beautiful dragoness, ripe for the plucking, and this idiot was believing tales about Princess Keita and spies. Honestly, what was *wrong* with him?

Although, when Meinhard thought about it, it was enjoyable to see his cousin acting a little less cold and standoffish, and a little more like a true Northlander. Possessive, erratic, and dangerously unstable.

To clarify what Ragnar was telling them, Meinhard asked, "Yes, you know for a fact that she's fucking spies? Or yes, you *think* she's fucking spies because you're being kind of a horse's dick?"

"What exactly are you having trouble believing about her?" Ragnar demanded. "The spying or the fucking?"

Meinhard looked at Vigholf, and together they replied, "The spying."

Ragnar began rubbing his forehead, and Vigholf said, "Look, brother, we're not saying the princess hasn't bedded spies. If they were male, chances are she's had her way with them. But giving them information? About her time in the Northlands? About her *mother*? No. I don't see that."

Ragnar got to his claws and began to pace. "What is this lofty pillar you two have her on?"

"We're not as snobby as you," Meinhard told him. "Don't need proof of virginity for a female to be in my bed. Actually . . . I'd prefer she wasn't. That's a lot of responsibility."

"And can be bor-*ing*," Vigholf sang under his breath.

"This has nothing to do with her virginity or lack thereof," Ragnar snapped.

"Then what is it? What is it about her that bothers you so much?"

Appearing more and more frustrated, Ragnar came out with, "What she could be getting herself involved in could be dangerous, and she's not bright enough to see that."

Meinhard shrugged. "Seems bright enough to me."

Ragnar cleared his throat, and Meinhard and Vigholf again looked at each other.

"Oh, I see," Meinhard reasoned. "She's not as smart as *you*."

"That is not what I'm—"

"Or your precious Lady Dagmar," Vigholf added.

"We're not talking about her either."

"Why don't you just get it over with?" Meinhard finally asked his cousin.

"Get what over with?" And the bastard had the nerve to look confused.

"Instead of accusing her of all manner of horse shit I'm not sure even you believe—just fuck her."

Ragnar took a step back. "Pardon?"

"Fuck. Her. Fuck her like you've been in Uncle Adalwolf's dungeons for the last century. Fuck her until your eyes roll to the back of your head and you can no longer walk. Fuck her and get it over with so we can get past this ox shit, dump these royals off, and get back to the Northlands where we belong."

"And that's your answer for how to handle this?"

"Handle what, cousin? Other than your overwhelming desire to fuck this female and that ungodly itch you've got going on with your chest, I don't see anything else to handle."

"Well, *cousin*, thank you for that evaluation but I have no desire to—"

"What?" Vigholf cut in. "You have no desire to what? Fuck her? Because we all know you're bloody gagging for it."

"I am not!"

"You are such a liar. Does Mum know what a bloody liar you are?"

"And let's face it, cousin, we all want to fuck her." And of the three of them, only Ragnar's eyes narrowed dangerously at Meinhard's words. *Yes. Definitely possessive.*

"Oh, really?" Ragnar asked.

"Whether it's that human ass or that She-dragon tail, I'm drawn in. Both look delicious."

"And who wouldn't want both?" Vigholf suggested.

"Exactly. But see," Meinhard continued, "we're not the ones gettin' in your way. *You're* gettin' in your way. You're bloody over-thinking it."

"Like you do with everything," Vigholf agreed.

Ragnar's jaw clenched. "I do not over-think anything."

"You do, you are, and you're letting her get away," Meinhard argued.

"And you're that sure she just has to have me?" When the cousins went out of their way *not* to look at each other,

Ragnar quickly pointed a talon. "What? What aren't you telling me?"

"We're telling you," Vigholf bit out between clenched fangs, "that if you want her, you can get her."

"And how would you know that? And don't lie to me."

"The Blue was a little concerned about, uh . . . what were those words he used, Meinhard?"

"Uh . . . inter-territorial relations. I think."

"What about them?"

"He didn't want his sister damaging them."

"And how would she do that?"

"Well, the lad says there may be a little"—Meinhard raised his front claw, wiggled his talons—"wager going on between the princess and that foreign friend of hers."

"Apparently that's something the two of them do when they're bored," Vigholf said.

"Wager? What kind of wager?"

"To see whether she could get you into bed or not," Meinhard answered.

Vigholf shook his head at the expression on his brother's face. "And look at ya. Pissed off. Over this."

"Of course, I'm pissed off over this!"

"Why?" Meinhard asked. "You've got yourself a She-dragon of royal blood, laid out on a slab for you to fuck, and you're pissed? Is there something wrong with you?"

"They're wagering on my cock!" Ragnar exploded, front claws going high in the air as if he didn't understand his kin at all. And he didn't. As they didn't understand him. Not when it came to this sort of thing.

"So? I'd let that dragoness wager on my cock daily."

"If it were me," Vigholf said, three talons clicking together to drive home his point, "I'd let her *win* that wager. I'd let her win it over and over and *over* again. Until neither of us could move or possibly breathe. That's what I'd do."

"Because you're both bloody worthless!" Ragnar roared and marched off into the trees.

Meinhard glanced at Vigholf and asked, "Did he just yell at us?"

"I think he did. Several times."

"I don't think I've ever heard him yell about anything."

"Good point." Meinhard scratched his head. "But still, the loss of all those tightly controlled emotions . . ."

"It's like I said." And Vigholf yelled the rest at Ragnar's retreating tail, "He's bloody *gagging* for it!"

Meinhard only had a chance for a short laugh before he was dodging that boulder his own blood had chucked at his and Vigholf's heads.

To Keita's eternal surprise, the warlord didn't complain at all when she and Ren eventually returned from the city. They'd taken their time walking back, planning out how they'd handle the next step in their search for Esyld. Yet the warlord said nothing. Nor did his brother or cousin. And, of course, all Éibhear cared about were the new books she'd brought with her from Gorlas's store.

"Aw, Keita. You're the best!" Éibhear said, grinning at her.

"Sorry about coming back so late," Keita sweetly offered while removing her fur cape and silk gown so she could shift.

"Not a problem," Ragnar grumbled back, shocking her.

"What?" Keita was sure she'd heard incorrectly.

"I said not a problem. We've already camped for the night." Then he walked off, leaving her standing there, utterly confused. So Keita grabbed Ren's hair and yanked him close.

"Ow!"

"What's he up to?" she whispered.

"I don't know. Probably nothing. And unleash me, female!"

She did. "What do you mean 'probably nothing'?"

"Probably nothing."

Now her eyes had narrowed on Ren. "What do you know?"

"In what sense?"

"In . . . what? Don't toy with me, Ren of the Chosen."

"You won't like it."

"I don't care."

He moved her farther away from the group. "He followed us into town this afternoon."

"He did what?"

"Don't worry. There was nothing for him to see, and if he asks, you were in a nice, clean, *boring* bookstore and I was getting that necklace evaluated."

"But how dare he follow me?"

"Let it go, Keita."

"Like one of the hells, I will." And with that Keita followed Ragnar out to the nearby lake.

He sat on his haunches by the water's edge, gazing across the placid surface. But he wasn't alone.

She stood just behind him for rather a long time before his entire body tensed.

"Sneaking up on me, princess?" he asked.

"Didn't realize I had," she lied. As her mother had pointed out on more than one occasion when startled by Keita, "sneaky as a snake, that one."

Keita moved up alongside him. "Are you aware there's a black bird on your head?" she asked.

He turned his gaze to her.

"Yes," he replied. "A crow. And I'm aware."

"Did it mistake you for a statue?"

"No."

She watched both dragon and bird a bit longer before asking, "Are you going to leave him up there?"

"He's not causing me any bother."

"But you have a bird on your head."

"Yes. We've established this. Although I don't know why that surprises you so. You seem to have your own entourage."

When Keita frowned, he motioned behind her. Keita glanced at what nuzzled her tail. "Oh. Them."

"Yes. Them. Do packs of wolves often follow you around?"

"Just the males."

"Pardon?"

She smiled. "What can I say? Males love me. Every breed, every species. It's not my fault. I do nothing to lure them, but they come anyway."

Shaking his head a little, Ragnar coldly replied, "I see."

When he said nothing else, Keita thought about pushing for more information but decided against it. She didn't like the warlord's mood. It made her uncomfortable. She didn't like to feel uncomfortable. "Éibhear says dinner will be soon," she offered, turning away from him to head back to camp.

"Tell me something, princess."

Keita stopped.

"What were you doing in the Northlands when my father found you?"

The question threw Keita off because she hadn't been expecting it. Two years ago she'd expected it, but not now. Not here. And what in all the hells did that have to do with him following her into Fenella?

Keita smiled, tossing her hair off her face. "Just being rebellious. You know how mothers and daughters can be."

"There are too few daughters in the north for parents to afford alienating them, but I have some idea. Still," he went on when she took another step away, "it was a risk. Wasn't it? Being in enemy territory?"

This dragon was digging, and Keita was in no mood to give him what he wanted. So she did what she always did best when she wanted to throw someone off. . . .

She became sneaky as a snake.

* * *

Ragnar didn't know what appalled him more at the moment. That a royal would involve herself with spies—most likely out of pure boredom—or that she'd been wagering on his cock? Perhaps he was appalled by both. What kind of royal spent her time trying to seduce males for sport when she wasn't visiting spy guilds in nearby cities? One not worthy of the loyalty and lust she seemed to have earned from Ragnar's idiot brother and idiot cousin.

Keita's claw slid across Ragnar's chest, the talons scraping against his scales. Startled, Ragnar jumped a little, his bird visitor flitting off to the trees. Leaving Ragnar alone—with her.

"Princess—"

She brushed her head under his chin and nuzzled his neck. "What is it you want from me, Lord Ragnar?" she asked, her voice husky. "You ask so many questions, but I don't know what you want. Or perhaps I'm merely being difficult. Perhaps I want you to drag the information from me." She went up on the tips of her back talons, her snout brushing against his throat, her voice whispering in his ear. "Perhaps it would be better for both of us if you'd tie me up—and *make* me give you the answers. Or chains," she purred, a little breathless. "Imagine what we could do with a few hours alone and chains."

Ragnar had her by the shoulders, was already pulling her to his body, when he realized exactly what he was doing. What she'd *gotten* him to do. With some gods-damn nuzzling and the mere mention of chains!

Viper!

Ragnar shoved her away, and instead of being angry, she laughed. Her façade of sexual abandon slipping away to show the hardened dragoness beneath. "What's wrong, warlord? Are chains not the way to go with you? Do you like the coquettish ingénue more? Or the struggling virgin who keeps saying 'no, no, no' but really means 'yes, yes, yes!'?" Her laughter rang out across the lake.

"What I like, princess—"

"No, no. Don't tell me. I'll bet you like the whole regal majesty thing, yes? Tail up, head down, ready to take one for the future survival of one's bloodline?"

She was irritating him, and he needed to leave. "As a matter of—"

"That seemed to be," she cut in, her tail picking up a stone and tossing it into the lake, "what your father favored." She sat back on her haunches and raised her front claws. "Not that I'd know personally. But is that it?" she asked. "Is that what you like?" She smirked, brown eyes sizing him up, purposely going for his weakest spot. "Are we having a 'like father like son' moment?"

And that's when something inside Ragnar broke. Even though he knew on some level she was merely taunting him to distract him from the questions he'd been asking, he could not hold his anger at bay. Not over *this* insult.

"No, princess," he replied, his voice low. "What I like, what I've always liked, is someone with the ability to think, to reason, to have a life that those in the future will consider meaningful. Don't get me wrong. I have no problems taking a working whore to bed, because I appreciate any female who understands business and the use of coin. But a vapid virgin with nothing in her head is as bad as a vapid slag with nothing in her head. Because when the fucking ends, and all you're left with is each other, then what do you do?" He gave a small shrug. "I guess what *you* do is leave. You know, before some male looks *too* close—and sees absolutely *nothing*."

He expected talons to claw across his face. They didn't.

He expected tears, accusations of hatred. They never came.

He expected rage, storming off. None of that either.

Instead her gaze was steady, her back straight, her voice even and calm. "I guess I should be grateful you don't have your sword tied to your back, because clearly I touched a nerve. But that's all right." She stepped around him. "We played a game that went too far. Now we know the boundaries." She headed back to camp, saying as she walked, "Although if you call me a slag or whore again—I'll have you killed. I only let my sister and mother get away with that, and that's because they're more dangerous than you could ever hope to be, warlord."

She left him standing there, staring at the ground. Never before, not once in his life, had Ragnar lost control of his tongue. Words had always been his weapon as much as Magick and good steel, because most of his kin, especially his father, were unable to fight Ragnar on that level. But, he used to think with pride, he never went for the easy strike. He never used words simply to hurt, to destroy. When he used them, it was to get what he wanted. Yet suddenly, in the middle of some Southland forest, he'd used words like his father once used his favorite warhammer. Brutally and with no care for the outcome.

Disgusted with himself, Ragnar again sat on his haunches at the water's edge and tried hard to convince himself that the look of pain he'd seen in Princess Keita's brown eyes was not nearly as bad as it had seemed.

Chapter Eleven

He wished he could say that for the next two days of their trip she wouldn't speak to him, refused to look at him, that she flounced off every time he asked her a question, that she hissed at him, or told him to piss off anytime he opened his mouth.

Ragnar *wished* he could say Princess Keita had done all that. That she'd played the wounded royal to the hilt. Too bad her way of getting even was much more artful, much more brutal.

Keita did in fact speak to Ragnar. Very politely. When she asked for something, she always followed her request with "please." When he told her to do something, she did it without question and followed what he said to the letter. She joined into conversation only when spoken to directly, and her replies were never too short or too long.

She kept her back straight, her head high, and even borrowed one of her brother's books to read during their breaks.

Ragnar soon realized that Keita had become everything he'd always expected and wanted out of a proper royal princess. He also now realized how much he hated a proper royal princess. He never thought he'd miss her laugh or the way she flirted with his kin or himself, or those annoying giggles and the way she teased her brother. But he did miss all that. At the very least, he missed them from Keita.

But she'd frozen him out, hadn't she? Like an avalanche of snow burying him beneath a cliff.

The others knew something had happened. They all watched the etiquette-correct moments between him and Keita and they knew something had changed, but none knew what. Except the Eastlander. He glared at Ragnar every time Keita's back was turned.

Not that Ragnar blamed either the Eastlander or Keita. He'd been unable to sleep the last two nights, flinching each time he remembered what he'd said to her.

So by the time they arrived in a safe place early that evening—the foreigner asking them to cut their daily trip short in the middle of nowhere—Ragnar was exhausted, cranky, and dangerously annoyed with himself and the world.

He sat down on the ground, his back pressed into the small hill behind him, his wings spread out so they could get a good stretch after so much flying.

"Éibhear." The Eastlander tapped the Blue's shoulder. "I'm taking your sister over to that lake about a half-mile away. She wants a bath."

The Blue nodded and pulled out one of the books his sister had picked up for him.

After the pair walked off, Vigholf crouched in front of Ragnar. "What's going on?"

"Nothing."

"She's become like one of those boring royals we always made fun of, and you've become a mean bastard. Something must have happened between you two. What did you say to her?"

"Nothing I want to discuss. So let it go, brother."

Now Meinhard crouched in front of him. "If you hurt her feelings, cousin—"

Unable to stand a second more, Ragnar stood and walked off, picking up his travel bag before he left camp.

Perhaps a good calming spell would ease his tension. And gods! Anything to stop the itching, which had gotten considerably worse since his last meeting with Keita by that lake. Ragnar stopped at a tree, shifted to human, and, leaning against it, scratched where the itching was the worst. Scratched so hard he feared there might be blood. This was becoming intolerable!

Moments from tracking Keita down and demanding she remove whatever spell she'd included when she'd impaled him with her gods-damn tail, Ragnar caught sight of the princess walking off alone through the trees. She was human now, dressed in another gown he'd never seen before, a fur cloak, and no shoes.

Ragnar scowled. For a She-dragon who loved human clothes as much as she did, he'd think shoes would be a given.

And exactly where did she think she was going in the middle of nowhere? Alone, human, and shoeless?

Keita stood in front of the big gate that surrounded Castle Moor.

Unlike the more fortresslike castles that the Southland territorial lords lived in, Castle Moor was like a palace. There were guards, but only a few strong ones to throw out any who might get out of hand after too much drink and pussy or cock, but there was nothing else to protect against a raid or army attack.

Then again, Lord Athol Reidfurd didn't need that kind of protection. At one time he may have been called a mage or a sorcerer or a wizard, but these days none who followed those paths would claim Athol as their own. It was said he'd gone down a darker path, perhaps sold his soul. Keita didn't know, and she'd rarely worried about it. She didn't have enough Magickal power to interest someone of his stature, and what went on behind his castle walls whenever she was in attendance seemed to have one focus and one focus only— pleasure.

The gate slowly swung back, and Athol, with his personal assistant, met her there.

"Keita."

"Athol." She walked into his outstretched arms and gave him a hearty hug.

"It's been too long, my beauty." He lifted her chin with two fingers. "And you are still beautiful. I do hope you plan on staying."

"I actually can't. Not for long anyway."

"Too bad," he murmured. "I have such entertainment planned for this evening. I'm sure you'd enjoy it."

She probably would, but that wasn't why she was here.

"Perhaps another time?"

"As you wish." He released her. "Where's Ren?"

"I don't really know," she lied. Against Ren's wishes, Keita had insisted on leaving her old friend behind. She had to. The tension between Ren and Athol had always been a problem. They tolerated each other because of Keita, but barely. If she wanted to get anything out of the elf, she couldn't have Ren there, needling Athol to death. Something the Eastlander was very good at.

"And your friend?" Athol asked.

Unclear what he was talking about, she asked, "Friend?"

Athol raised his chin, motioning to a spot behind her. Keita looked over her shoulder and had to work very hard not to show her shock at seeing the warlord standing right behind her. How long had he been there? Why hadn't she noticed him following her?

Ragnar stepped forward. "Brother Ragnar of the Order of the Knowledge, my lord. I'm accompanying Lady Keita on her current trip."

"A monk?" Athol asked, his gaze on Keita.

She quickly took Athol's arm, her mind scrambling. "He hopes to save my soul," she finally said, keeping her voice low. "And I hope to take his."

Athol laughed. "Ahhh. My scandalous little Keita. I'm so glad to see you haven't changed." He gave her a wink before bowing before the warlord. "I am Athol Reidfurd, brother, lord of this manor." Athol motioned them both in with a wave of his arm. "And you are both more than welcome here."

Ragnar couldn't believe the power of this place once he walked past that gate. It was as if the Magick he carried around with him had been locked into his skin, making most of his spells ineffectual. The loss of power was so great, Ragnar knew he'd be unable to shift back to his dragon form or unleash his lightning, no matter how much he might want to. Even his physical strength wasn't as strong—it was as though he'd become truly human. And what really astounded Ragnar was that all the power that protected this place emanated from one source and one source alone—Lord Reidfurd himself.

He followed the elf lord toward his palace home, Keita dropping back so that they walked side by side.

"What are you doing here?" she softly asked.

"Watching your back."

"I don't need you to watch my back." And for a brief second he thought he had the old, intolerable Keita back. Until she added, "Although it's greatly appreciated, my lord."

Dammit! "Keita—"

She hastened her step and entered the doors with their host.

Traveling behind them, Ragnar walked inside but had to stop at the very entrance. He'd heard of places like this, but had never seen one. Even the human queen's castle looked nothing like this. The entrance hallway to this place was made of pure marble, the intricate designs etched into the wall accented with pure gold. Standing gold torch-holders lined the hallway as did lit crystal chandeliers overhead, setting the entire space ablaze with light. And framing the entranceway—two six-foot-high phalluses.

"Something you need, brother?" Reidfurd's assistant asked him.

"No. Thank you."

"Then if you'll please follow me."

Ragnar followed the small group down the incredibly long hallway, passing room after room, each with a closed door or doors. Yet it took him only a moment to recognize the sounds coming from behind those closed doors—the sounds of fucking. Plus the smell of sex permeated everything, making it clear what kind of castle this was. Gods, had Keita been so angry and hurt at what he'd said that she'd come here, looking for solace? Looking for cold, anonymous sex?

Then again, if he was honest with himself—and for the last two days he'd been forcing himself to be brutally honest with himself—that didn't seem Keita's way, did it? Getting cold, anonymous sex might be her way, but to do it because she'd been hurt or angered by his stupidity? No. Keita's way seemed much more direct—likely she'd stab him with her tail again. Or wait until he was asleep and roll him off a mountain. Yes. That was more Keita the Viper's style, he now realized.

Then why the hell were they here?

Eventually they reached a private room at the end of the hallway. A den for Reidfurd himself, it seemed. Once inside, the assistant closed the door and offered chairs to Ragnar and Keita. When they were all sitting comfortably in the leather chairs, Athol asked, "So what brings you here, my beauty?"

"I'm looking for someone, and I heard they'd been here a number of times in the last few months."

"Lots of people come to Castle Moor, Keita, you know that."

"And you know each and every one who does. So let's not play games."

The assistant held up a decanter of wine, but Keita waved it away. He offered the same to Ragnar, and after the long day he'd had he seriously considered having a glass until he saw Keita give a very quick shake of her head.

He dismissed the assistant with a wave.

"No wine, brother?" Reidfurd asked, watching him closely.

"No thank you."

"Fruit then?" Athol held a plate of freshly cut fruit in front of Ragnar. Hungry but knowing something could be slipped into food just as easily as wine, he shook his head. "You sure? These are from the trees surrounding the manor. I have fresh ones picked every day," he told Keita. "They've become big hits with many of my guests."

"No thank you," Ragnar said again.

"As you like." Athol dropped the plate onto the side table and sat back in his chair. "So, old friend, who are you looking for?"

He seemed amiable enough, but as Keita opened her mouth to speak, Ragnar saw her change her mind about what she was going to say. He didn't know why or what it meant, but she suddenly came out with, "Any Sovereigns been by?"

"Sovereigns? From the Quintilian Provinces?"

"Do you know other Sovereigns I'm not aware of, Athol?"

"Ahh, yes. Your sarcasm. One of my least favorite uses for that mouth of yours."

Gods, she'd forgotten what an annoying twat Athol could be. And while that had not changed about him, something else had. She simply didn't know what. But he made her uneasy when, at one time, he'd made her feel anything and everything *but* unease. So she handled him carefully, not taking his attempts at insult too much to heart and ignoring the Northland battle dog growling at Athol from his leather chair. Keita held up her hand to silence Ragnar and said to Athol, "I know, I know. My sarcasm always annoyed you as your tiny cock always disappointed me. These are things we've decided to overlook in the name of friendship."

Athol's smile faded away, and Keita giggled and said, "I'm only teasing, old friend. You know that."

"Yes. Of course." Although he didn't look too sure. "I'm sure a Sovereign or two has made his or her way into my home. I get many willing to risk much just for a night here at my manor. But you know I don't share names, Lady Keita. People come here for private pleasure. Not everyone is as forthcoming as you about where you go and who you fuck."

"I refuse to feel shame about who I fuck or don't fuck, but that's just my way."

"Perhaps if you give me the name of this Sovereign you search for . . ."

"I have no name, but he would have been here in the last six months or so."

"Well, you know, old friend, so many come . . . and come and come." Athol glanced at Ragnar and said, "Old joke."

Ragnar's response was to stare so intently at Athol that for the first time Keita could remember, Lord Reidfurd shifted uncomfortably in his chair, and not even because someone was naked and being whipped for his entertainment.

"But you wouldn't mind if we look around, would you, Athol?" And she made sure to pout just the tiniest bit. "Please?"

Keita watched the elf's every move, how he breathed, what his hands did, if parts of him twitched. She watched it all so that when he replied, "Of course not," she knew he was lying. He did mind. Too bad she didn't care.

She clapped her hands together. "Excellent!"

* * *

All Keita said to him before they started off on their journey through Castle Moor was, "Eat and drink *nothing*." Ragnar knew being poisoned was only part of her worry. She also didn't need Ragnar taking some aphrodisiac that had him writhing on the floor like a big cat.

With that warning given, they went from room to room, and floor to floor—searching for what, Ragnar still didn't know. Yet he soon stopped thinking much about that as he became distracted by all that was going on around him. He hadn't seen so much fucking in one place at one time since he'd participated in a mass sex Magick ritual several decades ago. And although all the sex around him had his cock hard and his eyes fastened to Keita's perfectly proportioned ass with no hope of relief, he was still glad he'd followed his instincts and come with her. Like the wolves who'd snuggled her tail the previous eve, the males in this place were drawn to her. They'd pull their wet or oiled cocks out of orifices and prowl right over to her, hands reaching, mouths open.

She handled each male—and some females—easily, though. With a smile and a wave or a shake of her head or by yanking someone naked and good looking in front of herself to distract those who wanted her attention.

She dismissed another eager male from her presence and looked around the large first-floor ballroom they'd reached. If she saw all the sex going on around her, she certainly didn't show it. Instead her brow furrowed over eyes that studied everything.

That's when Ragnar recognized something in Keita's gaze that he'd only seen in a few others. His mother, Dagmar, and a few of his cousins.

And that something was cold, ruthless calculation.

"What are you hoping to find?" he asked.

"My aunt."

Perhaps, but Keita wasn't merely searching for her aunt—she was searching for answers. Answers about her aunt, yes, but more than that. It was a subtle difference, but still enormous in its complexity.

Ragnar looked around him. "Here? You hope to find Esyld *here*?"

She huffed, hands going on her hips. "And what's *that* supposed to mean?" Although Ragnar had no intention of walking into that trap, Keita held her hand up as if he'd been about to. "Oh, no. I bet I can guess. Only a whore would come here, right? And unlike me, my aunt is not a whore."

"I never said that."

"So my aunt *is* a whore?"

Wait. "And I never said that."

"So then only *I* am a whore and Esyld is a saint?"

"I didn't say that either."

Keita "humphed" at him and walked off. Ragnar moved to follow, but a young woman dropped to her knees in front of him.

"A monk," she purred, leering at him. "What a naughty treat."

She reached for his robes, and Ragnar caught her hands, terrified he wouldn't make her stop once she got her hands on him. He was just a dragon—not a saint.

"No, no," he said quickly. "No touching."

"Are you shy?" she teased.

Shyness wasn't his issue—and something told him he'd never leave this room if he told this woman he was a shy monk—but losing sight of Keita as she went around a corner definitely was.

"Not shy. Cursed." Her eyes lit up over that, too, so he quickly added, "Cursed with disease. A contagious one." She jerked her hands away, and Ragnar stepped around her and followed Keita.

He could see her down at the end of the hall, where a naked male had hold of her arm. But unlike before, where Keita had eased her way out of those awkward situations, this male wasn't releasing her. And, even more disturbing, he yanked her toward and out the back exit door.

Head lowering, Ragnar followed and burst through the same door, but he stopped short—had to with all those swords pointed at him.

"And who's this then?" Lord Sinclair DeLaval demanded when Ragnar came charging out that back door like an angry bull. "Another lover?"

"An innocent monk," Keita soothed. "Nothing more."

Gods, what a mistake DeLaval had been. Twelve years and the human still hadn't let their one night go. She didn't see him often, but when she did, he tried cajoling, gifts, and charm to get her back. Anything to get her to return to his bed. But one night had been enough. It wasn't that it was bad. In truth, it had been an enjoyable night—if she remembered correctly. Yet the ones who insisted on clinging after it was over always made her nervous.

And this was why.

Keita smiled at Sinclair, but her gaze was focused on the gate behind him. Right now neither she nor Ragnar could return to their true forms or use any of their natural gifts. Athol ensured that because he didn't like any surprises at his manor. Yet once past that gate, nothing could hold the two dragons back. The problem, however, was getting to the gate. DeLaval, as a noble, was allowed by Athol to bring his small contingent of guards inside the manor as protection. And because DeLaval paid so well, he had free run of the place. Now that she thought about it, Keita realized one of the many reasons she'd stopped coming to Castle Moor was because of DeLaval, and his needy, desperate ways. But she'd been so focused on her aunt, her mother, and the damn Lightning, she'd forgotten about DeLaval altogether. Now both she and Ragnar were trapped.

True, she still wasn't talking to Ragnar—few had pissed her off as he had and he'd done it twice!—but getting the dragonlord of the Northlands killed while on Southland territory would not help Keita's relationship with her mother. And, she'd admit to herself, she didn't want him dead. Groveling perhaps, but not dead.

"Return with me, Keita," DeLaval told her. "Come home with me. Just to talk."

The man stood there, naked, his cock hard and still covered in someone else's bodily fluids, and he just wanted to talk. Really, all he was doing was once again showing Keita why she hated the clingy ones!

She knew she had to get out of this and get out of it quickly. Unable to shift, she and Ragnar were awfully vulnerable to those sharp weapons.

"Sinclair, luv." She pressed her palm to his cheek. "I'd adore doing that, but I must return home first. We can meet later."

DeLaval's jaw clenched, and Keita realized too late that she should have lied outright to him, if only to get him to take her beyond the damn gate. But instead of just another incident of DeLaval begging, groveling, and giving gifts until Keita walked away from him—which was what had always happened before—this would be very different. Especially with his men watching.

DeLaval's grip tightened on her bicep, making Keita wince from the bite of it.

"Let's discuss this inside," he said, pulling her back toward the door while Athol watched and did nothing.

Keita quickly glanced around to see if there was an easy way out of this, but except for Athol's assistant—who seemed quite concerned, but feared his master so much that he'd never intervene—she saw no one else willing to help a lone female and her monk companion, which was exactly what DeLaval thought she and Ragnar were. The noble had never known the truth about her—many human nobles didn't. And they rarely connected her with the royal dragons living with the human queen of Dark Plains. Still, would no one in this damn place help her?

Then again, this *was* the kind of entertainment she'd heard that many of Athol's guests lived for. Rumors she'd always dismissed because she'd never seen the proof of it—until this moment. Until she saw the look on Athol's face as he coldly watched DeLaval try to drag her back inside.

Unlike DeLaval, Athol knew exactly who and what she was. Knew what Ragnar was, too, even if he didn't know his title or bloodline. And Athol knew that this situation could easily go either way, depending on how well Ragnar could fight as human and how fast DeLaval could get chains on her.

If she'd known the truth about Athol, she would have taken delight in burning the building down around the elf's head long ago. But it was too late for that now. Too late for regrets.

"Keita?" She heard the question in Ragnar's voice; saw what lay behind the pious folding of his hands and bowed head. A dragonmage he might be, but one who knew how to use a sword, a battle ax, a pike—as dragon *and* as human. Knowing she wouldn't have to worry too much about the Lightning did ease things up for her slightly. But only slightly.

"My men will keep you company, monk," DeLaval told Ragnar. He yanked Keita again, but she'd dug her bare feet into the ground and refused to be moved. For she knew that once she was in that house, DeLaval would have all the help he needed to get her chained to one of Athol's many performance stages.

DeLaval stepped toward her, his breath hot on her face. "I'll kill your monk, my lady. And I'll let my men have such fun with him before they do."

And sighing heavily, Keita knew what she had to do to end this—although she hated the thought of it.

* * *

Ragnar kept his eyes on the men holding weapons on him and on Keita. She refused to be moved, but that wouldn't last long. Even more appalling, the lord of the manor stood by and did nothing. That would make sense if Keita could shift back to her dragon form and easily save herself, but Athol had already ensured that wasn't possible. Leaving them both with only one option.

Keita lowered her eyes, her head dipping, and her body pressing into the noble who held her. Raising one hand from her waist, she pressed her palm to the noble's face, fingers slowly trailing along his jaw, forefinger pressing against his lips until he sucked it into his mouth.

"I'm sorry," Keita said, her voice very soft. "But I don't like to be forced to do anything. You used to know that about me—and respect it."

She pulled her finger out of his mouth, and DeLaval blinked down at her, groaned, took a step back. Then his entire body began to shake, and he dropped to his knees, his hands around his throat.

His men turned toward their lord, and Ragnar caught hold of the arm of the guard closest to him. He twisted the wrist holding the sword until the weapon dropped into his free hand; then he twisted harder until he heard bone breaking from the wrist straight through to the shoulder.

DeLaval's men returned their focus to Ragnar, but it was too late now. He had a weapon and nearly two centuries more training than the ones who'd been ready to kill him on order. He tossed the man with the destroyed arm out of his way and gutted the male in front of him. Internal organs spilled on the ground, and Ragnar pulled the blade out, spun and took a head, spun back, went low—successfully avoiding the short sword aimed for his neck—and brought his blade up and into another guard's groin. Ripping the sword out, he used his free hand to grab the throat of another guard coming toward him and crushed all those small neck bones until the man could no longer breathe.

He dropped the struggling man and stepped away, the blade low at his side but ready. There were four guards left, moving out around him. Keita stood off to the side and watched him while the noble writhed at her feet. If only the human had realized earlier that she'd lost interest in him—and accepted that fact—he probably wouldn't be dying now.

Ragnar raised his gaze to the remaining guards. "Come for me," he said. And, when they only stared at him, *"Come for me!"*

Keita jumped a little at the Northlander's bellow. She didn't know the snobby bastard was capable of being so . . . barbaric.

She liked it.

Too bad about those poor, stupid guards. Had they really been fooled by the monk's robes? Even worse, once Ragnar had gutted and beheaded several of their comrades, they still didn't run. Why, she couldn't fathom. What with their lord shaking and rolling on the ground at her feet, foam pouring from his mouth—it would soon be blood, though—he'd be dead any moment now, so what was the point of continuing to fight?

Perhaps it was a male thing, because Keita never had qualms about walking away from any dangerous situation when she had to. Then again, neither did her brother—and Gwenvael was male . . . mostly.

And, as stupid males will do, they ignored logic and charged Ragnar. Keita, wincing a little, watched the Northlander tear into them with absolutely no mercy and no regret. A head rolled by, and Keita quickly wrapped her cape around her body to protect her gown from stray splashes of blood.

The second guard was cut in two. The third lost both his

arms. The fourth got the back of Ragnar's fist. Just once, but it was enough to completely decimate the man's face.

With all the guards dead, dying, or incapacitated, Ragnar focused his attention on Athol.

Keita ran on her tiptoes—and around an endless amount of blood—over to Ragnar, sliding in front of him, her hands pressing into his chest.

"Leave it."

"He did nothing to help you," Ragnar said.

"Leave it."

She watched the Dragonlord, covered in blood and bits of human, pull back his rage and gain complete control of his emotions. When he was calm, he nodded, and Keita motioned to the gate. He headed out, and Keita walked over to Athol.

As if nothing had happened, she said, "Well, I must be off."

"So soon?"

Keita controlled her urge to bite the elf's face off. "Unfortunately. I do need my beauty sleep, and we have an early start tomorrow."

"And did you find who you were looking for, my beautiful Keita?"

"No. But perhaps I can return at another time and search again?"

"Any time you'd like, old friend. You know that."

Friend? Really? But Keita would say nothing about that either. Someone like Athol had his uses. Plus, he wasn't like the humans. He wouldn't be an easy kill for her or Ragnar, not here on his territory.

Athol kissed the back of Keita's hand, winked at her. *Bastard.* But Keita did give his assistant a small nod of respect because she could see the true regret in the youngster's face. She knew he'd wanted to help, and understood why he couldn't. He might not wear a collar and leash like some of Athol's guests did, but that didn't mean he wasn't just as yoked into submission.

She walked out of the gate and onto the road. She immediately felt the loss of Athol's power, and it shocked her that she'd never realized how oppressive that power was until now. When the gate closed behind her, she let out a shaky breath and rubbed her forehead.

"Are you all right?"

And what she didn't need right now was for Ragnar to be nice to her. She still had no idea where her aunt was or if she'd betrayed the throne; and there was also at least another day of flying ahead and her mother to face at the end of it.

Lashing out at the Dragonlord was one option, one she briefly considered, but she simply wasn't in the mood to do that either.

"I'm fine," she said.

"What did you do to him?"

"DeLaval?" She raised the forefinger she'd let him suck on. "Loeiz herb. I always keep a little in my pockets."

"To poison people?"

"When they get pushy . . . yes."

Ragnar studied the dragoness before him, realization slowly creeping upon him.

She'd handled that noble and the elf without a bit of panic or fear, although she was essentially trapped in her human form. And she not only knew about the rare Loeiz herb, but had some hidden on her and understood how to use it. He knew this because putting Loeiz in food or drink made it completely ineffectual. It needed to interact directly with saliva or mucus to kill quickly, or be put in a small bleeding cut if one needed time to leave before death occurred. And very few knew the poisonous uses of the herb because it was hard to find and could only be plucked moments before blooming. Too early and it was a wonderful smoking weed. Plucked too late and it was a delicious herb on cooked meats.

Ragnar stepped closer, looked into her eyes. She was too tired to play any games. Too angry to tease or taunt him. And when he looked, he saw only the truth. Perhaps if he'd looked closely before, he wouldn't feel like such a fool now. Because his cousin and brother had been right all this time—Ragnar had misjudged Princess Keita. He still believed she would bed any and all in her path, but this dragoness was far from stupid. Dangerously far—as that noble lord bleeding out on Athol's cobbled courtyard now knew.

"Is there something else you want to ask, my lord?"

Hoping to open up their conversation again, he asked, "What about Esyld?"

She looked away. "I don't know." Then, under her breath, "But I think he knows something."

"Who knows something? Lord Reidfurd?"

Keita began to speak, looking as if she planned to confide in him, but she stopped and forced a safe, bland smile. "It's nothing," she replied to his question.

And in an instant, they were back to the boring noble and the insulting warlord . . . again.

Ragnar couldn't stand it.

"Keita—"

"We should get back. More travel tomorrow and I do need my sleep." She gave a small bow of her head as royal etiquette would dictate—and it made him want to throttle her—and said, "Thank you so much for your assistance this evening, my lord. It was greatly appreciated."

But he didn't want to end it like this. He was, in all honesty, becoming desperate. A feeling he was not used to and did not enjoy. "Keita, if you'd only talk to—"

But without waiting for him to finish his thought, she headed off down the road, and Ragnar was forced to follow. Again.

* * *

Keita found Ren hovering a few inches off the ground, meditating. How he did that, she didn't know. She needed actual wings to fly.

Without her saying a word, he sensed her presence and lowered himself to the earth.

"How did it go?"

She shook her head and pulled off her clothes. She dove into the lake, shifting from dragon to human several times before settling on her human form and swimming up to Ren's side. He'd also shifted to human and waited for her in the water by the lake's edge.

"Athol played games," Keita said when she broke through the surface. She had no intention of telling her friend about what had happened with DeLaval. It would only upset him, and there was nothing to be done now, was there? "I didn't like it."

"You think he knows something?"

"Perhaps. I don't know. He was always a little odd."

"Maybe he hoped you'd barter as some of his guests do."

Keita chuckled. "I can say with all honesty, I've never bartered my pussy or any other orifice on my body, and I'm not about to start now."

She rested her arms on the lake's edge, resting her cheek on them. "Perhaps when we get home I can send word to Gorlas. Maybe he can get the truth for us."

"Perhaps." Ren kissed her shoulder. "What else happened there?"

"Oh, nothing much. That idiot followed me, though."

"Good," Ren said, surprising her. He'd been livid with the warlord ever since Keita had told him their wager was off and why. "I didn't like you going there alone." And Ren had been right to be concerned.

"Athol wouldn't have trusted you, Ren."

"But it went all right, though? With the Northlander by your side?"

"He came as a monk. So it worked out perfectly." And, Keita realized that in the end, she'd been quite grateful for Ragnar's presence. He'd protected her and kept her safe.

Too bad, though, he still hadn't apologized to her. Instead he kept trying to "talk" to her. She hated that. If Keita fucked up, she said she was sorry and tried to make it right. What she didn't do was try to explain away what she'd said or how she'd meant it or any other load of centaur shit that males like Ragnar came up with rather than simply apologizing. Until he did that, she'd have no reason to "talk" to him. No matter how pathetically sorrowful he might appear.

Ragnar found a quiet spot close enough to the campsite to deal with any problem, but not so close that the constant chatter of a big blue dragon would distract him. Once he'd settled down, thankfully back in his dragon form, he did what he always did when he felt this way—although he didn't think he'd ever felt this bad. Ragnar opened his mind and called out. A few seconds later, came a reply.

My son.

Mother.

What's wrong?

Ragnar sat down on the ground, his back legs bent at the knees, his elbows resting on them so he could drop his head into his claws.

I'm an idiot, he told her simply.

He heard his mother's sweet laugh inside his head, felt eased by it. *Oh, my sweet boy. There's nothing I can do about that, I'm afraid. It's in the bloodline. Like the lightning.*

Chapter Twelve

Fragma heard the warning horn blast through her tiny Ice Land village and, terrified, she caught hold of her youngest daughter. The other women of her village all did the same thing. They grabbed the youngest of their female children and quickly took them into their homes, away from the streets, away from the danger they knew lurked hundreds of leagues behind the mountains framing the north side of their village.

But they were coming closer, down through the dangerous mountain pass and through the village, smashing all in their way that might deter them—even for a second—from their final destination. Or, even worse than that, perhaps they'd stop. Perhaps Fragma's little village *would be* their final destination. Perhaps it would be Fragma's daughter that was claimed. Or her friend's daughter. Or her neighbor's daughter. It could be *any* of their youngest girls, and absolutely no mother Fragma knew was willing to take that chance. Because once anyone's daughter was taken—she was never seen again.

Another warning blast rang out, and Fragma ran into her home with her daughter held tight against her. She slammed the door behind her with her back pressed against it.

They'd be coming now. And all Fragma could do was pray

to her gods that they'd keep riding right through—and that it would be someone else's child they'd come for. But not hers. Please, gods, not hers.

Taking the hand of her mate, Morfyd the White Dragonwitch left their room and walked down the hall to the stairs. Before they reached their destination, Brastias stopped, and when Morfyd turned to him, he kissed her. She sighed, her mouth opening under his, her eyes closing while a fresh wave of desire coursed through her.

His big hand caressed her throat, her jaw; and when he pulled back, he asked, "Do we really have to go down today? Can't we stay in bed?"

"We both have work to do. Besides"—she gripped his wrist, smoothed the pad of her thumb against his work-hardened palm—"if we stay in bed today, we'll want to stay in bed tomorrow and the day after and the day after."

"I don't see a problem with that," he teased.

As hard as Brastias was trying, he couldn't fool her. She knew he wanted to cheer her up, keep her distracted. And he was doing that for one reason and one reason only—the return of Keita the Family Darling. Or, as Morfyd liked to call her, Keita the Momentous Pain in Morfyd's Ass.

It had always bothered Morfyd how easy it was for Keita to get under her scales and pluck away at the last nerve she possessed. From the moment their mother had brought Keita back to Devenallt Mountain from the hatching chamber, Morfyd's sister had the unmistakable ability of pissing Morfyd off at every turn. And every time she did, Morfyd was blamed for it. Keita would toss all that red hair, smile at their father as if butter wouldn't melt and the next thing any of them knew, Bercelak the Great would turn to his eldest daughter and gently remind Morfyd that she was older and she should be taking care of her little sister—"not trying to

throw her off the mountain when you know she can't fly yet."
Which, if Morfyd remembered correctly, had only happened
one time and the little brat damn well deserved it!

But they were adults now. And they would act like adults,
even if Morfyd had to twist that snotty little cow into a knot
and rip the scales from her body to ensure it!

Morfyd wouldn't worry about that now, though. Not when
the man she loved was smiling at her, teasing her, doing
his best to make her happy. Honestly, she could never ask
for more.

"You, my lord," Morfyd teased back, "will not lure me into
a life of laziness."

"Why should we be different from everyone else in this
house?" he asked, kissing her again when she laughed.

"Must," a voice snapped, startling them out of their embrace, "you do that right here in front of everyone?"

Morfyd glared up at her brother, all gold and beautiful this
morning, as he was every morning. "Must *you* do that every
time you see us? You could simply walk away."

"You're my sister, Morfyd, not some whore. He's treating
you like a whore!"

"You treat everyone like whores."

Gwenvael the Handsome shrugged. "And your point?"

Brastias, rarely taking her brothers seriously these days,
pulled Morfyd around a glowering Gwenvael and toward
the stairs that led into the Great Hall. As they walked down,
she saw that most of her kin were awake and halfway through
their first meal.

As soon as they stopped at the bottom step, Brastias released her hand and walked around so that the dining table
separated them. Keeping inanimate objects between them
seemed to lessen the glares from Briec and Fearghus. After
two years, she'd thought her brothers would become used
to her choice of mate. But for some reason they all seemed
to feel "betrayed" by Brastias. She didn't know why, and she

didn't care. The arrogant bastards would simply have to accept their union . . . one day. In the next thousand years or so.

"Annwyl?" Brastias asked the entire table, reaching between Talaith and Briec to grab a loaf of fresh bread.

"Training," Fearghus mumbled, his attention on the parchments in front of him.

"My, my," Gwenvael said, his big body dropping into a chair beside Morfyd, "she certainly does train a lot these days."

Fearghus raised his eyes from the papers in front of him. "Meaning what exactly?"

"Just an observation, brother." Gwenvael reached for his own loaf of bread and ripped it into several pieces before adding, "Although we never actually *see* her training. Not like we used to. She simply disappears for hours before returning all sweaty and looking rather used. I wonder where she goes . . . and who she goes with."

Morfyd opened her mouth, a caustic reply on her tongue, but Talaith—Briec's mate and, although human, a fellow witch—beat Morfyd to it, a big, round fruit winging its way across the table and slamming into Gwenvael's nose.

"Owww!" he cried out. "You callous viper!"

"Sorry," Talaith hissed with no obvious remorse to back up that apology. "But it seemed like your never-closed mouth needed something to fill it! Tragically, my aim was off."

Briec threw his head back and laughed until black smoke snaked from Gwenvael's nostrils. Then Briec sneered, silently daring Gwenvael to do something. Gwenvael, of course, sneered back, and then they were both reaching across the rather wide table for each other's throats. Morfyd leaned in, swinging her arms wide to separate them.

"Stop it! Both of you, just stop it!" They pulled back—neither willing to hit her in the face—and Morfyd again wondered how much longer they could all tolerate living under one roof. As humans no less!

"Honestly!" she complained, tugging her witch's robes

back into place. "Lately all of you have been acting like fighting dogs in a pit."

"Dagmar doesn't let us do that anymore," Gwenvael uselessly reminded her. "She says it's wrong." He glanced off. "Although I still haven't figured out why."

Morfyd slapped Gwenvael in the back of the head.

"Ow! What was that for?"

"For being a prat!" She pointed her finger across the table at Briec, cutting his laugh off. "You, too! Either both of you start acting like you've got some sense"—she moved her finger to Gwenvael to stop the next words out of his mouth—"even if you have none, or you find somewhere else to live."

"You can't throw us out," Briec argued. He'd never liked being told what to do.

"I bloody well can. I'm vassal of Queen Annwyl's lands, and I can toss anyone off them that I see fit. So don't *push me*!" she finished on a healthy bellow.

"You mean Queen Annwyl who's always off"—Gwenvael cleared his throat—"training?"

Morfyd had her fist pulled back, ready to pummel the whelp, when Brastias grabbed her arm and dragged her from the hall and out the enormous doors. He didn't release her until they were down the stairs and around the corner.

"Brat! He's such a brat!"

"He's restless. So's Briec, I think."

"That's not my problem!"

"Sssh," Brastias crooned softly, big, calloused fingers gently brushing against her lips, across her jaw. Only Brastias knew how to settle her. The gods of mercy knew he had the kind of skills most males would kill for, and she thanked those gods every night for giving his heart to her. "Don't let them trouble you so."

Morfyd took a breath and released it. "You are right, of course. It's simply that we haven't spent this much time together as a family since we were hatchlings. Now you can understand why Mother insisted on having a nanny and armed guards around us on most days. And when she didn't—there went Gwenvael's tail, Éibhear's hair . . . Briec's back fangs."

Brastias chuckled, kissed her mouth. "What I see is you protecting Annwyl." His head lowered with his voice. "Is there need to protect Annwyl?"

Morfyd couldn't answer that, not honestly, so she didn't answer at all. Instead she kissed Brastias until his arms wrapped around her, and he pulled her to his chain-mail-covered chest.

"You have work to do," she finally reminded him when she pulled away, both of them panting.

"You're right. Even if the legions are going nowhere at the moment, I need to make sure they keep up their training." He kissed her forehead. "Perhaps we can meet later this afternoon . . . in our room? A quick luncheon."

Morfyd grinned. Her day already looked brighter. "That sounds perfect."

Brastias walked off, and, as she always did, she watched him. And, as he always did, he looked back at her and smiled.

As a group, they landed on a plateau that held steps leading directly into a mountain. Devenallt Mountain, the seat of power for those who ruled the dragon Clans and Houses of the Southland. And hundreds of leagues below was Garbhán Isle. The seat of power for the human queen.

"You two wait here," Ragnar told his brother and cousin.

"You sure?" Vigholf asked. The idea of letting Ragnar go in alone bothered his brother, but it was for the best.

"I'll be fine."

"Don't worry," Keita said, patting Vigholf's shoulder. "Ren will stay here with you in case there's trouble."

"I will?" the foreign dragon asked. "You sure you don't—"

"It will be easier and quicker to get through this if my mother doesn't have you to fawn over. Besides, I need you to make sure my kin don't mistake dear Vigholf and Meinhard for problems."

"What fun for me."

She laughed, a sound heard rarely during the last of their journey. "We won't be long."

"Better not be."

"Come on!" the Blue demanded, sounding like the eager pup he was. "Let's go!"

"All right," Keita told him, waving him on. "We're coming."

"Good luck," the Eastlander told her as she headed up the stairs behind the Blue. Ragnar glanced at him as he passed, but the foreign dragon turned away, giving him his back.

Of course, Ragnar had been told he'd deserved that and more.

"Good," his mother had said. "You should feel ashamed. It was horrible what you said to her."

"I know," he'd responded.

"You'll have to apologize to her, my son."

"She won't make that easy."

"You can't apologize on your own terms, Ragnar. That isn't really an apology, but a perfunctory action simply meant to appease. To make *you* feel better. If you truly are sorry about what you said—"

"I am."

"You'd better be, because I didn't raise you to be mean, my son. And we both know that was mean."

He did know. That's what ate at him. It was one thing to be cold and calculating, a necessity when dealing with politics and world rulers. But it was another thing entirely to be mean and cruel because he had issues over his long-dead father. So whatever he had to do to fix this with Keita—in all honesty, he could care less about the Eastlander, except for his connection to Keita—he would do. If only she'd give him the chance.

And, for the remainder of their journey, she hadn't given him a chance. Since he and his kin planned to head home as soon as they were done here, he had no choice but to push the issue now. He refused to return to the Northlands with her hating him.

Ragnar met her at the top step before entering directly into the mountain. He touched her shoulder, and she stopped. After a moment, she faced him. He wanted to look away from her. All that royal coldness staring down at him made his shame even worse because he knew he had no one to blame for it but himself.

"Yes, Lord Ragnar?"

"Before we go in," he said, "I want to tell you how sorry I am. About what I said to you. It was wrong, and I understand if you can't forgive me, but I do hope that you'll at least accept my apology."

For a moment, Ragnar wasn't sure he'd said those words out loud. Nothing about her changed. Neither the expression on her face nor the coldness in her eyes. She showed no anger, no sorrow, not even boredom.

And without saying anything, Keita walked away from him and inside the Dragon Queen's mountainous court. Ragnar followed, sighing heavily. It appeared as if he'd be going home with Keita hating him after all.

Another set of stairs awaited them, and the Blue stood in the middle of them, tapping his front claw and glaring. "You two are taking forever."

Keita walked up to her brother and stood beside him on the step.

The Blue's impatience turned to concern. "Are you all right, Keita? You've been looking like this the past couple of days. You're not worried about Mum, are you? You know how she is sometimes. She doesn't mean half of what she says."

Keita didn't respond to her brother, instead focusing on Ragnar, who now stood at the bottom of the stairs.

"You were saying, Lord Ragnar?"

Damn. He knew she wouldn't make this easy, but . . . damn. Ragnar briefly closed his eyes, girded his loins, and said again, "I'm sorry, Keita, and I do hope you can forgive me."

The Blue frowned, his gaze bouncing back and forth between them. "Sorry for what?"

Keita continued to stare at Ragnar. She wouldn't answer her brother's question, but instead patiently waited for Ragnar to do so.

Never before had the desire to run away like a panicked cub filled him like this. But he remembered his mother's words clearly: "You can't apologize on your own terms, Ragnar."

As always, his mother was right. So, while gazing into Keita's dark brown eyes, Ragnar admitted to the brother who adored her more than life itself, "I made the crude and completely reprehensible suggestion that your sister is a slag."

Again, Keita's expression didn't change, and, even when that blue fist hit Ragnar with the power of a rampaging herd of cattle, he kept his gaze locked with hers.

Ragnar stumbled to the side, but didn't fall. It wasn't easy. It was a shame the cub didn't have more of an edge—he had the power and strength to be a hell of a warrior, if not the skill and will.

A black talon pointed at him from a blue claw. "You talk to my sister like that again, and your brother and cousin won't find enough of you to put on your funeral pyre. Do I make myself clear?"

Moving his jaw and trying to get feeling back on that side of his face, Ragnar nodded. "You do."

"Good. Now"—the Blue huffed a little—"I strongly suggest we keep this between us. If our father gets a whiff, we'll be back to Lightning versus Fire all over again with the alliance completely destroyed." The Blue gently placed his claw on his sister's shoulder. "Are you all right with that, Keita?"

She nodded, and, after one more disgusted scowl in Ragnar's direction, the Blue said, "Let's go then," and headed up the rest of the stairs.

Ragnar continued to gaze into Keita's eyes, still hoping for the forgiveness he had no right to ask for. Her smile, when it came, bloomed into Ragnar's life like the two suns abruptly moving past dark storm clouds and lighting the world around him.

"Now," she said with a wink, "I'll accept your weak little barbarian apology."

Chapter Thirteen

"Do you need a refresher on court etiquette?" Keita asked Ragnar, still shocked the Lightning had apologized to her. And not some stiff-upper-lip, "I apologize if I offended you, my lady" kind of apology. But an actual "I'm sorry" that he'd meant. And because he'd meant it, she had happily accepted. Because Keita simply didn't believe in holding grudges unless it was necessary. Why sit around loathing someone because they had a moment of stark idiocy? Such a waste, in her opinion.

And as long as the Northlander meant what he said to her—and she knew he had because she could always spot a lie or a liar—she wouldn't hold it against him.

Of course, if he said something like that to her again, she'd poison his drinking water and giggle at his deathbed. But that seemed only fair.

"Perhaps a small reminder wouldn't hurt."

"Don't walk beside me," she reminded him, "but only because it's your first time here. Don't approach the queen unless she summons you. Don't touch her unless she touches you first. Don't even think of unleashing your lightning inside these walls—it will be the last thing you ever do. Refer to her as 'Your Majesty,' even if she's pissing you the bloody hells off, and my father as 'my lord.' Oh. And no challenging stares to my father. Although that's not so much etiquette as good sense."

"I'll keep all that in mind."

"Good." They turned a corner, and Keita stopped. "For everything else follow my lead and you should be fine."

"I will."

This corridor led to the first floor of the queen's court, the walls lined with her armored guards, each holding a pilum in one hand and a long shield in the other. As they walked through the hallway, none of the guards looked at them or noted their presence. Keita kept her gaze fixed firmly on the floor. When she was younger, she used to play a game to see which of her mother's guards she could get to pay attention to her, but when a few lost their positions, Keita stopped. It was only fun if everyone got a laugh out of it. She had no desire to ruin someone's dream or career because she was bored.

The trio reached the far end of the hallway, and the final two guards stepped away from their post and moved in front of the opening, blocking them from entering the next chamber. These guards still had the sharp metal tip of their pila aimed at the ceiling, their shields held in front of them but not in battle position.

"Princess Keita," one of them said. "We weren't aware of your returning."

"I adore surprises, don't you?" She motioned to Ragnar. "He's with us. Mother summoned him."

The guard looked her over, searching for any obvious signs of weapons. Her mother's personal guard always did this to her. As Gorlas had said, Keita might protect the throne, but it was the Queen's Royal Guard, led by her cousin Elestren, who protected Her Majesty. Even if it meant protecting her from her own children.

"He leaves his weapons," the guard finally said.

Keita turned to Ragnar and held out her claws. She feared

he'd spew some Northland nonsense about never putting down his weapons, but, without a word, he pulled off the sheathed sword and battle ax tied to his back, and removed the warhammer he had tied at his waist. With a grin, he dropped them in Keita's arms, and she nearly buckled under the weight of all his crap.

"Éibhear," she squeaked, and her brother quickly removed the weapons. The fact that her baby brother held those weapons easily did nothing but annoy her. "Rude," she hissed at Ragnar, and he had the nerve to laugh.

Once Éibhear placed the weapons aside, the two guards moved out of the way, allowing them to enter.

Gods.

Up to this point, Ragnar had been a bit disappointed with the queen's court. All stark, dank walls and cold caverns. But this . . . *this* was what Ragnar had expected to see all along: mountain walls plastered in pure gold, the history of the Fire Breathers etched into each section; chalices, made of gold, crystal, or ivory, held by dragons of noble birth, some of them wearing items made of the finest metals and gems; the floors lined with furs so the nobles' precious talons wouldn't be forced to touch actual stone; fresh meats turning on spits over big fire pits while uncooked and unseasoned meats rested a few feet away so the royals had their choice of meals.

It was as decadent and wasteful as Ragnar had been led to believe by his kinsmen, making him wonder how much of a threat the Southlanders could possibly be to his kind. Ragnar couldn't imagine even one of these pampered lizards raising a claw in defense against a dragonfly much less a powerful Dragonlord Chief of the Hordes.

As the small group walked by, the royals turned away from their conversations to watch them. The females focused on the Blue, their cold eyes turning calculating at the sight of him; the males focused on the princess. Then one male, a Red, pushed through the others, his expression angry, his demeanor threatening. Ragnar felt the way he had when dealing with that human noble at Castle Moor. But this time Ragnar wasn't trapped in his human form. He wasn't weakened by another's Magick. So when the Red moved too close in Ragnar's estimation, Ragnar faced him and slammed his tail down between them.

The strength of the Northland tail ensured that the metal spiked tip tore through the fur they stood on and straight into the stone floor beneath.

"Move out of my way, low born," the Red ordered.

"You need to calm yourself and step away."

Frustrated, the Red yelled out, "Keita! Don't walk away from me!"

Keita stopped, her front claw barely catching hold of her baby brother's forearm before he could run over and beat the Red to death.

"I know," she said, without turning around, "that you didn't just bellow at me as if I were some barmaid."

"You will talk to me."

"Tragically for you, I've never been desperate enough to take orders from anyone. Now if you'll excuse us, our mother awaits."

The Red tried again to pass Ragnar, his rage exploding when Ragnar shoved him back, determined to keep him away from Keita.

The Red swung his fist at Ragnar, but a black-scaled claw closed around it before it could connect, black talons engulfing red ones and squeezing.

The sound of cracking and breaking bones echoed through the now-silent hall. Having met the black dragon once before, Ragnar recognized the Queen's consort and Keita's father. Bercelak the Great, as he was known in the South—in the North he was still called Bercelak the Vengeful and Bercelak the Murdering Rat Bastard Scum—did not warn others off. It simply wasn't in his nature, although Ragnar guessed that was especially true when it came to Bercelak's daughters.

The older dragon, without saying a word, kept up the pressure on that red claw until he'd completely crushed it, leaving the Red weeping like a babe on the fur-covered floor. The Fire Breather's gaze moved from the sobbing noble to Ragnar. He studied him closely with those cold black eyes before motioning to a set of stairs. "My Queen waits for you, Lightning. She doesn't like to wait."

Now Ragnar remembered why striking directly at Queen Rhiannon's court was something even his father had avoided. Not because of the nobles—they seemed relatively worthless—but because of their battle dogs: Lord Bercelak and the Cadwaladr Clan.

The nobles should be grateful for the presence of the low-born dragons, because they were the only ones who kept the wolves from the door, to use a common human phrase.

Ragnar moved around the Queen's consort and walked up another set of stairs. At the top stood the Blue and Keita. She waited until Ragnar was in front of her and her brother entered the next chamber.

"He seemed attached, that Red," Ragnar observed, looking over his shoulder to see the Queen's consort eyeing everyone until they looked away.

"Don't blame me," Keita contested. "I promised neither him nor DeLaval anything and was very honest from the beginning about what they would get from me." She reached up and brushed her claws against Ragnar's shoulders as if she was wiping away lint on clothes he wasn't wearing. "Most appreciate my honesty, but there are some who think they can get around that, that they can change my mind." She looked up at him through her lashes, and he knew this was more about him than that idiot Red or DeLaval.

"Some of us at least have to try, my lady. But there's a

definite line between being determined and just being a pushy prat."

Keita laughed and headed into the next chamber. "I'm glad to see that you apparently know the difference."

Keita stepped into the chamber. This one had a few nobles but many more of her father's Clan in attendance, which, in her mind, always explained the presence of more weapons and guards and less high-priced royal trappings.

Instantly, Keita saw her mother at the other end of the hall. The queen had her arms around Éibhear, hugging him to her.

"My sweet, sweet hatchling," Rhiannon crooned. "I'm so glad to have you home, safe and alive."

"I missed you, Mum."

"And I missed you." For the first time with any of her off-spring, Queen Rhiannon raised herself on the tips of her talons in order to reach Éibhear's forehead and kiss it. Then she kissed each cheek before pulling back and looking him over. "By the gods, son. You've gotten huge! You're looking more and more like your grandfather every day."

"Thanks, Mum."

Crystal blue eyes focused past Éibhear and onto Keita. Mother and daughter's gazes locked, the same way they had—rumor had it—when Keita broke out of her shell at hatching. It was said that although Keita had no fire at the time, she sent a ball of smoke at her mother's head. Something Queen Rhiannon had yet to forgive her second-hatched daughter for.

As always, Keita braced herself for what was about to happen, which was the same thing that happened every time mother and daughter met. The same horrifying, ridiculous display that, if unleashed, could destroy the innocent minds of an entire countryside of peasants.

"Remember, warlord," she softly warned Ragnar, watching

her mother step around Éibhear and move toward her, "that no matter what you see here, I am no more or less than what you thought of me before."

"What in all the hells does that mean?"

Keita let out a breath. "You'll see."

Rhiannon, still safely across the hall, lifted her mighty white head, pulled her lips back over bright white fangs, opened her arms, and cried out, "Keita! My lovely daughter!"

Keita opened her arms and shouted back, "Mumsy!"

Ragnar watched in fascination as the two females moved across the hall and made what seemed to be an attempt to hug each other but then not quite bothering. Instead they kept their arms held out and kissed the air around each other's heads rather than cheeks.

Rhiannon stepped back and, looking her daughter over, said, "Keita. Look at you. You look absolutely . . ." Ragnar waited for the queen to finish that compliment, but instead she finished with, "You!"

"Mumsy," Keita replied, the queen's eye twitching the tiniest bit. "Look at all that beautiful gray in your hair. It really does fit your face . . . now."

"And you, my sweetest daughter. With all that fiery red hair! Like a blessing from the gods!" She lowered her voice—a little. "It seems they even blessed your chin a bit."

"Nothing that can't be plucked away! Like you do with your chest!"

Smiles still firmly in place, the two females looked at each other and said as one, "*You!*"

"Don't I get a hug?" Bercelak asked from beside Ragnar, and the smile that was on Keita's face now was as warm and true as any he'd seen from her before.

She ran back across the hall and into her father's arms, each hugging the other tight.

But it was while he had his daughter in his embrace that the queen's consort mouthed at She Who Rules These Lands, *Be nice!*

The queen shrugged and mouthed back, *I am!*

When Keita stepped away from her father, the queen motioned to the Blue beside her. When Bercelak said nothing, the queen gestured again until her consort let out a great sigh and mumbled, "Boy." The queen scowled at her mate, and Bercelak added, "Glad you're home."

The Blue's eyes crossed. "Gee. Thanks, Dad."

Queen Rhiannon patted her son's shoulder. "Now I have to talk to Lord Ragnar for a bit. So why don't you and your father go chat?"

Ragnar had to quickly look away because the expression of pure panic on the Blue's face was so hilarious he knew he would be unable to keep the laughter in if he kept watching.

"Talk?" the Blue asked, his voice nearly cracking.

"Yes." She pushed her hatchling toward Bercelak. "We won't be long." She motioned to Ragnar with a snowy-white talon, and he moved across the hall, those in the chamber watching him closely. Again, he was reminded that the royals weren't the worry when it came to the Southlanders. It was these dragons. All of them—even the females—were warriors, fighters, killers.

He'd neared the queen when she said, "You stay, too, Keita."

Keita stumbled on her claws; she'd been following her father and brother out. "Me? Why?"

The queen laughed, placing her claw on Ragnar's forearm. "Isn't she funny, my little hurricane wind? Pretending she doesn't know how to follow orders from her queen. She always makes me laugh."

Bercelak motioned to his daughter and, her shoulders slumping a little, Keita walked toward her mother and together the three of them moved into the queen's private chamber.

Chapter Fourteen

Queen Rhiannon, ruler of all Southland dragons, dropped down onto her throne and gazed at her daughter and the handsome Northland dragon with her. "So where is my sister?"

"I'm sorry, Your Majesty," the Northlander replied, "but when I arrived she wasn't there."

"I see. She just disappeared, then?"

Keita snorted. "More like she escaped before you could get your claws on her."

Rhiannon snarled a little at her brat, but the Lightning quickly stepped in front of her. When she heard Keita gasp and demand, "What do you think you're doing?" Rhiannon had to fight hard not to giggle.

"From what we could tell, Lady Esyld had not been in that house for some time, Your Majesty."

"There was nothing that told you where she might have gone?"

"We looked. There was nothing."

"Was she captured?"

"Wouldn't you know that, Mother?" Keita demanded behind the Dragonlord.

"And what is that supposed to mean?"

Keita walked around Ragnar. "It means, how long did you

know she was there? How long have you been plotting to have her killed?"

"Your Majesties—" the Lightning began, but Rhiannon cut him off with one raised white talon.

"I knew she was there from the first time you went to see her. Was it worth it?" Rhiannon demanded. "Betraying me for that backstabbing little whore?"

The brat sighed out of pure boredom. "I never betrayed you, Mother."

"You knew where she was, Keita. You never said a word. Not even to your brothers."

"I didn't see a point. She wasn't hurting anyone."

"That doesn't matter, you twit! You knew where a suspected traitor was, and you said nothing. You've broken the law. You've put yourself and your kin at risk. Why? To protect a female who wants me dead?"

"Och! If you feel that way, call a meeting of the Elder Council, have them find me guilty of treachery, have me sent to the Desert Mines."

"I should do that. It wouldn't be any less than you deserve!"

"Then what are you waiting for?" Keita demanded, holding out her front claws. "Have your guards take me away and let us end this ridiculous conversation!"

Annoyed as only her damn daughter could annoy her, Rhiannon slapped Keita's arms down—and Keita slapped her back across the shoulder. Mouth open, stunned her daughter would do that to her own mother, much less the queen, Rhiannon stood and slapped Keita's shoulder. They were in full slapping swing by the time the Lightning pushed his way between them.

"*That is enough!*" he bellowed, shoving the females apart. "*Both of you cut it out!* I've never seen mother and daughter act like this before. You two bite at each other like snakes in a pit!"

Rhiannon's guards burst into the chamber, led by Bercelak, but she held up her claw. "It's fine, my love."

"Rhiannon—"

"It's fine, it's fine. Go back and talk to your son."

Bercelak's eyes crossed. "Must I?"

"Bercelak!"

"All right, all right."

Her consort grudgingly left with the rest of Rhiannon's guard.

"My, my," Rhiannon said once the three were alone again, slowly walking around the Northlander, "my little lightning bolt has a bit of a temper."

"He does," her daughter chimed in, walking around Ragnar as well. Keita's anger, as always, quickly forgotten. It was a gift none of Rhiannon's other offspring possessed.

As they moved around the suddenly tense Dragonlord, the pair grinned at each other as if they shared a delicious secret. Her daughter truly liked this one; Rhiannon could tell. "When he gets really frustrated," Keita explained, "he says horrible things. But he apologizes and takes a punch to the face from a protective brother like a true dragon should."

"That's very nice to hear. Nothing is worse than those who will not apologize. Of course, I never apologize, but I don't have to. I'm the queen!"

Ragnar was dragon enough to admit he was unnerved by the two She-dragons circling him like a wounded bear.

"What else have you noticed about him?" the queen asked her daughter.

"He broods sometimes. But not enough to make him painfully boring. He's very loyal to his brother and cousin. And he's more powerful than he's willing to admit."

"So he's not a show-off then?"

"Oh, no. Not at all."

"Or like his father?"

"Ewww. Gods, no."

"More like your mother then?" the queen asked him, her spike-tipped tail brushing his shoulder. "She raised you better perhaps. I knew she would."

Ragnar studied the queen. "You knew my mother?"

"I knew her quite well. Her disappearance from her kin's cave was what began the war between our people during my mother's reign."

"I'd heard that."

"So you're a Southlander as much as a Northlander."

Ragnar couldn't help but smirk. "We're not raised that way. No matter where your mother may come from, you are your father's child—a Northlander."

"With all those codes and rules and dying with honor?"

"And purple scales and lightning. It's all part of the package."

Rhiannon smiled at him. She was large for a dragoness. Nearly his height and width. Her daughter, much smaller, stood by her mother's side now, appearing tiny in comparison, her dark-red scales bright beside her mother's white ones.

"Tell me, Keita . . . can this Northlander be trusted?"

To Ragnar's surprise, Keita answered without hesitation, "Aye. He can."

Unable *not* to ask the question, he put in, "How can you say that about me?"

"Because I know, and be grateful I do, warlord. It's the only reason you're still alive." Keita abruptly turned to her mother. "How long have you known?"

The queen placed a talon to her lips to silence her daughter and said softly to Ragnar, "Seal the room."

Ragnar had no idea what was going on between the royals, but he did as the queen bade. Her eyes widened in surprise. "Gods, child. The Dragonlord *is* powerful."

"Told you."

"Aye, daughter, but I thought you were talking about these

mighty shoulders of his." Rhiannon returned to her throne. "How much time, my dark cloud?"

"Ten minutes. But less if you insist on using all those nicknames."

"I love your nicknames, my swirling tornado." She sat down on her throne, gazed at her daughter. "What was your question again?"

"How long have you known?" Keita repeated.

"About you?" The queen let out a little laugh. "That's simple, child—I've known since you killed my brother."

The thought of running crossed Keita's mind, but she'd never give her mother the satisfaction.

"Which brother?"

"Let's not play games, child. At least two of them!" Rhiannon's laugh rang out, and she clapped her front claws together. "Don't let her beauty and seemingly intense lack of brains confuse you, Lord Ragnar. My second-born daughter is *nothing* like what she seems."

"What I did, Mumsy"—and she loved how her mother's eye twitched when she called her that—"I did to—"

"Yes. I know. You did it to protect the throne. And what I'm about to ask you to do is so that you may continue protecting the throne."

"Which is what exactly?"

"Someone will approach you, daughter, with an offer. You are to accept it."

"What kind of offer?"

Rhiannon grinned. "To be the next Dragon Queen."

"Oh." Keita glanced at Ragnar, her brown eyes crossing. "Right."

"You don't believe me."

"Oh, no, no. There are lots who want to see me as queen.

I hear it all the time. Of course, that's usually from drunk males trying to look up my tail."

"Keita, you've managed to hide the truth about yourself very well. Most of the human nobles don't know you're a dragon *or* of your connections to Annwyl. And the dragons think you'd love to see me dead."

"Well—" Keita began, but Ragnar's tail slammed into her ass, cutting her off. "What I mean is," she quickly corrected while glaring at him, "the dragons think I'm vapid and stupid and vain. So who in their right mind would think to make me queen?"

Ragnar answered instead of Rhiannon. "Someone who wants complete control of the throne and the Southland dragons."

Rhiannon raised a claw to him. "See how smart he is? Smart and handsome and—"

"Your brothers are too independent and too loyal to their mother," Ragnar cut in, interrupting her mother's list of his attributes, and for a second there, Keita adored him like the suns. "And your sister—"

"Right," Keita said, sniffing in annoyance. "She's perfect and would never do such a thing." Her sister's perfection was something Keita had heard about since hatching.

"About her perfection, I do not know. But with her powers, she's too dangerous. She'd have to be killed as well."

"Lovely." And Keita couldn't help feeling a little de-pressed. "Everyone thinks that I'd betray my entire family to their deaths so I can have," she sneered, "*that*."

"I adore my rock," the queen said, shifting around on it. "I look very regal on it."

"Pardon my questions—"

"No, no, Lord Ragnar. Ask. We may not have time like this again before this all plays out."

"It just seems a dangerous situation to put your daughter in, my lady." And Keita felt her heart stutter a little before she remembered that all Northlands males were protective of females in that way.

"Oh, but my daughter lives for risk. Don't you, Keita?"

Knowing exactly where Rhiannon was about to go, Keita said, "Mother—"

"Now, now. There's no shame on your part, child. Everything my Keita has done has been in service to my throne. For instance, my brother Oissine, who'd fled to Alsandair after I became queen, had hired assassins to kill me. Too bad about that *food poisoning*, eh?" Then she winked at Keita.

Mortified, Keita sighed, "Oh, Mother."

"And Muiredach, brother number two, had gone into the Northlands. It took her some time to track him down, but she must not have liked what she saw or heard when she found him because he seemed to have had a tragic fall off one of those Northland mountains of yours, young Ragnar. He was so high up, apparently, that it was a fall no dragon could survive . . . drunk and unconscious, that is. Tell me, Keita, did you use your father's ale to get him that drunk before you shoved him off that mountain? Or did you find that stash of your grandfather's drink that we keep when we need to strip skin off a horse carcass?"

Keita could feel Ragnar's eyes on her, could feel him sizing her up. She'd never felt so exposed before. Those who knew the truth—her father, Gwenvael, Ren, Gorlas—had been with her from the beginning. They had seen her training, her growth as one of the Protectors of the Throne. The small, eclectic group of dragons and humans that made it their life's work to do anything and everything necessary to keep the Southland thrones safe from those who would take them.

And discussing what she'd done among those who already knew the truth had never been something that made Keita uncomfortable. Yet discussing it with Ragnar and her *mother*? Here? Now? She'd be less uncomfortable naked and spread eagled in the Garbhán Isle market.

"My third brother is also said to be hiding somewhere in the Northlands and Keita was quite determined to find him until your father found her first." When Ragnar said nothing, Rhiannon asked, "Didn't you ever wonder, Ragnar, why my daughter was in your territories? Alone? Why your father was able to get his claws on her?"

"You told me it was because she went to see Esyld."

"And she did. Often. But she only had to go as far as the Outerplains for that. She went farther, however, for one reason only. To find my brothers and sort them out. Like she'd sorted out Oissine. You see, Dragonlord, my daughter was able to do what entire legions of my Dragonwarriors could not. Track down and exterminate those who are a danger to me." And before Keita could correct her, she said, "Sorry. I meant a danger to my throne."

"Interesting," Ragnar said, and Keita flinched a little at his tone. Until he added, "So she searched for and found proof that at least two of your brothers were preparing to strike against you, and she acted accordingly. Then logic would dictate that she did the same due diligence with your sister and found that Esyld was not a threat. That she was not a risk to your throne or to you."

Shocked, Keita stared up at the Northlander, while her mother leaned back in her throne and studied him hard.

"I find it fascinating, Dragonlord, that you don't seem shocked by any of this."

"I've misjudged your daughter in the past, Your Majesty. And I don't make the same mistakes twice."

"I see. Then I shall be honest here, now. I don't know if my sister has betrayed me. All I do know is that my throne is in play, and I need your help, Keita. For you will be the one they come to. *You* will be the one they try to set against me."

Keita couldn't think of a time when her mother had ever asked her for anything—other than not being "such a twat all the time!" And now, between her mother asking her for help and Ragnar's words about misjudging her, Keita felt a little overwhelmed.

She swallowed, found her voice. "I know what to do."

"I know you do. But still, keep your true temper in check and remember who and what you're playing. A spoiled royal, but one with boundaries. If you act as if you're willing for them to do anything to get you the throne, they'll know you're lying, that you're setting them up. Let them lead. Let them lie. They'll tell you what they think you'll want to hear, but if they bring up your brothers, your sister, definitely your father—you insist they must be kept safe, alive. Feel free to waffle on me, however."

"Oh, I plan to."

"Once the traitors contact you, you must contact me."

"I will."

"Immediately, Keita. Don't try and handle this on your own. Not this. Understand?"

"Aye. I understand. I'm not new to this, Mum."

"You also need someone to watch your back."

"Ren's here with me. He can—"

"I'll do it," Ragnar cut in.

Keita ignored her mother's smirk and said, "I've done this sort of thing with Ren for years and—"

"That's exactly the problem," he cut in again. "He's too close to you. Too close to the throne and your family."

"He's right, Keita."

"Yes, but Ragnar's an outsider."

"But the foreigner isn't?" Ragnar asked.

"Stop calling him that!"

"It doesn't matter," Rhiannon said, raising her front claws to calm them. "It really doesn't."

"Why not?"

"Because Lord Thunderclap is right. You and Ren *are* too close. Plus they know about the loyalty of the Eastland dragons to the throne and to me. They know Ren won't risk his father's wrath if he's involved in betraying me. They won't trust him."

"Yes, but—"

"And, more importantly, this is Lord Ragnar's problem too."

Ragnar blinked. "It is?"

"It will be."

"Threats again, my lady?"

"Not threats, my darling cyclone. But word has come to me that your cousin near the Ice Land borders has been approached."

"My cousin? Do you mean Styrbjörn?"

"I thought he was dead," Keita said.

"That's Styrbjörn the Loathsome. His son, Styrbjörn the Revolting, has since taken over the Borderlands."

"Such interesting names in the north," Keita muttered.

"Who has Styrbjörn been approached by, my lady?"

And when her mother didn't answer immediately, Keita focused on her. "Mother?"

Rhiannon cleared her throat. "I believe it is . . . Overlord Thracius."

Keita dropped back on her haunches, her mind on that damn Sovereign necklace they'd found at Esyld's. "The Irons?" Keita said, trying to sound disbelieving when she no longer knew what to believe. "You think the Irons are coming after your throne?"

"Why do you sound so shocked? The Irons have wanted this territory and the Northlands for centuries."

"Then why haven't they moved before now? What are they waiting for?"

"Thracius is not his father. He won't make rash decisions. He wants everything in place before he moves. You on the throne, me dead or imprisoned, the Elders in his pocket. If he gets all that, he won't have a massive war campaign to fight, he'll have more of an insurgency to tamp down. Something much easier to manage."

"And I'm sure revenge against Thracius for past offenses has nothing to do with this."

"A war against Thracius won't do me any favors."

"But he killed your father, Mum. You've always wanted revenge for that."

"I have, but protecting my throne is more important than getting even with that bastard. Wouldn't you agree?"

"You know I do."

Her mother's damn smirk returned. "The seal is fading from this cavern, daughter. So decide now. In or out, Keita?"

"You already know my answer, Mother."

"I do. But I won't lie, daughter. You'll be on your own until this is done."

Stating a simple truth, feeling neither anger nor pride, Keita admitted, "I've always been on my own."

But then Ragnar, quietly standing next to her, said, "Until now."

Chapter Fifteen

They heard the yelling seconds before a livid Keita stormed out of the throne room.

"I'm leaving!" she said, coming quickly down the stairs, with Ragnar behind her. "Give my siblings my love."

"Oh, Keita—" Éibhear began, but his father caught hold of him and held him back.

"You'll stay," Éibhear's mother said from behind Keita and Ragnar, "because I *insist* you stay."

The thin tether that held Keita's anger in check must have snapped, because she spun on her heel and hissed, "I'll not stay, you overbearing harpy. And you'll not order me to."

"I'll do any damn thing I want to. I am the queen."

"You're a broken-down old field horse with wings is what you are!"

In retaliation—and to Éibhear's shock—Rhiannon raised her claw, flames shooting from her palm. But Ragnar stepped between the flames and Keita, raising his own claw. He drew the flames in and closed his talons into a fist. After a few moments, he opened his claw, and the flames the queen had thrown at Keita fell to the ground in bright-colored crystals.

Surprise flitted across his mother's face before she mused,

"My, my, we are *protective*, my little winter storm. Tell me, what did my innocent daughter do to make you so protective?"

Growling, Keita tried to shoot past Ragnar, but he caught her and pulled her back while the Royal Guard moved into place around the queen.

Ragnar ignored the queen's words and said, "This doesn't have to get nasty, Your Majesty. I'm sure it wouldn't hurt to stay for a little while."

"I don't—"

Silencing Keita with one glare, he reminded her, "Your kin have missed you. I'm sure they'd like to spend time with you before you head back out."

"Och! Fine," Keita told him. Then she sneered at their mother and stormed off.

Ragnar briefly bowed his head to the queen and followed after Éibhear's sister.

"Bitch," his mother growled, before she returned to her chamber.

"Go with your sister," his father said.

"But Dad—"

"Did you learn nothing in the north about taking orders? Don't argue with me. Just go."

"All right." Éibhear followed his sister, glancing back to see his father head up to the queen's chamber. Maybe his dad would ease things. Keita had never gotten along with their mother, but it was time to put all that behind them, wasn't it?

Rhiannon sat inside her private chamber, her mind turning.

"Well?" Bercelak asked, his claw taking hers. "Is it done?"

"It is."

"Are you sure about this, Rhiannon?"

"No. She's impulsive. Hot headed. I've always said so." She glared at him. "What are you grinning at?"

"Nothing. Just the way you describe Keita sounds like someone else I know."

Perplexed, Rhiannon asked, "Who?"

"It doesn't matter. But our Keita, she's smart and well trained. She's one of the best agents we have, and you know that."

"Of course I know that. But this will be a dangerous game for her to play. Especially where your kin are concerned."

"I could warn them—"

"No. Rumors will spread. They all talk too much, Bercelak. We'll just have to let it play out. Keep it from them as you've kept it from me all these years."

"You found out anyway."

"Not found out—knew. There's a difference." She sighed. "Besides, it's time for her to be truly tested."

"You keep saying that."

"I do."

"But why? It clearly has you worried."

"It must be her," she said, feeling suddenly exhausted. "She needs to do this. She needs to meet this challenge."

"Why, Rhiannon? Why Keita?"

Rhiannon stood and headed to her bedchamber. "Because," she said simply, "one day she *will* be queen."

With that, Rhiannon stepped out of the throne room, but went back when she realized Bercelak was not behind her. When she saw the expression on his face, she rolled her eyes and added, "I don't mean *now*, low born. I'm talking *years* down the line."

Bercelak let out a breath. "I thought you meant . . . and with the others ahead of her . . . and her penchant for poisons . . . gods-dammit, Rhiannon! *You scared the life from me!*"

Realizing that Bercelak thought she'd seen her time—and apparently the times of their offspring—ending much sooner than she had any intention of tolerating, Rhiannon began laughing and couldn't stop. Even when he caught hold of her and lifted her up, carrying her back to their bedchamber, snarling the entire time, she didn't stop laughing.

Chapter Sixteen

The trip from Devenallt Mountain took them straight down to Dark Plains below. They landed about two miles away from Garbhán Isle, in the surrounding forests. What was strange, though, to Vigholf was that for the entire trip, Ragnar, Keita, and that foreigner argued. In hushed whispers, but it was arguing. Something that Vigholf rarely saw his brother do. Ragnar didn't believe in arguing. He gave his orders, and he expected them to be carried out. If they weren't, he gave the task to someone else, and he forgot the existence of the one who'd failed him. It may not sound like much, but it was enough. His brother's coldness rivaled the icy mountaintops of their home.

Yet here Ragnar was. Arguing. First with Princess Keita alone. Then the foreigner joined in. They never raised their voices. Not like Vigholf and Meinhard were known to do, but still. It was an argument.

Vigholf shifted to human, put on his clothes, and watched the three continue to argue. He didn't know what they were talking about, and he didn't care. He was ready to go home. This place with all its greens and heat. Gods, it was warm here even though the Southlands were nearing their winter, the princess pulling out a fur to cover her long-sleeved gown illustrating the chill that at least *she* felt. Did they even have snow in this country?

Not that it mattered. Once his brother stopped arguing, they'd take the pup and the princess to their kin and they'd be on their way.

"What's going on?" Meinhard asked him.

"I have no idea."

"We shouldn't let them argue," the pup said. He was always worried about everyone being upset, this one. He prided himself on all the arguments he stopped. Although it wasn't his soothing words that halted fights among Vigholf's kin. It was his size. Lightnings were well known for their size, although they had a tendency to be slower than the trimmer Fire Breathers. But the pup, he had the size of any Northlander, but the speed of his fire-breathing kin. Shame he wasn't much of a fighter. Ragnar had already written him off and didn't want him sent back to the Northlands anytime soon. Although Meinhard was quietly working to change that. He'd taken to the oversized hatchling, though Vigholf simply didn't know why.

"I wouldn't get in the middle of a Ragnar argument, if I were you."

"We should do something."

Seeing that he was going to debate this, Vigholf caught hold of the pup's arm and dragged him from the trees to the road. "Let's wait here until they're done."

Vigholf and Meinhard went through their travel bags while the pup paced from one side of the road to the other.

"Think we can get more supplies before we leave?" Meinhard asked. "Dried beef will help when we go through the Outerplains again."

"The princess promised to replenish our supplies."

"They're still arguing!" The pup shook his head. "I can't let this go on."

"Wait—"

"Let him go, Meinhard," Vigholf said, standing. "He'll interrupt, Ragnar will slap him around, he'll learn not to do it again."

Meinhard stood, his gaze down the road.

"What?" Vigholf asked. Meinhard gestured with a nod of his head, and Vigholf followed.

It was a woman walking down the road, her hand holding on to the reins of an enormous black horse. She stopped and stared at them.

Smiling, wishing he'd remembered to put on his cape sooner—he hated explaining his purple hair to humans, all that horse shit about tragic curses and such—Vigholf waved. "Greetings!" he called out.

The woman, tall with long golden brown hair, released the reins of her horse and walked closer. Her eyes narrowed, her head dipping down.

"What is she doing?" Vigholf muttered to his cousin.

"I have no idea," Meinhard muttered back. "Maybe she's lost. Or scared."

"Or crazed," Vigholf added, seconds before the crazed bitch—he'd been right, by the gods!—unsheathed one of the swords she had tied to her back and silently charged.

"This is the way it is to be," Keita said to Ren—again! She didn't like having to repeat herself, and just because Ren was a noble in his own bloody country, didn't mean he had any more right to ignore her than one of her mother's subjects.

"I don't like it. I don't like him." Ren glared at Ragnar. "He looks down on you, and he just hurt you again."

"And that," the Northlander said through clenched teeth, "is *still* none of your business."

"What do you hope to gain from this, barbarian? Perhaps you and Keita's mother have a plan that she knows nothing about. Perhaps you plan to betray her."

Ragnar lifted his hand, sparks flicking off the tips of his fingers. Ren did the same, only it was flames that charged from his. Keita, used to much more physically reacting males, ordered, "Stop it! Both of you! This is ridiculous!"

"What's going on?" Éibhear demanded, storming over to them. "Why are you all arguing?"

Keita glanced at the two other males, shrugged, and said sweetly, "We're not arguing."

"Keita!"

"A discussion does not an argument make, Éibhear."

"What aren't you telling me?" He looked from one to the other. "What's Mum up to?"

"Nothing. She was just being herself. You should be used to that by now."

"Don't lie to me, Keita. You know you can't lie to me." He was right. She couldn't lie to any of her brothers because none of them were distracted by a random touch or secret smile. "There's something going on, and I want to know what."

"Go back to Meinhard, boy," Ragnar ordered.

Keita held up her hand. "Don't order my brother around."

"Fine then. We'll let him stay."

"Don't get that tone with me, warlord. I can handle my own brother without any help from you."

"Handle me? You need to handle me?" Éibhear repeated.

Her patience waning, Keita said, "Stop. Everyone just . . ." She frowned, her head tilting to the side. "Ren? What's wrong?"

He pointed at something behind Keita. "Don't we know that horse?"

Keita glanced over her shoulder. "Looks like Annwyl's horse," she said, scratching her ear.

A moment later, she froze at the sound of steel against steel.

"Gods," she said, turning to her brother.

Together they shot off, heading for the nearby road. They

ran past the trees, and Keita squealed, falling back onto her rear, the blade of a sword nearly taking off what she'd always considered her very precious nose.

Hands lifted her from the ground and put her back on her feet. "You all right?" She expected it to be Ren, but it was Ragnar who stared down at her with concern.

"I'm fine. We need to stop them."

"My brother would never kill a woman."

"That's not a woman," Keita said. "Not specifically."

Meinhard raised his shield, and the bitch's blade slammed into it, pushing him back. Gods! What strength she had.

And yet she was human.

He lowered his shield to see that the woman had her back to him, busy now with his cousin. Meinhard thrust his sword forward, aiming for her side. His intent to wound, incapacitate. Not kill. But she turned at the last second, his blade moving past her. Meinhard stumbled forward. That's when she slammed her elbow into his face, shattering his nose.

He barked, and she went low, her foot slamming into his calf. To Meinhard's shock, he heard bone break, felt something go "pop" in his leg, and he went down hard on one knee.

The pain would be tolerated. The break would heal. But the humiliation—that would not be borne!

Meinhard watched his cousin force the woman back toward him. She was less than a foot away when he swiped his shield at her back. It hit her on the side, sending her flying into a close-by tree. She crashed into the trunk hard, bounced away from it and onto the ground, rolled to her feet, and went at Vigholf once more.

Vigholf swung his blade, but she went up and on his back, her short sword raised high.

"*Annwyl, no!*" Princess Keita screamed while Éibhear caught the vile woman and yanked her off Vigholf from behind. At the same time Ragnar caught hold of Vigholf and pulled him back.

Keita stood in the midst of them all, her hands raised. "Everyone calm down!"

"Calm down?" Vigholf demanded. "That crazed bitch attacked us!"

Meinhard felt hands on him and looked up into the strange face of the foreign dragon. Without a word said between them, Meinhard allowed Ren to help him to his one good foot.

"My Lord Vigholf," Keita said soothingly. She turned to face him. "Please accept my . . ."

Eyes wide, she stared at Vigholf, and Meinhard quickly followed her gaze, terrified that he was about to see his cousin bleeding to death from a wound they hadn't noticed. But it was worse than that. Far worse.

Keita covered her mouth with her hand, her brown eyes wide. Unsure what he'd find, Ragnar looked at his brother—and released him.

"Oh."

"What?" Vigholf asked. "What's wrong?"

"Uh . . . uh . . ."

Poor deformed Vigholf looked down at himself. "What are you all looking at?"

"Perhaps," said a cold female voice, "they search for this."

Vigholf raised his head as the human female held up the long, single braid of thick purple hair that once belonged to him.

"Sorry about that," the woman said, grinning. "I was trying for your entire head. But you move much faster than your oxlike size would suggest."

"*Oxlike?*"

"Don't worry." She swung the braid back and forth. "This

will look amazing in my helm when I ride into battle. Purple's never been my color, but I think it'll work just fine."

"*You mad cow!*" Vigholf screamed, and Ragnar caught hold of his shoulders, barely managing to hold his raging brother back. Not that he blamed him.

"Come," the human laughingly challenged. "Let's finish this, *Lightning*."

Keita moved closer to the woman and slammed her hands against her shoulders. "Stop this right now!"

The woman frowned, staring at Keita. For a moment, Ragnar feared for the royal's safety until the woman asked, "Keita?" Then she smiled, pushing the Blue's hands off her waist. "Keita!" The woman dropped her blade—if not the braid—threw her arms around Keita, and hugged her tight. "Gods! I'm so glad to see you!"

Keita let out a breath, gave a small nod to Ragnar. "And I you, sister."

"It's been too long."

"And what about me? Do I not get a hug?"

The woman spun around and faced the Blue. "Éibhear!" She threw herself at him, wrapping long legs around his waist and arms around his neck. "Oh, Éibhear!"

Laughing, the Blue hugged her back. "That's the welcome I was hoping for."

"She mutilated me," Vigholf said to him. And he wasn't far off. Although no Northland male would ever wear his hair as long as the Southlanders did, they still prided themselves on what they did have. Before any major battles, related females or mates would put the Dragonwarrior's hair into war braids. When the battle or war was over and had been won, another ritual took place where the braids were taken apart and the long single plait was returned. It was a simple, unadorned thing, but meant much to many.

But the truth of it was that they were in dangerous and foreign territory. Retribution for the damage this female had done could not happen. "Not here, brother. Not now," Ragnar whispered.

"Then when?"

"Whenever you like, Lightning," the woman offered, finally crawling off the Blue. "Now, if you so choose."

Vigholf snarled, but Ragnar held him back with his hands against his shoulders. "Calm down."

"Don't hold him back. Unleash him so I can finish what I started and then"—the human female pointed a finger at Ragnar—"I can finish the rest of you."

"What is wrong with you?" Keita demanded of the human. "Why are you acting like this?"

"You don't think I know? That I hadn't heard what they did to you?" Green eyes glared at them from under uncombed hair. "They kidnapped you, Keita. Trying to force a female into what they want. And for that"—the woman bent her head from one side to the other, the sound of bones cracking radiating across the road—"they lose their heads."

She pressed forward, and Ragnar turned so he faced her. Not willing to let anything happen to Vigholf, Ragnar prepared to unleash a spell, but again Keita got between Ragnar and his kin and this crazed human female.

"No! You're wrong. That's not what happened."

Keeping her eyes on Ragnar, the human asked, "Then what did happen?"

Keita cleared her throat. "These were the ones who rescued me from Olgeir."

"Bullshit."

"Do you think I'd really protect anyone who had a hand in my kidnapping?"

"It wasn't them?"

"I assure you, Annwyl, it wasn't—"

"Annwyl?" Ragnar repeated, suddenly remembering that Keita had said the same name before they'd burst out of the woods. "This is Annwyl?" Ragnar looked the woman over, from her absurdly large feet to the top of her unkempt head. "*This?*"

This human who had more muscles than seemed necessary for any royal and watched him and his kin with what he could only term as the mad eyes of a diseased animal.

Keita lifted her hand to silence him, her intense gaze warning him. He noticed that she made no large moves, kept her voice even and controlled. "Queen Annwyl of the Dark Plains, please allow me to introduce you to Ragnar the Cunning, his brother, Vigholf the Abhorrent, and their cousin Meinhard the Savage. My lords . . . this is Queen Annwyl, human ruler of these lands and my eldest brother's mate. Now, before we go any further, just let me say—"

The human held up her hand. "Wait. I'm sorry. Your name is . . . Vigholf the *Abhorrent?*"

"Annwyl—"

"Why don't we have names like that in the Southlands?"

"It used to be Vigholf the Vicious," the Blue decided to add for some unknown reason, "but in the last war it became Vigholf the Abhorrent."

"Now see, I'm just Annwyl the Bloody. That's bloody boring is what that is. But Annwyl the Abhorrent? Now that has a lovely ring to it, don't you think?"

"Annwyl." Keita pressed her hand to the woman's forearm. "Lord Ragnar and his kin are here under my and Éibhear's protection."

"Really? Even though they kidnapped you . . . twice? First this one's father and then him."

"I already told you, he rescued me from Olgeir. And the gods know we can't charge him with what his father did. You, Annwyl, should know that better than anyone."

"So when I'd heard he'd taken you to barter with your mother . . . ?"

"Nothing more than a silly misunderstanding and absolutely no reason for there to be any anger."

"Silly misunderstanding? Really?" The queen's grin spread across her face, making her appear even more insane. "Then I guess we can call all this"—she swung the braid in her hand—"a silly misunderstanding as well? Eh?"

She laughed, kissed Keita on the cheek, and waited until the Blue lowered himself so she could kiss his cheek. "I'm glad you're both home. Perhaps you'll stop my mate from roaring so much these days." She clicked her tongue against her teeth, and her horse came forward. "Be sure to see the children. Tell Fearghus I'll be back later."

The human queen tucked Vigholf's braid into the belt around her waist, slung her sword and shield on her back, and somehow managed to mount a horse that would be too big for many Northland men. "I look forward to seeing you all at dinner."

With another laugh, she spurred her horse and rode off.

"*That's* your human queen?" Ragnar asked again. "*Her?*"

Keita shrugged. "She has moods."

"She took my hair." Vigholf drove his sword into the ground. "*My hair!*"

"My lord." Keita took Vigholf's hand and held it between her two smaller ones. "Please forgive her. So much weighs on her, and she only did it for me. I promise to do all I can to make this up to you."

Ragnar knew it took a lot for his brother to say, "It's not your fault, princess. Think no more of it." But his strength of will was as strong as any Northlanders'.

"Come." She tugged at Vigholf. "Let's get you settled." She smiled at a wounded Meinhard. "And get you a healer."

"And what do I get?" Ragnar asked her.

"My patience."

And her response made him laugh.

"Welcome to Garbhán Isle, my lords," Keita said to them all. "I can, at the very least, promise you that not a moment will be dull."

Chapter Seventeen

"Sister!"

Morfyd gritted her teeth. She could do this. She *would* do this. Not merely because she'd promised Brastias, but because she'd promised herself.

Forcing a smile to her lips, she faced her sister. "Keita."

"Oh, you look lovely!"

Morfyd instantly scowled. "And what's *that* supposed to mean?"

Her sister scowled in return. "That those plain white robes you wear every day bring out the dark circles under your eyes?"

"Snake."

"Birthing cow."

"Keita."

At the chastising tone coming from behind her sister, Morfyd gave a genuine smile. "Ren!" She kissed the Eastland dragon on both cheeks. "How are you, old friend?"

It was a fact among the House of Gwalchmai fab Gwyar that sweet Ren of the Chosen Dynasty was much beloved. Even by the likes of Briec, who loved no one but himself, and Bercelak, who loved only their mother. Ren had come to them nearly a century ago, sent by his family to learn about the

Southland dragons while one of their cousins who was on the Dragonwitch's path had gone east in his stead.

Morfyd hadn't given much thought to the arrangement. It had been done before and had always worked out well, but those who came from the east rarely stayed. Why would they? They left behind a much calmer, much simpler, and much more extravagant life in the east than the one they found among her mother's court. And yet, Ren had stayed. He stayed because he managed to become an accepted part of a family that could barely tolerate each other, much less outsiders. Even Fearghus had been known to invite Ren to his cave in Dark Glen for drinks. Fearghus didn't even invite his brothers there. They'd show up randomly, but they'd never been invited.

Morfyd had to admit, though, she'd worried in the beginning when Ren became so close to Keita. Although Keita was barely thirty winters old at the time, she already had quite a reputation among some of the males. It wasn't that Morfyd cared about who her sister bedded. How could she question what Keita did when no one questioned Gwenvael? But Keita was known for leaving a trail of broken dragon hearts in her tail's wake, walking away from males as easily as Morfyd beat Briec at cards. She had not wanted the same for the powerful mage who, unlike most of their brethren, never took his power for granted, nor flaunted it to seem more important than he was. Yet after a short time, they all realized that Keita and Ren were far from lovers. They were fast friends. It eased their brothers' concern about Keita's welfare, knowing Ren often traveled with their youngest sister and could, at the very least, alert them if she got into any trouble.

But it still amazed them all that after so many years, Keita and Ren were still traveling companions and friends. Loyal to each other as any blood-related kin might be.

"I'm fine. And Keita was supposed to be securing your assistance, not pissing you off."

"She started it," Keita complained.

"You insulted me."

"Only after you dare question my compliments! Do you think I compliment everyone, you whining sow?"

"Keita!" Ren smiled at Morfyd. "Maybe this will be easier if I say that *I* need your assistance, good lady."

Yes. It also helped that, without being annoying, Ren was a magnificent peacekeeper.

"Of course, Ren. Anything for *you*." She took Ren's arm. "What can I assist you with?"

"Our Lightning guests had a slight run-in . . . with your queen."

"Mother?"

"No. The other insane monarch you have running your lands."

Morfyd gasped. "Gods, are they dead?"

"No. But there were some injuries. Tell me"—he began, leading her over to the waiting Northlanders—"I'm at a loss myself. Do you happen to know any spells for growing hair?"

Hands on hips, Keita glowered after her traveling companion and that vindictive, petty vestal virgin. She did not follow. She was too annoyed, and she knew what would happen. Ragnar would slobber all over her sister. Her perfect, glowing, Magickally-infused sister. In no mood to witness that, Keita waited, and, as she knew would happen, Ren returned.

"How long were you going to stand there—seething?"

"Until the end of time," she said, making sure to sound particularly snippy.

"I thought you'd want to keep an eye on your Lightning."

"Don't start, Ren."

"I'm worried. I don't trust him."

"All that should matter to you is that I do trust him."

"At least tell me what's going on."

"Later. Not here." Keita glanced around and saw a contingent of soldiers heading her way and waving—several held flowers. "Gods, Ren," she whispered. "Get me out of here."

Ren put his arm around her, and steered her through the crowd. When the soldiers glared at him and came closer, Ren unleashed a line of flame that had the men all diving for cover.

"Now," Ren said, clearly in no rush with the soldiers currently running for their lives, "are you going to leave your Lightnings all alone? I think Lord Ragnar won't like that much with him as your great protector."

"Don't like the tone," she sang. "And he'll have Morfyd to keep him company. They can discuss moving mountains and melting trees with their great skills."

"I hope you're not testing him, Keita."

"Why would I do that?" she said a little too quickly. "Besides, I'd hate to think of my brothers seeing the warlord and his kin before I've had a chance to ease the way."

Thankfully accepting that excuse, Ren asked, "Is it my imagination, little one, or is your family very 'kill everything first, ask questions later and if we're in the mood' types?"

"Some might suggest that . . . you know, if their victims could speak with their heads lopped off and all."

So this was her. Morfyd the White.

She was beautiful, as Ragnar had always heard. Although the scar on one side of her face, tore at him. Marked as a witch when the human Southlanders were still doing that sort of thing. It was a weak leader that couldn't appreciate the power of others. Power that could be used to his benefit. Thankfully, the She-dragon's blood had helped the scar to fade, but it was still there, clear to Ragnar's eyes.

Although of royal blood and heir to her mother's Magickal power, if not her throne, the princess still crouched before Meinhard like any healer and examined his leg. They were right outside the gates that opened to the town of Garbhán Isle, Meinhard sitting on one of the wood benches lining the path that led to the gates, Ragnar and Vigholf standing behind him. Eyes closed, the princess held her hands around Meinhard's calf without touching it. A true healer, unlike Ragnar, who could mend his brother's bone, but it would be difficult for him to place it so perfectly that Meinhard would have no limp without causing his kin more pain.

After several minutes, the princess leaned back.

"It's definitely broken. But I can heal it quick enough if you don't mind staying human for a while. Their bones are easier to heal than ours, I find, and healing the one usually affects the other."

"That's fine," Ragnar answered for Meinhard. "We'll be staying for a bit."

"Even now?" Vigholf asked, his hand constantly straying to where his hair now rested by his ears.

"Yes, brother. Even now."

Morfyd stood. She was taller than her sister, but leaner, even under those robes. "I am sorry about all this. I apologize for my brother's mate. She's quite cautious these days. But I can assure you all the best accommodations and anything you may need."

"None of that's necessary, but thank you, princess."

"Morfyd. Please. I've always felt that once you've been unfairly attacked by one's family, a more casual etiquette should come into play."

She smiled, and Ragnar returned it. "That sounds like an excellent plan."

"Good." She motioned to several guards. "These men will take you to your rooms."

"I can walk," Meinhard said, pushing himself to his one good foot.

"I'd prefer you not try."

"A Northland dragon is only carried when he's dead, my lady."

"Well that's"—Morfyd cleared her throat—"a rather hopeful ideal."

Ragnar saw the Blue coming down the road—alone. They'd left him and Keita speaking to some locals while Ragnar and Meinhard searched for a place to let their cousin rest his leg. But only the Blue returned.

"Is something wrong?" Morfyd asked.

"Do you know where your sister is?"

"Knowing Keita? In the guards' barracks, picking up where she left off perhaps?" The princess blinked and took a step back. "I'm . . . I'm only joking."

Ragnar realized he must be scowling, and he worked to control it.

"Morfyd!"

The dragoness spun away from Ragnar. "Éibhear!" She lifted her robes and ran toward her brother, throwing herself into his arms.

"The way these women act toward him," Vigholf complained, "explains so much about this pup."

"Leave him alone," Meinhard said through clenched teeth.

Vigholf walked over to their cousin and put Meinhard's arm around his shoulder. "Lean on me." When it looked as if Meinhard would throw that stupid Code in his face, Vigholf added, "It'll make us look good to the pretty She-dragon with the blue eyes. You'll look needy and I will look giving."

"I hear she's taken," Ragnar tossed in.

"By a *human*," Vigholf said before both he and Meinhard snorted in unison.

Laughing now, Ragnar turned from his cousin and brother, only to spot something off in the distance. Something that, although he'd never seen it before, he still recognized from a long-ago discussion with a warlord's very reasonable daughter.

"You two go in. I'll meet you."

"Go in? Without you?" Meinhard sounded terrified that he'd be forced to act as the Lightnings' representative. And considering how poorly he did in those situations, it was probably best he didn't act as representative for anyone.

"Don't worry. I won't be long. You two can stay out of trouble for five minutes, can't you?"

Vigholf pointed at his head. "You look at the two of us and you have the nerve to ask that?"

Ragnar walked away from his kin and headed into the thick trees surrounding the well-used road. Although he could see the house easily from the gates, the walk took him several minutes. Several minutes that allowed him to worry.

Had she been dismissed out here? Already tossed aside by that whorish dragon she was now mated to? No longer of use to the Mad Queen of Garbhán Isle, so they'd banished her to live alone in the woods? Like some useless old spinster? Had he led her to the wrong path?

The fear that Ragnar had been wrong, once again, in less than a week, nearly choked him as he approached the small house. It reminded him of Esyld's little house, although there was no herb or vegetable garden. Just flowers and bushes that lined the walk and surrounded the house itself. Not only that, but there was Magick here. Strong protection Magick that would keep most beings out.

Most beings but him.

With a wave of his hand against the unseen boundaries, he tore a hole that was large enough for his human form to walk through and stepped onto the stone path leading to the front door.

He walked up to the entrance and worked hard to keep control of his growing concern. If they'd tossed her aside, he'd fix it. He'd take her from here. Take her to a place where her mind and skills could and would be truly appreciated. He'd not let her end up as his mother had until his father's death.

That would not be the life for her. No matter what he had to do to make it happen, Ragnar would fix this.

Resolved, he knocked once on the door before opening it, not even thinking he should wait to be told to enter. He stepped into the warm interior, a pit fire built into the wall blazing brightly and fresh tea sitting ready to be poured on the small dining table. With a single glance, he took in the one-room home with its tiny kitchen, dining table, large bed, and books and papers piled high in nearly every corner. Except for the corner that held the desk. The sound of a quill quickly and efficiently scratching against paper made him smile and the low "woof" of warning from the dog sitting beside small, bare human feet had Ragnar raising his hand to silence the large beast.

Before he could announce himself, the female who sat at the desk with her back to the door said without turning around or pausing in her writing said, "You, dragon, promised me four solid hours of work time this afternoon. So you can take that randy cock of yours and sheathe it until I'm done."

Shocked more than he could possibly admit, Ragnar finally managed, "It's actually quite sheathed, my good lady."

Entire body tense, she slowly looked over her shoulder in Ragnar's direction. Then, after a moment, she squinted in an attempt to see him better.

"Your spectacles," he reminded her.

Her cheeks turning a charming crimson, she reached desperately for the spectacles resting on the desk beside her arm. She put them on and again looked at him over her shoulder. Her sight now clear, they stared at each across the small room.

"Uh . . . Lord Ragnar?"

"Lady Dagmar."

"Uh . . ."

"Hhhm . . ."

"You—"

He pointed at the door. "I should have—"

"No. No. Not necessary. I just . , . didn't . . . uh . . ."

"This is our first time, eh?" he finally said and, when her eyes grew wide behind her round spectacles, Ragnar quickly added, "Awkward moment. This is our first time having an awkward moment. I think we're both well known for causing others to have awkward moments, but for us to avoid them quite nicely."

"Oh. Right. Yes. Right."

They were silent for several long moments, and then Dagmar Reinholdt admitted, "Do you know that even when Gwenvael the Ruiner is not here, he still manages to embarrass me beyond all reason. It's a gift he has. Or an illness."

"Like the plague?"

A rough snort passed Dagmar's nose, and their first awkward moment ended as quickly as it had begun.

After passing through another set of gates, Keita and Ren entered the courtyard of the queen's castle. As they neared the stairs that led to the Great Hall, it was Gwenvael who charged out to greet them. A bright, welcoming smile on his handsome face, he ran down the stairs and straight to them.

Keita opened her arms for a big hug from her brother. "Gwenvael!" she cried.

And Gwenvael replied, "My old friend!" while shoving Keita aside so he could hug Ren instead. "It's so good to see you!"

"And you, Gwenvael."

Barely stopping herself from hitting the ground, Keita dropped her arms to her sides and spun on her heel to face them. "What about me?" she demanded, not used to being ignored by anyone but especially not by her own kin!

Placing one arm around Ren's shoulders, Gwenvael turned and peered down at her. "Do I know you?"

"Oh, come on now!"

"I remember someone who looked like you. A sister, I

believe. But it's been so bloody long since I've seen or heard from her—not even a letter," he said to Ren. "That I wouldn't know what she looked like these days."

So he was going to play *that* little game, was he? Well, he could play it alone! "If you're going to be that way about it, I'm leaving!" Keita turned, ready for her grand exit, which would involve a great deal of flouncing off before shifting and majestically flying away into the two suns, but the black eyes she now faced scowled down at her so hard, she immediately stopped in her storming-off tracks. "Oh . . . Fearghus."

Arms folded over his chest, legs braced apart, her eldest brother said nothing.

"You look well," she tried again.

And, though she hadn't thought it possible, his scowl increased tenfold.

Deciding not to push her luck, Keita used what would not work on Gwenvael or Morfyd. She let the first tears fall. "Are you angry at me too?" she whispered, and, instantly, Fearghus pulled her into his arms.

"Come now. Don't cry."

Keita turned her head slightly and gave Gwenvael a good sneer.

Gwenvael rolled his eyes and demanded, "How come my tears don't work with you lot?"

"Because," Fearghus shot back, "your lying tears always involve mucus. So I'm too disgusted to care."

Another voice said from behind Fearghus, "Forgiven her already?"

"She started crying. What was I to do?"

Keita took a step back from one brother and looked up at another. The silver-haired Briec. He'd be harder than Fearghus.

"Two years," Briec accused. "Two years and no bloody word."

"I sent gifts," she offered. "And my love."

When this one's scowl got worse, she pressed herself closer to Fearghus.

Ragnar sipped his hot tea and watched Dagmar search the cabinets of her tiny kitchen for more cookies than the few that were currently on the plate.

"I can't believe he ate all the other cookies," she complained while searching. "I can't believe how selfish he is! Who eats like that?"

Eating the last cookie on the plate, Ragnar replied, "Dragons."

"Reason preserve me." She slammed another cabinet door and walked over to the large and sturdy bed. She knelt beside it and pulled a small trunk from underneath. After using a key that hung from a set attached to her girdle, she opened the trunk and pulled out a tin. Locking and returning the trunk to its place under the bed, Dagmar walked back to the table and opened the tin, offering him more cookies.

"I trust that dragon with my life and the life of my kin," she said. "But I'll never trust him with my food." She glanced down at the purebred dog who'd followed her around the tiny room, his long and thick whiplike tail threatening to knock over everything in his wake. "Or Canute," she added. "I'd never trust him—or his brothers—with my Canute."

"I probably wouldn't trust his youngest sister either," Ragnar added, thinking of that guard dog in Bampour's dungeon. "As a precaution."

Ragnar took a handful of cookies. Dagmar sat opposite him, her dog settling at her side so that he faced the door but could still keep his eye on Ragnar. The woman did know how to earn loyalty.

Never one to waste time on niceties when unnecessary, Dagmar got right to it. "What brings you back into the Southlands, Lord Ragnar?" He remembered when she'd called him "Brother Ragnar." When she'd believed him to be a human monk. At the time, he had honestly thought she could never understand or handle who he truly was. He'd been wrong. He still felt regret for that mistake. Immense regret.

"Escorting Keita and . . . uh . . . the boy."

Dagmar nibbled on a cookie. She probably limited herself to one or two a day at the most, used to the rules of economy that the Northland humans believed in rather than the excesses of the South. The Hordes had similar ideals—but not when it came to food. "What boy?"

"The blue one."

Her smile was quick and warm. "Éibhear's home?"

Ragnar studied the warlord's daughter before he relaxed back in his chair. He appreciated the fact that the furniture had been built for dragons in human form. Nothing more embarrassing than leaning back in a chair and having the damn thing break on you. "What is it about him that makes all you females eager to see him?"

"Blue hair?"

"Mine's purple."

Grey eyes that had always reminded him of the finest steel peered at him through spectacles he'd made for her many years ago. "A bit jealous, my lord?"

Ragnar couldn't help but pout a little. "No."

"I can't believe you're yelling at me!" Keita wailed. "*Do I mean nothing to you?*"

"Don't try that with me, Mistress Mayhem. *You* were the one who cut off contact with us. *You* were the one who blamed us for getting caught unaware in Northern territories," Briec reminded her.

"I never blamed you," she insisted. "Who said I did?" But as soon as she asked the question, her eyes narrowed, and she accused, "Mother."

"Don't blame her. She didn't tell you to cut off contact with us."

"I had some things to take care of," she argued.

"So you run off with that"—Briec sniffed in Ren's direction—"foreigner?"

"Oy! Be nice to the foreigner!" Gwenvael cut in. "Him I know."

"What's going on?" a voice asked from the castle steps, and Briec immediately rolled his eyes and let out a long-suffering sigh.

"Nothing to worry yourself about, my precious sweet tart," he replied.

A brown hand caught Keita's arm and dragged her out of the big-brother pile she'd been trapped in.

"Talaith!" Keita cheered, hugging the acid-tongued witch tight. "It's so good to see you."

"And you, sister." They pulled away from each other, and Talaith gave Keita an astonishing smile that lit up her whole face until she faced her mate and that smile quickly turned to a scowl that even a demon spawn would fear.

"I thought we discussed and *agreed*," Talaith bit out between clenched teeth, "that when we saw Keita again, none of you were to pounce and yell at her. Instead, we were all to have a nice, friendly, family chat to discuss and resolve any issues."

"There was no discussion," Briec said. "You, heart of my heart, just talked, talked, talked like you always do and I ignored, ignored, ignored, like I always do. Did you really think I heard or bothered to listen to a word you actually said on something regarding *my* baby sister?"

A damning finger pointed at Briec. "If I thought, for one moment, that either of your daughters would forgive me, I'd cut off your tongue and wear it around my neck as an amulet to ward off your idiocy!"

"Isn't your one, constantly yammering tongue enough for even *you* to handle, Lady Never Quiet?"

"Not when a day doesn't pass that you don't torture me with your insanity, Lord Stick Up His Ass!"

Keita stepped between the bellowing couple. "Must you two do this out here?" she asked desperately. She dropped her voice to a whisper. "The servants are watching."

There was a moment of silence, and then Keita and Gwenvael burst out laughing, earning themselves several sighs of disgust.

"Battle Lord?" Ragnar asked again. "She made you Battle Lord?"

"Annwyl made me *Chief* Battle Lord. All Battle Lords of Dark Plains report to me." Dagmar sipped her tea. "Your mouth is open, my lord."

"I . . . uh . . ." Ragnar put his tea down . . . and closed his mouth. "I must admit. I saw this house and thought that you'd been forced here. Of no further use to the Mad Queen of Garbhán Isle and the Fire Breathers who rule with her."

"I guess there's always that risk with Annwyl, but she likes me."

"And fears you as well?"

"Why would she fear me? As long as she does what I tell her without question there is nothing to fear."

"I don't know if you're joking."

"Oh," she said. "That's unfortunate."

To think, for a few brief minutes Ragnar had worried that Dagmar had been tossed aside as many brilliant females often were, but he should have known better. If there was one survivor he knew, it was Dagmar Reinholdt. The Thirteenth Offspring of the Reinholdt, Only Daughter of the Reinholdt, and now shockingly powerful Battle Lord of Annwyl the Bloody, Mad Queen of Dark Plains. He should have known Dagmar would never allow herself to be tossed aside by anyone. He should have known.

"And you enjoy what you do?"

"Quite a lot."

"So then . . . you're happy?"

She pursed her lips, hands wrapped around her cup of tea, her gaze on the ceiling.

Finally, Ragnar added, "Happy for a Northlander."

"Oh! Oh, then yes. Quite happy."

"I'm just glad you're home," Fearghus said, kissing the top of Keita's head and hugging her close again.

"And I'm glad to be back. I've missed almost all of you."

Fearghus laughed. "And you say that I hold a grudge."

"You do hold a grudge—as does your mate."

"Annwyl?" Fearghus leaned back a bit. "What did she do?"

"Nearly took the head of Lord Vigholf and crushed the leg of poor Lord Meinhard."

Fearghus pulled her to his chest again. "That's . . . that's too bad. I'll talk to her about that later when I see her."

It was too quiet.

Keita pushed away from Fearghus and found all her kin— and Ren!—laughing. Silently, but still! "This is not funny!"

"Yes!" Briec crowed, ending their silence. "It is!"

"Do you know the jig I had to do to calm the situation? We can't afford to make them enemies because you can't control your mate, Fearghus."

"Control Annwyl? I don't try to control her, baby sister. I unleash her on the world like a devastating storm from the sea."

"Here they come," Gwenvael noted, shaking his head. "And just look who leads them."

Briec sniffed. "I see two years has not given that idiot more sense."

"They're his friends now, I'm sure." Fearghus sighed, looking and *sounding* more like their father every day.

But Keita wouldn't stand for it. Always picking on little Éibhear! It was unforgivable!

Keita stood before her three brothers, hands on her hips. "Listen well to me, you uncaring lizards. You be nice to our brother! All he's talked about the entire trip was seeing all of you, and you *will* make him feel welcome or I will do all in my power to make you suffer in ways that even the gods will fear."

"What happened to our wailing little Keita?" Gwenvael asked.

And that's when she punched him in the groin, dropping her brother to his knees. "I said be *nice*!" she snarled at her now-wailing older brother. "Now everyone smile! And welcome him!"

Keita took a breath and called out, "Talaith?"

The witch, who'd gone back into the castle a few minutes before, came out.

With a nod of her head, Keita motioned behind her. "Look who's here."

Talaith stepped around her mate and Fearghus. "Gods . . . Éibhear?"

"He's grown a bit," Keita teased.

"Éibhear!" Talaith cheered, throwing her arms in the air before charging down the stone steps and over to their youngest sibling.

"See?" Keita pointed out. "*That* is welcoming."

Fearghus and Briec looked at each other, shrugged, and threw their arms in the air. "Éibhear!" they both cheered in high-pitched voices that made her stamp her foot.

"That is *not* what I meant!"

Another stunning woman charged over to the oversized pup and threw herself into his arms.

"What does that boy have?" Vigholf asked. As if *Meinhard*

would know. He worked hard simply not to have human females run from him screaming. As his sister once put it, "That permanent scowl you wear and the fact you can't really see your neck because of your shoulders just makes human women think you only want to rape and pillage their villages. But once they get to know you . . ."

"Talaith!" the pup said, spinning the female in a circle.

"I'm so glad you're home." She kissed him on the cheeks, then the mouth. "And look how big you've gotten."

"It's not that bad."

"If you dropped me from this height, I'd be dead by the time I landed."

"Stop it, Talaith."

She hugged him again, laughed. "You look wonderful, and all I care about is that you're home."

"I'm glad to be home."

Princess Morfyd walked up behind her brother, patting his back. "Does my brother not look handsome, Lady Talaith?"

"Gorgeous, Lady Morfyd."

"Stop it." The Blue's cheeks turned red, and he ducked his head.

"Is he blushing?" Vigholf asked.

"I think so," Meinhard said.

"Have you ever blushed?"

"Not that I know of."

"You're forgetting your manners, brother," Princess Morfyd lightly chastised.

"Oh. You're right." Éibhear carefully placed the woman in his arms down. "Talaith, Daughter of Haldane, this is Lord Vigholf and Lord Meinhard."

The woman smiled, and all Vigholf and Meinhard could do was stare.

She cleared her throat and asked the royal, "Should I be running for my life?"

"No, no. I just think they've never met anyone from Alsandair before."

"Ahh. I see."

No. She couldn't see. But Vigholf spoke for them both when he sighed out, "By the gods of war and death, my lady, you are astoundingly beautiful."

Her grin grew, and she curtsied a bit. "Why thank you, fine sirs."

But before Vigholf and Meinhard could fight to the death to see who would claim her hand, they suddenly had some Southland dragon in human form standing between them and their prize.

"Lightnings," he sneered.

"Fire Breather," they sneered back.

He jerked his thumb over his shoulder. "This one's mine."

"Oy!" came the woman's voice from behind him.

"Tragically, this one doesn't have wings for you to hack off anyway, but feel free to go for the one that took your hair."

Vigholf roared at the insult, and Meinhard, hopping on one leg, reached for the battle ax tied to his back.

But good Princess Keita rushed between them. "No, no, no! All of you promised me!"

They had, and, as hard as it was, the cousins immediately apologized. The Fire Breather, however . . .

"I promised you *nothing*, baby sister."

"You most certainly . . ." The princess's words faded, and she studied Vigholf and Meinhard closely. "Where's Ragnar?" she asked them.

Suddenly that detestable Gold known among their people as the Ruiner caught his sister's arm and swung her around to face him.

Meinhard reached for his ax again as the Ruiner demanded, "That purple-haired bastard is here?"

Éibhear pulled his sister away from the Gold and said, "He is, and you will not act like an idiot."

"Where is he?"

"He went off."

The Ruiner grabbed his brother's nose and twisted until he had Éibhear bent at the waist. "Where, you idiot? Where did he go off to?"

"I don't know! Toward some house in the woods outside the main gates!"

"Bastard!"

The Ruiner snarled and took off running.

The silver dragon, laughing, yelled after him, "Run, brother! Run before that Lightning snatches her out from under you—again!"

"And on that note . . ." Princess Morfyd clapped her hands together. "Let's get you upstairs, my lords, and get you settled."

"I still didn't agree to their stay—" a black dragon began.

But both princesses quickly barked out, "I don't want to hear it!"

"Can you take care of our esteemed guests?" the beautiful Talaith, Daughter of Haldane, asked Princess Morfyd.

"Aye."

"Good." She caught hold of Princess Keita's arm and dragged her toward the fortress steps. "Because this one has something to do that she's left far too long."

"We're not going in there alone, are we?" Princess Keita asked, making Meinhard worried for her safety. "Shouldn't we have guards or something to do this?"

"Stop it, Keita. They're just children. It's not like they bite . . . enough to cause permanently disabling injuries or death."

Children?

"Explain to me why we can't go home?" Meinhard asked.

"Because my brother's an idiot," Vigholf replied.

"That's what I thought."

* * *

"So explain this house to me, Lady Dagmar. I saw it, and I somehow knew you'd be here."

Dagmar's gaze roamed the room, and her accompanying smile was soft and very sweet. A smile once reserved for Ragnar alone, but now—he knew—it was strictly for another.

"I mentioned once to Gwenvael—after too much of his father's wine, I imagine—that I'd always dreamed of having my own little house on my father's lands. A little spinster home of my own. I said that I guess I wouldn't get that now that I had a mate. A mate who, according to him, wasn't going anywhere, anytime soon since he knew how much I adored him and couldn't live without his presence." She laughed at an arrogance most couldn't tolerate for two seconds. "A few months later, Gwenvael brought me here. He'd had the royal builders make this just for me. And it's perfect, isn't it? Exactly how I imagined it. I was concerned it was too close to the castle, but I am continually amazed at how lazy you dragons are. If I'm sitting right in the Great Hall, you'll stop and talk to me or around me for hours. But to traipse a few hundred feet away from the gates to chat . . . that takes a taller order, apparently."

"You forget, my good lady, that you can't group us all together. There are many dragons, with all sorts of differences, and we hate each other equally."

She laughed. "Good point. I always forget that."

Ragnar reached across the table and took her hand, his gaze fixed on where his fingers stroked her knuckles. "I'm very glad to see you happy here, Dagmar. And I am sorry about how things ended for us." No. This wasn't right. He couldn't look away from what he'd done. He had to face it directly as he'd done with Keita. "I'm sorry," he said again, this time making his eyes meet hers. "For how I lied to you all those years about who I was and what I was. I truly never saw a choice and—"

"Stop," she cut in.

Dagmar looked off for a moment, and he knew she was getting her thoughts organized as she liked to do. No dramatic emotional moments for her, and that was fine with him.

When she returned her gaze to his, it was calm and controlled. Just like her. "I'll admit that finding out that you'd lied to me did hurt. It hurt me in a way, I imagine, no one else could have. But I've also come to understand why you did it. More importantly, I now know and understand that everything you've ever done for me, ever shown or taught me, has led me to this. Has led me to a place where I can be who I am without fear or worry. For that alone, Lord Ragnar, all past transgressions are forgiven, and I strongly suggest we leave the past where it is and move on from there."

A weight that had been on his shoulders for far too long lifted. "Do you understand, my Lady Dagmar, that you will always be one of my greatest triumphs?"

Her smile was small but powerful, yet whatever she was about to say in return was cut off when her dog got to his feet and began to bark hysterically at the front door. A moment later, the gold dragon who held Dagmar's heart threw the front door open and stormed in.

Ignoring the frothing dog right in front of him, Gwenvael the Ruiner focused on Ragnar. "The Liar Monk has returned, I see."

Since it appeared they would not even pretend to honor the basic rules of greeting, Ragnar replied, "Ruiner."

Gwenvael's eyes locked on where Ragnar held Dagmar's hand. "I'm beginning to feel the need to start hurting things," the Fire Breather announced.

"Quiet." And it took Ragnar a moment to realize Dagmar was actually talking to Canute. The dog stopped barking, but he kept growling, his eyes fixed on Gwenvael's throat.

Noticing the dog, the Fire Breather leaned in and asked it, "Miss me, old friend?"

The barking started again, and with a sigh, Dagmar pulled

her hand away from Ragnar and walked to the door. She held it open and gestured to Canute. "Out. Now."

Snarling and reluctant, the dog went outside, where it would most likely stare at the door until it opened again and he could be near his mistress once more.

"Why do you taunt him?" Dagmar demanded, slamming the door once the beast had gone.

"I wasn't. That was me being nice to him."

"Then we have much work to do, I fear. Because while *you* may be replaceable, Defiler, Canute is not!"

"It's Ruiner! Even this idiot gets it right! And another thing," the Gold went on, "when I gave you this house, my lady, I never expected you to entertain peasant males who may come wandering in unannounced, and I have to say I am extremely displeased at . . . cookies!"

His apparent rage gone as quickly as it had come, Gwenvael walked to the table and reached into the tin. And that's when Dagmar slammed the lid on his hand.

"*Ow!* Viperous female!"

"You're lucky I didn't add blades to the lid so that they'd remove your fingers altogether."

Sucking on his wounded body parts, the Fire Breather said around them, "As much as you love what I can do with my fingers? You'd only be hurting yourself in the long run."

Dagmar slashed her hands through the air. "And now we're done!" She grabbed the tin of cookies and held it to her chest.

Gwenvael snorted and leered, his eyes focused on Dagmar's chest. "Like that'll stop me."

Not really wanting to see any of that sort of thing, Ragnar stood and said, "I guess I'll be—"

"Why are you here, Lightning?" the Gold asked.

Ragnar had thought Keita's moods and whims were impossible to follow. But *this* dragon . . . Ragnar had no idea how Dagmar tolerated the bastard.

"Your mother sent for me," he replied.

"Are you her puppet warlord chief now—ow!" He grabbed his forearm and glared at his mate. "Pinching? Now we're pinching?"

In even less of a mood for a fight than for leering, Ragnar confessed, "She asked me to pick up her sister Esyld in the Outerplains."

The couple stared at each other for a moment before slowly focusing on him.

"Why did she want Esyld?" Dagmar asked.

"And you dragged her here?" Gwenvael demanded.

"I have no idea why she wanted to see Esyld," he told Dagmar. "And I didn't drag her anywhere," he explained to her mate, "because she wasn't there to be dragged."

"She's gone?"

"And has been for some time. Your mother seemed concerned about that. As did Keita. Perhaps you should talk to them about it."

"I'm talking to you, Lightning."

Ragnar smirked at Gwenvael. "Challenge me if you dare, Ruiner. Although I'm sure Keita will miss your presence greatly. She seems fond of you."

"That's enough," Dagmar said softly. "From both of you."

She gestured toward the door. "Let's return to your brother and cousin, my lord. And then we can talk to Keita."

The two males continued to glare at each other until Dagmar added, "Please don't make me get terse."

Ragnar could see from the Gold's expression that he understood—as Ragnar did—that Dagmar's terse was equivalent to a dragon army destroying an entire continent. They gestured to the front door and said to Dagmar together, "After you."

Chapter Eighteen

"Here." Talaith shoved the bundle into Keita's arms. "Say hello to your newest niece since you couldn't be bothered to come and meet her when she was born."

"I thought you weren't mad at me," Keita complained, barely glancing at the child.

"And when, pray tell, did I say that? You fly off in a pouty princess rage and leave me, Dagmar, and Annwyl to deal with all that gods-damn brotherly whining that followed. You're lucky I didn't lock you in a room with those three."

"It's not like I lived here, Talaith. All of you rarely saw me anyway."

"Very true. But your brothers have always been in contact with you. At least once every few moons or so. But this time . . . nothing." Wearing simple black leggings, a sheathed dagger tied to her right thigh, black leather boots that reached her knees, and a rather large grey cotton shirt, Talaith dropped into a chair. Considering how she dressed and, to a degree, how she acted, it amazed Keita that Talaith, Daughter of Haldane, was one of the most beautiful females she'd ever met. "And why is it that we haven't heard from you exactly?"

"If you must know," Keita said, holding the blanket-covered baby in her arms but staring out one of the windows and the bright sky just out of reach, "I guess I was embarrassed."

"I didn't know any of you were capable of being embarrassed."

"Only the females have that issue," she said without much thought.

Talaith laughed, and, as Keita glanced over to smile back, an impossibly tiny brown hand touched her chin. Something strong and electric shot through Keita's system, and she immediately focused on the babe.

Wide violet eyes gazed up at her from a tiny brown face surrounded by curly silver hair. Not in all her years had Keita seen anything quite so beautiful. Quite so . . . clear. Yes. That was the word for it. Clear. Pure and clear and untouched by centuries of anything.

Voice thick with emotion, she said, "She has Briec's eyes. And his hair color."

"Aye," Talaith agreed, watching Keita closely. "She does. And you do know what that means for the rest of us, don't you?"

Keita winced in sympathy, knowing exactly what it meant. "It means that as far as her father's concerned, she's the most perfect child ever to walk the world if for no other reason than she came from his loins?"

Talaith briefly raised her hands. "Now you see what you've left us to deal with all this time. For that alone, we should oust you from the family ranks."

Grinning, Keita asked, "Has my brother been completely insufferable?"

"He's always been completely insufferable. Now he's also intolerable." The displaced Nolwenn witch rested the heel of her foot on the chair and wrapped her arm around her bent leg. "He adores that child as wolves adore the moon. All day, every day, we all hear about how perfect she is. 'Look how she perfectly squeezes my finger. Look how she perfectly throws up her breakfast. Look how she *perfectly* shits her diapers.' It's endless!"

Keita laughed.

"Of course you laugh. You don't have to live with it. And what will I do if she believes him? I mean arrogance in a man is one thing, since few of us take them seriously anyway, but in a woman? And if she becomes even a tenth as arrogant as Briec, then she'll be well on her way to becoming—"

"My mother?"

Talaith agreed with a nod of her head and a flip of her hand. "Exactly."

Keita walked over to one of the bigger windows so she could get a good look at her niece in the bright light of day. She was an astoundingly beautiful child and barely a year and a half old, but it wasn't her beauty that snared Keita. Nor was it the fact that she had her father's eyes. It was what Keita saw in those eyes for someone so young. Intelligence. Vast intelligence and kindness. A benevolence and understanding that Keita had rarely seen in adult beings, much less the eyes of a child.

"Talaith . . ."

"I know. I know. Those eyes stop everyone in their tracks. And it's not the color, is it? It's like she can sense everything you feel or will ever feel."

"If there's truth to that, my friend, her life will not be easy."

"I know that as well."

Wincing that she had to ask the question because she had not been here to witness it or help, "Was it a hard birth for you?"

"Do you mean did I die, only to be brought back from the other side by a god so that I could slaughter a herd of Minotaurs trying to kill my child?"

Laughter wiped the awkward moment away, and Keita nodded. "That's *exactly* what I'm asking."

"Sorry. Nothing so exciting as what happened to Annwyl.

Just your typical, miserable labor with lots of screaming and swearing blood oaths at your brother for doing this to me. Very similar to my Izzy's birth." Talaith studied the babe in Keita's arms. "But this time no one took my daughter from me. This time I can hold her whenever I want to. She's mine to raise as I like."

Knowing the human female spoke of how the god Arzhela had secured Talaith's obedience for some sixteen years by holding her now-eldest daughter hostage, Keita said, "Gods, Izzy must be so excited by this. Her own little sister."

When Talaith didn't answer, Keita looked away from her niece's intense little face. "Talaith? You have told her, haven't you?"

"Well, like you, Izzy hasn't been home in two years."

"*So you haven't told her?*"

"Don't yell at me!"

"How could you not have told her?"

Talaith rubbed her forehead with her fingers. "It just never seemed the right time."

"Well, two years later is certainly *not* the right time. It's bad enough she didn't even know you were pregnant, but when she finds out there's been a child and no one told her—"

Talaith slapped her hand against her leg. "You know, for someone who hasn't deigned to reward us with her presence in two bloody years, you certainly seem aware of what's going on. And have opinions!"

Iseabail, Daughter of Talaith and Briec, Future Champion of Rhydderch Hael—probably—Future General of Queen Annwyl's Armies—She hoped! She hoped!—and sometimes Squire to Ghleanna the Decimator, kept her head down and tried hard not to show any reaction at all. She'd learned this approach after the first time her unit had come into one of these small towns, only to find it decimated by one of the

barbaric Western tribes. When she'd first arrived as a new
recruit for Queen Annwyl, the troops often went into towns
just like this one, either to protect the residents or to deal with
the aftermath, if they were too late. But even when they were
too late, they usually found only the men dead. The women
and children were taken off to be slaves, and more than once,
some of the units were able to rescue them before they'd been
sold at the slave market.

But in the last eight months or so, things had changed. Instead of finding a lot of dead men, they'd been finding dead
everything. Men, women, children, pets, cattle, crops. Nothing had been spared. And seeing a dead child for the first time
had taken Izzy by surprise, leading to silent but noted tears.
By the end of the evening, after cleaning up the bodies, she'd
been called in front of her commander to be told not to be "so
damn weak." Izzy knew her commander was being intention-
ally cold. There was no other way to get through a day when
you had to put one, let alone many, corpses of children on
funeral pyres.

So Izzy had taught herself to stare at something innocuous.
A tree. A cart. Today it was the bushes surrounding a burnt-
out husk of a house. It was strange how the house had burned,
leaving the lower-left frame standing but nothing else.

Grumbling about "bastard barbarians," her commander
began to snap out orders to the young recruits. "Grab this, get
that, burn them . . ." It was all the same.

Not exactly the glamorous battle life Izzy still dreamed of,
but she knew everyone had to start somewhere and it was her
dreams of earning more that made getting through the set-up
of more funeral pyres for the innocent tolerable.

"Iseabail," her commander ordered, "check the rest of the
houses."

"Uh-huh," Izzy said without thinking, her gaze catching
something buried in the dirt by the burned house she'd been
focusing on. She walked over to the husk and crouched down

by what was left of the bushes. Curiosity getting the better of her, Izzy dug her hand into the dirt and caught hold of the strip of red leather. She pulled it out and brushed at it, trying to see the emblem.

"Iseabail! Daughter of Talaith! *Do you hear me?*"

In the back of her mind, Izzy knew she should be jumping at her commander's bellowing, but she didn't know how. To say she'd been through more than most of the recruits was kind of an understatement, and after facing down gods, dragons, and, most terrifying of all at times, her mother, some bellowing unit leader who could have the skin stripped off her back for insubordination really didn't worry her much.

"Commander?" she said, running over to him. "What do you make of this?"

The commander, always annoyed Izzy didn't jump in terror at a mere word from him, snatched the leather from her hand. He wiped at the emblem with his thumb, his scowl suddenly fading away. "Where'd you find this?"

She pointed. "Over at that house there. In the dirt."

The commander slapped the leather back in Izzy's hand. "Take this to the general."

Izzy grinned. "Can I get a horse?"

"No!" he bellowed back. "You cannot get a horse. You haven't earned one!"

"I was just asking," she muttered.

Bringing two fingers to his lips, the commander whistled. Izzy shook her head. "No. Please, sir. No."

Her commander leered at her. It was the one way he knew to get to her. The one thing that set her teeth on edge. Because it was the one thing Izzy had absolutely no control over.

"Enjoy the ride, Iseabail."

Before Izzy could beg more, the dragon's tail wrapped around her waist and lifted her out of the small town. As always, she screamed when that happened. Begged to be put down, because she knew *exactly* what would happen when they arrived at their destination. Because it happened to her at least once a day now. Sometimes more, rarely less.

Yet the cruel beast holding her was no different from all the others who did the same to her—heartless and relentless, thoroughly enjoying the pain she suffered. And usually— family!

"No!" she begged, as she always begged. Especially when she saw the expansive camp that belonged to Annwyl's troops, right outside the Western Mountains. "Don't!" Izzy tried again as they flew through the camp. "Please!"

"Hold on!" was the only warning she got before the tail pulled back and then flicked forward, tossing her through tent flaps and inside the tent.

"Bull's-eye! Ten points!" the dragon cheered.

Izzy flailed wildly, trying to find a way to land that wouldn't shatter a shoulder or knee. But before Izzy could fly out the other end of the tent, where she was often grabbed by another tail and tossed somewhere else, big hands plucked her out of midair.

Panting, relieved, she looked up into a face she knew well because it looked so much like her grandfather's.

"Honestly, Izzy," her Great Uncle Addolgar chastised. "What are you playing at?"

"*Me?*" Why did they think it was always her? True, she'd been known to throw herself from one dragon back to another while hundreds of miles above the earth, but that was her choice, wasn't it? *This* particular game was *not* her choice, but it had turned out that those dragons she thought of as cousins and kin, didn't care. They insisted on treating her like a human shot, and no one seemed to care! Least of all her great aunt and great uncle.

"Don't start all that caterwauling," her uncle warned.

"I do not cater—"

"Why are you here?"

"My commander sent me back. He wanted you to see this."

She held out the strip of leather, and her uncle took it, then dropped her. Izzy's ass hit the ground hard, but she kept in her grunt of pain. It wasn't easy.

"Where'd you get this?"

"From that little town you sent us to check out. The barbarians had already been and gone. I found that in the dirt by a house."

"Oy. Ghleanna. Look at this."

Izzy's Great Aunt Ghleanna got up from the chair she'd been sitting in, drinking her afternoon ale. With her hand still around the battered mug, she took the leather from Addolgar and studied it. "Shit and piss," she finally said.

"What is it?" Izzy asked, trying to get another look.

"Mind your own," Addolgar told her, pushing her back by planting his excessively large hand against her forehead and doing just that—pushing her back.

She hated when he did that.

The siblings walked over to a corner and talked in hushed whispers while Izzy tried to listen without appearing to. Eventually, as they sometimes did, the pair began to argue, but for some reason Izzy got the feeling they were arguing about her. That was strange. It seemed as if they barely noticed her these days.

"It's a mistake," Addolgar said to his sister's back as she walked up to Izzy. But, like most days, Ghleanna ignored him.

"You were coming back with us to Garbhán Isle, yeah? When we leave in four days?"

Izzy nodded and held her breath. She'd feared this would happen. That something would come up and she'd be unable to return home. She wanted to go home so badly. Not to stay, of course—she had too much to do—but she hadn't seen her family in two years. She missed them all, but especially her mum. She wanted to see her mum.

"Looks like you'll be going back earlier."

Izzy bit the inside of her cheek so she wouldn't smile. "Oh?"

"Yeah. But before you go, *I* think there's something you should know first."

"And I think you should stay out of it," Addolgar snapped.

"Shut up, brother."

Izzy began to panic. "Is everyone all right? Is Mum—"

"She's fine, Izzy. She's fine." Ghleanna handed the leather to her. "When you get back, give this to Annwyl. Tell her it's the fourth bit like this that we've found. She'll understand."

"All right."

Ghleanna placed her hand on Izzy's shoulder. "But about your mum . . ."

"Is she coming back for the celebration?" Keita asked, slowly pacing around the room with her niece still in her arms. The entire time the babe's gaze never left Keita's face.

"They all are. Ghleanna, Addolgar, all their offspring. Some of your father's cousins who work the desert borders will hold the line in the west until after the celebration." Talaith watched her for a moment, then asked, "I'm glad you came back, luv. If nothing else, I know Izzy will be overjoyed to see you. She writes about you often."

Keita couldn't help but smile. "Does she?"

Talaith snorted, rolled her eyes. "You are joking? She's adored you since the first time you two met and you said in that cultured lilting voice of yours, which none of your other siblings have, 'Well, by the gods, isn't Briec's daughter absolutely beautiful.'" Talaith sneered and added, "Suck up."

"I wasn't lying, your daughter is beautiful. Besides, it worked, didn't it?"

They both laughed until Talaith's youngest daughter suddenly focused her intense gaze on the door.

"Should I be flying her to safety?" Keita asked when all on the other side of the door remained quiet.

"No. It's merely this incredible sense she's had since birth to know when her cousins are nearby."

As if on cue, the nursery door opened, and Fearghus walked in.

"You came to see Briec's offspring before mine?"

"Her mother led the way. *You*, however, were too busy laughing at Gwenvael."

He snorted. "Well, that was funny."

"Where are they?" Keita asked, trying to see over and under his excessively wide shoulders by moving about. "With the nanny?"

Her brother snorted again. "They lost her hours ago. They tracked me down themselves."

Fearghus looked over his shoulder and said, "Well, get up here. Meet your Aunt Keita."

Keita watched as two sets of eyes—one a vibrant green, the other an endless black—peeked over their father's shoulders.

So sweet, she thought. *They're shy.*

At the sight of her, those green eyes rose, and a filthy little boy raised himself up, his hands firmly placed on Fearghus's left shoulder. He sized Keita up with one long glance—and grinned.

Keita blinked, her gaze going to Fearghus, who quickly stated, "I won't discuss it. I just won't."

"Yes, but—"

"Not discussing!" he barked.

And that's when the child on the right launched herself at Keita, a small wooden training sword tight in her meaty little fist.

Thankfully, however, Fearghus was fast and caught hold of his equally filthy daughter by the back of her shirt.

"What have I told you about random attacks?" he asked the black-haired toddler. He sounded so bored by the question that Keita felt certain he'd had this discussion with her nearly every day since her birth. Disturbing enough, but the fact that the girl continued to swing her sword at Keita while snapping tiny baby teeth—definitely, much *more* disturbing.

"Is that normal, brother?"

"It's about to get stranger still," Talaith warned.

"And how is that possible?"

To answer the question, Talaith's daughter reached out her tiny hand toward her cousin, then placed it against Keita's chin. A moment later, Fearghus's daughter instantly relaxed, her sword lowering to her side.

"She didn't like you holding her cousin," Talaith explained, "until she got her cousin's approval, that is."

Taking a step back, Keita asked, "What in all the hells has been going on here?"

"We don't know," Talaith said on a yawn. "Though we've all asked ourselves that question often enough."

"But we had to stop," Fearghus continued. "Because to be quite honest—"

"—we were getting a little bit terrified by it all."

"But on the plus side," Fearghus quickly added, "none of them has a tail."

"Or scales."

"So superficially they seem quite normal."

Keita frowned. "And that's fine with you?"

Fearghus and Talaith exchanged glances before answering together, "It could be worse."

Branwen the Black was busy braiding her older brother Fal's hair when she saw Izzy. She looked well enough, even though one of their cousins had tossed Iz into Branwen's mum's tent. Branwen knew it for the compliment it was—that the Cadwaladrs thought Izzy tough enough to stand the abuse they'd dole out to any young dragon—but that didn't mean Iz liked being tossed about. Then again, Branwen didn't like it much either, and she could fly.

"Izzy doesn't seem to be in a very good mood," Fal observed.

Izzy was scowling so hard, she almost looked like Uncle Bercelak, which was strange since none of them were actually related to Izzy by blood. It didn't matter, though. They were all kin now. And after two years and countless battles, Branwen had grown impossibly close to Izzy. She was nicer than any of Branwen's sisters and more understanding than any of her brothers. True, they were more than six decades apart in age, and Iz was tragically human, but it wasn't something that mattered. Not to them.

Branwen released her brother's hair and stepped over the log he sat on. "Izzy?"

Izzy stopped, faced her cousin. "Did you know?"

"Did I know what?"

"You mean about your mother?" Fal asked, looking all sorts of bored. He shrugged. "I knew."

"You knew what?" Branwen demanded of her brother, but he never got a chance to answer. Izzy picked up one of the logs they used for sitting and with one good swing, knocked Fal up and back into their brother Celyn, who'd come up behind him to find out what was going on. Both dragons hit the ground hard, and Izzy tossed the log down, the ground shaking a bit from the weight of it.

"Can you take me back to Dark Plains?" Izzy asked her.

"Aye, but—"

"General Ghleanna wants me to give something to my queen as soon as possible, so it'll be faster this way."

"Anything, Iz, but—"

"Five minutes then?" And not bothering to wait for Branwen's answer, Izzy walked off.

Celyn stood next to Branwen now, both ignoring their groaning brother with the broken jaw. "What's going on?"

"I don't know, but I'll find out."

"I'll take her back to Dark Plains," Celyn offered.

"Like hell you will."

"Yeah, but—"

"Don't be stupid," she whispered and motioned to poor Fal. "Take care of our brother. I think his jaw's broken."

"Then maybe he should have kept his mouth shut for once."

"There she is!" Briec walked into the room, and for a moment, Keita actually believed he spoke of her. She was wrong. "There's my perfect, perfect daughter." He removed the child from Keita's arms without asking permission. As always, her brother was rude!

"Isn't she perfect, Keita?" He motioned to Fearghus and his offspring. "Unlike those two."

In response, Fearghus's little girl pulled back her arm to toss her wooden blade at her uncle's head, but Fearghus yanked it away from her before she could carry through.

The baby clung to Briec, small arms wrapped around his neck. But, for the first time, Keita noticed that she didn't smile.

"Does she not smile?" Keita asked, and she knew it was the wrong question when both Talaith and Fearghus winced and Briec snapped, "She'll smile when she's gods-damn ready!"

"Don't bark at me!" Keita snapped back. "It was a simple question."

"Well, if you'd been here, you wouldn't have to ask those bloody questions!"

"Bring that up one more time, Briec, and I'm—"

"Flouncing back to your cave?" Fearghus asked.

"Oh, shut up!"

"You know what we haven't told her?" Talaith suddenly asked, a big grin on her face as she jumped to her feet. "The children's names." Talaith stroked her hand down Fearghus's girl's black hair. "This is Talwyn." Then she tickled the boy's cheek. "This is Talan." She held up her hands and, as if she were offering something for sale, she announced, "And this . . . this is Rhianwen."

Keita's eyes narrowed, and she stepped away from her safe window, barely noticing Fearghus's twins were crawling away from her until they again hid behind their father's shoulders. "Rhianwen?" Keita all but roared. "You named her Rhianwen?"

Briec raised a silver brow. "Is there a problem with that, sister?"

"Why not just curse her with the name Despair? Or Bringer of Misery?"

"I happen to *like* the name Rhianwen. And before you say it, Rhianwen is not *that* similar to Mother's name."

"You're pathetic!" Keita accused her brother. "Always sucking up to that she-cow! At least Fearghus had some backbone with his naming!"

Briec turned on her. "Well, when you breed some hatchlings of your own, Mistress Whine, you can name them what you'd like! But as far as I'm concerned, any perfect offspring that are sprung from *my* loins deserves a majestic name—*and that majestic name is Rhianwen!*"

Disgusted beyond all reckoning, Keita stormed out of the room and down the hallway to the stairs. She was cutting through the Great Hall when Ren caught up to her.

"You look ready to roast an entire town. What's wrong?"

"Rhianwen!" she exclaimed. "That suck-up named his daughter Rhianwen!"

"Rhianwen?" Ren exclaimed back. "Why not just call her Misery or She Who Despairs?"

Keita stopped, turned, and threw her arms around Ren, hugging him tight. "This is why I'll always love you, my friend."

Laughing, he patted her back. "I know, old friend. I know."

Talaith shook her head. "That went well."

"She started it," Briec stated before holding his "perfect"

daughter out to Talaith and announcing, "She looks to need nourishment. Unleash your breasts for her."

"Would you stop saying that!" she yelped over Fearghus's laugh. "I hate when you say that!"

"Do you? I hadn't noticed."

Talaith snatched her child from her mate. "You do realize that when I'm finally forced to kill you, no one will blame me for it?"

"I know I won't," Fearghus tossed in, busy holding his children upside down by one leg each, grinning when they laughed and squealed. Although neither of his children spoke. They never spoke. Except to each other and only in whispers . . . and in a language no one understood. The family had finally admitted it to each other when the twins were about one and the truth could no longer be avoided. But again, there were worse things that could happen with them, but it was still strange. The twins were strange.

Talaith walked across the room and sat in a rocking chair Briec had made for her right before Rhianwen had been born.

"Whatever you two do, please don't scare off your sister before Izzy arrives in a few days. You know she'll want to see Keita." And, Talaith hoped, Keita might be the one being who could defuse Izzy's rage when she found out the truth about Rhianwen.

Talaith hadn't been lying to Keita when she'd told her no moment seemed to be right to tell Izzy about her sister. There was so much going on in the west, and the last thing Talaith wanted was for Izzy's mind not being on her task. She didn't want to send a letter with all the information, only to find out her daughter was ambushed a day later by barbarians because she wasn't paying attention. Because she was worrying about her mum. That was how it felt in the beginning; then after the baby was born, it just seemed wrong to tell her in a letter. But Talaith had thought Izzy would have been home by now. That she would have told her by now.

But when Izzy got home in the next few days, it would be the first thing Talaith did. She'd make sure of that.

"We're not going to scare her off," Briec informed Talaith. "We're simply making it clear that what she did was unacceptable and will not be tolerated again."

"And how well that has worked for you in the past, eh?"

"Don't try to tell me how to raise my baby sister."

"Raise her? She's nearly two hundred years old."

"Not yet she's not."

"Och!" Keita barked, stepping out of the Great Hall and into the late-day suns. "I simply can't believe Briec named his poor hatchling after that slithering pond scum!"

"Shouldn't you just call her Mum when we're on her territory?"

"Only when she's directly in earshot."

Keita watched as Ragnar returned with Gwenvael and some servant. "There you are! You can't just go wandering off, warlord. Unless, of course, you were hoping for a haircut so you can match your brother."

"Is it my imagination or is that concern in your voice?" the warlord asked.

"Hardly. More like annoyance." She continued down the steps and grabbed Ragnar's forearm. "Come. We need to talk."

"Where are you going?"

"Don't question me, Gwenvael."

"But Keita—"

"Later. I need to talk to Ragnar." Keita stopped by the servant. "Please ensure our Northland guests have all they need. I believe they were taken to the third floor. Make sure they have food. My sister has a tendency to forget that sort of thing." She glanced at what stood behind the servant, a large bone held in its mouth. She'd seen a lot of those around the territory. More than she'd seen before. *Must be an overpopulation issue.*

Something she could help with. "Dog might do. Roasted. Not heavy on the salt." She sighed longingly. "Roasted dog. Yum." She pressed her hand to her stomach and realized how hungry she was. "Send some up to my room as well. We'll be back in a bit."

Keita hopped off the last step and looked back at Ragnar. Shocked at the warlord, she could only ask over his laughter, "What's so funny?"

"Keita—" her brother said.

"What?"

Gwenvael put his arm around the servant, and Keita sighed softly in exasperation. Why her brother felt the need to protect every female, especially now when he had some barbarian warlord mate of his own, was beyond Keita's reckoning. It wasn't as if she'd battered the female into submission or something. She'd given her simple orders to follow. That was her job, wasn't it?

"I'd like you to meet Dagmar Reinholdt," Gwenvael said.

Really? Now there had to be proper introductions to servants? But Keita didn't want to argue any more with her siblings. Even Gwenvael. "Nice to meet you, Dagmar. You can call me Lady Keita."

That seemed to make Ragnar laugh harder, when the dragon rarely laughed at all. He especially didn't laugh like this.

"*What* is so funny?" she demanded.

"Dagmar Reinholdt," her brother said again, as if she hadn't understood him the first damn time. "Thirteenth Offspring of The Reinholdt, Only Daughter of The Reinholdt, Chief Battle Lord of Dark Plains, Adviser to Queen Annwyl, Human Liaison to the Southland Dragon Elders, and my *mate*."

Oh.

Shit.

Oh, shit!

Shit, shit, shit, shit, shit!

Pulling from nearly two centuries of royal training, Keita

broke out her most dazzling smile. "Of course she is!" she said with a laugh. "I was merely teasing."

She went back up several steps until she was close enough to the Northland warlord's daughter. Keita grasped one of the human's tiny hands between her own. "I am so glad to meet you, my Lady Dagmar! It's taken far too long for us to meet."

"It has," the human said. For the first time, Keita noticed that the female wore little round pieces of glass held between two wires that she had perched on her nose. Whatever for? Was she blind? "I've heard so much about you and have longed to meet you. You are truly as beautiful as all the *many* men throughout the land have said."

Another laugh escaped the barbarian dragon, and Keita briefly thought about flipping him over the stair banister. "And you are," Keita said in return, "well . . . *you*. And I'm sure you're the best you that you can be."

At this point, Ren now headed back into the castle and Gwenvael forced the two females' hands apart.

"All right then!" her brother said with an obscene amount of forced cheer. "That's enough greeting, don't you think?"

He turned his mate toward the doors and shoved Keita back down the stairs. Keita barely kept her snarl in—and on her feet—but before she could stomp away, the human maneuvered around Gwenvael and said, "Oh, my Lady Keita, one other thing."

Keita stopped and faced her, keeping that cheery smile on her face. "Aye?"

"Dogs . . . off limits."

"Are they now?"

"If you hadn't heard, it's a rule of the land. And I'd hate to see you get into trouble over it with your mother."

"My mother?" Keita asked, unable to keep the surprise out of her voice. "My mother agreed to a law banning the eating of dogs?" The same dragoness who wouldn't even agree to a written ban on the eating of humans? Instead she felt it was something her dragon subjects should simply know not to do "unless they can get away with it."

"In fact, she agreed happily."

Knowing when she was beat, at least in one area, Keita said, "Of course. The gods know I wouldn't want to go against my mother."

"Then I'm sure we won't have any problems."

Normally Keita would argue the point, but she was starting to feel terrible about the whole thing and decided it was best to simply walk away.

Reaching up, she caught hold of Ragnar's hand and pulled him off toward the gate's east-side exit. And it wasn't until they'd gone about twenty feet or so that Keita heard the warlord's daughter snap, "Canute!"

She and Ragnar stopped walking and looked behind them. The dog that had been with Lady Dagmar now stood behind them. He dropped his bone and pushed it toward Keita with his snout. Lifting his massive head, his tongue hanging out, he grinned at her.

"Ohhh," Keita exclaimed. "Aren't you sweet?" But before she could pat the dog's head, Ragnar yanked her away, sniffing in disgust.

"Well, don't get mad at me," she argued. "Is it my fault males always want to give me things?"

Chapter Nineteen

Ragnar got as far as a copse of trees outside the fortress walls before he decided to stop and face the princess. She gazed up at him with those brown eyes and asked, "That went badly, didn't it?"

And that's when the laughter started all over again. So bad, he couldn't stop. He just sat down in the grass and let the laughter roll right through him.

"It's not funny!" Keita yelled, stamping her bare foot. "You could have bloody warned me!"

"You didn't give me or anyone else a chance! I don't know which was better. The look on your face or the look on hers!"

Keita paced away from him, her hands twisting against each other. "How was I supposed to know *that* was Dagmar Reinholdt? A warlord's daughter? I thought she'd be huge! A snarling, snapping hound beast!" Ragnar pushed himself up on his elbows and studied her. She gave a small shrug. "My brother has . . . interesting tastes."

She continued to pace. "I feel horrible!"

That surprised him. "You do?"

"Of course I do. I never wanted to hurt her feelings. But with that headscarf, those pieces of glass on her face, and all that grey . . . how was I to know?"

"Those pieces of glass on her face are spectacles."

Keita, appearing horrified, briefly covered her mouth before asking in a desperate whisper, "She's blind, isn't she? I mocked a blind woman!"

Laughing again, Ragnar fell back on the ground.

"It's not funny!" She stood over him, scowling. "Don't you see? She's probably crumpled at my brother's feet right now—sobbing hysterically!"

Stretched out on their bed inside their fortress sleeping quarters, Gwenvael asked, "Does this mean I can call you my sassy servant girl now?"

"No, it does not." Dagmar sat on the edge of the bed and pointed a finger at her dog. "And don't you come over here. I'm still not speaking to you."

Whining, the dog lay down on the floor, tucking his muzzle between his paws.

"How about blind slave girl?"

"No."

Gwenvael moved over until his head rested in her lap. "How about saucy serving wench?"

Dagmar plucked lint off the sleeve of her gown. "All right, but only when we're alone and you're naked."

"Shouldn't you be naked as well?"

She sighed, in desperate exasperation. "If I'm already naked, then you can't very well rip off my clothes and demand I service you with my mouth or you'll bring in your many brutal guards to force me to comply—now can you?"

Gwenvael shivered, his hand reaching up and sliding into Dagmar's hair before pulling her down to him. "How in all the hells did I forget the best part?"

* * *

"I've devastated that poor, wee thing and destroyed her will to live."

"You really have not been in touch with your kin at all these last two years, have you?"

"I was busy!" She paced away from him, returned. "I'll go straightaway and apologize. It's the least I can do."

She hadn't even moved yet, but Ragnar caught her arm. "I wouldn't do that."

"Why ever not?"

"Because you'll only show Dagmar weakness, and she will prey on that weakness the way one of your relatives is preying on that carcass over there."

Keita looked off into the east field and raised her free arm. "Hello, Uncle Amhar," she called out loudly so he could hear her from the distance between them.

The older dragon lifted his head, blood covering his snout and dripping down his fangs. "Hello, my lovely niece! All well?"

"Aye! Enjoy your meal!" She returned her attention to the Lightning at her feet and tilted her head to the side. "You were laughing," she observed.

"Yes."

"I didn't know you were capable." Keita sat down beside him, spreading her gown out around her. "So apologizing is out."

"Definitely. I taught Dagmar well, and she'll only see your apology as something she can use against you later."

"Taught her?"

"I've known Dagmar many years. I met her when I was traveling through her father's lands as a monk."

"How old was she?"

"Ten, maybe."

"And what, exactly, were you teaching her?"

Ragnar pulled his legs up and rested his arms on his raised knees. "Please don't make me destroy . . . everything."

"Sorry, sorry. I've just known a few dragons who've done

that sort of thing. They don't touch their humans until they're of age, but the grooming starts much sooner."

"It was never like that."

"Good. When I've discovered that sort of thing in the past, it was very upsetting."

"I can well imagine. What did you do?"

"Told my father." She picked a flower that had managed to bloom before the winter set in. "And he killed them."

Ragnar's head fell forward, and he let out a breath. "Is that the answer your kin have to everything?"

"Yes."

He studied her for a long moment. "Is that why you're an assassin?"

Insulted, "I am *not* an assassin. I am a Protector of the Throne. And have been since I was thirteen winters."

"You couldn't even fly when you were thirteen winters."

"All right, fine. If you're going to be literal. I knew I was *going to be* a Protector of the Throne. I didn't actually pledge myself until years later. There. Happy?" Ragnar began to answer, but she cut him off because she felt the need to make something clear. "But I am *not* an assassin." She brought the flower to her nose, sniffed it. "That would be Talaith."

"And who's Talaith?"

"My brother Briec's mate. She's from Alsandair."

Ragnar visibly winced. "Alsandair? Does she have a daughter? Tall girl?"

"Aye. You've met them?"

"I think so." He scratched his jaw, and Keita noticed for the first time the scar he had on it. It was long but so low on his jaw, it wasn't immediately obvious. "They killed my father."

"Huh . . . dinner tonight might be awkward."

"Not really. As you well know, he deserved it. But best not to mention it to my kin."

"I'm glad you told me. Izzy will be here in a few days, and I'll need to get to her before she says something completely inappropriate to Vigholf and Meinhard. She won't mean to, of course. But it won't matter."

"So I'll still be here in a few days?"

"I'm guessing."

He leaned forward a bit, resting his cheek on his knees. "Tell me what you really think about all this with your mother."

"I think I truly appreciate your not mentioning that necklace we found."

"Right now your mother is unsure of Esyld's loyalty. I sensed you were right, though, and her opinion would have changed quickly if I had told her about it." He reached over and took one of her hands in his. "Tell me about your people and the Irons."

She took in a breath. "During my ancestors' time, the Iron dragons were just Southland dragons. They had wings and talons and fangs and breathed fire just like the rest of us. But they always wanted more. They began to segregate themselves from the others, and there were rumors of inbreeding in order to keep their blood lines 'clean,' was the word I heard used. Unlike the rest of the Southland dragons, their scales were all one color. The color of iron. Even you Northlanders, you're all varying shades of purple, but the Irons were just one shade. And any that deviated, I'd heard, were destroyed at birth. They change their horns too. Use some contraption when their offspring hatch to curl their horns around their heads. They were finally forced out by my great grandmother, who had no tolerance for that sort of bizarre behavior, and they moved into the west. When my mother was young, the Irons attacked only once. My grandfather and his troops met them before they even cleared the Aricia Mountains. We won the day, of course, but my grandfather was captured and taken back to the Quintilian Provinces—the capital of the Sovereigns now, but then it was still just a lone province. He was tortured for days, they said. Until his execution." Keita turned her hand over in his, pressed her thumb against the back of his hand. "Although we tell others he was killed in battle. Only the family knows the truth about his death."

"And that truth will never leave me."

She believed him and gave him a small smile. "My mother loved her father dearly. He protected her from her mother, and his death was a great loss to her."

"Do you really think she only wants revenge? That she'd instigate a war with the Irons just for that reason?"

"My kin hold grudges like the ocean holds water. Forever, until a giant wave slams into the shore and devastates absolutely everything."

"That doesn't mean she's wrong about this, Keita. You can't say you don't feel something barreling down on us."

"I dreamed . . ."

"You dreamed . . . what?"

Keita shook her head. Was she really going to sit here and tell Ragnar about ridiculous dreams involving demon horses? What exactly did that have to do with the Irons anyway? "Forget it. But you're right. I do feel something coming. But I also know my mother embraces war. The Elders have much less power when there's a war."

"And Esyld?"

"If my mother can use Esyld to get her war, she will—but I want to stop this before it goes that far. I need to protect the throne."

Ragnar sat up. "Gods, tell me you don't think the Irons can be reasoned with."

"I won't know that until I meet with them."

"Meet with them?"

"Calm down. I don't mean now."

"You better not mean ever."

"I can't promise that. If I get the opportunity—"

"Have you lost your mind?"

"It's so sweet of you to ask that like it's not possible . . . even after meeting my kin."

* * *

"Now the bigger issue—"

"There's a bigger issue than your insanity?" Ragnar demanded, wondering what this female was thinking.

"Surprisingly—yes! And that bigger issue, of course, is what are we going to do with you?"

"Pardon?"

"Well, in the past when Ren and I—"

"Yes. Your perfect Ren. How could I forget him?"

"That sounded an awful lot like sarcasm, but I'm choosing to ignore it. Now, I've thought about this all the way from Devenallt Mountain. And we need a good, solid reason for you to be around me. You can't just follow me like a puppy. So, after some thought, I think the best idea is for us to be lovers." She smiled. "Isn't that a lovely idea?"

Gods! This female!

"What?"

She had the nerve to look insulted. "You don't have to look so panicked. We can just fake it if it makes you more comfortable."

"I'm not panicked—I'm trying to keep up." He scratched his head as it dawned on him that she hadn't said they would pretend to be lovers, which meant what exactly? "Do you *want* to be lovers?"

"Sure. Why not? You know, while we're here."

She was truly trying to drive him into drinking every day until he blacked out, wasn't she?

"It's kind of a 'two mountains, one boulder' sort of thing," she explained. "It will give us something fun to do while waiting to stop a war that may devastate our entire continent."

"Uh-huh."

"*And*," she continued, smile widening, "everyone will be disgusted that I'm willing to lower myself to actually bed a barbarian lightning breather. A definite win-win, wouldn't you say?"

"How is that a win-win?"

"They'll all assume I'm doing it to torment my mother, not realizing my mother could give a blessed shit, which will draw the traitors out sooner rather than later. See? It's brilliant."

Ragnar began to rub his temples with one hand. "Let's try this again. Do you *want* to be with me?"

"You mean actually fuck you?"

Ale. He needed ale so badly right now. "Sure. Why not?"

Keita leaned back and studied him. "Aye. I think I'd enjoy fucking you." Her eyes narrowed. "Is there something wrong with your chest?" Ragnar slammed his hand down, and Keita leaned farther away. "You don't have scale fungus, do you?"

"I do *not* have scale fungus! If you want the truth, this is *your* fault!"

"My fault?"

"You stabbed me, and this damn thing hasn't healed in two years. Did you use a poison on your tail?"

"Of course I di—" Keita abruptly stopped talking, her hand covering her mouth.

"*You did, didn't you?*" Ragnar bellowed. "*You did bloody poison me!*"

"It shouldn't have lasted this long," she argued while not trying very hard not to laugh. "I just rubbed it against an iustig plant before I—"

"Assaulted me?"

"If you want to be literal. But the itching should have stopped ages ago."

"Well, it didn't. Dammit, Keita! I thought I was losing my bloody mind."

"I'm sorry."

"Like hell you are."

"No. Honestly. I *am* sorry."

Ragnar shook his head. "Maybe we should talk about this later."

"No, no." Keita crawled into his lap, facing him, and

pressed her hand against the scar. There was a shirt between her flesh and his, but he only felt Keita. "I am sorry, and I can get you an antidote."

He grunted, looking off.

"Don't be angry with me now—we were just getting along. For once."

He still said nothing, and that's when she asked, "Have you ever kissed as human?"

Was it possible for her to stay on one topic at a time? He didn't think so.

"Once or twice."

He'd been joking when he replied, but she winced, just a little. It was enough.

"Are you any good?"

"As a matter of fact—"

She raised her hand, cutting him off. "That's all right. It's not a large issue."

She settled against Ragnar's waist, her knees on either side of him. "I love kissing as human," she explained. "I love fucking as human, too. Hope that won't be a problem for you." He again didn't reply, not knowing what to think of any of this. "And the most important thing to remember is not to choke me to death with your tongue."

"I'll keep that in mind." Although he was sure he would have sounded much ruder if he wasn't panting just a little. But damn her, she was naked under that gown. He'd forgotten.

"Good."

Keita closed the gap between them and pressed her mouth against his. Small kisses at first, nothing rushed or too forceful. It surprised him how innocent those first few kisses felt. Taking his supposed "inexperience" to heart, she didn't push him, simply continued with those small kisses, lengthening them by degrees. As each kiss grew in intensity, the damn itching of the scar she'd given him flared to life again. He clenched his hands into fists to stop himself from scratching the area until there was blood.

"It's all right," Keita whispered against his mouth. "Just relax. You're doing fine."

No. He wasn't doing fine. How could he concentrate on this kiss or any other when the itching was driving him beyond reason? He needed that damn antidote before he went any further.

Ragnar began to speak at the same time Keita came in for another kiss. Finding his mouth open, she slipped her tongue inside, brushed up against his. Ragnar's body shuddered, and his hands unclenched so he could grip her waist and pull her closer to his body.

And that irritating scar on his chest? Momentarily forgotten.

The pious Lightning was a fast learner, his tongue boldly moving around hers while his arms held her tight against him.

Keita tilted her head to the side, relaxed into him, and let the kiss go on. Perhaps not much experience at this sort of thing while human, but definitely a quick learner.

Her body heated under her dress, her nipples hardening, and her pussy clenching with the need for something to fill it. When she started to squirm on his lap, Keita pulled out of their kiss.

Both panting, they stared at each other. Keita had no idea how long, it felt like hours.

"Keita!" she heard from near the fortress. It was her brother, Éibhear.

She closed her eyes and reached out to her brother with her mind. *What?*

Where are you?

In the west fields. What is it?

Dinner in the hour.

And?

Well . . . I know you like to dress for that sort of thing, so

I'm letting you know beforehand so you don't yell at me later that I didn't give you enough time!

Don't get testy! I'll be right there.

All right. Oh. And have you seen Lord Ragnar?

Why?

Vigholf was looking for him, and Briec, being a right bastard, said, "Oh, you didn't know? We took him down to the river and drowned him." And Vigholf went for his weapon, and Fearghus said, "Do that, Lightning, and I'll let my wench cut off the rest of your head." And I said, "Can we not do this now?" And then I told Fearghus, "And don't call Annwyl wench." And he shoved me. So I shoved him back. And that really pissed him off, and then he and Briec ganged up on me. And I said, "I'm telling Mum!" And then they laughed at me, and I don't think that was fair at all.

Keita's baby brother went on, but it was the shaking beneath her that had her opening her eyes and staring at the warlord she had her arms wrapped around. The *laughing* warlord.

Éibhear, she cut in. *Don't let them worry you. I'll be back in a bit. Ragnar's fine.*

All right.

Her brother ended their communication, and Keita grabbed hold of Ragnar the Cunning by that one braid his brother no longer had.

"Ow!"

"Were you listening?"

"My gods, he whines so!"

She yanked.

"Ow!"

"How do you do that? How is that possible?" Only direct kin could hear each other's thoughts.

Ragnar caught her hand and pulled it off his hair. "Neither of you shield your thoughts. Any good mage, this close, could hear you two like you were screaming in his ear. Especially with that level of whining."

"My brother does not whine." She grabbed his braid again, yanked.

"Ow!"

"Stay out of my head, warlord!"

"Try to control where your thoughts go, princess."

"And that sounded like prince-ass!"

He smirked. "Are we going back before your baby brother starts sobbing?"

She pointed a warning finger at him. "Never, and I mean *never*, pick on my brother."

"Isn't he a little big to coddle?"

Keita slid off Ragnar's lap and stood. "You will stay out of my head."

"Why? What are you hiding from me?"

"Nothing, but it's rude and invasive. And as powerful as you *claim* to be, you should have as easy a time blocking out what you hear as you do hearing it."

"If you say so."

"I do. Now can we go?"

The warlord got to his feet, moving with an ease belied by his size. To be honest, she always expected him to lumber a bit more.

"Now remember," she told him, smoothing down her dress, her hair, "just let me take the lead on this and all will be well. We can decide later if we want to take that kiss further."

Ragnar's arm wrapped around her waist as he walked by, pulling her into his chest. "You're trying to drive me insane— I won't let you."

"I am not—"

"And we *will* damn well take that kiss further."

"Oh, you think so, do—"

He kissed her again, stunning her with the power of it. But as quickly as he started, he ended it, releasing her with a hard swat to her ass.

"Let's go, princess. You have to get dressed for dinner and get me that damn antidote."

"I'll have to have it made, so you'll get it after dinner or to-morrow. And I'm still hearing prince-*ass*!" she shouted.

Amhar the Blood Drinker watched his niece follow after that Lightning. He'd been so focused on the carcass at his feet that he'd thought she'd gone inside long ago. But when he lifted his head, she was just standing up in the tall grass and the Lightning was right behind her.

Amhar didn't like the looks of all that. Especially that swat to the ass. The kiss meant nothing to him; it was the ass swat that he saw as a stronger message of intent.

Although his niece might be freer than most with males—she took after a lot of his sisters on that score—no respectable female in their family would ever lower herself to bed down with some barbarian snake with wings. And as one of the royals, Keita had to know better than that.

Then again, the only thing Keita the Viper knew better was how to get herself into trouble.

Worried, but not one to deal with a female issue himself, Amhar decided to discuss it with one of his sisters first. He definitely wouldn't be the one to bring it to Bercelak's atten-tion. One of his nephews had lost the fangs on the left side of his head because he'd suggested that Keita should be locked away in a nunnery so she wouldn't bring shame on her kin. Not that Amhar could blame his brother. Bercelak protected his daughters like Amhar did, as their father had taught them to. Some of his nephews either needed to learn to keep their mouths closed or put up a better fight.

Deciding what his next course of action would be, Amhar went back to his nearly devoured carcass and thought no more about it for the moment.

Chapter Twenty

Dagmar smoothed her grey gown into place and glanced at herself in the extremely tall standing mirror. *Good enough*, she reasoned and stepped away, only to be pulled back by her mate.

As he liked to do, he tugged the front of her gown down to reveal more cleavage.

"Is this necessary?"

"I'm already beautiful—you want to at least keep up."

He turned her around and lifted the back of her dress until it rested over her rear.

"What are you doing?"

"I think you should wear your gown like this to show my mark."

"And why, by all reason, would I do that?"

"So your Lord Ragnar knows who you belong to."

"He's not my . . ." Dagmar stopped, gazed at the floor. After a moment, she lifted her head and asked, "Are you jealous?"

"I prefer the term proprietary."

"You're jealous . . . over me?"

"You are mine. I thought I made this clear long before I marked your ass. Perhaps I need to mark it again to—"

Dagmar raised her hand, silencing her mate. "Please. Allow me a moment to enjoy this."

It wasn't merely that the most arrogant and vain male she'd ever known was jealous, it was that *any* male was jealous over *her*. She'd long ago accepted the fact that beauty was not something she could count on to get her through life.

Still, moments like these did manage to surprise and delight her when they happened—and they happened more than she'd thought possible with her impossible dragon.

"I do not trust that smile of yours." His arm slipped around her waist. "Back to bed. I sense I need to exert my dominance yet again."

She attempted—rather weakly, she'd admit—to pry his arm from around her waist. "I will not leave my Northland comrades alone with your brothers at dinner tonight."

"When did they become comrades?" Gwenvael tossed her onto their bed. "Spread your legs, woman. Prepare yourself."

Dagmar began to laugh.

"You're not helping your case." He crawled onto the bed, raising himself over her. "But you'll have no one to blame but yourself."

He reached for her, snarling when a knock came at the door.

"Go away. We're fucking."

Dagmar, wondering how she'd learned to tolerate any of these dragons, countered, "Come in, and we're doing nothing of the sort!"

"Yet."

The door opened a bit, and Gwenvael's youngest sister peeked around it. "Are you sure? I don't want to interrupt my brother doing something wonderfully vile."

"Not when she can listen at the door."

"I didn't listen!" Keita smiled, looking more like Gwenvael than anyone should. "I merely sold tickets. Made a fortune that night."

Gwenvael relaxed on his side. "Did you come here to bow

before the mistress of my heart, who you cruelly believed to be a mere servant, and beg her forgiveness?"

"No." Keita stepped fully into the room. "I did, however, bring her a dress."

Dagmar winced. Considering the bright and sparkle-infused light blue gown the princess currently wore, Dagmar had no desire to see what kind of dress the royal had brought for her. "That's very kind of you, princess—"

"Keita, sister. Call me Keita. We are family now, are we not?"

Dagmar studied the royal closely. She trusted few beings in this world, and although Gwenvael and his brothers thought highly of Keita, Dagmar had yet to see any evidence that she was anything but a spoiled royal with expensive taste in clothes. *Are those real diamonds she has sewn on to her dress?*

"Of course we are," Dagmar said, not believing a word either of them spoke.

The princess giggled. "Such a little liar, Dagmar Reinholdt. But I'll overlook it because you make my brother happy. Now, tell me what you think."

She pulled out the dress she had hidden behind her and held it up for Dagmar's inspection. Although ready to hate it on principle alone, Dagmar knew she couldn't.

Sliding off the bed, she walked up to Keita, her hand reaching out and carefully touching the gown.

"It's . . . beautiful."

"I know you prefer grey," Keita said, pulling Dagmar over to the mirror. "But silver and steel work just as well. This color is called 'sword steel' among the shop owners"—she stood behind Dagmar and held the gown up in front of her—"and perfectly brings out your eyes, which are quite striking, I might add. I bet my brother adores your eyes."

"And you'd be right," Gwenvael said from the bed.

"See? I know my brothers quite well. Now, go. Try it on."

"Yes!" Gwenvael cheered from the bed. "Strip naked for me *and* my sister."

Keita sniffed. "You don't think I planned for that, my disgusting brother? Knowing how you turn everything into something inappropriate?" She walked to the door and opened it. "Bring it in."

One of the servants brought in a tall screen and unfolded it. Once the servant was gone, Keita pulled Dagmar behind it. "Try it on."

Without questioning, something Dagmar did about nearly *everything* in her life, she did as the royal ordered.

Keita sat on the bed next to her brother while his little human put on the dress she'd chosen for her. "Remember me now?" Keita demanded, making sure to flare her eyes in a terrifying manner.

Gwenvael laughed. "I don't know how I managed to forget you."

"Nor do I. I am, in a word, unforgettable."

Putting his arm around her shoulders, Gwenvael kissed her forehead. "Everything all right, little sister?"

"We need to talk," she murmured softly.

"About Esyld?"

Keita blinked, looked up at her brother. "How did you know?"

"That Lightning told us earlier. Why would Mother send him to fetch her anyway?"

"Long story. And, of course, there's much more to it."

"Of course. But tell me, are that Lightning and his barbarian entourage going back soon . . . as in tonight?"

"No. Because Esyld is only part of it."

"What's the other part of the problem?"

Keita scratched her cheek. "Irons. Possibly."

"Iron what?"

"Iron dragons, you idiot."

Gwenvael's arm fell away, and he gawked at his sister. "What about them?"

"Our mother seems to fear they may be planning war."

"You can't be serious."

"I am. At the very least Mother is."

"Mother hates them. Would love a chance to kill them all."

"Exactly. She wants war, but I'm hoping I can prevent that."

"Do you really think it's wise to get between Mother and her love of carnage?"

"This has to stop. First she used the Northlanders to get her war, now she's aiming at the Irons."

"Or she's right and they're aiming at us."

Keita shrugged. "I guess anything is possible." She frowned at the screen. "What are you doing back there, luv?"

"It's very bright. I feel like I can be seen for miles."

Keita raised her hands to the ceiling. "Why? Why do you all question me?"

A long sigh came from the other side. "If I didn't know you were his sister before . . ."

"Come! Let us see!"

After several moments, the warlord's daughter stepped out from behind the screen, and Keita clapped her hands together. She *did* have an eye, didn't she?

And when she heard her brother's sharp intake of breath, she knew she wasn't the only one who thought so.

True, it didn't make Dagmar Reinholdt any less plain of face, but it brought out her eyes and her eyes were stunning.

Keita moved closer to Dagmar, pulling the skirt of the gown out for the full effect. "You look almost perfect," Keita told her.

"Almost?" Gwenvael repeated in disbelief.

Keita stood behind Dagmar again and removed her head scarf. She grabbed a brush from the dressing table and swiped it through the Northlander's hair until it fairly glowed, the locks reaching to her small waist. "*Now* she looks perfect."

Keita pushed her in front of the mirror again. "I know the bodice is a bit low cut," she said, quickly placing small flowers she'd brought with her into Dagmar's hair before the Northlander could tell her to stop, "but I know my brother's taste. Figured I'd throw the lusty bastard a bone."

"It is a lovely gown, Keita," Dagmar said. "Thank you."

"Of course. An average grey gown for the day-to-day is absolutely fine, sister, but you don't want anyone at important royal dinners thinking you're a servant as well." She winked at Dagmar in the mirror and received what suspiciously appeared to be a smile in return.

Keita turned Dagmar to face her again and removed the spectacles from her face. "*Can you see without these?*" Keita yelled.

"No," the warlord's daughter snapped, her smile vanishing as she snatched the spectacles back and put them on again. "Nor am I deaf! Is there something wrong with your family I've not been alerted to?" she asked.

And Keita replied with pure honesty, "You'll have to be much more specific than that, I'm afraid, Lady Dagmar."

Ragnar glared at his brother and cousin. "You're going to make me go down there alone?"

Meinhard pointed at his leg. "Still healing."

"Shut up." Ragnar looked at Vigholf. "And you, brother? What's your excuse?"

"I've been disfigured!" he yelled, pointing at his hair. "What more do you need?"

"For you to stop being such a girl," Ragnar muttered.

"What?"

"Nothing." Resigned to sitting through an entire meal with self-important Fire Breathers, Ragnar walked out of the room—making sure to slam the door behind him—and headed down the stairs.

They'd placed him and his kin on the third floor, far away from the family rooms, which was fine with him. He made it to the second floor and walked down the hallway to reach the next set of stairs. A door opened, and Ragnar stopped, allowing the occupants to go by him.

Gwenvael walked out, the smile on his face fading when he saw Ragnar. "Oh. You're attending dinner?"

"I thought about allowing myself to starve to death," Ragnar replied, "but decided against it."

"Lord Ragnar." Keita slipped past her brother and latched on to Ragnar's arm. "As always you have perfect timing. Show him," she said. But when there was no reply, she released Ragnar and stalked back around her brother, and into the room. Two seconds later a flustered and embarrassed Dagmar Reinholdt stumbled into the hallway. Ragnar could only assume she'd been pushed.

"Does she not look lovely?" Keita prompted after taking his arm again.

Surprised at The Beast's new look—and knowing exactly how uncomfortable she was with it from her expression—Ragnar replied, "Lovely." He took Dagmar's hand and kissed the back of it. "Very lovely."

Dagmar gave a small laugh. "Why, thank you, my lord."

Gwenvael yanked his mate's arm back. "I swear by all the gods, I'm going to tear that Lightning's arm off and beat him to death with it."

"Don't be surly, Gwenvael," Keita chided her brother, and they began to head toward the stairs. "You don't look very handsome surly."

"I *always* look handsome," her brother argued.

"Isn't my brother adorable?" Keita asked Ragnar.

"No. Not even a little." Ragnar glanced down at where

Keita's hands clutched his upper arm. "So has the game begun?" he murmured, so only she could hear.

"And I thought you knew, my lord." She smiled. "The game is *always* being played."

It was a quiet dinner tonight. The Cadwaladr Clan had remained at the lake since the rest of the kin were beginning to show up. Keita didn't mind. It was easier to get caught up with her brothers without the distractions of her aunts, uncles, and cousins. She even had the chance to spend time with Fearghus's twins. Talwyn was proving herself to be her mother's child by challenging anyone and everyone with her training sword—*who gave her that bloody thing anyway?*— and Talan crawled into Keita's lap after he finished eating, buried his face against her bodice-covered breasts, and dropped right off to sleep.

At that point, everyone—even Ragnar—looked at Gwenvael, who quickly denied any involvement. "It wasn't me! I didn't teach him that."

"It seems more like the boy is taking after his father." Briec took his own babe from his mate's arms. Whether he was doing it to give her a rest or annoy her was anyone's guess and impossible to tell with those two. "You do seem to have a fetish, Fearghus."

Now they all looked at Annwyl. Unlike everyone else, she hadn't dressed up for dinner, but wore what she'd worn all day. She also wasn't paying attention, her gaze focused on her lap. When the silence continued, she finally lifted her head. "What?"

"You've got a book under there again, don't you?" Dagmar accused.

"What if I do?" Annwyl slammed the book onto the table. "What of it?"

"We have a guest," Dagmar snapped back.

Annwyl glanced at Ragnar and shrugged. "So?"

"Despite the fact you tried to kill his brother and cousin—"

"I told you I didn't know who they were!"

"That's a lie. You could at the very least, your royal worship-ness, give him the respect he deserves as Chief Dragonlord and representative of the Northland dragons. *Is that asking too bloody much?*"

"When I'm this bored . . . *yes!*"

"Uh . . . excuse me," Ragnar interrupted and, dying to see what he'd actually say, Keita turned in her chair to look directly at him.

"Yes, Lord Ragnar?" Dagmar asked, attempting to keep her voice calm.

"Well . . ." He reached under the table, pulled something out, and slammed it onto the table. A book. "All right. Fine. You caught me."

Dagmar's back, already painfully straight, managed to straighten more. "Ragnar!"

"I'm sorry. I was bored, too. It was all this chatter about relatives I didn't know, never intend to meet, and couldn't care less about. So I smuggled in a book."

Queen Annwyl, human ruler of all the Southland territories and one of the most feared warriors to ever live, pointed her finger across the table at Dagmar and screamed, "*Ha!*" Then she raised her fists in the air and cheered, "Yes! Yes! *Yes!*"

"Oh, shut up!" Dagmar looked at Ragnar. "You do understand, my lord, that I am *trying* to train her on basic etiquette?"

"I'm not one of your dogs, barbarian!"

"No, you're not. Because my dogs are *smarter.*"

Annwyl gasped. "Savage beast!"

Ragnar had to admit he was intrigued. He'd never seen Dagmar Reinholdt get into a verbal argument with anyone. Not one that involved actual voice raising. And he remembered clearly how she was around her sisters-in-law. A catty, vicious group of hags who took delight in making her life miserable. Too bad for them doing so was near impossible because Dagmar didn't care. She didn't care what they called her, she didn't care how they treated her, she didn't care if they liked her or not. All Dagmar cared about was the safety of her people and of her father, The Reinholdt himself.

Yet it could only mean one thing for Dagmar to unleash vicious insults and barking rage at the obviously insane human ruler who bored easily—that she was comfortable. Not comfortable in a sitting-in-a-soft-padded-chair-after-a-long-walk way. But comfortable enough around these humans and dragons to reveal her true nature and thoughts while trusting that Annwyl's insults would go no further than "barbarian" and "savage beast"—words and phrases Dagmar would only take as compliments.

Focusing on the queen, Ragnar watched her chant "Boring! Boring! Boring!" over and over again while Dagmar tried to explain how visiting nobles and dignitaries should be treated during meals. Dignitaries and nobles that he sensed did not visit too often. Obviously the human queen ran her court very differently than the Dragon Queen ran hers. In fact . . . he took a quick glance around the enormous Great Hall. Nope. Just this small group and the servants. No nobles or dignitaries anywhere in sight. For some reason the realization made Ragnar like the human queen.

Like a true warrior, Annwyl had scars. Lots of them. On her face, hands, arms. He was sure there were more under her sleeveless chainmail shirt and leather leggings. She also brandished the marks of her Claiming by Fearghus with great pride, wearing no bracelets or armbands on her forearms to hide the branded dragons she had there. She didn't seem to have the same issues as Keita did about being Claimed and he was finding it harder and harder to dismiss Annwyl as just another insane monarch.

Ragnar leaned forward a bit to look at the book she'd slammed onto the table. He studied the cover and laughed. The queen's green eyes turned to him, and he could understand how anyone's first impression of her was of someone insane. It was that scowl combined with those wild green eyes and the fact that she always seemed to be glaring through her hair. But now Ragnar was beginning to see her as he'd seen Dagmar all those years ago. The warlord's tiny daughter that he'd almost dismissed as shy and probably a little slow—until he realized she simply couldn't see more than a few feet in front of her. Once that issue had been addressed, the real Dagmar had made her very dangerous appearance.

Finding the connection with Dagmar had been easy back in those early days. He'd brought her a puppy he found. It was the equivalent of handing some a gold-filled cave.

With Annwyl it was even simpler. He held up his book. She scowled at it, read the title, and then grinned. And gods, what a grin!

"Isn't his writing amazing?" she asked, suddenly eager to talk to him when only an hour before she could barely be bothered to smile and nod in his direction.

"I agree. But I didn't enjoy his last book."

"But didn't you see? He wanted you to look deeper. He was *challenging* the reader."

"Perhaps, but his third book is still my favorite. With that amazing line: 'If I knew then—"

"—what I know now—"

And together they finished it: "—I would have killed the bitch when I had the chance!'"

They laughed until they realized everyone was staring at them.

Annwyl shrugged. "*Gorneves, Royal Spy to the Queen.*"

"A spy novel?" Dagmar asked. "You two are talking about a spy novel?"

Annwyl threw her hands up in the air. "Not *just* a spy novel!"

"It's much more than that," Ragnar argued, and when Dagmar gawked at him in disgust, he added, "I can't read deep, meaningful, thought-provoking philosophy *all* the time."

"Exactly. Sometimes you have to read about a completely amoral hero whoring and killing his way across an unnamed land in the name of the queen that he'll always love—"

"—but never have." Then both Ragnar and Annwyl sighed a little.

Dagmar briefly closed her eyes. "I think I'm going to vomit on my new gown."

"Oh, no, dear," Keita counseled. "Don't do that. Just aim to your left."

Now the Ruiner threw up his hands, as he was sitting to Dagmar's left. "Was that *really* necessary, Viper?"

Chapter Twenty-One

Morfyd packed up her equipment, put out the pit fire, and headed back to the castle. She'd spent longer than she'd originally planned casting protective spells around Garbhán Isle and her nieces and nephews, but to be honest, she hadn't been ready to go back. Not yet. Especially when she'd gotten word that Brastias would be late this eve. But she'd run out of things to do and knew she couldn't stay out by this small stream much longer.

She trudged back to the castle and, after taking a deep, fortifying breath, headed up the stairs. The dinner was already winding down, which she was quite grateful to see. Walking into the Great Hall, Morfyd smiled, nodding at her kin and their guest. She wasn't surprised to see that only one of the Northlanders had made it to dinner. The one with the broken leg—*uh, Meinhard . . . I think*—would need the night for her Magick and his natural power as a dragon to heal that damage. And she knew the other one—*Vig-something or other*—was still morbidly embarrassed about his hair. Not that she could blame him. Although she hoped the Northlanders would be far from here when Annwyl received her new helm. She'd already handed the braid of hair over to her blacksmith and told him to add it.

Morfyd rested her hands on the back of Gwenvael's chair and smiled. "How was everyone's meal?"

"Did you eat yet?" Talaith asked after everyone agreed the food was delicious. Her ability to mother seemed innate some days, as she always checked up on all of them to ensure they'd eaten, slept enough, and spent enough time with the children. "There's more than enough—unless your brother plans to unhinge his jaw again and inhale what's left."

"I was starving," Briec returned, "after a whole day of putting up with you."

"Putting up with me?" Talaith demanded. "*Putting up with me?*"

"All right," Morfyd cut in, her hands raised. "Perhaps we can table this next Talaith–Briec argument to a time when we don't have guests."

"But we were so looking forward to another one of their arguments," Gwenvael muttered.

"Quiet, snake," Talaith shot back. She pushed her chair out and stood. "I'll get you something to eat," she said to Morfyd.

"Oh, don't bother." Morfyd waved her off. "I'm not hungry."

"Are you sure? It will only take me a moment."

Actually Morfyd was starving, but she had other plans for this evening with her mate in their room, and sitting with her family, eating cold food wasn't one of them. But she wasn't about to go into any detail on that in front of her brothers and, more importantly, Chief Dragonlord of the Lightning dragons, Lord Ragnar.

"No, no. I'm fine."

And that's when Morfyd heard it. A sigh. A soft, *annoyed* sigh. Her gaze moved to where her sister sat between Lord Ragnar and Éibhear. And, as timing would have it, caught her sister at the midway point of an eye roll.

"Something wrong, sister?" Morfyd asked sweetly, already tired of Keita's presence in her home.

"No, no. I'm fine."

"Are you sure? It seemed there might be some issue? Something you'd like to discuss?"

"Sisters," Fearghus said low, the warning in his voice clear.

"It's all right, Fearghus. I'm just trying to find out if there's something I can do to make my precious baby sister's stay here at Garbhán Isle all the better. I do hate to see her unhappy."

"Unhappy? Me? Oh, no, sister! I'm deliriously happy." Keita ran her hands through her dark red locks before adding, "Although you might want to get off that sacrificial pyre . . . we need the wood."

"What does *that* mean?"

"'Oh, no, Talaith!'" Keita mocked her in an annoyingly high pitch that sounded nothing like Morfyd's voice. "'I don't want to eat. Just let me starve in my virginal white robes. You all go on without me. Honestly, I'll be fine—if I don't die first.'"

"That is not what I said, nor what I meant."

"Oh, really? Because that's what it sounded like to me, my Good Lady Dragoness of Suffering."

"Come now, sister," Morfyd lashed back. "Don't be so jealous."

"Jealous? Of *you*?"

"Of the fact that there are others who care about me, who like to take care of me. But I don't want you to worry. I know for a fact there are many who care about you. Even now I'm sure there's a bed set up in the middle of the barracks with a line of soldiers wrapped twice around the building, waiting just for *you*."

Keita stood up fast, her chair slamming hard to the floor, while Éibhear caught hold of their no-longer-sleeping nephew before he could tumble to the ground.

"Keita!" Fearghus snapped.

"What is it, sister, that really bothers you?" Keita asked, ignoring Fearghus. "The fact that I could pleasure every one of those soldiers in a way you couldn't even dream . . . or that your precious Brastias might be at the head of that line?"

To be honest, Morfyd didn't remember much after she let loose that roar.

Ragnar was so busy wondering if there was, in fact, a line of soldiers waiting for Keita that it never occurred to him to grab her. Besides, why would he have to? She was a royal, after all. Trained in the fine art of etiquette, proper poise, and all that.

Unless, that is, your sister just called you a whore in front of your entire family, which meant you had to return the favor by suggesting you're whore enough to fuck your sister's mate. Apparently the Southland dragon etiquette rules varied little from the Northland Dragon Code when it came to sibling fights.

Still, Ragnar knew he'd never have been prepared for any Northland female of his acquaintance to suddenly jump up on the table and charge across it as Keita was doing, only to meet her roaring sister in the middle, the two of them colliding. Their bodies spun as they hit, both of them grabbing on to the other's hair and pulling, screaming obscenities at each other like drunken Northland sailors on leave. No. Ragnar would never have been prepared for that—and he wasn't prepared for it now.

And what were their kin doing? Nothing. They mostly looked bored while the Blue just kept saying, "We have to do something!" But he wasn't actually doing "something." Even the human queen had gone back to her book. Only Dagmar seemed shocked, her hand over her open mouth, her eyes wide behind her spectacles.

Realizing none of Keita's kin were going to do anything to stop this, Ragnar stood and climbed up onto the table.

"You don't want to get into the middle of this," Fearghus,

the queen's eldest and seemingly most useless offspring, warned. He'd quickly retrieved his wandering children and was holding them securely on his lap, but that was all he seemed in the mood to do.

Yet Ragnar didn't *want* to get in the middle of this, but the Fire Breathers had left him little choice.

He had just gotten his arms around Keita's waist when a human male rushed in from another exit. "Damn," he muttered before he dropped his shield and ax and joined Ragnar on the table. He took firm hold of Princess Morfyd, and, together, they pulled the two royals apart. Too bad the females still had each other by the hair.

"Let her go, Keita."

Keita's response was to scream. She didn't scream words, just screamed. It was a little disconcerting.

"Morfyd! Please!" the human practically begged. But she wasn't much better than her sister.

Desperate, Ragnar pulled one arm away from Keita's waist and touched her hand. He unleashed the lightest of lightning bolts, but it was enough. The bolt shot through her fingers and into her sister's hair, directly into her scalp. They both screeched and released the other, allowing the two males to pull them apart.

"Whore!" Princess Morfyd screamed.

"Frigid cow!" Keita screeched. Then one slapped the other, and the other slapped the first and Ragnar had had enough! He stepped down from the table and carried Keita from the Great Hall and out into the cool night.

Brastias took Morfyd into their room and closed the door. He placed her on the bed, returned to the door, and locked it, then went back to their bed and sat down beside her. She had her elbows resting on her knees and her face buried in her hands.

"The door's locked," he said.

"You sure?"

"Positive."

Then Morfyd burst into tears, and Brastias pulled her into his arms, letting her cry herself out.

Ragnar placed Keita down, and she immediately began to head back toward the castle. "Ungrateful, spiteful—"

He caught her arm and pulled her back. "Let it go."

"Let it go? I'll let nothing go including my righteous disdain!"

And Ragnar honestly couldn't help it when he started to laugh.

"I'm sorry!" he lied, grabbing firm hold of the stalking-away royal. "I am so sorry."

"You are not sorry! You agree with her, I'm sure. Let's take the whore down a peg."

"Don't tie me into this fight with your sister. This is between the two of you. I'm merely an innocent bystander." Ragnar sat down on a bench and pulled Keita until she flopped down beside him.

"Miserable old cow," she muttered.

"Now, now. Don't be so hard on yourself."

Her small fist jammed into his arm.

"She always does this, you know," Keita said. "She starts a fight with me."

"*She* started the fight?"

Keita glared at him. "Are you saying that *I* started the fight?"

"I'm saying that to my eyes both of you are equally guilty."

"I should have known you'd side with her."

"I side with no one."

"Liar!" She stood and began to untie the bodice of her dress.

"What are you doing?"

"Getting away from all of you. I knew I should never have returned."

"Keita, don't go." If nothing else, don't leave him here alone.

"I'll not stay where I'm not wanted."

"And who said that? Your brothers *and* their mates seemed quite happy you've come back."

"Too bad!" She practically tore the dress off her body before flinging it at Ragnar. He had yet to understand exactly what he'd done to earn her rage as well.

"Where are you going?"

She stormed naked to the middle of the courtyard and shifted to her natural form. "Away."

"But what about—" She flew off, and Ragnar sighed out, "The plan?"

He gazed down at the dress in his hand. It had been quite pretty on her.

"That color will bring out your eyes," the foreign dragon said from behind him, making Ragnar jump a little.

"Where the battle-fuck did you come from?"

"Everywhere. Nowhere." Ren moved his hand through the air. "I am one with all that is around us. The land, the sea, the—"

"You smell like pussy."

Ren's hand dropped, and he sat in the spot on the bench Keita had left. "I smell like several pussies actually, but thanks for noticing." He grinned, motioned to the dress. "Keita flounce off?"

"You could say that."

"Must have been her sister, yes?"

Ragnar answered by sighing again.

"Don't let it bother you. That's what they do."

"I'm not used to it. Northland females simply don't . . . act that way."

"He's right." Dagmar sat down on the other side of Ragnar.

"We don't act that way. Instead, we're quietly catty, vindictive, and vicious. But I will say this . . . if I thought I could pay both sisters to join forces and go to my father's fortress to start a fight like the one I just witnessed with my sisters-in-law, I would." Dagmar clenched her hands together. "I'd give up *everything* to make that happen."

Ren laughed while Ragnar scratched his head and said, "This has been such a long day."

Keita debated heading to Fearghus's cave in the middle of Dark Glen. There she had the option of seething by herself or teasing some of the guards who protected the cave at all times since the birth of the twins. Although when she thought about it, she wasn't really in the mood to tease, flirt, or fuck anyone. She was, however, in the mood to punch her sister in the face. *That* she'd like to do.

The bitch! The judgmental, callous bitch!

Deciding that going to her brother's cave was as good a plan as any, Keita tilted her wings and began to loop around toward Dark Glen. But when she caught sight of a pit fire on one of the hills, she adjusted her flight pattern and headed over. It was late, and she wanted to make sure everything was safe so close to her nieces and nephew. Yet when she took a good look, she immediately dived down, landing hard on her talons, the ground shaking beneath her claws. And as soon as she shook her hair off her face, a chorus of female voices cheered, "Keita!"

She moved closer, shifting to human so she could take the bottle of wine held out by one of her cousins and a blanket from one of her aunts.

"Heard you were back, little miss," said her Aunt Bradana, one of Bercelak's much older sisters. "You couldn't come and visit until now?" Bradana's voice was like wagon wheels over stone due, in part, to where her throat had been cut during a brutal battle nearly four centuries ago.

"Don't question me, aunt," Keita said, making sure to sound as imperious as possible. "I've had many royal things to do the last day involving cranky Lightnings and pouting brothers and gods-damn, evil bitch sisters!"

Grinning, all the females said, "Morfyd."

After a healthy gulp of wine, Keita said, "Is it my fault she's frigid? Is it my fault she could only find a human male who would tolerate all that piousness? Is it my fault she's a bitter, bitter hag?"

"Yes, it is," said one cousin.

"Shut up!" Keita sat down hard on the ground, her female kin laughing around her while she gulped several more mouthfuls of wine before handing the bottle off to someone else. "And can I just say I'm sick of everyone? Even you lot, and I haven't seen most of you in ages. I should have stayed away."

"You can't forget your family, girl." One of Bradana's favorite sayings and a direct quote from Keita's grandfather Ailean. "Because no matter where you go or what you do, they'll always be your kin."

"Kind of like a disease you can't get rid of," another cousin tossed in.

"Oy." Bradana's oldest daughter, Rhona, pointed at Keita. "Last I heard, you were training at Anubail Mountain with uh, Uncle Cadan's oldest girl."

"Elestren," another aunt offered.

Keita rubbed her nose. "Right. That didn't work out so well for me."

"Too much work for you, princess?" Rhona teased, already a little bit drunk. Not surprising when Keita did a quick count of the number of empty wine bottles tossed off to the side. "We all know how you royals don't like to do much."

"They wanted me up at the break of dawn . . . to *exercise*. Why was that necessary? What was wrong with mid-afternoon? Or early evening? And all right, perhaps swords, battle axes, warhammers, and long axes were not quite right for my particular . . . skill level. I didn't go there to learn how to fight with weapons anyway. I leave that amazing ability to you lovely She-dragons since you all seem to have a natural affinity for such things."

Another cousin shook her head. "No wonder your eyes are brown, you're so full of—"

"But apparently my skills were so lacking that I was summarily dismissed by one and all, which seems rather unfair. I worked so hard for days . . . nearly a whole week even! And they were ready to toss me out because they felt I wasn't learning fast enough."

"All very true." Bradana nodded in agreement and announced between sips, "But they really kicked you out because you took Elestren's eye."

Except for the crackling pit fire, all fell silent. Even the night animals. And all her cousins and aunts gawked at her while Bradana continued to drink from her own bottle of wine and chuckle.

"I did not take her eye," Keita gritted out. "Not on purpose. It was self-defense." Keita reached over several of her female kin to snatch the bottle back from another of the aunts. "And even though I told them all it was self-defense, they still banned me from Anubail for my lifetime because—and this is according to those Royal Guard Council bastards—I don't know or understand the rules of engagement, whatever the ass fuck that means."

"Accident or not," Bradana warned, "watch yourself with that Elestren, luv. She's mean and not one for forgiving."

"I can handle her," Keita said again.

"In other words you're completely avoiding her, eh?" Rhona asked.

"Perhaps a little," Keita muttered, taking another sip. Finally feeling the light buzzing in her head that came with most drinks manufactured by her father's side of the family, she nearly yelled, "And I'll have you know I sent that cranky twat an array of beautiful eye patches in a variety of colors so she could wear them for any occasion!"

When she found all the females still staring at her, Keita asked, "What?"

Rhona, clearly fighting a smile, glanced at all the cousins and aunts, before leaning forward and asking, "You sent her *eye patches*?"

"*I was being nice!*"

Chapter Twenty-Two

After checking on his cousin—sleeping—and his brother—brooding—Ragnar spent a little time in his own room reading a few letters he'd taken with him from the Northlands but hadn't had the time to review. Mostly from the commanders of different troops and units. And although the letters and missives were short, each filled him with growing unease until he was sure that Queen Rhiannon had been right. Whatever was going on in the Southlands greatly involved the Northlanders.

He also knew he wouldn't be falling asleep anytime soon. He decided he needed a walk to help clear his head, but first he returned to his brother—still brooding—and gave him the letters.

"Read them."

"All right."

"Then, tomorrow, start talking to people."

"About what?"

"Anything. Any rumors about enemies, wars. I don't care." His brother had a way with locals and servants that allowed him to find out all sorts of things. And Ragnar needed a sense of things among the Southland humans. As much as dragons often tried to pretend humans were no more than an additional food source, Ragnar knew that what happened in their world often directly affected what happened among the dragons. "Fill me in later."

With that taken care of, Ragnar headed out of his room, down the two flights of stairs, and through the Great Hall. There were lakes and streams all over this territory, and he'd find a nice, calm one that would help him think and figure out what he should do next.

But before he could even get down the steps, something tumbled past him. Whatever it was landed hard in the middle of the stairs, and Ragnar stepped in closer to get a good look.

"Keita!" He crouched beside her. She was still human and only wore a blanket. She could easily have been killed, coming from that height.

Carefully Ragnar turned her over. Her nose was bleeding, and she wore what appeared to be a homemade eye patch. Two, actually. One over each eye. But she was breathing, her heart still beating.

"Keita? Can you hear me?"

Ragnar pulled the blanket off, fighting desperately to ignore the beauty of the human body beneath, instead focusing on any damage she might have. He ran his hands over her ribs to her hips. He didn't find anything broken, but she did have a nasty bump on her forehead, and again . . . the eye patches.

He was reaching for them, about to remove them, when Keita coughed. Ragnar pulled back. "Gods of thunder, how much have you been drinking?"

Keita held up four fingers and slurred, "Two ales."

"You all right, cousin?" a dragoness yelled-slurred from above.

Keita's four fingers turned into a thumbs-up aimed at the sky.

"Good. And tonight at dinner you should introduce us to your handsome friend."

"Get your own Lightning!" Keita yelled back. "There are two more, and they're not half bad."

"Selfish cow!"

"Callous vipers!"

The laughter faded with the She-dragons heading off, and Ragnar was left with a drunk, naked royal.

Ragnar leaned over her. "Keita—"

His next words were cut off when Keita's hands slammed into his face. "I'm blind!" she cried, her hands grasping. "I cannot see! Why have the gods cursed me so?"

"Quiet! You'll wake everyone." He pushed her arms down and yanked the eye patches off.

"Oh." Blinking several times, she finally focused on Ragnar. "Hello, Éibhear."

Now he was insulted. "I'm Ragnar, you twit."

"What are you doing with my sister?" the blue royal asked from behind him.

Knowing how this must look, but not really caring, "I was about to see how much I could get for her on the slave barges. She's pretty enough, I guess."

"*You guess?*" Keita demanded. "And you," she said to her brother, "where the hells have you been anyway?"

The Blue pointed off to town. "At the pub."

"Well, while you were getting your sword polished by some bar sluts, brother, our cousins were forcing me to drink endlessly. For hours."

"Forcing you, Keita? Really?"

"What does that mean?"

"Nothing." He reached for his sister. "I'll take her back to her room."

"No, you will not." Keita pointed at Ragnar. "He will."

"Must I?"

"Yes, barbarian, you must." She held her arms out. "Carry me."

"Can't I just drag you by your leg?"

"When I vomit up whatever's in my stomach, I will aim it right at your face."

"How enticing." Ragnar picked Keita up in his arms. "I've got her." Ragnar started to walk off, away from the castle. But after a few feet, he stopped and without even looking at the young dragon warned, "And don't glare at me, boy."

"Yeah!" Keita yelled to no one in particular before she passed out completely.

Keita woke up with the night sky above her and the sound of running water right by her.

It was a lovely view, but she couldn't enjoy it. Instead she flipped over and quickly crawled to the nearest bush so she could vomit up what was left of all that damn wine!

It wasn't until the fourth or fifth heave, her arms braced, her palms flat on the ground, that she felt a hand against her back, pressing through the shirt someone had put on her while another hand held her hair back.

"Feel better?" a low voice asked.

She tensed, forcing herself to recall the last few hours. She didn't *think* she'd done anything that would require her to soothe some male's damaged ego. Perhaps because she'd thankfully left drunken trysts behind a century and a half ago. She always hated waking up to soft smiles, flowers, and first meal in bed with a male whose name she couldn't even remember.

Needy bastards.

"My nose . . ."

"Broken."

She grasped the hand held out for her and let Ragnar help her up. Slowly, they walked to the stream. Keita kneeled down and took a few moments to rinse out her mouth. After that, she girded her loins as any good royal knows how to do, then stuck her entire head into the freezing cold water.

When her face was numb, she sat back up, flipping her wet hair off her face. "Now."

Ragnar crouched in front of her, held her nose between two fingers of each hand, and jerked it back into place. Keita closed her eyes and let out a shuddering breath.

"Thank you." She stood but just as quickly sat down again, Ragnar's arms catching her before her ass could hit the ground.

"Close your eyes," Ragnar murmured. He placed his hand on her forehead, the palm pressed against her skin, his fingers gently massaging her scalp. She heard him chant softly, felt his breath brush her lips. And, in moments, her pain eased off.

His hand slid away, and he studied her closely. "Feel better?"

"Much. Thank you," she said again.

"You're welcome." He sat down beside her.

"Why didn't you do that for your cousin after Annwyl broke his leg?"

He smiled a little. "Healing is a skill for females."

"Is that your opinion or theirs?"

"It's not mine, but I've never seen the point of enduring excruciating suffering. Then again, my father always referred to me as the 'soft one.'"

"Your father . . . not the brightest dragon I've known. I was there only two weeks, and I had him convinced to gut out an entire section of his mountain for me."

Ragnar peered at her, frowning a little. "Is *that* what happened to Olgeir Mountain?"

"Uh-huh. I told him I couldn't live in an undecorated cavern like some bat. How could I ever be happy?"

"We store armor in there now. How did you convince him?"

"It was easy. Told him what he wanted to hear, acted like he wanted me to act, flattered him, charmed him—took me three days. And that was only because I spent the first day there sobbing softly and wringing my claws."

"You weren't scared at all, were you?"

Keita gave a small shake of her head. "When they didn't take my wing right away . . ." She smiled. "Your brothers and cousins weren't too bad. A little thick. In the head, I mean." She winced. "Thick in the head on their *shoulders*, I mean."

"I understood your first reference." Ragnar grabbed her hand gently in his, lifted it, and studied it for a long moment. After a time, he said, "Can I tell you something?"

"You watched me vomit for ten minutes and shoved my broken nose back into place so I can breathe again. I'm of the mind you can tell me anything."

"I fear your mother may be right. About the Irons . . . about my cousin Styrbjörn. I think the Irons are planning to strike the Southlands through Northland territories."

"Why would they do that?"

"Because it would be foolish to come through the Western Mountains. There's no place to hide. No way to craft battle plans that allow for any flexibility in attack. Once they'd come over the Western Mountains it would be a head-to-head fight with the Southlanders. A fight even my father wouldn't risk. A fight the Irons already lost once before."

"They could go south and cut through the Desert Lands."

"And deal with the Sand dragons? No one's that fool-hardy."

"Then the north it is."

He took in a breath. "I realized they could come up by the Borderlands that dissect the Northlands and the Ice Lands from each other. Cut through the Mountains of My Mother's Misery and—"

Keita placed her free hand on Ragnar's knee. "I'm sorry but . . . the Mountains of My Mother's Misery? That's the actual name?"

Appearing more embarrassed than she'd seen him before,

Ragnar gave a small shrug. "Naming things . . . not our strong suit in the Northlands."

"I see that now. So you think the Ice Land dragons will help?"

"There are no Ice Land dragons. There are the Snow dragons, who consider the Northlands a hot jungle of heat and misery. Somehow I doubt they'd be invading anytime soon."

"Oh."

"And then there are the Eternal Ones. The immortals who chose eternal life over family. There are only a handful of them, but they are dangerous."

"Do you think they'll help the Sovereigns?"

"They hate everyone. Eternal life has not made them happy from what I've heard and read. But if they decide to aid Thracius, as well, they would be a definite problem—they spew acid."

"Ew." That sounded so unpleasant, Keita thought no more about it. "So you really think your cousin . . ."

"Styrbjörn."

"Yes, Styrbjörn. You think he would really help the Irons?"

"No, Keita. I think he already has."

Keita, so surprised by his admission, tried to pull her hand away, but Ragnar was in no mood to release her. He was trusting her at this moment. Trusting her more than he'd trusted anyone before, except for his brother and cousin.

When he didn't release her hand, she relaxed and asked, "What do you mean he already has?"

"My commanders near the Borderlands believe Styrbjörn had a small battalion of Irons escorted through the territory. A dragoness was with them, and much coin must have been exchanged for them to have not tried to take her."

"Styrbjörn would betray his own for the Sovereigns?"

"It's said that the closer one gets to the Ice Lands, the more one realizes that coin can buy you much. Especially loyalty."

She squeezed his fingers with her own. "Where was this battalion taken?"

"As far as the Southland borders. After that—my commanders don't know."

"Fuck me," she said in a low voice.

Ragnar gazed at the stream. "I worry there may not be time to wait for those who will betray your mother, and the throne, to come to us."

Hating that he had to do this but knowing he had no choice, he raised his gaze to Keita's.

Her smile was sweet. "It's all right, Ragnar. I've been thinking the same thing. But mostly because after my fight with Morfyd, I'm more than ready to get this over with so I can flee her judgmental glare."

"Doing this will be dangerous, Keita. To let others know you knew Esyld's whereabouts and purposely didn't tell your mother . . . I mean, Rhiannon was right after all. You *were* breaking Southland law, and that is dangerous."

"Good games are always dangerous."

"This is hardly a game anymore. Especially when it can turn your kin against you."

"My kin will shake their heads in disgust and say, 'That Keita. She hasn't got a bit of sense in her head.' And mother already knows. She was my biggest threat."

"Your brothers?"

"Fearghus and Briec will yell and snarl and spit fire. . . . That's what they do. But they'd never harm me. And Gwenvael has known Esyld's location for two years now. Besides, if we can lure out the ones who would betray the throne— then it's worth the risk. Not to mention that all this sitting around, *waiting* for something to happen . . ."

"I know. Boring."

"Bloody boring. And who knows? If we time this right, we

can get this resolved in no time and once the feast is over, you and your kin can head back to the north and I can head off . . . anywhere."

"Is there no place you call home?"

"The *world* is my home."

"Your home is huge."

"I need space." She rubbed his shoulder with her free hand. "Good. You're laughing."

"Laughing or not, I'll not leave your side until this is done."

"Then you best take me back so you can be caught sneaking out of my room when the two suns rise."

"And why is that necessary again?"

"Because it'll appear much more devious if it looks like we're hiding our relationship. Something I never do. Everyone will wonder why I'm hiding it this time. Add in the truth about Esyld, and it'll look like a plot against my mother."

And that's what worried him. Terrified him. Not for himself, for Keita. "This is dangerous."

"Oh, don't worry. I won't allow you to fall in love with me if that's your worry."

"It's not. I'm talking about the danger to you when the truth comes out."

"Come, come now," she teased. "We both know that what you're afraid of is falling in love with me. And you should be. I am *astounding*."

"You're something, all right."

She studied him for a moment, then said, "Here, we'll make a pact."

"What kind of pact? A you-won't-let-me-fall-in-love-with-you pact?"

"No. You'll just have to suffer your broken heart when I go away—and I will go away."

"Then what?"

"That until this is over, we're loyal to each other."

"Meaning what exactly?"

"That we'll do nothing tricky to betray the other. We're on the same side with this. I do trust you, but when it's my life in play . . ."

"I understand and always like extra precautions myself. But I will never betray you, Keita." And he knew he meant every word of that.

"Then you won't mind committing yourself to me."

"Not at all." But when she lifted her hand to her mouth, palm up, Ragnar quickly added, "But if you spit in your palm, I'm not shaking it."

Her hand dropped. "So picky." She studied the ground around them, then stretched her body over his lap and dug into his travel bag.

The shirt he'd put on her had ridden up to her waist and he had what could only be called the most adorable ass of all time staring him in the face . . . wiggling. "What are you doing?"

She shimmied off his lap, which he didn't appreciate at all because he was appreciating it too much, and opened her hand. "What are these?" she asked.

"Rune stones. I use them for spells and seeing possible futures."

"Do they mean much to you?"

"They're my mother's."

"Then they mean much to you." She examined them closely and finally chose one. She handed him the rest and held the one she'd picked in the middle of her palm. Seeing the one Keita chose, Ragnar couldn't help smirking a little.

"What?"

"Nothing."

"It's cursed or something, isn't it?"

"Of course not."

"Then what's that look on your face?"

"I'm just amused by your choice."

"Because it's cursed?"

"No. It's the Fire Rune Stone. It represents heat and power."

She smiled, examined it.

"And sex."

Her smile grew into a leer.

"And love."

Her leer turned into a sneer. "Must you ruin everything?"

She started to toss it away, but he caught hold of her hand with both of his, the stone trapped between them.

"Keita the Red," he said, using the name she'd been given at hatching. "I swear on the power of this stone and in the name of my ancestors never to betray you in word or deed or in my heart."

Her entire face scrunched in disgust. "*Must* you go that far?"

"Now your turn, princess."

"Ragnar the . . ."

"Fourteenth."

Her eyes grew wide. "Seriously?"

"And I'm a middle offspring."

"Och! That's enough. I'll hear no more." She shuddered. "Ragnar the Fourteenth, I swear on the power of this stone and in the name of my ancestors never to betray you in word or deed."

"Or in your heart."

"I'm not going that far."

"In your heart," he pushed, trying not to laugh.

"All right! Fine! Or in my heart."

As soon as she snapped the last word at him, power radiated from the stone, through their hands, and straight through them like a hard gust of wind, blowing their hair back.

Keita looked around before glaring at him. "What was that?"

"I have no idea."

"You must have an idea. You're a mage."

"Yes, but that's never happened before when *I* used these."

"You've cursed me, haven't you?"

"What is your obsession with curses?"

"That isn't an answer."

"No. I didn't curse you."

"Better not have."

"Or what?"

"Trust me, warlord. As much as I know how to give plea-sure, I also know how to take it away. Now"—she stood, man-aging to look regal in his shirt—"let's get back so you can be caught sneaking out of my room in the morning."

Ragnar cleared his throat, raised a brow.

"What?"

He made his brow go a little higher.

"Oh, fine!" She slapped the rune into his hand.

"You Southlanders are such thieves."

"If you didn't want me to have it, you shouldn't have let me take it out of your bag."

"You're blaming me for your thievery?"

"Yes!" She stormed off, yelling over her shoulder, "Well come on! I don't have all bloody night! And stop staring at my ass!"

"It's almost too large to miss." And he did think he quietly muttered that remark until that ball of flame nearly took his damn head off.

Chapter Twenty-Three

Keita woke up and wondered who'd buried her alive. Probably Gwenvael. *Bastard*. Then she realized that she'd been buried under something breathing.

The Lightning. That's right. He'd taken care of her last night. Even with the vomiting and broken nose. *Damn aunts and their damn homemade ale*.

It was odd. She was really starting to like Ragnar. Despite the fact her mother seemed to like him as well and her sister seemed to respect him.

She chuckled a little to herself, and the big body lying on top of her moved, rolled off, and stretched.

She turned on her side and, lowering her voice to a husky purr, said, "Good morn to you, Lord Ragnar."

His smile was sleepy, his dark purple hair, out of its plait, a wild mane around his face.

Then he fully woke and just looked panicked.

Keita fell back on the bed, snickering.

"How did I get in your bed?"

"I asked nicely, and you agreed."

He lifted the fur over his body. "And why am I naked?"

"You ask many questions in the morning. Are you sure that's wise when you're dealing with me?"

"Good point." He sat up, yawned. "How do you feel?" he asked.

"Surprisingly well, considering." She pressed her hand to his shoulder. "And thank you for last night."

He studied the hand touching him, then her face. "You're more than welcome."

"Gods," she said, tossing the fur off her body. "You have such a voice so early in the morning."

"Do I?"

"Aye. The kind that can get me into all sorts of trouble if I'm not careful." Keita walked over to her dresser and swiped up the small jar that had been placed there the evening before. She'd noticed it when they'd first walked in after their time by the stream, but had been too tired to deal with it. "Let's get this done, shall we? So your torment can end."

"What an interesting way you have of suggesting sex," he noted dryly. "It makes me all tingly."

Keita returned to the bed and crawled onto Ragnar's lap, a fur the only thing separating Keita's bare ass from the warlord's bare cock. "I'm not talking about bedding you. At least . . . not yet." She held up the jar. "The antidote."

"Thank the gods."

She held up a dagger, enjoying the way Ragnar's eyes grew wide in panic. "Now just lie still."

He caught hold of the hand holding the blade. "Isn't there another way?"

"Tragically for you, no."

"Then let me do it."

"Don't be such a hatchling. I know what I'm doing."

"I'm sure you do." He wrestled the dagger from her. "But that doesn't make me any less wary."

Ragnar pressed the blade to the wound on his chest and stopped, blue eyes glaring at her. "And stop grinding against my cock."

"Oh. I didn't realize I'd been doing that."

"Liar." She was definitely a liar.

With a quick flick, he opened up the old wound and Keita slathered on a healthy amount of the ointment, making sure much of it got inside the opening, as well as covering the entire area.

"Done."

Ragnar nodded and with a chant, re-closed the wound, the ointment seeping into his skin.

Using a rag, Keita cleaned up the small amount of blood, her hands, and the dagger. "That should do it," she said, sliding off his waist and placing everything back on the dresser.

"I hope so. This damn thing has driven me mad for two bloody years."

"You poor thing you."

"I heard absolutely *no* remorse in that statement."

She walked around the bed and stretched out beside him once more. "That's because there was no remorse in that statement."

The pair stared at each other for a long moment before Ragnar shook his head and threw his legs over the edge of the bed. "I should go."

"All right."

Ragnar stood, using the fur to cover the front of him. Keita was just reaching over to palm the warlord's amazing-looking ass when she heard one of the servants at the door with the hot water for her morning bath. Instead of his ass, Keita grabbed hold of the fur Ragnar held and yanked it away at the same moment the servant walked in, took one look at the naked warlord, and quickly walked out again, closing the door.

Keita grinned at the glowering—*and gods! Is he blushing?*—dragon.

"And so it begins, my lord."

Annwyl wished she could say she was up just before the two suns rose because she was simply an early riser. But anyone who knew her, knew what a lie that would be. Instead, she was up and dressed for training because she'd had that nightmare again. The nightmare she told very few about because she didn't know if the dream was caused by a general sense of fear for her babes or because she'd suddenly started having prophecies. She hadn't even told Fearghus. How could she, after he'd been through so much? She still caught him looking at her in that way that told her he could still remember her on her death bed after the children were born. And that he feared he'd find her there again. No, she wouldn't put him through any more. Not when there was absolutely nothing he could do about it. And she knew, in her heart, there was nothing he could do.

Anyway, the bottom line was she couldn't sleep. So she'd left her warm bed—and her even warmer mate—and headed out. She carefully and quietly closed the door behind her and went to the room next door. She stepped in and smiled at the babe already awake and standing tall in her crib.

"How's my little Rhianwen this morning?" Annwyl asked her niece. She reached into the crib and picked the babe up. "You can't sleep either, little one? Unlike your cousins?" Annwyl glanced over at her snoring twins. They slept in separate beds these days out of necessity. Too many times Annwyl had walked in to full-on fist fights between the pair when they'd shared a crib. And the last time she'd tried to separate them, her son had ducked and her daughter had nailed Annwyl with a right cross that left bells ringing in her head. After that, the little nightmares were separated for good.

They'd also tried to put Rhianwen in her own room, but all three of the babes had screamed and cried until she was returned. Since then none of the adults had bothered to separate them.

A tiny hand reached up and stroked Annwyl's cheek. "Don't worry," Annwyl told that concerned little face that broke her heart on the best of days. "I'll be fine. You needn't worry so." But she knew Talaith and Briec's little girl did worry. There was something about her that practically screamed, "I worry for everyone!"

"We have to teach you to smile, little one," Annwyl said before placing her back in her crib. "Your father is getting impossible about it." She pulled the blanket around the babe and leaned in, kissing her head. "Get some more sleep."

Annwyl faced her own children. Her son, smirking even while he slept, and her daughter, who looked so much like Fearghus it made Annwyl's heart ache. She knew most mothers would make sure to be there when their children woke up. They'd make sure that they fed them each and every morning and helped them learn all sorts of new things. That's what most mothers would do.

But, instead, Annwyl kissed both their sleeping heads and, with her two swords tied to her back, stepped away from their beds. Because instead of doing all those wonderful things for her children, she'd train. She'd train until her muscles ached and her body felt drained. She'd train until she bled from accidental wounds and her head throbbed from accidental blows. She'd train until she knew that no matter what horrors came for her children, she could take them all on. That she could fight until nothing was left standing but her and her babes.

Fighting her urge to feel guilty, Annwyl faced the door but immediately stopped.

"Morfyd? What are you doing in here?"

Morfyd yawned and stretched her arms over her head. "Just watching them. It's nothing."

"Where's the new nanny?"

"Annwyl—"

"Where is she?"

"Gone."

"Why? What happened?"

"Does it matter?"

"The fact that we can't keep a bloody nanny in this place makes it matter."

"I'll figure something out."

"Fearghus doesn't want any dragons but blood. He doesn't trust the others," Annwyl reminded her.

"I know."

"And the females of your line aren't exactly nanny material."

"I have sent messages out to a few of my younger cousins who have no designs to be warriors and—"

"If they're too young, Fearghus is not going to like that either."

"I'll handle Fearghus." Morfyd motioned to the door. "Go. Get in some training."

Seeing no point in arguing with her, Annwyl walked out the door and quietly closed it. Then she stomped away from the room. Before she reached the stairs, another bedroom door opened and Dagmar stepped out. She caught Annwyl's arm.

"What's wrong?"

"We lost another nanny, didn't we?" Annwyl looked past Dagmar at the naked male stretched out, face down, on the bed in the room behind her, long golden hair reaching to the floor. "How do you listen to that noise?"

Dagmar closed the door, but it only toned down some of the snoring. "It's amazing what one tolerates for love."

"I don't think I could tolerate that for anything."

"Probably not. But what I will ask you to do is leave the nanny situation to me and Morfyd."

"She's trying to get one of her younger cousins to do it. Fearghus is not going to—"

"What part of 'we'll handle it' are you not grasping, my lady?"

"Don't get huffy with me, barbarian. It's my little nightmares that are scaring off the townsfolk."

"They are lively, fun-loving children who merely need a good, solid, and loyal nanny to help raise them."

"You mean as opposed to demons sent from the underworld who need a good solid exorcism?"

"Must you be this way?"

"I don't know how else to be."

"Annwyl, just trust me, would—" A door opened behind Annwyl, and Dagmar's eyes grew wide behind the little round pieces of glass she wore.

One hand reaching for her sword, Annwyl spun to face whatever was behind her. But her hand fell away, and her mouth fell open.

The purple-haired dragon stood in Keita's bedroom doorway, his shirt thrown over his shoulder, his hand on the door handle, his gaze fixed on Dagmar's.

"Ragnar?" Dagmar whispered. Annwyl would assume so, but she couldn't tell one purple-haired bastard from another. They all looked alike to her. Just one more head begging to be lopped off.

"Uh . . . Lady Dagmar."

The poor thing looked caught, ready to spring back into the room. But Keita yanked the door open wide. She wore only a fur around her body, her normally smooth and flowing dark red hair a mass of uncombed curls and knots.

"You forgot this." Keita put a travel bag in the dragon's hands and went up on her toes, kissing his cheek. "I'll see you later," she murmured. "Now go."

"Keita . . ."

"What?"

Ragnar motioned to Annwyl and Dagmar, and Keita glanced over. Instead of grinning, as she had done a few years back when Annwyl had caught Danelin, Brastias's second in command, trying to sneak out of Keita's room, the She-dragon's eyes grew wide. She looked almost panicked.

Strange, since Annwyl couldn't remember a time Keita had panicked over anything.

"Uh . . . Annwyl. Dagmar. Good morn to you both." Her smile was forced, brittle. She nudged Ragnar, and, reluctantly, he walked off.

Once he was gone, Keita whispered, "You won't tell anyone . . . about that . . . will you?"

Now Annwyl was truly confused because Keita usually suggested, "Make sure to give all the details to my sister. Let me know if you need drawings!"

Was she really hiding this? And if she was . . . why?

"We won't tell," Annwyl said, since she had her own secrets.

"Thank you." Then Keita slipped back into her room and closed the door.

"Is no one safe from that female?" Dagmar asked.

Annwyl shrugged since she had no answer and left Dagmar staring at Keita's closed doorway. She headed down to the Great Hall where she found food already out and the other two Northland dragons eating at the table.

She walked over and dropped into a chair across from them. She said nothing until she'd filled her own plate and begun to eat. Then she asked, "Did you both sleep well?"

They nodded while they kept eating. A few years ago she might have been insulted by that. But after the Northland battle in which she'd fought beside the mighty Reinholdt and his sons, she knew this to be the way of things when Northland warriors ate.

"And how's your leg, uh . . ."

"Meinhard, my lady," one of them answered while still managing to chew his food. If she was going to remember their names, she'd have to find something distinctive about them, especially since the other one's hair would eventually grow back.

"Call me Annwyl."

"As you like."

"And your leg?" she prompted.

"Better. Healed up nice during the night."

"That's perfect." She loved how dragons could heal quickly with a little help from a witch or mage. "I was going to get some training in—you both can train with me."

They paused in their feeding and lifted their heads. Just like two oxen at a watering hole that had sniffed out a predator nearby.

What could Annwyl say? They weren't too far off.

"I'm not sure that's such a good idea, *Queen* Annwyl," the one with short hair answered, and Annwyl had to laugh. She loathed when people used that stupid title, but she knew he was doing it for one simple reason: to point out that perhaps fighting with a queen who'd already tried to take his head might not be the smartest decision. Normally he'd be right, but they were under Éibhear's protection and their brother was—secretly at least—fucking Keita. So unless Annwyl heard otherwise, she wouldn't bother killing them.

"We'll use the training ring right around the corner of this building. And I promise I'll not hold anything that happens in the ring against either of you, your brother, or your people."

"Why us?" the other ox asked. He bore a scar from his hairline to below his eye. It had faded with time, but it was clear enough to remind her that "eye scar" was Meinhard, meaning the other was . . . uh . . . *shit. What's his bloody name again?*

Rather than ask him that—she'd tried to take his head, but she couldn't be bothered to remember his name . . . tacky—she admitted, "No one else will train with me these days. Even the Southland dragons. Unless, of course, Northland dragons are too afraid of me to take the risk as well . . ."

Meinhard sneered around his food while the other's purple brows peaked.

Knowing how to close this deal, she added, "Besides, wouldn't you like a chance to get even over your hair?"

When she saw fang, she knew she had them both.

Keita skipped down the stairs to the Great Hall and hopped off the last step. So far only Gwenvael, Dagmar, Morfyd, and Talaith had made it down to breakfast. Keita, making sure her smile was exceedingly happy and bright, threw her arms wide, and said with no small amount of cheer, "Good morn, my lovely family!"

"You're fucking Ragnar the Cunning?" Gwenvael barked at her.

Keita dropped her arms to her sides and glared at Dagmar, hoping to look appropriately betrayed. "You promised me you wouldn't say anything."

Gwenvael refocused his scowl onto his mate. "You knew?"

"I know lots of things."

"*You knew?*"

"Don't yell at me, Defiler."

Keita was surprised the warlord's daughter hadn't said anything. But this was good. The rumor was spreading even faster than she'd thought it would, and Dagmar apparently could be trusted. *Excellent.*

"Is it beyond you"—Morfyd pushed her chair back and stood, stalking around the table—"to keep your legs closed, sister?"

"Beyond me? No. But why would I? He's gorgeous."

"He's a Lightning," Gwenvael reminded her. And Keita had to admit she was a little shocked. Of those she'd thought would be upset about this, she'd never imagined it would be Gwenvael. Who she fucked was not something her golden brother had ever cared much about unless a problem arose.

"Yes. He is. And so were those slags you fucked during the war that got you the name Defiler."

"It's *Ruiner*! And I never tried to hide what I'd done. Why are you?"

"I don't have time for this." Keita headed toward the Great Hall doors, which stood open, giving her a glimpse of early-morning freedom. But just as she stepped outside, Gwenvael caught her arm and swung her around.

At least, she *thought* it was Gwenvael. Gwenvael, who was much taller than Keita, so that when she swung her arm at him and slapped him with her hand, she would really only hit his side and do very little damage.

Too bad, though, it wasn't Gwenvael but Morfyd who'd grabbed her. And Morfyd's face was right in line with Keita's open palm.

The sound ricocheted around the courtyard, and Morfyd's cheek turned red where Keita's hand had collided with it.

A moment of stunned silence from both of them followed, poor Dagmar rushing up to them yelling, "*No, no, no—*"

But it was too late. Much too late. Screeching, they grabbed onto each other's hair and stumbled down the steps while trying to kick the other while trying to yank every strand from the other's head.

Dagmar tried desperately to separate them, the human guards wisely deciding not to intervene between two She-dragons who could shift at a moment's thought and crush them in the process.

"Stop it!" Dagmar yelled, her tiny little human hands trying to pry them apart. "Stop it right now!"

It was strange, in the middle of a sister free-for-all as Gwenvael always called it, that Keita could hear anything but her own yells and Morfyd's, but she did hear it. A familiar voice coming from across the courtyard and heading their way.

"Wait!" that voice begged. "Would you just wait? Please!"

Keita wanted to pull away from her sister to see what was going on, but Morfyd wasn't letting go.

But then they had no choice in the matter because something incredibly strong—and, she was guessing, incredibly pissed off—yanked the pair apart with one pull and shoved them in opposite directions before walking on through.

Keita looked down at the strands of white hair she still had in her fists, then she gazed up, mouth dropping open, when she saw all the red ones in Morfyd's.

Raging, Keita yelled, "You big-handed—"

"Izzy! Please wait!"

The plea cut off Keita's words, and she could only stare as Keita's young cousin Branwen shot past them while desperately pulling clothes over her human form.

"By all reason—" Dagmar began.

"—*that* was Izzy?" Keita finished.

"It's been two years since we've last seen her," Morfyd said, "but . . ."

The trio gazed at each other a moment longer before Keita and Morfyd dropped each other's hair and charged up the stairs, Dagmar Reinholdt pushing past them both and beating them inside.

Chapter Twenty-Four

Talaith had heard all the yelling and screeching, but she'd learned not to get into the middle of a Morfyd–Keita fight long ago. Even Gwenvael—surprisingly annoyed since he didn't seem to get annoyed by much, but especially not by anything Keita did, or who she fucked for that matter—had walked out the back door of the hall.

"Aren't you going to help?" she'd asked him as he passed her.

"They'll wear themselves out eventually," he'd replied and was gone.

Perhaps they would, too. Yet unlike Dagmar, Talaith wasn't about to abandon her breakfast to find out the truth of that. She would stop the brothers from fighting when necessary, but she wasn't about to get between sisters. She'd grown up with women, and she above all knew exactly how mean they could be.

Talaith heard someone coming down the steps and smiled when she saw her mate. He might be able to get his sisters to stop fighting without her getting a black eye in the process. Yet he stopped midway down, his gaze locked on the entrance to the Great Hall. His mouth dropped open, his eyes widened, and a look of shock crossed that perpetually bored dragon's face.

Concerned his sisters had finally really harmed themselves, Talaith followed his gaze. But those angry light brown eyes glaring at her from across the hall belonged to no dragon.

"By the gods . . ." Talaith breathed out, slowly pushing herself to her feet. "Izzy?"

Her daughter. Iseabail. Back, alive and well, among her own after two very long years, and with all her important parts still attached. But Talaith's Izzy had . . . matured. She'd developed curvy hips, and breasts that had nearly doubled in size, proving Izzy was a late bloomer like her mother. But that was only part of what had happened to Izzy since Talaith had last seen her.

There also wasn't an ounce of fat on Talaith's daughter, but she was far from skinny. Instead Izzy was layered in hard-edged muscles rippling powerfully under a short-sleeve tunic and brown leggings. She was also taller—even taller than Annwyl—and her shoulders were strong, wide, and powerful, making Talaith feel puny and weak. It seemed that Izzy had taken after her birth father's people more than Talaith would have ever thought. Now Izzy was built like the warrior women of Alsandair. Tall and broad and oh-so-very strong.

Even more dangerous, Izzy had become quite beautiful. Beautiful and, if Talaith was a gambling woman, she'd say completely oblivious to it. Izzy got that from her father, too. He'd been stunningly handsome but had no idea about it and to the day of his death always seemed shocked Talaith could love him as much as she did. He had never believed himself worthy.

"Forgot me already then?" Izzy slammed her hands flat on the table, leaned in, and with a bellow that rocked the castle walls, accused, "*Because you've replaced me with another?*"

That bellow snapped Talaith out of her shock. "What the hell are you talking about?"

"You didn't even bother telling me! Do I mean so little to this family?"

Talaith cringed when she realized why her daughter was so angry, and looked to her mate. But he'd turned around and was heading back up the stairs.

Deserting bastard!

"You never said a word," Izzy went on, ranting and pacing, her cousin Branwen standing behind her, looking unusually distraught. "You all conspired to lie to me!"

"Izzy, you don't understand—"

"Don't interrupt me!"

Insulted—she was still this ungrateful brat's mother—Talaith stormed around the table and over to her daughter. "Don't you *dare* talk to me like that! I'm still your mother!"

"Barely!" Izzy crossed her arms over her chest. "Were you hoping I wouldn't come back?" Izzy asked, haughty. "So you could pretend you never had me? Was I such a burden?"

Enraged the brat would even suggest such a thing, Talaith exploded.

"How dare you say such a thing to me!"

"How dare *you* not tell me the truth!"

"*I see being away hasn't made you any less impossible!*" Talaith screamed.

"*Like mother, like daughter, it seems!*" Izzy screamed back.

"Izzy?" Briec said from the bottom of the stairs, Rhianwen in his arms. "Don't you want to say hello to your sister before you say good-bye to us all?"

Izzy faced her father, cleared her throat. "No. I don't."

"You're being impossible," Talaith snapped.

"*I'm* being impossible?"

Briec had walked around until he stood beside Izzy and Talaith.

And for the first time that Talaith could ever remember, their younger daughter didn't seem to be content in her father's arms. Instead she reached for Izzy with both hands, fighting to be held by her.

"I don't think it's me she wants," he said softly.

Izzy rubbed the palms of her hands against her thighs and took a step back. As stubborn as always—Talaith had no idea where her daughter got that from—Izzy silently refused to touch her own sister. And if the surprise and hurt on her father's face didn't knock some sense into her, Talaith was at a loss as to what would.

"Tell her the name," Keita suddenly piped in.

Briec scowled at his sister. "Are you still on that?"

"I'll be on *that* until the end of time. You might as well have cursed the poor child. Rhianwen he named her. Can you believe it, Izzy? Trying to get in your grandmum's good graces by selling the babe's soul."

"The names aren't even that close," he argued. "And leave off, already."

"Leave off?" Keita came forward, yanking Rhianwen out of her brother's arms and shoving her at Izzy, giving the stubborn girl no choice but to grab hold of her sister or let her drop to the floor. "I'll not 'leave off,' as you so eloquently put it. But what I will do is call you the suck-up that you truly are. It's like you have no shame."

"Me? You're calling me a suck-up?"

While the siblings argued, Izzy held her sister away from her. But Rhianwen wasn't having it. She continued to reach for Izzy, little hands grasping desperately.

Holding her breath, Talaith watched her two daughters. She could live with Izzy being mad at her, but not at her sister. Rhianwen had done nothing wrong except be born into a very strange situation.

"My daddy adores me!" Keita was yelling at her brother. "And your jealousy over that bores me!"

"You bore me, and yet I tolerate you well enough!"

"The world bores you, Briec, because you think you're better than everyone else!"

"I *know* I'm better than everyone else. If you'd only admit it, you'd be so much happier with your inferiority!"

Frustrated she couldn't reach her sister, Rhianwen began to cry, and Talaith was a moment away from taking her daughter back.

"Shh-shh-shh," Izzy soothed, pulling the babe to her. "It's all right. Don't cry." Izzy began to walk in small circles, bouncing her sister in her arms. "And you two," Izzy said to her father and aunt, "pack it in. You're upsetting the baby."

The arguing stopped instantly, and the siblings glanced at Izzy, then at each other. Keita winked at her brother and smiled at Talaith.

Thank you, Talaith mouthed at the dragoness.

The crying subsided, and Rhianwen leaned her head back so she could do to Izzy what she did to everyone: study her with that almost painfully intense gaze. What did her little one see, Talaith always wondered—and worried—when she looked so closely at others?

Whatever Rhianwen saw this time, however, it was more than enough. In fact, it was as powerful as Izzy's shoulders. Because, for the first time since her birth, Rhianwen did something she'd never done before.

She smiled.

A smile so bright and happy that Talaith felt it like a punch to her chest. Even Briec had to take a step back, his gaze searching out Talaith's.

Izzy grinned in return, completely unaware of what she'd managed to do in thirty seconds that no one else had been able to do since Rhianwen's first breath in this world.

"She's gorgeous," Branwen offered, moving up behind Izzy to get a closer look.

"Of course she is," Izzy snapped back, sounding more like her adoptive father every day. *The horror.* "She's *my* sister."

"Och! I love the little human ones." Branwen reached around Izzy. "Let me hold her now."

"Back off." Izzy turned so her cousin couldn't touch her sister. "Your hands are dirty."

"No dirtier than yours."

"I had gloves on for the trip."

"Just let me hold her for a second," Branwen begged, and Talaith felt bad for the young dragoness.

Especially when Izzy bellowed back, "Unclean!"

"Fine! I'll wash me hands then."

"You need a bath. You're filthy."

"You ungrateful little—"

"Why don't I make this easy for all?" Dagmar cut in. She gestured with a crook of her forefinger and Fanny, who was still in charge of the servants but had somehow become Dagmar's personal assistant, suddenly appeared.

"Yes, Lady Dagmar?"

"Fanny, could you get these two settled? A hot bath for both, and food."

"Of course, my lady." Fanny smiled at the pair. "Welcome home, Lady Iseabail and Lady Branwen. Please follow me."

"Come on, Rhi," Izzy said to her sister, "you'll come with us." She started off behind Fanny and Branwen, but stopped and glared at her parents. "And don't think you two are off the hook."

Talaith opened her mouth to tell her spoiled brat of a daughter what she could do with her "hook," but Keita, Dagmar, Briec, and Morfyd all covered her mouth with their hands. She stamped her foot, but they refused to take their hands away until Izzy and her cousin disappeared up the stairs and down the hallway.

"Brat!" she yelled once they released her.

"She was hurt," Briec said. "I warned you—"

"Shut. Up."

"And normally I'd be fine with her being mad at you—but

she's mad at me too. That's not acceptable. My daughters adore me. I won't have that ruined by you."

Keita gazed up at her brother. "Do you really think this is helping?"

"Helping? I'm supposed to be helping?"

"She's so stubborn!" Talaith snarled, pacing. "I don't know where she gets it from."

Now they all stared at her.

"I can't believe you had the nerve to say that out loud," Briec remarked.

"And what's that supposed to—"

They all jumped, the sound of squealing young females reaching them moments before Izzy and Branwen shot back down the stairs, over the dining table, and right out the Great Hall doors.

"Gods!" Talaith exclaimed. "Where's the—"

"Rhianwen is fine," Fanny called out. A few seconds later, she appeared at the top of the stairs, a giggling Rhianwen in her arms. "I've got her."

"What's going on?"

"Don't know. They looked out the window of their room, tossed, uh, *handed* me the baby, and ran for the door."

"What in all the—"

Gwenvael ran into the hall. He was so overwhelmed with whatever was going on, he couldn't even speak. He just kept pointing.

Dagmar placed her hands on her hips. "What is *wrong* with you?"

Gwenvael took a breath, then spit out, "In the main training ring. Outside. Annwyl . . . and the Lightnings." He held up two fingers. "Two of 'em. She's taking on *two* of them."

There was a moment of stunned silence as they all glanced back and forth at each other; then everyone ran for the door, leaving Talaith and Dagmar behind.

"Wait, wait, wait!" Dagmar yelled. The group of them stopped and faced her. "You have to stop them," she ordered.

Briec snorted first and charged out the door, the rest of them following while Talaith went to check on Rhianwen.

Ragnar sat under a tree and stared off across the tall grass. He had a book open on his lap, but he'd barely glanced at it since he'd sat down. He had far greater things on his mind at the moment.

He couldn't get the looks on Dagmar's and Queen Annwyl's faces out of his mind. Not because they thought he'd bedded Keita. That was part of her grand plan, after all.

No, Ragnar was upset because Keita then had to face the rest of her immediate kin on her own. Of course, it hadn't been his choice to walk away. She'd made it clear that was how this all had to be played, but that didn't mean it felt right to him. And although he could pretend his desire to protect Keita was something instinctual among all Northland male dragons, he knew better. He knew there was more to his feelings for her than mere instinct.

Still, Keita understood her kin better than he ever could, but even knowing that didn't ease his concern.

Dagmar charged up to him, skidding to a stop. She was out of breath, and she'd obviously *run* to get here. *Dagmar? Running?*

"Ragnar—" she began, but her gaze snagged on the small tornado spinning in the middle of the field. "By all reason, what is that?"

"Oh. Sorry." Ragnar unleashed the winds he'd called to him, and the tornado quickly ended.

"You did that?"

"It's nothing. It just helps me think."

"Yes, but—"

"Is there something you need, Dagmar?"

She blinked hard behind her spectacles, one hand pressing against her chest. "Uh . . . yes. Yes." She took a breath, calmed her nerves. When she spoke again she was in control once more. "Your brother and cousin are in the training ring with Annwyl."

"Doing what?" he asked.

One brow rose over cold grey eyes and plain steel-framed spectacles and Ragnar could only sigh, "It's as if they want me to flay the scales from their bones."

Keita had always loved a good fight. She avoided fighting herself, but she did love to watch it. And this . . . this was good fighting.

Using only one shield and one sword, Annwyl had managed to keep both Lightnings at bay while landing in a few good shots here and there. All three were bleeding, but nothing major had been cut, torn, or removed. Besides, that was the rule in the training rings on Annwyl's territory. They were for training only, not killing.

But Keita knew enough of fighting to know that these two Lightnings were not exactly holding back on their swings. She'd bet gold they had in the beginning. Fighting females was not something any Northlander liked to do—mostly because there was no honor in it—but after five minutes in the ring they'd probably realized Annwyl was not some queen who merely liked to *believe* she could fight, who presented a symbol to her men as something to fight for.

No. Not Annwyl. She was and always would be a fighter. A warrior who led her men into battle and to possible death.

"What's going on?"

Keita looked up at her eldest brother. "I believe it's training."

Fearghus shook his head. "She'll fight anyone these days."

"And she's learned some new moves," Briec tossed in.

"Wonder who taught her all that?" Gwenvael added, and Keita slammed her foot onto his. "Ow! What was that for?"

Fearghus briefly glared at his brother before focusing back on Annwyl. "She practices every day now. Sometimes nine to ten hours a day."

And all that work showed. Keita had marveled at Annwyl's muscles when she'd first seen her, but watching her fight two males much stronger and bigger than she was a mighty sight to behold. Annwyl also seemed to understand she wasn't as strong as either male so she used her speed and smaller size to her advantage. It was working, too. These two mighty Northland warriors were barely holding their own against this one woman. They were probably confused and a little ashamed by this. They shouldn't be. Keita's own kin had accepted that Annwyl was, and would always be as long as she had breath, a dangerous opponent. The Cadwaladr Clan actively refused to fight her and had no shame over that decision.

A shadow covered Keita, and she looked over her shoulder to see Ragnar walk up. Behind him ran an out-of-breath Dagmar. *Did she have to race to the Northlands to retrieve him?* The woman appeared exhausted.

Ragnar pushed between Keita and Fearghus. "Do they not listen to a word I say?" he asked her.

"Apparently not," Keita replied. "But don't worry. They can't kill each other in the training ring. It's a rule or something."

"And yet that doesn't make me feel better."

"Are you going to go in and stop them?"

"They made the decision to travel down this road," Ragnar explained, "now they must see it through to its end."

Without looking away from his mate, Fearghus said, "In other words, you're not about to get in there and risk your own head."

"Those words work, too, but mine sound much more honorable."

Inside the ring, Vigholf used his sword to rip the shield from Annwyl's hand. She stumbled back and stumbled back again. Now she was between Vigholf and Meinhard. Both males moved at the same time, and Annwyl jerked aside at the last moment, forcing both to pull back their weapons before they hacked into each other.

Annwyl took the moment to kick the same leg on Meinhard that she'd broken the day before. The dragon roared in pain, lightning strikes spraying out. Keita ducked, not in the mood to get shocked, but Briec quickly unleashed a spell that brought up a shield, protecting them all.

With Meinhard temporarily taken care of, Annwyl charged into Vigholf's legs, taking him to the ground. She quickly got to her feet and rose over him, her sword grasped between both hands and raised over his belly.

Moments from bringing that blade down on the dragon— and Vigholf most likely moments from shifting back to his dragon form so he could stomp Annwyl to oblivion—Annwyl glanced over at her audience, back at her prey, then over at them again.

"Izzy?"

Izzy raised her hand, waved.

"Izzy!" Annwyl slammed her sword into the ground by poor Vigholf's head—forcing the dragon to grit his teeth, most likely to stop himself from screaming like a startled baby—and charged across the training ring. Annwyl leaped over the fence, all of them scrambling back, and right into Izzy's arms.

"Iseabail!" Annwyl cheered, swinging her niece around. "I'm so happy to see you!"

Gwenvael leaned in and whispered in Keita's ear, "It's like a battle of the giant females."

Before she could laugh, Briec slapped Gwenvael in the back of the head.

"Ow!"

Annwyl put Izzy down, but still held her hands. She took a step back and looked her over. "You're looking so well. How's it been going?"

"I'm still in formation," Izzy whined.

"And you will continue to be until your commanders feel you're ready for advancement. You want too much too soon."

"You didn't expect that to change, did you?" Izzy muttered, making Annwyl laugh.

"No. I didn't expect that. I also didn't expect you back this early."

"Oh, well, I came here to confront my mother about her betrayal."

"Izzy," Briec warned.

"Still not talking to you either," she said without looking at him. "And to bring you this from Ghleanna."

She dug in to the top of her boot and handed over a piece of leather. Annwyl took it, examined it, and her expression changed almost instantly.

"Where was this found?" she asked, no longer the loving aunt but the demanding queen.

"A small town near the Western Mountains. The town had been attacked by barbarians a few days before. By the time we got word asking for help, it was too late."

"Any survivors?"

Izzy shook her head. "No. It looked as if they killed everyone. Men, women, even children. If they took any as slaves, we couldn't tell."

Annwyl's hand closed tight around what she held. "I'm glad you're back, Izzy," Annwyl said again. "We'll talk later, yes?"

"Aye."

"Good. Good." Annwyl motioned to Fearghus before

starting off to the castle. He followed, stopping long enough to kiss Izzy on the cheek and give her a hug.

Before Annwyl disappeared around the corner, she called out, "Oy! Barbarian. Witch. We need you two as well."

Morfyd, with a nod to the Lightnings, headed off after Annwyl, and Dagmar let out a weighty sigh before limping off after them all.

"I need to get her into better shape," Gwenvael muttered. "She's as weak as a kitten."

"Only physically," Keita clarified.

Gwenvael chuckled and stepped in front of Izzy, hands on hips. "What?" he demanded of his niece. "You return and show me no love whatsoever?"

"I'm not sure I'm talking to any of you." Izzy folded her arms over her chest. "In none of the letters I received did any of you tell me about Rhi."

"Who's Rhi?"

"Rhianwen," Keita said. "You idiot."

Focusing back on his niece, Gwenvael said in confusion, "But I didn't write you at all. So that should alleviate me of any accusations of being a liar." When everyone only stared at him, "Well, it should!"

Vigholf ignored the hand held out to him and managed to get to his feet on his own. He did, however, take the jug of water his brother offered.

"You all right?" Only Ragnar asked that question after a fight. But this time, finishing off half the water and handing it to his cousin, Vigholf didn't think Ragnar's question was out of order. No, not this time.

"I didn't know females could fight like that," he admitted. "Sure she doesn't have some demon in her?"

"She doesn't." And Ragnar would know. "It just seems like she does."

Vigholf looked up to see two females approaching them. One was a very young dragoness, the other a human female, her skin brown like Lady Talaith. Beautiful like Lady Talaith as well, making him think they were of similar bloodline.

"That was amazing," the human said. "Do you think you could teach us some of that?"

"Some of what?" he asked, a little amused.

She reached down and picked up his battle ax. He'd used it for a bit with the queen, but she'd gotten it away from him early on. Of course, the queen had only managed to knock it from his hands. When she'd tried to pick it up later, she'd struggled with the weight of it so much, she'd tossed it down and dove for Meinhard's dropped sword instead. Yet this . . . *child* hefted it in her hands with what seemed to be ease.

"Teach us how to use battle axes. We haven't gotten to that yet."

"Izzy's still on spears and swords," the dragoness said. "She's a bit bored."

He watched the human swing his favored weapon in short arcs with one hand. "This is nice, isn't it?" She stopped, blinked up at Ragnar. "Don't I know you?"

"Uh . . ."

Princess Keita appeared, popping up, it seemed, out of nowhere. "Excuse us a moment." She grabbed the human by the collar and pulled her a few feet away.

"What's going on?" Vigholf asked his brother.

"Nothing."

"Are you lying to me?"

"Only a little."

"Ohhhhh." The human looked over at them, cringed. *Sorry*, she mouthed at Ragnar.

"There's absolutely nothing subtle about that one, is there?"

Ragnar shook his head. "Not really."

The princess and the human walked back up to them, and the human held out Vigholf's ax to him. He took it.

"Nice weapon," she said.

"Thank you."

He waited for her to push to learn more about it, but she stood there saying nothing and wiping her hands on her leggings.

"Well," the princess said, "why don't we all—" Her head snapped up, and she suddenly blurted, "Shit. Shit!" Then she dove behind Ragnar.

"Should I ask what you're doing?"

"Avoiding some . . . uh, people."

"Male people?" And Vigholf noted how annoyed his brother sounded.

"Don't get that tone with me, warlord." Tugging on Ragnar's shirt, she made him turn a bit so that he continued to block her. "Stay here. Don't move. I'm going to make a run for it."

"Where are you going?"

But the princess had already lifted her skirts and took off running, heading toward the main town.

"Oy! Foreigners!" Sneering, all three of them looked at the human male soldiers standing on the other side of the rail, several holding flowers. "Where's the lovely princess then?" one of them asked. "We just saw her."

Meinhard, trying to work out the newest pain in his leg, suggested, "I say we kill 'em all."

"Ooh!" the young She-dragon suggested. "Use the battle ax!"

"Or!" the human cut in, shoving the She-dragon aside and focusing on the soldiers, "You lot can piss off."

"No one's talking to you, muscles."

And the young female lowered her head, raised her eyes, and balled her hands into fists. It was enough.

"All right, all right," the man said, raising his hands. "No need to get nasty."

The men walked off, and the girl faced the Lightnings

again, smiling. "All talk, that one. But if you have any more problems, you just let me know. I'll take care of it."

And Vigholf was torn between laughing and believing she would take care of it. Quite well, as a matter of fact.

"I better track Keita down," Ragnar finally said, sighing a little.

"Suddenly the princess is your responsibility, brother?"

"Sure there's nothing you need to tell us, cousin?" Meinhard asked.

"Yes."

"You lying?"

"Maybe a little."

He walked off, leaving Vigholf and Meinhard alone with the two young females.

"I'm Branwen," the young She-dragon said. "This is Izzy. She ain't blood, but she's me cousin."

Too complicated. These Fire Breathers lived lives that were simply too complicated.

"Good for you then," Vigholf said, hefting his ax onto his shoulder. "Me and Meinhard train every day at dawn," he told the pair. "And we'll be training here in this ring as long as we're at Garbhán Isle. What you do with that information is down to you."

They headed back to the castle and perhaps some ointments for what Vigholf was sure would be many aches and pains.

Dagmar placed the strip of leather, looking like a piece torn off a sword belt, onto the long table covered with maps and correspondence from the different legion commanders.

"It could have been there for years," Fearghus said, his gaze straying to his mate. Annwyl stood by the window, her back to them, arms folded over her chest, staring out.

"It appears relatively new," Dagmar said. Then, with a sigh, she walked over to a small trunk she kept in the room. She kept important correspondence or important but not-often-used maps and items in there. She was the only one with a key; none of the dragons bothered to ask for one since they could tear the trunk open without it. She pulled out the keys she kept around her girdle and unlocked it, removing several items from inside. She placed those on the desk alongside the newest piece. Two were strips of leather, emblems burnt into them, another was part of a necklace, and another was a gold coin. All received from Addolgar in the last few months.

Fearghus and Morfyd moved in closer, taking a look. Fearghus's cold black gaze lifted to Dagmar's. "You're just telling us of this now?"

"There was no reason to alert anyone until I was sure. I have my people out getting as much information as they can, and Ghleanna and Addolgar are on top of the matter."

"And?"

Dagmar dropped into a chair on the other side of the desk. "There's still nothing definite. No witnesses. No sight of the Sovereigns before or after the attacks. Nothing."

"But this?" Morfyd asked, gesturing to the bits Dagmar had collected.

"Evidence it could be, but it's not exactly damning."

"We can send more legions into the west to look for them. To find out if it is the Sovereigns, and act accordingly."

Fearghus, his head down, said, "It's not the Sovereigns we need to find."

"Why not?"

"It's been said," Dagmar explained, "that the human Sovereign forces are no more than puppets for their dragon masters."

"The Irons," Fearghus filled in.

Morfyd shook her head. "Do you really think Thracius would dare move on us?"

"Outright?" Fearghus shrugged. "Doubtful. But to have

Thracius's human attack dog, Counsel Laudaricus and the Sovereign legions, wear away at our troops? Keep us busy, splintering our legions, while we look away from what's going on—perhaps right in front of us? That I can see, sister."

"I don't understand."

He pointed at the map he had on the table. "Fearing an eventual attack by the Sovereigns after discovering all these conveniently placed bits of evidence, we move all our human troops here"—he pointed at the Western Mountains—"and send our dragon units over the mountains and into the valley territories between the Western and Aricia Mountains."

"All right."

Dagmar leaned forward and pointed at the northern portion of the map. "While the iron dragons sweep through the Northlands and Outerplains and wipe this land clean before any of the troops can make it back."

Morfyd stared down at the map until she suddenly announced, "Mother knows."

"Why would you say that?"

"Why else would she bring Ragnar here? After two years, his war almost over? She's up to something."

Dagmar placed her elbows on the table and cupped her chin with her hands. "Another war would put her in a better position with the Elders, but that doesn't mean she's actively working to make a war with the Sovereigns happen."

Morfyd began to pace. "The Sovereigns are not like the Northlanders, you know. Splintered by terrain and old grudges. The entire Sovereign Empire, dragon and human, all bow before that bastard Thracius. He rules with an iron claw, and if Mother lets this play out until the Elders have no choice but to declare war . . . it might be too late."

"Then we don't wait for that," Fearghus said. "Human and dragon legions attack first. Before the Sovereigns' or Mother's plans has a chance to play out."

"No."

Fearghus's eyes briefly closed at his mate's softly spoken, but adamant, proclamation.

"Annwyl—"

"No, Fearghus. That's what they want. For us to leave the children."

"It's not like we'd be leaving them alone in a field to fend for themselves."

She faced them all, and Dagmar couldn't help but wince when she saw the human queen's expression. It was . . . fixed.

"I'll not leave them. I can't make it any plainer."

They watched her walk out, none of them jumping when the door slammed behind her. The queen was a notorious door-slammer.

"I'll talk to her," Fearghus said.

"You've been talking to her, brother. We all have. She won't hear us."

"She dreams," Dagmar said, telling them what had been said among the servants. "She dreams someone is coming for the babes."

"And?" Fearghus pushed. "Is she right?"

Dagmar and Morfyd exchanged glances before Dagmar admitted, "Yes. We think she may be."

"There will always be someone coming after the babes," Fearghus said, taking up the spot his mate had left. He even crossed his arms over his chest and stared out the window. "Everyone wants them dead."

"Trust me, Fearghus, if what Annwyl has been dreaming, if the details I've received are correct, then she has good reason to be concerned. We all do."

Chapter Twenty-Five

Ragnar was heading down a side street when he saw the pub. Although it wasn't the pub that caught his attention, but the men going into it. Practically running.

He sighed. Honestly. The things he was reduced to.

He stepped into the pub, moving past tables, punters, and barmaids until he reached a small table in the back. That's where he found Her Majesty holding court, human males surrounding her.

"Lord Ragnar!" she cheered when he stood in front of the table, towering over the other males. "Gentlemen, this is Lord Ragnar. Lord Ragnar, these are my gentlemen." She giggled at that, and he debated pulling her out by her hair. But that sounded too much like something his father would do—making it impossible for him to do the same. "What brings you here, my lord?"

"I've been looking for you. Thought you could return with me to the fortress."

"But I'm having such fun," she said, raising the pint in her hand. Gods, how much ale had she had since she'd run off? It hadn't taken him *that* long to track her down.

"It's time for your fun to end, I'm afraid."

"But I don't want it to end," she pouted, and damn her for looking so adorable while doing so.

"I don't care—"

"Why don't you leave off?" one of the men snapped. "Just go—"

Ragnar held up his hand in front of the man's face, silencing him and the entire pub with a thought.

"Don't annoy me, my lady. Just come along."

Oblivious, Keita said, "But I don't want to go."

She was testing him, and he didn't like it.

Glancing at the man who'd been so protective of her, Ragnar ordered, "Bark like a dog."

And when he did, Keita's eyes grew wide, her mouth dropping open.

"Stop it," she told him.

Ragnar glanced at the man to his right. "Quack like a duck."

"Ragnar!" she squeaked over the quacking and barking. "Stop it!"

Curious, he asked, "Why do you care what I do to them?"

"Because what you're doing is wrong. Can't you see that?"

He could; he was just surprised that she could see it as well.

"What do you do that's so different from what I do?"

"You must be joking." And he realized she wasn't drunk at all.

"Not really. These human males would crawl across broken glass to entertain you."

"Of their own free will. I force no one to do anything and *would you stop the quacking and barking!*"

"Stop."

They did as ordered, and Keita's eyes narrowed. "Can you do the same to me?"

He laughed. "Dragons are never that easy, princess. But lusty men have to be the easiest of all."

"Which you're saying is my fault?"

"You certainly don't help." He held his hand out to her. "Now, are you coming, or should I have them start mooing?"

Keita stood and walked around the table. She took the hand he held out to her, but wouldn't move. "Release them, Ragnar."

"As you wish."

He did as she bade, everyone returning to what they'd been doing without missing a beat.

The men, realizing Keita was leaving, begged her to stay.

"I'm sorry, all. I must go. But I'll be back." She let Ragnar lead her to the front door and outside. "That was mean!" she said, snatching her hand away.

"So is your testing me."

"I was not."

"Weren't you? To see what I'd do with you surrounded by so many men?"

"I do not call them to me. And do you really think I'm that petty?"

"Yes. I do."

Keita gasped, outraged, and pulled her fist back to assault him with one of her weak pummelings when her sharp gaze caught sight of a blonde wearing a dark blue cape and moving quickly down the street. "It's her!"

"It's who?"

"Come."

"Pardon?"

"We can't let her get away!" She caught his hand and tried to drag him with her. When he only gawked at her, refusing to be moved until she told him what was going on, she dropped his hand, lifted the skirt of her gown, and followed the woman.

Who knew that sleeping late would cause Éibhear to miss a second fight between Annwyl and Vigholf and Meinhard?

And this time he wouldn't have had to worry about stopping them and possibly losing his head in the process or being responsible for a small territorial incident because it had all taken place in the training ring. But according to the servants who'd brought him something to eat earlier, he'd missed quite the battle. Typical.

But he was home and he was glad to be.

He walked down the stairs and into the Great Hall. No one was around; even the servants off doing something else, somewhere else. It didn't help that he was bored and still feeling the effects of all that wine from last night. Still, he'd had quite the good time at the pubs with a few of his male cousins and several of the barmaids.

He debated what to do now, and decided that heading into town would work. He could stop by the booksellers and see what was new and interesting—which would probably be everything since it had been ages that he'd purchased a new book. The Northlanders were not big on books and on very few occasions did he get a chance to stop by a bookseller or library. And gods, when he suggested it, he only got blank stares from the others.

That did sound perfect, though, didn't it? A good book and a hearty meal at one of the local pubs.

Checking his pocket for coin—he'd stolen some from Briec's room, it's not like his brother needed so much—Éibhear set off.

He walked outside and immediately winced from the light searing his brain. It didn't deter him from his goal, but it reminded him that drink was not always his friend. He simply didn't handle it as well as his kin.

Taking his time and only able to keep one eye open, he walked down the Great Hall steps. As soon as his feet touched the cobblestones of the courtyard, he turned toward the side exit and started off.

"Hello, Éibhear."

Éibhear stopped and looked back at the stairs. He'd thought he'd passed someone on the steps, but he'd been so focused on just getting down them without throwing up, he hadn't really paid much mind.

Squinting, he leaned in a bit to get a better look. Gods, he might never drink again at this rate.

"Uh . . . hello."

"Gods . . . have I changed that much in two years that my own *uncle* doesn't recognize me?"

Éibhear's eyes opened wide—both of them—and he ignored the pain doing so caused as he stared at her. "Izzy?"

Her smile, as always, lit up her face and his world. He hated her for that smile. On those long, lonely patrols in desolate Northland territory, it had been that smile he couldn't stop thinking about.

"How . . . how are you?"

"Fine. Found out my parents and entire family are"—and this she yelled up at the castle walls—"*complete and utter liars!*"

"Oh, get over it already!" Talaith yelled back from somewhere inside.

"But other than that," Izzy went on, "I'm fine. How about you?"

"I'm fine."

"The Northlands have treated you well, I see. You're bigger. All over."

Don't say it. Do not say it!

"Lots of hard work. How's army life?" he asked quickly to change the subject.

"I'm still in formation," she complained, rolling her eyes. "I move trees. A lot."

She laughed. "Don't worry. I'm sure in a few more years we'll both be forces to be reckoned with."

Éibhear pointed at her. "What have you got there?"

She held up the ball of fur. "Puppy."

"You didn't get that from Dagmar's kennels, did you? She'll have your hide."

"So telling her I found him wandering around outside won't work?"

"Not even a little."

She brought the puppy closer to her face, her nose to its wet snout. "But he's so cute."

"And in a few more months, he'll be able to take your face completely off."

"Then I definitely want him."

Éibhear chuckled. "I see you haven't changed, Izzy."

"It depends on who you talk to."

It hit Éibhear at that moment, watching Izzy with her puppy, still wearing travel-soiled leggings and a sleeveless tunic, dirt on her cheeks and neck . . . he was over her. All those inappropriate feelings he'd had for her—and the gods knew how he loathed all those damn, uncontrollable feelings—were gone. He still couldn't see her as his niece, or even a cousin, but she was still Izzy. Izzy that he had no interest in whatsoever.

The realization made his headache fade away, and he stepped a little closer. "I was about to go into town, stop by the booksellers, then get something to eat. Maybe you'd like to—"

"Oy!"

Éibhear looked across the courtyard and smiled at the sight of his cousin Celyn. He and Celyn used to be quite close when they were both younger until . . . well, until Celyn had met Izzy. But that didn't matter now.

"Celyn?" Izzy asked, gazing at Éibhear's cousin as if the dragon had somehow magically appeared. "What are you doing here?"

Celyn stopped in the middle of the courtyard, gave a "why do you think?" shrug that had Éibhear's back teeth grinding a bit. He wasn't still trying to seduce little Izzy, was he? He had to know that was wrong and that Briec would kill him. He couldn't be *that* stupid, could he?

"I came here to check on you, didn't I?" Yeah. That's right. Celyn *could* be that stupid.

Izzy placed the puppy down on the step and stood. She kept standing, too, the human female having grown at least three or four inches since Éibhear had last seen her. That didn't seem normal for a human female, but Izzy was far from normal. Even worse was that her height wasn't the only thing that had continued to grow on little Izzy. She'd filled out—a fact that made Éibhear hate her just a little because no one who called herself a warrior should have those kinds of curves.

Izzy charged over to Celyn and launched herself at the idiot. Even more offensive was how her legs went around Celyn's waist and her arms around his shoulders while Celyn used Izzy's innocent and playful show of affection as an opportunity to put his hands all over her ass.

What in all the hells was Izzy doing anyway? Without even realizing it, she was giving Éibhear's lecherous cousin all the wrong signals. And, as usual, Izzy was completely oblivious!

"Oh," Celyn said to Éibhear as if he'd just spotted him. "Hello, cousin."

"Celyn."

Celyn's grip must have tightened on Izzy's ass because she squealed and slapped at his hands. "Stop that!" She jumped down and laughed, punching Celyn in the shoulder.

"Ow."

"Did you come alone?" she asked.

"Fal came with me. He's around somewhere." He tapped the tip of her nose with his forefinger. "But I came looking for you. You all right?"

"Did you know? About the baby?"

"You know I would have told you if I had. I would have risked my mother's wrath for you, my sweet Iseabail."

Izzy rolled her eyes, not believing the lying bastard any more than Éibhear did. "Somehow I doubt that."

"True enough, but would you have blamed me?"

"Not really. But I am glad you came."

"Me too."

Éibhear knew he couldn't stand any more—not without throwing up first—so he gave a little wave. "I'm off," he said.

"I thought we'd track down Brannie and go get something to eat together," Izzy offered.

"Not right now. I have to be somewhere."

"That's too bad," Celyn said. And, yeah, he looked completely destroyed by that.

But Éibhear wasn't going to get into it here, now, with his cousin. He didn't have to. He'd simply talk to Izzy tonight. She was still an innocent, that one, and she didn't understand that she was getting in way over her head with his idiot cousin. But Éibhear would put a stop to that. Because he should. He was still her uncle, wasn't he? Not by blood, of course, but he was her uncle. And because they weren't raised together as uncle and niece, it would be easier for him to explain to her the way of things when it came to dragons like Celyn.

Until then, he'd get a few books, some food, and something from the local healer for this bloody headache that had tragically returned.

Ragnar had no idea where she was going, but he knew he had to follow. It was too frightening to think of the trouble she'd get into without him. And he could no longer escape the fact that he found Keita more entertaining than anyone else he'd known.

She was stalking after some human female, following from a distance. Any time the human stopped and looked to see if she was being followed, Keita blended into the shadows of a building or into the crowd. After a while, Ragnar had to admit that she was very good at what she did, each day moving farther and farther away from the image he'd originally had of her as a dim-witted royal.

She abruptly stopped and held up her hand to halt him.

"What are we doing?" he finally had the chance to ask.

"She's the slit that killed Bampour," Keita replied in a whisper. "Now she's here. It can't be a coincidence." She carefully looked around the corner of a building and gasped, glancing back at Ragnar.

"What?" he asked. "What is it?"

"I don't believe him!"

"Who?"

Rather than answering as any logical dragon would do, she shot off, forcing Ragnar to follow her since he had no idea what she was up to. She slid to a stop in front of what appeared to be an old warehouse. She held the door with one hand, waited a few seconds, then snatched it open.

"Whore!" she accused, which Ragnar thought a little harsh since Keita didn't actually know this woman. But when he stepped into the warehouse, he saw who the woman was standing with and knew that Keita was right. Definitely a whore.

The Ruiner grabbed hold of the barmaid, dragging her in front of him to use as a shield.

"Protect me, Dana!" Gwenvael begged, and Ragnar could only hope he was joking. "Before this merchant of evil and her dim-witted henchman destroy us both!"

Ragnar went ahead and assumed that *he* was the dim-witted henchman.

"You whore," Keita said again. "What about your mate? What will she say when she finds out?"

"You can't tell her!" Gwenvael wailed. "*She'll kill us all!*"

"How can I not tell her the truth?" Keita argued. "How can *I* betray womankind everywhere?"

The woman pointed at Keita. "She's the one who threw me out the window."

Gwenvael stared down at his sister, his wailing and crying stopping instantly. Both brother and sister were performers, but Keita was much better at it. "You threw her out a window?" Gwenvael asked.

"I was saving the ungrateful goat's life. Remind me next time not to bother. Honestly, if I'd known she was just one of your whores . . ."

She certainly did toss that word around.

The woman stepped closer to Keita. "I am no whore, slag. And I knew I should have killed you when I had the chance."

"Perhaps, but you were too busy wiping that old man's come off the inside of your thighs to have the time."

Gwenvael snorted, and both he and his sister burst out laughing.

"Ignore us, Dana." Gwenvael, wiping tears from his eyes with one hand, gave the confused human a coin pouch with the other. "As promised."

"Thank you, my lord." Eyeing Keita coldly, clearly seeing her as the bigger danger, the woman backed away until she got to a side door and slipped outside.

"I'm doubting she'll be back," Ragnar said.

"She works for me, and I pay her well," another voice said from the shadows. "She'll be back."

Dagmar Reinholdt's dog, Canute, stepped into the light, and Keita backed into Ragnar. "Good gods! The dog speaks." Ragnar only had a moment to cross his eyes before Dagmar stepped in behind her dog. Keita let out a breath. "Thank the gods that was you, sister. What a relief. Can you think of anything stranger than a dog being able to speak?"

Dagmar's eyes studied the three dragons in human form standing before her and, eventually, shook her head. "No, Princess Keita. I can't think of *anything* remotely stranger than that."

* * *

Keita grinned. "There's that sarcasm again."

"Me? Sarcastic? Never." And the words couldn't have been spoken with a flatter inflection if the woman had been dead. With her pale hands clasped together and resting against the skirt of her gown, the warlord's daughter appeared almost . . . virginal. A young spinster who'd joined one of those nunneries. But for her eyes. For Keita, those cold, missed-nothing eyes were the giveaway.

Which added up to one thing for Keita the Viper—she was truly beginning to enjoy her brother's choice of mate! Dagmar Reinholdt was so blatantly ruthless and mean, so direct with it that once Keita bothered to look past all that grey . . . Honestly, how could she not adore the human female?

"Why are you here, princess?" Dagmar asked.

"I live here," Keita explained. "These are the lands of my people."

"Is that the game we're going to play?"

"I do love games."

"Keita," her brother chastised.

"Oh, fine. I recognized the girl and wanted to see who she was working for. Imagine my surprise to find out it was you two. . . ." She let her grin grow wider, her gaze bouncing back and forth between the warlord's daughter and Gwenvael. "I had no idea you two enjoyed those kinds of games. Very nice choice, brother."

"Isn't Dagmar *wild*? You should see her when she's training her dogs!"

"Stop it. Both of you."

Keita placed her hand on Dagmar's arm. "There's no shame in hiring a whore to satisfy your needs, Lady Dagmar. I'd do the same if I couldn't decide which I preferred more, a cock or a puss—"

"You and I both know Dana is no whore."

"Perhaps murderess is more apt a title?"

"What does that make you then?" Ragnar asked Keita.

"Loyal to my people. Now shut up."

"Was it your loyalty that led you to Lord Bampour's room that morning?" Dagmar asked.

"I was merely concerned for poor Lord Bampour's health. He wasn't well at all at our dinner."

Dagmar's lips twitched into what could almost be called a smile. "She's a much better liar than you, Defiler."

Gasping in practiced horror, Keita pressed her hands against her chest. "Are you suggesting I'm *lying*, Lady Dagmar?"

"I'm suggesting you wouldn't bother using truth if it promised to erect a temple in your honor."

Keita held up one finger, waved it. "I beg to differ on that." She shrugged at Ragnar. "I've always wanted a temple."

"Where males from all across the land could come and worship you!" Gwenvael cheered.

"Yes! And they'd have to bring me gifts because I would be a god." She sighed. "I love gifts."

Dagmar gazed over Keita's shoulder at Ragnar. "Have you been putting up with this for the last few days?"

"Yes." He frowned. "I've been enjoying it, too. . . . That's not a good thing, is it?"

"Don't worry," Dagmar told him. "It only hurts a little in the beginning."

Ren of the Chosen Dynasty stepped into the Dragon Queen's chamber. She smiled at him, showing many rows of fangs, and gestured him over with a wave of her claw.

"Hello, my friend."

He rose up on his hind legs, then dropped to one knee and bowed his head. "My queen."

"Oh, for the sake of the gods, Ren. Who's that performance for?"

Ren sat back on his haunches, tossed the fur that fell into his eyes. "I like to err on the side of etiquette, Rhiannon."

She laughed and waved her claw again. This time, it released a collar she wore, the chain that was linked to it, attached to a wall. It was a game the queen and her consort played. A game Ren never questioned. Mostly because it was none of his business, but also because what went on between the pair was something pure and white hot. And, to Ren's kind, explained how things had changed so much among the Southland dragons of the west. Only a love like that of Rhiannon and Bercelak could transform everything the dragons of this land had known.

"You summoned me?"

"I did." She sat down and patted a spot next to her on the slab of rock. Of course, this was not her official throne. That was in another cavern that had room enough for the Elders. Nor was this her bedchamber. It was, simply, the Queen's Chamber, where many world-altering decisions often took place.

Ren sat down, and the queen said, "I want to thank you for watching out for my Keita. Being good at what she does makes her a target, and knowing you've often supported her has brought me great comfort."

"Excuse my boldness, but I didn't think you gave two shits what your whore daughter did. Or were those not the exact words you said to her sixty-eight years ago—correct?"

"I won't explain the relationship I have with my daughter to anyone. Not to you—"

"Not to her."

"Not to anyone. What I do and why I do it, is mine to know and understand."

"I see. Then perhaps we should address what you want with me."

"I need you to head west and—"

"No." Ren shook his head. "I'll not leave so you can have Keita at the will of that Northlander."

"He worries you."

"He was able to hurt her when no male I've known has ever managed before."

"Which means what to you?"

"That she's vulnerable to him. I don't like it."

"It's not yours to like or not like. Keita may be vulnerable to him, as you put it, but I have no doubt that will only make it harder for him to get near her. But separating you two isn't my goal here."

"Then what is your goal? What can only *I* help you with?"

"I need you to look into something for me."

"Which is?"

She tossed something at him, and Ren caught it in his claw. He studied it. "A gold Quintilian coin."

"A *Sovereign* coin. There is a difference." He knew that. A Quintilian coin could be found anywhere and was used throughout the lands. A Sovereign coin, which held vastly more value because it was pure gold, was only found in the Quintilian empire and usually only among the nobles. "It was found buried under the remains of another town destroyed by what we had believed to be one of the barbarian tribes."

"But you no longer think it's the barbarians?"

"Whoever is doing this kills everyone and take no slaves. Barbarians of the Western Mountains always take slaves. That's how they make their money."

"You truly think it's the Sovereigns?"

"I know it's the Sovereigns. But I need hard proof. Not only for the Elders, who have never felt good about my alliance with the Lightnings, but for my offspring. They think I only want war."

"Don't you?"

She threw her claws up, reminding him of her daughter. "Yes! But only with those I *know* I can destroy—and that, my friend, is *not* the Irons."

Chapter Twenty-Six

"You are a Protector of the Throne?" Dagmar nodded at Keita's admission, and leaned close to Gwenvael. "What is that exactly?"

It was so rare that there was something—*anything!*—his mate did not know, he would admit he took a moment to enjoy the sensation. Until she said, "Well?"

"They're like . . . special agents to the throne, I guess."

"You mean spies?" Dagmar asked, focusing on his sister. "You? You're a . . . spy?"

"I prefer Protector. Spy sounds so sordid, don't you think?"

"*You?*" Dagmar said again, forcing Gwenvael to bump her with his hip. So far Keita seemed to like Dagmar; he wanted to keep it that way. He'd ended up on the wrong side of Keita's rage more than once, and spending three days doing nothing but vomiting up whatever she'd slipped into his food or wine was not a fate he'd want his lovely mate to endure. "It's just . . . you seem so vapid."

Gwenvael flinched, but Keita only laughed. "I do, don't I? And mostly I am. Except when it comes to the throne. I will protect that with my dying breath, if necessary."

"Hopefully, it won't be," the Lightning cut in, and Gwenvael couldn't help sneering at the bastard.

"What do you have to do with anything?" When the Lightning didn't reply, Gwenvael looked at his sister. "Keita? What's going on with you two?"

"I'm simply using him for sex."

"Of course you are. But that doesn't explain why you've still allowed him to hang around you once you're done."

"He's very good?"

Dagmar pressed the back of her hand to Gwenvael's chest, her gaze on Keita and Ragnar. "Is this about the Sovereigns?" she asked, and when both their expressions turned perfectly blank, Gwenvael knew his mate had guessed right.

Keita studied the human Gwenvael had mated himself to. "How much can she be trusted?" she asked her brother.

"I've already trusted her with my life and the lives of everyone in this family. Her loyalty is not in question. Even Father trusts her."

Surprised, Keita raised a brow. "Indeed?" She nodded. "Then I'll make this quick and what I tell you goes no farther than these walls." When they all agreed, she continued. "There's a distinct chance Overlord Thracius hopes to put me on the throne. Mother thinks he's already secured the assistance of someone in her court. She believes they'll approach me soon, but to speed that process up a bit . . . I need it to get out that I've known where Esyld has been all this time."

Her brother shook his head. "Are you insane? If the family finds out—"

"It's a risk I have to take. And I think you can help me, Dagmar."

"You want me to get the rumor about you and Esyld out?"

"Can you think of anyone better to make that happen?"

Dagmar smirked. "Not really."

"I don't like this, Keita," Gwenvael said.

"I know you don't, but I need the traitors to present themselves much sooner. I fear we're running out of time."

Gwenvael began to argue, but his mate cut him off.

"She's right." Dagmar let out a breath. "We've become fairly certain the Sovereign human troops are raiding small towns and villages near the Western Mountains. Dividing Annwyl's troops, hoping to pull more dragon troops there to help."

"And it seems Styrbjörn the Revolting may be helping Thracius," Ragnar added. "Everything is moving into place. As much as I hate this as well, we must push this along."

"And what about the safety of my sister?" Gwenvael demanded, glaring at the Northlander but making Keita feel a touch more special than she had a few minutes ago.

"I will protect your sister with my life. I swear it on the Code and the name of my kin."

"Which means what to me?" Gwenvael demanded.

"Everything," Dagmar told her mate. "It means everything."

"Keita?" Gwenvael asked her. "What say you?"

"I trust Ragnar the Cunning as I trust you . . . or actually more like I trust Ren."

Gwenvael pouted. "You trust Ren more than me?"

"At least he's reliable."

"You can't seriously still be blaming me for that, little sister! I was late one time!"

"And I nearly lost this *amazing* head! If it hadn't been for Ren, my perfection would have been lost for the ages. I still don't know how you live with yourself after that!"

"Because *my* perfection would have remained. And that's all that matters!"

They eventually left the warehouse, the pairs separating. As they headed back to the castle, Gwenvael took his mate's hand.

"Well?" he asked.

"I can't believe you never told me."

"It wasn't my information to tell. And she's my sister."

"Reason help me, she is *so* your sister, Gwenvael."

"What does that mean?"

"I hope Ragnar understands what he's about to get himself involved with."

"He's already fucked her—how much more involved can he get?"

"He hasn't."

"He hasn't what?"

"As you so eloquently put it, fucked her."

Gwenvael stopped, pulling his mate to a halt. "How do you know that?"

"Instinct. Body language. Your sister is very smart. She knows having a very secret relationship with Ragnar, a low-born enemy dragon—no matter how many alliances your mother agrees to, many of your kin and other noble dragons still consider the Northland dragons enemies—Keita comes off even more of the bored royal itching for her mother's throne. She plays stupid because it makes her seem control-lable. Too bad she's more like her mother than either of them seems to realize."

"Don't ever say that loud enough Keita can hear you. She'll rip your throat out."

"I'll keep that in mind." She tugged, and they began to walk again. "But they will be soon enough, I'm guessing."

Gwenvael had learned over the years that his mate had a tendency to jump from conversation to conversation because that's how her brilliant mind worked. Most beings could barely manage one or two cohesive thoughts at a time; Dagmar seemed to manage hundreds.

"They will be soon enough what?"

"Fucking."

Gwenvael stopped again. "I thought you just said they weren't?"

"They're not. Although I don't know why it bothers you so much."

"What if he's just toying with my sister because he's good and pissed I got you?"

"I think it would be very hard for any male to toy with your sister and live to enjoy it. But it doesn't matter because that's not Ragnar's way."

When Gwenvael could only manage a grunt, Dagmar stroked her free hand against his chin. "And I'm with you, not with him. He understands that."

"He better."

"Besides, I'm sure once he beds your sister, he won't think about me for another second."

"How are you so sure that'll happen?"

"Do you need my spectacles to see, Defiler?" She tugged him into moving again. "They're both gagging for it!"

Keita was heading out of town with Ragnar when she saw him. He stood by a blacksmith stall, talking to a pretty young girl. He held the girl's hand and leaned in close.

She stopped, stared, rage singing through her veins.

"Keita?" Ragnar slid his hand down her back. "What is it?"

Unable to answer, her anger too great, she marched across the street until she reached the pair. Lifting both her hands, she slammed them into the human male, shoving him to the side. She grudgingly had to admit she was impressed. Although hitting her brothers like that would do little more than annoy them, she had been known to break a few bones of the human males. This one, however, just stared at her.

"Keita?" he asked, obviously shocked.

"Do you think," she snarled at the bastard, "that you can do this and get away with it? That *I'd* let you do this?"

The general of Annwyl's armies and her sister's worthless

human mate frowned, *appearing* confused; then his eyes grew wide. "No, no. You don't under—"

Unable to look at him without wanting to set him on fire, she spun on the girl. "You. Whore. Get from my sight, or I swear by all the gods that I'll destroy *everything* that you love!"

The girl, rightly terrified, burst into tears and ran off, allowing Keita to focus on the man behind her.

She faced him, pointing a finger. "I should rip the flesh from your human carcass, you low-born—"

"She's my cousin," he cut in.

"Yeah. Right. Nice one. Like I've never heard *that* line of centaur shit before."

"I was asking her to be our new nanny."

That had a ring of truth to it, didn't it? "New nanny?"

"We lost another nanny, and Morfyd asked me to see if my young cousin would take the position. The young cousin you just sent screaming and sobbing back to my aunt and uncle, who will probably never let me see her again."

Keita lowered that accusing finger, knowing he spoke the truth. "Oh."

"You can ask Morfyd, if you'd like. She knows my whole family. They adore her."

"Brastias, I'm so . . . very . . ."

"No, no. It's always wonderful when your fourteen-year-old cousin is called a whore on the street and you're accused of betraying the mate you adore. And in front of the blacksmith, too."

Keita looked over, and the blacksmith gave a happy wave.

"Truly, I am so sorry. I just—"

"You and Morfyd go at it like cats and dogs," Brastias said, "but something always told me I never wanted to be on the wrong side of that." He walked past her. "Now I know I was right."

He headed off down the street, back to the castle, and tossed over his shoulder, "Some of the Cadwaladrs are dining with us tonight. With Izzy back, there will probably be dancing. I thought you should know."

Keita buried her face in her hands. Mortified. She was absolutely mortified!

So when Ragnar put his arm around her shoulders and led her out of town, she didn't even ask where they were going. She didn't even care.

He took her deep into the forests, leading her along until he got to a small lake behind some large boulders. It was secluded and quiet, a place he'd stumbled upon when he'd been here two years before. Less than a mile away was the spot where Keita had stabbed him with her tail. She didn't go into a rage often, but when she did . . . there were always so many victims.

He brushed off one of the smaller boulders and led her to it. "Sit."

She did, planting her elbows on her knees and her face back in her hands.

"You all right?"

She answered, but he couldn't make it out with her hands in the way, so he crouched in front of her and pulled them away. "What?"

"I said I'm mortified."

"Is that a new experience for you?"

"Kind of."

Ragnar brushed her hair from her face. "All right. So you called a child a whore and accused your sister's mate of betraying her . . . I'm sure it could be worse."

"What are you doing?"

"Trying to make you feel better?"

"You're not very good at it."

"I know. Sorry."

"Don't apologize." She gave a little laugh. "I think it's endearing."

"Like the village slow boy who brings flowers to the pretty neighbor girl?"

"Pretty much . . . but I must say you have managed to make me feel better." Keita sat up, scrutinizing the dragon crouched in front of her.

"What?" he asked. "Why are you looking at me like that?"

"You know . . . you have a beautiful face."

"Thank you?"

Reaching out, Keita framed his face with her hands.

"Has no one said that to you before?"

"Of course. My brother said it just the other day before he bought me a pretty new gown . . . and earrings."

"You Northlanders do love your sarcasm."

"It gets us through the day."

"Would this help you get through the day?" And then she kissed him, pressing her lips to his, stroking her hands across his jaw.

To Keita's surprise, unlike their first kiss, there was no response from Ragnar. She might as well have been kissing the boulder she was sitting on.

Feeling a little idiotic, she pulled back and found those strange blue eyes watching her.

"Was I too forward, warlord?"

"No. But I'm no Southlander."

"Which means what exactly?"

"Something about you tugs at me, Keita, and I won't be shooed away like some irritating fly once you bed me. You can play that game with your Fire Breathers, not with me."

"So should I hand my wings over now or wait until you come first?"

His smile was a little sad as he took the hands she still

had pressed against his face and gently pushed them back into her lap. "If that's the best you think of me, perhaps you should find yourself someone else. A safer distraction for Her Majesty than a wing-removing bastard of a Lightning."

He rose to his full height, towering over her with all that power and muscle. As a dragoness, she should feel wary. Ready to fight or flee at the slightest move from the Northlander who made her feel so uncomfortable.

"It's all right," he said. "To the rest of the world we'll be ravenous lovers."

He took a step away, and Keita reached out, catching hold of his inside thigh. Keeping her hand there, she stood. She only reached his shoulder, but that was enough.

"How about we make a deal?" she suggested.

"What kind of deal?"

"I promise not to shoo you away like a . . . what was it? An irritating fly? And you promise not to force a Claiming." She pressed her hand hard against his thigh. "Seduce me, if you like. Charm me, if you can. But no more than that. If that's amenable to you."

Ragnar turned toward her, stepped in close. Her hand automatically moved up until it pressed against the sizable cock he had hidden behind his leggings. His big hands slid into her hair, fingers massaging her scalp while he tilted her head back.

"That's a deal I can agree to," he murmured, his gaze searching her face.

"Then kiss me, warlord. I think we've both waited long enough."

He knew he'd made a dangerous decision as soon as he took her mouth with his own. Nothing had ever tasted sweeter to him, nothing had ever felt so perfect. And what kind of deal had he agreed to? A deal that, at the moment, felt impossible to abide by when all he wanted to do was toss her over his shoulder and fly her back to his Northland home. Yet he knew that the one way to lose Keita forever was to break his word to her. And not the everyday things that males promise their females—"I know I said I'd clean up the ox carcass from the dining hall, but I've been busy!"—but this deal in particular. It was a test, and they both knew it. Because what Keita wanted above all else was her freedom. The freedom to go where she liked, when she liked, with whomever she liked. That meant everything to her. Of all the commitments they'd made to each other over the last few days, some that risked life and death and the future of their territories, this was the one that could make Keita his or push her away forever.

For that reason alone, he should stop this now, get this situation that might or might not involve the Sovereigns out of the way. Then, when the time was right, Ragnar would return and court this dragoness of royal blood properly.

That's what he *should* do.

But as soon as he ripped her bodice open to get at her breasts, any hope of doing what he should rather than what he wanted ended.

He sucked her nipple into his mouth and she moaned, her hands digging into his hair, her small fingers quickly undoing the braid that fell past his shoulders, and he knew they were both beyond the point of stopping and thinking rationally.

Rationally? He would have laughed if he wasn't busy falling on his back and bringing Keita with him.

Rational thought was for when one courted someone one was interested in, but who didn't heat the blood. Someone safe and pretty and not remotely challenging. Keita was dangerous and stunning and more challenging than that nest of ice snakes he fell into once. Ice snakes, which could grow so big and long that they could wrap around a dragon his size seven or eight times, and crush every bone he possessed in less than a minute. And that five-hour fight Ragnar only managed to survive because of Vigholf and Meinhard—not nearly as challenging as Keita.

Then again, nothing ever would be, and he understood that now.

He'd torn the bodice of one of her favorite dresses and she didn't care. He'd dragged her to the lakeside dirt rather than easing her there slowly, seductively—she didn't care. And his grip on her was like steel as he held her close, locking her in place while his warm mouth sucked one nipple, then the other, teeth scraping, hands digging into her hips—and she loved it.

She hadn't dared to hope that someone as methodical as Ragnar the Cunning could ever be so passionate. Then again, maybe she should have known. The way he looked at her, watched her.

He released one arm so that he could reach between them and get at his leggings. She knew then there'd be no foreplay this first time, no soft caresses, no sucking his cock to make him hard, no licking her to get her off, before they got to the finale of it all.

And, for once, it didn't matter. As soon as he'd kissed her, she'd grown wet, nearly desperate. A desperation she hadn't felt in a very long time for any male, no matter how handsome or powerful he might be. At the moment, Keita needed none of those extras, yanking herself from Ragnar's grip so she could unleash human-sized talons and shred the leggings from him until his cock reared up free. She caught hold of it and rose up on her knees, moving her body until she was over it. She spread her thighs, took a breath, and dropped her weight down.

Her pussy engulfed all that male hardness in one shot, both Keita and Ragnar groaning, writhing. He filled her, expanded inside her even more.

Ragnar caught hold of her hips, pulling her in tight while he drove up.

Keita's head fell back; she laughed even as she moaned. Gods! That felt so good.

She couldn't explain why, didn't care. She just knew she loved it. Every inch of his cock driving into her—nothing had ever felt quite this good.

His hands moved up her sides and pulled her down, closer. Ragnar sat up a bit until he could reach her breast. His mouth surrounded it, and then, she felt it. Little lightning strikes against her breast. Little lightning strikes that had her entire body clenching, her eyes opening wide in surprise.

She panted, twisting hard against him, her hands pressing against his shoulders. Not to get away—at this moment, she was sure she'd *never* want to get away—but because she'd lost control. A control she prided herself on having when it came to males. He moved to her other breast, released more little shocks against her flesh, and Keita screamed out, the first orgasm ripping through her, followed closely by a second.

Shaking, covered in sweat, she held on to him as he continued to fuck her, using his mouth and tongue on her nipples until he did it again. Until he sent those tiny lightning strikes into her body and Keita cried out once more, her entire body clenching. But this time his cry joined hers, his hands squeezing her so tight she wondered if he'd crush her ribs. He came inside her, his hips rocking into her as each new ejaculation shot into her hard and hot.

When, finally, his arms wrapped around her waist and her head crashed into his chest, she knew with absolute certainty that making a deal with this dragon was perhaps the *dumbest* thing she'd ever done.

Panting, head slowly beginning to clear, Ragnar realized he had Keita in his arms and a short amount of time to figure out how to keep her there.

The first step, though, was not to let her know that was

his intent. If he even showed a hint of making what they had permanent, she'd run off like a startled rabbit.

So he wisely kept his mouth shut and leaned back against the lakeside dirt with Keita held against him. He waited until they could both breathe evenly again before he asked, "Is there any way to get out of the dancing portion of tonight's dinner?"

She laughed, and he heard the relief in it. Knew she was expecting a litany of praise for what had just happened and promises of commitment for all time. He had no intention of being so obvious. Besides, he never understood the after-sex chatty ones who felt the need to analyze every thrust, gasp, and shudder.

"Not really. But you could try sacrificing your kin while you make your escape."

"They'll hate me for that." He shrugged. "But it might be worth it."

She lifted herself up, resting an elbow on his chest, her chin in her palm. "You can't dance?"

"I have been taught the skill, but that doesn't mean I enjoy it."

"You'll have to at least dance with me."

"If I must."

Lips tightening, she punched his arm. "There are males who'd kill for a chance to dance with me, but I'm allowing you the privilege. You should feel honored."

"Oh, I do." He rolled over until she was beneath him, his cock instantly stirring back to life. "We should bathe in the lake before we go back," he murmured, trying to brush the rest of the dress away from her body. "Might as well do it here."

"You ruined my dress," she remarked.

"Hhhm." Ragnar gripped what was left of the bodice and tore the gown down the middle, giving him complete access to her body.

"You should buy me another."

"You ruined my leggings," he replied, pulling his hands away from her long enough to pull his shirt up over his head and toss it off into the grass. "That makes us even."

"Dammit." She pressed her hands against his chest and stroked his flesh. Ragnar's eyes closed, his head falling forward, his cock more than ready to begin again. "My evil plan for a new dress foiled again." Her fingers grazed the skin where she'd stabbed him with her tail, and Ragnar shuddered.

"I hurt you that day."

"You poisoned me."

"You deserved it. But it has healed, has it not?"

"It has, finally."

She leaned up, licked the scar. "Good thing I'm so damn forgiving, warlord."

He caught her shoulders and, with much more force than he ever planned to use, slammed her back into the ground. Keita only smiled.

"I thought we had to bathe and get back to the castle," she reminded him.

"Later." His gaze locked with hers, he pinned her arms to the ground and began where he'd left off, thrusting his hard cock inside her.

Grinning, Keita tossed her head back, her eyes closed, her body meeting his thrusts with her own. "Later works for me. Much later sounds even better."

Chapter Twenty-Seven

Izzy dropped the dress, faced her cousin, and both burst out laughing, the puppy she still refused to return to the kennel barking happily.

"I think I've outgrown it a bit," she said.

"Gods, Iz!" Branwen crouched by her and tugged at the bottom. It barely reached her shins. "At least you'll be able to dance in it."

They laughed harder.

Although Izzy would never admit it to her mother—at least until she was done being good and self-righteously pissed off—she was happy to be home. And it was home. Her home. The one place she'd always be welcome.

"I'll talk to Keita," Branwen offered, standing tall.

"How does that help? She's a tree gnome compared to me."

"True, but she has an eye. She can track down a dress that'll make you look bloody stunning in seconds."

Branwen went to the door, pulled it open, and yelped. "Don't bloody sneak up on me!"

"I wasn't."

Her cousin stepped out, and Izzy's "uncle" stepped in.

Izzy turned back to the mirror, but kept her head down a bit to get control of her smile. She *knew* he'd be back. After the way he'd looked at her earlier in the courtyard, she *knew* it.

"So what do you think?" she asked him once Brannie had left.

Éibhear blinked. "Uh . . . it's a bit short." He scowled at her chest. "And a bit tight."

She looked down at herself. Her tits were bulging out of the bodice. "I seem to have grown out of it since I last wore it."

"I haven't fared much better with my own wardrobe." He closed the door behind him. "Izzy?"

"Hhmm?"

"I think we should talk."

This was it! This was it! He'd finally admit how much he'd missed her, and that's all she needed—at this moment. He could tell her he adored her and wanted her forever and ever, tomorrow . . . or later in the week. But for now, a simple, "I missed you" or, even better, a simple "I missed you, can't live without you—by the gods, you're the most beautiful woman I've ever known" would do just fine.

"All right then. Let's talk."

He walked up to her, took her hands in his. And blood and fire, he had big hands!

"Izzy?"

"Aye?"

He let out a breath. "You need to be careful."

Careful? Careful of what? His overwhelming love and adoration?

"I need to be careful about what?"

"Celyn."

"Celyn? What about Celyn?"

"I know you don't understand, that you think he's just being friendly or a good cousin, but I think he wants more from you than that."

Izzy couldn't believe it. He was still playing protective uncle. But she already had protective uncles! Plus a protective grandfather, protective great uncles, protective aunts and great aunts, and protective cousins! What she didn't need, what she would *never* need again, was another god-damn protective *anything*!

Izzy pulled her hands away. "You're an idiot."

Éibhear stepped away from her. "What?"

"I said you are an idiot."

"I'm trying to watch out for you."

"I don't need you watching out for me. You haven't watched out for me for two years now and look." She held her arms out from her body. "I'm still here. In one piece. I will tell you this, though." She slammed her finger into his chest. "Celyn has watched my back in battle." She slammed her finger again. "Celyn has helped me wash blood out of my hair." Another slam. "Celyn also tore the arms off a bloke who thought it would be funny to jump me when I was out alone on night patrol." Another slam that had Éibhear backing up into the door. "So if you don't mind, I think I'll keep Celyn as a friend since he's been there when *you have not*!"

"I was trying to warn you!"

"You can stick your warnings up your ass!" She shoved him aside and yanked the door open. "Now get the fuck out of my room."

Éibhear stomped into the hall, but he spun around to face her. "Izzy—"

She slammed the door in his face and tore the stupid, too small dress off her body, chucking it across the room.

He had to be the most infuriating dragon she'd ever met, and it galled her that she might be trapped loving him forever!

"Are they having an execution?" Vigholf asked, watching as the Southlanders began to move tables out of the way to open up the floor.

"They don't do that sort of thing during dinner," Meinhard stated, then added, "The humans don't, anyway."

"But we've already finished eating." Vigholf kept his hand on his sword. "Maybe we should leave?"

Ragnar had kept it from them as long as he could, but now he had no choice but to speak the truth. "We can't leave."

"Why not?"

"Because we're invited. It would look poorly if we leave."

"Invited? For what?"

Ragnar took a breath to explain it all to his kin, but the musicians began to play and the Ruiner slid to a stop on his knees, facing the front of the hall. He was such an odd dragon. "Sister!" he called out.

"Brother!" Keita, looking dazzling in a light blue gown, her dark red hair threaded with light blue flowers, ran bare-foot up to her brother.

"Dance with me," he ordered. "My mate refuses."

Keita gasped. "Is she mad? Does she know who she turns down?" She placed her hand into her brother's. "When will she ever get a chance to dance with someone as beautiful and amazing as you?"

"That's what *I* keep telling her!" Gwenvael got to his feet and spun his sister out into the middle of the floor. "But she never listens."

"You bastard!" Vigholf growled at Ragnar through clenched teeth.

"I'm leaving," Meinhard said.

"Neither of you are going anywhere." To be honest, he didn't want to be left alone. "If I'm sticking it out, you are as well."

"We don't have to." Vigholf glared at him. "We're not the ones fucking a royal."

His brother and cousin had heard the rumors started by Keita. If they'd brought it up to him earlier in the day, he would have told them honestly—knowing they could be trusted—that it was all a lie. He couldn't really say that now, though, could he?

"You still follow my command, brother. And you will stay or I'll—"

The argument ended abruptly as the three males were approached by two females. Two *young* females. A little too young for them, in fact.

"Lady Iseabail," Ragnar said.

She smiled. "Just call me Izzy."

"And I'm just Branwen."

"Can we help you with something?"

"My cousin and I were wondering if you'd like to dance with—"

"No," all three Lightnings answered in unison.

"Well, you don't *all* have to bark at me."

The Blue walked up to them, scowling down at Izzy. She didn't even look at him. It seemed Izzy was the only female in Dark Plains who didn't feel the need to throw herself into the arms of the big bastard.

"We need to talk," the Blue said.

"Again? Haven't I been tortured enough this evening?"

"You took what I said wrong, and throwing food at my head during dinner just shows you haven't matured much at all."

"Oh, piss off!"

Vigholf choked back a laugh, and Meinhard took a drink of his ale.

"No, I will not piss off. Who do you think you're talking to?"

"Do you really want me to answer that?" she asked before walking off, the Blue following right behind her.

Branwen stood there a moment longer before she shrugged and said, "I have nothing to say to any of you." Then she disappeared into the growing crowd on the dance floor.

Vigholf nodded. "I like her honesty."

Meinhard slammed down his mug. "Their ale tastes like piss."

"More like watered-down piss."

"If all you two are going to do is complain—" Ragnar began, but again he was cut off. This time by Keita.

As soon as his brother and cousin saw her, they both stood straighter and smiled at her. "Lady Keita," they both said. They might not be pissed at Ragnar for having swooped up Keita, but since he hadn't Claimed her, she was still considered fair game by Northland standards. The cold-hearted bastards.

"My lords. I see that you're not a fan of the ale."

"Oh, no, no. It's fine." Meinhard picked his mug up again and forced himself to take another sip. "It's . . . smooth."

Keita laughed, bright white teeth flashing, smooth human throat stretching as her head tipped back. Gods, he wanted her so badly, he could barely breathe.

"I do appreciate you forcing that down, Meinhard," she said. "But don't worry. I have something that should help." She raised her arm and snapped her fingers. A servant carrying a tray rushed to her side. "My father's brew," she said, handing each of them a mug. "He's around here somewhere with my mother. Avoid him if you can. This ale is quite popular with his Clan and Dagmar, although my brothers wouldn't touch it if you held a knife to their throats."

Ragnar stared into his mug. "Sure it's not poisoned?" he couldn't help but tease.

"Only yours," she whispered back. "Now that I'm nearly done with you."

While he debated whether she was serious or not, his brother and cousin tried the ale. After a deep sip, they both nodded in approval.

"That's nice."

"Real nice."

Shrugging, Ragnar tried his. As it burned its way to his stomach, he thought the evil wench really had poisoned him!

Ragnar bent over and coughed, unable to hide the pain he was suffering.

"Don't mind him," Vigholf said, slapping Ragnar on the

back. Something that did not help his current situation. "He's always been kind of weak with his drink."

"I see that. Well, no worries." Keita took the mug from Ragnar and, while he watched through the tears in his eyes, drank all that brewed acid in one hearty gulp. When she was done, she slammed the mug on the table behind them and wiped her mouth with the back of her hand. "Ahhh. My father's brew has only gotten better over the years."

"Oy! Your royal majesty!" one of her brothers yelled from the floor. "You coming out here or what?"

"My kin call," she said with a laugh. "But I hope you three will stay and enjoy yourselves."

She smiled again before turning on her heel and moving out into the dancing crowd.

Ragnar quickly picked up the mug she'd put down, and all three of them looked inside. "She downed every drop of this bile."

Together they all looked up and watched her dance by with her silver-haired brother, Briec. She moved as if she hadn't had anything to drink, as steady as she ever was, making him wonder exactly how much she'd drunk that night with her cousins and aunts.

Then Meinhard said what they were all thinking. . . .

"She's absolutely perfect."

Fearghus grabbed his daughter and turned away before the girl's mother could get her hands around her throat.

"You little viper!"

"Annwyl—"

"Shut up!" She wiped the blood from her face. "Look what she did."

"I'm sure it was an accident." He was lying, of course. He'd seen his daughter grab hold of that eating dagger before he could and throw it with a skill he'd taken decades to master.

Barely two years old and her skills rivaled his, her mother's, even Bercelak's. The worst part was, he knew that Talwyn threw that dagger not out of rage, but curiosity. Hitting her target was her only concern. Although her skills in doing damage were far in advance of her age, her understanding that throwing knives, swords, plates, cups, chairs had consequences was still far from being grasped by her.

"Don't be hard on her," he told his mate.

"We need a nanny." Annwyl took the cloth one of the servants handed her and pressed it to her latest wound.

"We're working on that."

"Work faster."

Fearghus held his daughter up to her mother. "Say you're sorry, Talwyn."

"What are you doing?" Annwyl asked him. "You know she can't say it."

"Can't and won't are two different things. She talks to her brother more than enough."

"Whispering plots is not talking. It's whispering plots."

"I've said it before, and I'll say it again. You're too hard on—*ow! You treacherous little demon child!*"

Before Ragnar could kick the beast gnawing at his foot, Annwyl swept the little demon up in her arms and held him against her chest. "Don't you dare, you mad bastard!"

"He started it!"

"What's wrong with you? He's your son."

"He's *your* son, wench." He pulled his daughter to him. "She's mine."

"You can have her."

"Fine!"

"Fine!"

"That's enough." Rhiannon moved in and took her grandson from Annwyl while Bercelak took Talwyn from Fearghus. "You two dance or something before the Northlanders get to see the future heir to my throne having a sword fight with his own mate."

"When did you two get here?" Fearghus asked.

"Can't we come and visit our kin and our beautiful grand-children?" She smiled at the demon child, who sneered at Fearghus.

"Little bastard," he muttered, earning a slap to the back of his head from his father. "Must you do that?"

"Don't be an ass. Go. Dance. Fuck. Do something."

Fearghus grabbed Annwyl's hand. She kissed her son's head, scowled at their daughter, and smiled at his mother and then Bercelak. She started to walk to the dance floor when Fearghus yanked her back.

"What was that?" he demanded.

"What was what?"

"You. Smiling. At my father."

"Would you have preferred I spit at him?"

"As a matter of fact . . . yes."

Still holding his hand, she placed her other hand on her hip. "Fearghus the Destroyer, either dance with me or fuck me, but do *something*."

Before he could answer, Gwenvael leapt to Annwyl's side and said, "If he's not up for either, I'm sure I can—"

"Fuck off!" they both yelled.

Pouting, Gwenvael walked away. "You two certainly are moody these days."

Once alone, they both looked at each other and smiled.

"Your sister scared off the last potential nanny," Talaith complained as she dropped onto Briec's lap uninvited.

"How did that happen?"

"Not sure. Brastias was a little vague, but it looks like we're on the search again. Adding much to Annwyl's prophecies of doom."

"There's no nanny? So you've left my perfect daughter—"

"If you call her that one more time . . ."

"—alone and defenseless?"

"No. Your mother and father are taking care of the children. I think they only come to these things now so that they can take care of the children. And let's be honest, my love, our daughter and the twins are hardly defenseless. Although when I find out which one of you idiots gave Talwyn that damn training sword . . ."

"That idiot would be her grandfather."

"Oh."

"Oh?" Briec demanded. "All Bercelak gets is an 'oh,' but if it was me or Fearghus or, gods forbid, Gwenvael, you'd have torn our heads off and shit down our necks?"

"Yes. There's truth to that."

"How is that fair?"

"Because it's Bercelak. Sweet, caring, wonderful Bercelak, who takes excellent care of his grandchildren and—*ow!*" Talaith yelped as her ass hit the floor from Briec standing up and walking away without warning.

But what exactly did she expect?

Sweet? Caring? Bercelak?

Morfyd was debating between several of the sweet desserts when her sister asked, "Sure your hips can afford that, sister? You are beginning to look like Mum from behind."

Outraged, Morfyd spun around, a huge fireball ready to be unleashed, but Brastias stepped in front of her, his wide back blocking the sight of Keita's perfect, unmarred face.

"Keita, your Northland guests are beginning to look panicked. You may want to check on them before they run screaming from the building."

"Honestly," Keita complained. "It's only dancing."

Keita went off to rescue the Northlanders, at least one

of which she was currently—and stupidly—bedding, and Brastias slowly faced Morfyd.

"Isn't one slap fight a day enough for even beautiful dragons?"

"She starts it!" Morfyd accused.

"And you let her. Why? When you know she does it on purpose?"

"Because she deserves a good thrashing."

Brastias leaned in and kissed her forehead, but she got the feeling he only did it to stop from laughing at her. Not that she blamed him. She and Keita were too old for this sort of thing, but there was something about her sister that simply pissed Morfyd off.

"You look beautiful," he murmured against her skin, his kiss lingering longer than was necessary. Not that she minded. She didn't mind. In fact, she liked it very much.

"Thank you."

"Do we have to stay long?"

"No." She swallowed past the lump in her throat, her eyes briefly closing. "It's not a feast or anything. Simply an after-dinner get-together."

"Then why don't we"—he kissed her cheek—"head up to our room"—he kissed her jaw, her throat—"and retire for the evening?"

"That sounds—" Morfyd almost saw him too late. Gwenvael walking past and spying the pair, his eyes narrowing on Brastias's back as he watched the couple cuddle. Gods, he was being such a baby about all this! Gwenvael came to an abrupt stop, and she watched her brother pull air in his lungs to unleash flame at Brastias. Tired of her brother's ridiculous vendetta against her mate, Morfyd wrapped her arms around Brastias's shoulders, pulled him in against her with her chin resting on his shoulder, and unleashed the fire ball she'd been planning to use on Keita.

While her brother flew back across the room, she finished her thought. "Delightful. That sounds delightful. Let's go."

* * *

Ragnar and Vigholf stepped aside, watching the South-lander fly past them engulfed in flames.

Once he hit the wall, they moved together again and focused on the crowd.

"What else have you heard?"

"Lots of talk about attacks on small villages and towns in or near the Western Mountains. They try to make it look like the barbarian tribes, but the troops are finding evidence it's the Sovereigns."

Ragnar blew out a breath and nodded. "All right. Good work."

"You sure you're not just reading too much into those missives?"

"Perhaps, but I'd rather be sure, wouldn't you?"

"You sure this has nothing to do with your princess? A reason to keep her around maybe?"

"It has almost everything to do with her. But that doesn't change the fact that if the Irons come, they'll be coming down through the Northlands."

"You really think Styrbjörn would be that stupid?"

"Yes. I do."

"Then I'll see if I can find out any more."

"Good. Thank you, brother."

Vigholf nodded. "There's one other thing. It may be nothing, but . . ."

If it was nothing, Vigholf wouldn't bother to bring it up. "But what?"

He leaned in closer, dropped his voice even lower. "They say the human queen has been having dreams. About something riding down mountains of ice on horses with eyes of fire, giant dogs with horns running at their side."

Ragnar stared at the floor, his heart skipping several beats. "Are you sure?"

"It's what I heard, but the rumor is only now starting to spread." He shrugged. "They all think she's mad anyway, so few take these dreams seriously."

Because they didn't know.

"If it's them she dreams of, brother—" Vigholf began.

"Don't panic." Ragnar lifted his head, glanced around. "Let me see what I can find out. We'll talk more later."

"All right."

Ragnar motioned across the room to Meinhard, who'd found himself several females to talk to. "He seems to be doing all right for himself."

"He has all his hair," Vigholf muttered, making Ragnar want to punch his brother in the head.

"Perhaps you'd like hair like these royals. Past your ass, so you can look particularly enticing to other males."

"I didn't say I wanted that. I just don't want this."

"Be grateful you still have your head."

"Lord Vigholf!" Keita called out, stepping away from the dancing crowd. "There you are."

Considering he and his brother had not moved, Ragnar wasn't sure how hard it could be for Keita to find Vigholf.

With her hand on another She-dragon's shoulder, Keita said, "Lord Vigholf, this is my cousin Aedammair."

"My lady."

"It's 'captain,'" the brown dragoness gruffly corrected. "You wanna dance then?"

"Well, actually—"

"Good." The dragoness grabbed Vigholf's surcoat and yanked the poor bastard out onto the dance floor.

Keita leaned her backside against the table, her palms pressed against the wood.

"And what exactly was that about?" Ragnar asked.

"He looked depressed. Aedammair will help him with that."

"Tell me, princess, do you whore out all your relations to appease outsiders?"

"Only the cousins who tell me, 'I'll fuck that purple stallion over there. What's his name?'"

"Why does she get to bed a purple stallion without question, but you can't?"

"Aedammair is a low-born. *I*, however, am of royal blood. I can't be running around, bedding just anyone." She pursed her lips before admitting, "I *do*, but I'm not really supposed to."

Ragnar laughed, gazing down at her. "You look amazing tonight."

Her smile was bright. "I know. I put in all this effort for you, I'll have you know. It best pay off."

"I think I can arrange that."

Gwenvael had finally managed to get to his feet, stumbling up to the table while brushing dirt and flame residue off his still-intact clothes, proving whoever had set him aflame hadn't been trying to hurt him as much as make him go away.

"You're unreasonable!" the Gold yelled at someone across the hall.

"Do you think whoever he's yelling at was being unreasonable?"

"No, not at all." Keita spread her arms out a bit farther, and her fingers brushed against his.

Ragnar watched his brother cut through the crowd on the dance floor, trying to make it to an exit, the brown dragoness hot on his heels. "When can we get out of here?" Ragnar asked, keeping his voice low. "I have a great need to be back inside you."

"We could brazenly walk out with me over your shoulder like one of my cousins did with his mate. Although I'm fairly certain that may lead to your imminent death from my brothers before we make it out to the courtyard."

"I'd like to avoid that."

"So would I. Can't have my way with you if you're dead."

"That's an excellent point."

Vigholf charged back the other way, pushing Fire Breathers aside as he tried to make his escape.

"We could sneak out like my baby brother did a few minutes ago with one of the human nobles' daughters."

"If you witnessed him sneaking out, he wasn't sneaking out well."

Keita snorted. "That little bastard *wanted* to be seen. He's being so obvious about this whole thing."

"I have no idea what you're talking about."

"It's nothing. My brother's still young. He'll learn about females soon enough."

"I'm thinking your brother will be a thousand years old and *still* know nothing about females."

Vigholf suddenly appeared before them and whispered, "Help. *Me.*"

"Where'dya go?" the dragoness captain asked, getting a good hold on Vigholf and dragging him back to the dance floor.

"When I was your brother's age," Ragnar continued, "I'd already been in battle against one of my own uncles' Hordes, traveled into the Ice Lands to train for ten years with a small group of mages that believed they were neither good nor evil, and destroyed an entire monastery of monks."

"Gods," Keita said on a shaky breath. "It's like you want me to fuck you right here."

Briec walked up to them, his eyes locked on the dance floor.

"What's going on out there?" he asked, motioning to Vigholf, who was trying desperately to keep the brown She-dragon from getting as close as she'd like.

"Aedammair is helping poor Vigholf forget his tragic hair loss."

Briec shook his head at Keita, smiling. "You really are a heartless cow."

Instead of being insulted, Keita laughed and replied, "I know!"

"By the way," her brother said, and Ragnar wondered how one dragon could possibly sound so bored *all* the time. "Ren wanted me to tell you he'll be back soon."

"Wait. What?" Keita stood straight. "Ren left? When?"

"Sometime this afternoon."

"Where did he go?"

"I don't know."

"Did you not think to ask?"

"Do you actually think I care?" Briec asked, before walking off.

"Well, you don't have to be rude!" Keita began to play with the gold bracelet she had on her wrist.

"You're worried."

"It's not like Ren to leave like that. He always tells me when he's going off."

"Maybe he wasn't planning to be gone for long."

"Perhaps."

"You're obsessing."

"I don't obsess."

"You're obsessing right now."

"I am not." She quickly stepped to the side as Vigholf slammed into the table.

"By the sweet shit of gods, help me!"

The captain walked up to them. "What's wrong with him anyway?"

"He's shy." Keita leaned in and whispered, "And I think he's a little sweeter on Gwenvael than you."

"Oh. Like that, is it?"

"I'm afraid so." Keita pointed across the room. "But there's his cousin. Meinhard."

"Meinhard. I like that name." And off the Brown went.

"You are cruel, Princess Keita," Ragnar chastised.

"And here I was trying to be helpful."

Chapter Twenty-Eight

Éibhear let the duke's daughter lead him through the forest to a "deserted little spot" she knew. She was pretty enough, but, more importantly, she was nice! If he wanted to be talked down to and have food thrown at his head, simply because he was trying to be helpful, he could have stayed in the north.

But he wouldn't let thoughts of Iseabail the Bitchy ruin what he was sure would be an entertaining finish to a magnificently shitty night.

"Have you been here before, my lord?" she asked.

"No, I haven't." He was lying, of course. There were few places this close to his brother's cave and Annwyl's castle that he'd not explored. But the duke's daughter wanted to believe that she was showing him something new, and why should Éibhear disabuse her of that? Especially when she was pretty and eager. He liked eager.

She led him up a ridge that looked out over one of the many lakes in this territory. It was a quiet place, and he thought she'd chosen well until she stopped, tilting her head, and put her finger to her lips. "I think I hear someone," she whispered.

Together they continued up the ridge, but kept quiet. Éibhear had the distinct feeling the duke's daughter was a bit of a snoop. He'd have to tell Dagmar. She might prove useful to his brother's mate. Dagmar did like snoops.

As they neared the top, they dropped to the ground and crawled the rest of the way, both laughing a little as they did.

But Éibhear's laughter died in his throat when he saw it was Izzy by the lake—and she was alone with Celyn. Even Branwen was nowhere to be seen. Only that damn puppy he'd already told her twice to return to Dagmar.

Did she not hear a word he'd said? Did she not understand *anything?* And was she stupidly doing this *just* to get under his scales?

With the dress Keita had finally found her pulled up to her knees, Izzy had her feet dangling in the water, and Celyn swam from one end of the small lake to the other. When he reached her, he stopped.

"Are you going to be like this all night?" Celyn demanded.

"Yes."

"I don't know why you let him get to you this way."

"I don't know why you keep bringing him up."

"Because you're sitting here pouting about it."

"True, but I was pouting alone."

"You weren't alone."

"The puppy hardly counts, Celyn."

Celyn swam in a little closer. "You didn't tell him about us, did you?"

Izzy planted her palms flat on the ground behind her, the puppy lying against her hand. "About us?"

"About our relationship."

"We don't have a relationship."

"What would you call it then?"

"*Not* a relationship."

"Why? Because of him?"

"No. Because of me. I have no plans to get attached to anyone in the immediate future."

"Why was that again? Oh, right. You're going to be general one day, and you can't let me get in the way of that."

"I am going to be general." And she said it with such certainty that Éibhear believed her. He was glad she was being smart and not letting Celyn dissuade her from going after what she wanted. Although Celyn was being a little pushier than Éibhear would expect. *And what relationship?*

"One day," she went on, "*I'll* be leading Annwyl's armies into battle. But thank you so very much for your faith in me." She stood and tried to stomp off, but Celyn placed one hand on the lakeside dirt and reached up with the other, catching her arm and holding her there.

Éibhear's hands turned into fists when he thought his cousin might just be going over the edge from being pushy to downright forceful. He wouldn't let him force Izzy into anything.

"I'm sorry if I hurt your feelings, Izzy. I didn't mean to."

Izzy took in several deep breaths before she crouched down next to the lake. "I never lied to you, Celyn," she said. "I never promised you something I couldn't give."

"Couldn't or wouldn't?"

"Both. I won't let anything get between me and what I want. I told you that from the beginning. You said you understood."

"I do, but I never said I'd like it."

"Not liking it sounds like your problem. Not mine." And the teasing was back in her voice, the smile back on her face.

"You'd think you'd at least *try* to make me feel better," Celyn complained.

"I thought you were here to make *me* feel better."

"You're right. That is why I'm here." Celyn scrambled out of the water, the duke's daughter gasping a little when she saw his naked human body lit by the moon overhead. But all Éibhear could think was that Celyn was naked and Izzy was alone with him.

Laughing, Izzy made a weak attempt to run, but Celyn caught her and pulled her into his arms, holding her against him.

"You're getting my gown wet, and it's not even mine!"

"I'll get you another."

"With what? You have no money."

"I'll steal some from Brannie."

"And she'll rip your scales off."

"Will you nurse me back to health?"

"No. I'll let you suffer. It's wrong to steal from your own sister."

"Come on, Iz," Celyn practically begged, and Éibhear slowly rose up, ready to tear the pushy bastard apart for trying to force Izzy to do what she'd never done before when she wasn't ready to . . .

"Don't make me wait any longer. It's been weeks since we've been alone."

"Days, you big whiner." She giggled, Celyn nibbling on her neck, while the puppy wandered off to the woods as if to give them some privacy. A thought that absolutely horrified Éibhear. "We almost got caught that last time too."

Caught? Caught doing what exactly?

"The last thing I heard," Celyn said, "was my mother. 'Iseabail, Daughter of Talaith and Briec, what are you doing out here naked?' And your fast-thinking reply of, 'Uhhhh.'"

Laughing hard now, Izzy put her arms around Celyn's neck and brought her legs up and wrapped them around his waist. "I didn't know what to say!"

"Well." He stared at her lips. "We're alone now, Iseabail, Daughter of Talaith and Briec, and my mother is still miles away. You going to keep me waiting?"

"Not tonight, no."

She kissed him, and it was definitely not the kiss of some innocent who was desperately trying to hold on to her virginity.

Éibhear turned away, unable to watch a second more. He needed to be away from here. Far away. And he was halfway down the ridge before the duke's daughter caught up with him. He'd forgotten all about her, and she'd been right next to him.

"Are you all right?"

"Aye. Sorry. I need to get back."

"Oh." She looked disappointed, but he couldn't help her with that right now. Instead the most he could do was walk her back to her guest quarters and leave her to the care of her servants.

"Tell me, Lord Ragnar," Keita said low, as she circled behind him. "Have you ever had a Southland She-dragon's mouth on your cock?"

Ragnar locked his knees, cleared his throat. "No. I haven't had that."

"Would you like to?"

Gods, yes! "I wouldn't mind."

Keita chuckled and backed away from him. "Then you best come for me, my lord. So you can *come* for me." Her chuckle turned into a laugh, and she walked off into the thinning crowd. Ragnar started off after her, but he suddenly had three long-haired freaks in his way.

"You enjoying our sister, Lightning?" Fearghus asked him.

"I don't know what you mean."

"Do you really think you can hide what you're doing with our baby sister from us?" Briec demanded.

And Gwenvael tossed in a "Yeah!" But when Ragnar raised a brow, he added, "Just trying to help."

"We all know," Ragnar explained, "that there is nothing I can say at this moment that will prevent my pummeling. So I will have to use alternative means."

Briec, another who had, at least for a time, walked the path of Magick, cracked his knuckles. He most likely looked forward to a good mage battle right here in the Blood Queen's hall.

Too bad for them he had other options. "Talaith?" Ragnar called out.

"You bastard," Briec hissed at him, and Gwenvael laughed. "He's good."

The beautiful human witch walked over. "What's wrong?"

He leaned in and whispered, "I'm off for a secret rendezvous with Keita, but her brothers blocked my way. Can you help me?"

Fearghus stared at him with his mouth open. "Gods, you are *such* a bastard!"

"What is wrong with all of you?" Talaith demanded. "Why can't you leave him alone? He's so sweet!"

"Gods, Briec," Gwenvael noted, "she's been drinking."

"Not really," Talaith argued. "I only had two glasses of wine." But she held up four fingers when she said that. To help her, Ragnar folded down her pinky and ring finger. "That is sooooo sweet. You are sooooo sweet." Then she turned on the three Fire Breathers blocking his way. "*You leave him alone!*"

Eternally grateful to Dagmar Reinholdt for the helpful tip on how to handle Keita's brothers, Ragnar walked around them and headed out the way Keita had. Once outside, he sniffed the air and caught her scent. He started off after her, tracking her past dog kennels and horse stables. He knew when he neared Keita, her wonderful scent growing strong. But he stopped short and quickly stepped back into the shadow of an empty guard house.

She was hugging two older dragons in human form, both wearing long brown cloaks. One was a Blue, the other a Red.

"Elders Gillivray and Lailoken! How good to see you both!"

"My lady, please," one said. "Keep your voice down."

"Oh." Keita briefly covered her mouth with her hand. "Sorry." She stepped closer. "Is there a problem?"

"Not a problem. Not really," one said.

"Although we are glad to have you back at home. Where you belong. With your people."

"And I am glad to be back." She glared at the castle. "Although my mother doesn't make it easy for me to stay." Her face a study in concern, she caught the hand of each Elder and said, "I heard about the unfortunate event with Elder Eanruig. I am *so* sorry."

"Thankfully, neither of us was there to witness it, my lady."

"Nor I." She shook her head. "Still. *Such* a tragedy. He's always been so loyal to our kind and the House of Gwalchmai fab Gwyar." Ragnar's eyes crossed. Gods! Did the royal Southland names have to be so complicated? "I was shocked and, I must admit, disturbed when I heard what happened." She took a deep breath. "I'm afraid to ask, but . . . was my mother behind it?"

"There is no evidence of that, my lady," one of them said in a low voice.

"I didn't ask if you had evidence, Elders. What does your gut tell you?"

"What does your gut tell *you*, princess?" the other pushed.

She let out a breath and briefly gazed off. "You both know me well enough to know what *I* think. My mother's loathing of Elder Eanruig was known to any in earshot, and as you know, Elder Gillivray"—she motioned to the old blue dragon—"I've never understood that. He was always so sweet to me. So honest and sincere. And quite protective."

"The blood in you, princess, clearly flows from your grandmother's veins." The red dragon—Elder Lailoken, Ragnar supposed—grinned. "She would have adored you more than words can say."

"It hurts me I was never able to meet her. From what I've heard, she and I would have much in common."

"You do, princess." Lailoken stepped in closer. "And that is something that you'll need to remember in the coming months. Something that you must never forget."

"Why?" Keita asked, her eyes wide in apparent confusion.

The two Elders looked at each other, Lailoken nodding at Gillivray.

"It's time, princess," Gillivray explained softly, "for you to start thinking about your future among your people—and claiming your rightful place on the throne."

Keita's head lowered the slightest bit while her brown gaze swept the empty courtyard around her. When she was done, she leaned in a bit, her fingers carefully brushing her dark red hair behind her ear. "My *royal* blood connection to my grand-mother is something that I never have and never will forget, my great lords. But I do have grave concerns over the safety of my father and my brothers—"

Lailoken raised his free hand to stop her. "There is no need to fear there. In fact, if your mother understands that change is for the better, I'm sure something beneficial to all can be worked out."

"But how?"

"Don't worry about that. We're not in this alone, you see. And we've made sure our . . . friends are well aware of what your concerns and demands might be."

"And who are these friends, my lords?"

"That will come out in time. For now, my lady, you simply need to understand that your chance for true glory and power is nearly upon you. Are you ready for that?"

Keita nodded her head and stepped back. She glanced around again before saying, quite simply, "Proceed as you wish, my lords. I am ready for whatever the world has in store for me. Now go . . . with my blessing."

"Thank you, my lady."

The two males bowed low before the princess, and she re-turned the gesture with nothing more than a small bow of her head. Without another word, she walked off, heading toward one of the fields surrounding the human queen's stronghold. Once she was gone, the two Elders stared hard at each other before they turned away and headed off in opposite directions.

Keita stood and stared off at nothing but trees and more trees, her hands tight in front of her, her breath coming out in short pants. When Ragnar found her, he didn't touch her.

"Keita?"

"They dare approach me so close to my kin? They dare come *here* to do it? I thought they'd send for me. Or send some messenger."

"They're feeling safe."

"They shouldn't. They shouldn't feel safe at all."

"Keita—"

"I should have struck them down when I had the chance. I should have alerted Fearghus. He would have torn them to pieces before they could ever hope to fly away."

"And what purpose would that have served?"

Keita closed her eyes, trying hard to control her rage. "They approached me *here*, Ragnar, with my kin no more than a few hundred feet away."

"You need to get control," he said calmly. "You need to re-member why we're doing this. Why we're taking this risk."

Ragnar was right. If she let her rage loose now, she could ruin everything. Gillivray and Lailoken were minor players in this game. Puppets, who would probably be killed long before any real fighting began. She didn't think they wanted war either, but that's what would happen before Queen Rhiannon ever gave up her throne. Yet Keita still held out hope that she could stop a war. That she could stop the Irons. That she could stop them all.

It took her a moment, but she realized her breathing had re-turned to normal, her hands no longer clenched tight, and her body no longer shaking.

Ragnar also held her now, his arm around her waist, his

cheek pressed into the back of her head. He'd soothed her growing rage with only that.

"You need to tell your mother," Ragnar reminded her.

"Not yet."

"Keita, you promised."

"I know, but I was actually lying to her."

"You're going to test her patience."

"My mother has no patience. But I do. We wait to tell her. This has not played out yet, warlord. Not yet."

Finally smiling, she reminded him, "I made you promises for tonight."

"And they can wait."

Understanding deep in her soul that time was short, she knew that nothing that could ever mean anything to her could wait.

Chapter Twenty-Nine

Keita turned in his arms, her body much too close. Too close if he was going to be the bigger dragon here.

"That's very sweet of you," she said.

"I'm known for being very sweet."

"No, you're not."

"I could be."

"No, you couldn't." She giggled. "But I like you despite all that."

"Thank you. That's good to know."

Her hands slid around his waist, her leg wrapping around his calf. "You hold yourself back from me."

"I do."

"Why?"

"Why give you everything when you made it clear you will not take it?"

She shook her head. "I don't understand you Lightnings. The first female you meet, you're ready to settle down and have little hatchlings with."

"No, Keita." He brought his hands up and cradled her face. "It's not that easy. You are hardly the first female I've met. Definitely not the first female I've bedded. But you are the first who's truly caught my interest. Who's truly enticed me."

"It won't last. Every male gets bored."

"For Lightnings, life is too hard to allow for boredom. And only a fool would get bored around the females we've been known to choose. One gets bored, one lets one's guard down—and wakes up the next morning with a throbbing headache and a missing back claw."

"That's a lovely story."

"Tragically, for one of my cousins . . . it's a fact."

She snorted, briefly buried her head into his chest. "As entertaining a fact as that is, I'm thinking of you."

"Are you?"

She patted his shoulder and stepped over to a nearby tree. "I can't do it, you see."

"You can't do what?"

"Allow myself to be held captive, chained against my will, forced to live a life of lies."

"Most of us just called that Claimed. Humans call it marriage."

"And I can't do that."

"What can you do?"

"Besides be beautiful?"

"You're much more than that, Keita."

She smirked. "I never thought I'd hear you speak those words, warlord."

"How could I not?" he asked, stepping to her, watching as she took an immediate step back. She never backed down if someone was complimenting her beauty or her latest gown or threatening her with deadly physical harm. But his simple words practically had her running off into the dark forest behind them. "Every day you play a dangerous game with your kin, your mother's enemies, your mother's court. Every day you do all you can to protect the throne of your people, and protect your siblings from themselves." That made her giggle, even as she backed another step away from him. "And every day you show a caring for those around you without any of that unattractive weakness that annoys me beyond all reason."

"Éibhear isn't weak."

"Even now you protect the weakest of your Horde."

"We don't have Hordes, and Éibhear is not the weakest. I mean, he's not weak at all." Her back slammed into the tree behind her, and she stamped her foot. "Honestly! You're so mean to him."

"Convince me to be nice."

"Blackmail is so unbecoming to a dragon."

"That's not really blackmail. More like coercion," he teased, pressing his hands against the tree behind her, blocking her in. "And we Northlanders pride ourselves on being bullying scum when it's necessary." He leaned in, kissed her. Such a soft mouth and such a talented tongue.

Her hands reached up, clutched his jaw. And Ragnar knew he'd no longer be able to fight this.

Keita didn't know what to do with this dragon. He made no demands, except relatively logical ones. He promised her nothing, and gave nothing to her but himself. It wasn't fair. How was she to fight this? How was she to stay true to herself when he insisted on seeing her as no one else did?

He pulled out of their kiss and slowly dropped to his knees in front of her.

A move she didn't feel was fair at all, considering.

He pushed her gown up until he had it at her waist. "You're always naked under your clothes," he observed.

"Why wouldn't I be?" she asked.

Grinning, he pressed his mouth to her stomach, her hips, her mound, the inside of her thighs. Once he had her squirming, he placed his mouth on her pussy and slid his tongue inside.

Keita's groan was long and louder than she intended. She didn't care. It felt too good.

He thrust his tongue in and out, getting her wet, making her tremble like the virgin she had been a really long time ago. Then he dragged his tongue out, skimming up until he could swirl it around her clit.

When Keita felt her knees give, she gripped the back of Ragnar's head and pulled him away, yanking him off. Desperate, panting, she pushed him to the ground and climbed on top of him, dropping her pussy over his mouth while she heaved his cock out of his leggings and wrapped her mouth around it. She felt his growl against her skin, enjoyed the way his hands gripped her hips. He held her tight while he sucked her clit between his lips and whipped it with his tongue.

That's when Keita called up the lightest of heat to warm his cock, and felt his fingers digging even deeper into her skin. She smiled around the thick flesh in her mouth, pushing the warlord to give her everything he had.

Ragnar knew this game. The who-can-get-the-other-off-faster game. It was a matter of pride with her, wasn't it? Didn't she yet realize he had no intention of giving in that easy?

He suckled on her clit, relentlessly tugging at it until he heard her grunt each time. Then he released one hip and slapped his hand across her ass. Keita's head snapped up, his cock tragically slipping from her mouth, her voice crying out, her body convulsing on top of his.

He drew out her orgasm by slipping two fingers inside her pussy and keeping his lips working her clit. When he knew he'd wrung her dry, at least for the moment, he lifted her off him and got to his knees.

She was panting, gazing up at him. He caught hold of her gown and lifted it off her head, tossing it over her shoulder, the fine silk landing in the dirt. When she didn't even notice, he had to fight hard not to smile. He practically tore his leggings off the rest of the way, stripping as fast as he could. Then he turned her away from him, both of them still on their knees, and sunk into her pussy from behind.

Her head fell back against his chest, and he kissed her, letting her taste herself on his lips and tongue, inside his mouth. He stroked his cock inside her, his eyes nearly crossing at the way she clenched her muscles each time he pulled out, taking all of him with a smile and a groan when he slammed back in.

She caught hold of one of the hands he had gripping her waist, lowering it until his fingers were on her pussy, his forefinger teasing her clit. He loved how she showed him what she wanted, took what she needed.

His thrusts became more brutal, his teeth nipping at the side of her neck. He matched the tempo of his cock with that of the finger on her clit. Her hands clutched his, the nails digging into his skin.

He gave her what she wanted. He gave her everything, pounding into her until she screamed his name and he whispered hers. He emptied his seed inside her, and nothing had ever felt more amazing to him before—and he'd moved a mountain once.

Still on their knees, both of them gasping, sweating, clinging to each other, they said nothing. There was nothing to say. But when she gave him that kiss on the cheek, the sweetest kiss he'd ever known, he knew he wouldn't stop until he'd found a way to keep Princess Keita forever.

"She met with them near one of the empty guard houses."

"Did you hear what was said?"

"No. That Northlander was lurking about, and we didn't want to be seen."

"He was following her?"

Her lieutenant sneered. "I wouldn't worry. When she was

done betraying her mother, she fucked that Lightning like a well-paid barmaid."

"There's not much difference between the two."

"Do you want us to pick up Gillivray and Lailoken tonight?"

"No." She walked around the dragon. "First we deal with Her Majesty. *Then* we deal with those two."

"Are you sure about this?" her lieutenant asked. "Her mother is the queen."

"And she's a traitor. News about her and Esyld is spreading through the town like flame on dry wood. We need to make an example of her now before it's too late. Nothing else matters."

The lieutenant nodded, but before walking off he said, "By the way . . . that's a nice eye patch."

It crossed Elestren's mind to tear *both* the bastard's eyes out, but she'd wait to unleash all that rage on Keita the Traitor, Giver of Ridiculous Eye Patches.

Chapter Thirty

Ragnar woke up when he heard the snuffling. He smiled. "Good morn to you."

The mare brushed her muzzle against his head, giving him her blessing, before she lazily moved on to the next bit of grass nearby. Although Ragnar had woken up like this before, surrounded by mares and their yearlings, he'd never managed to wake up like this with a dragoness by his side. But this time was different. This was Keita, and she had her own entourage—all of them stallions. And all of them watching Ragnar closely.

Eventually Keita stirred on her own, brown eyes slowly opening, arms stretching wide.

"And good morn to you too." He kissed her forehead, felt her hand stroke his cheek. "Feeling better?"

"Aye. My rage has turned to cold determination."

"Then the world should quake in fear."

"Sarcasm so early in the morning?"

He brushed her hair from her face. "That wasn't sarcasm. It was honesty. I'll admit I misread you in the beginning, Keita, but I'll not make that mistake again."

Her hand slid around to the back of his neck. "And I thought I'd be so bored with you by now."

"I'm so glad I was able to disappoint you on that."

"So am I," she whispered, pulling herself up, her lips mere millimeters from his. Ragnar closed his eyes, waited for that kiss. When it didn't happen, he opened his eyes and realized she was staring off at the horses.

"What's wrong?"

"I can't believe I didn't think of it before." She looked at him, blinked. "I'm such an idiot."

"What?"

"We all are!" She scrambled away from him, quickly grabbing up her gown and yanking it over her head.

"Wait. Where are you going?"

"I'll catch up with you later!" she yelled at him, already running toward the castle, the stallions watching her go while the mares pushed their yearlings out of the way.

He stood, his cock hard and already dripping. "I can't believe you're leaving me like this!"

"Use your hand!" she said before she disappeared over a small hill.

"Exactly where are you taking us?"

"Oh, shut up," Keita ordered her sister, tired of her asking the same damn question over and over. Rousing the females out of bed and away from their mates had been a task of its own—except for Dagmar, who'd already been up and "plotting" as Gwenvael put it, which was true enough since rumors about Keita and Esyld had already begun to spread—but getting them to follow her several miles into the forest on the other side of the eastern fields took all her cajoling skills.

Keita felt a hand swipe at her hair, and she spun around, her own hands open and slapping at her sister until Annwyl reached between them and shoved them apart.

"Give it a rest!" she barked. "You two are worse than the twins."

Keita tugged her dress back into place. "This won't take long. I promise." Then she added with a little snarl, "I'm trying to help!"

"Then help," Talaith said. "We're right behind you."

Wanting to be done with this, Keita ignored her sister and continued on. When she reached a high ridge that looked over the Deep Canyons, she stopped.

"What are we looking at?" Talaith asked.

From out of the line of trees on the low plain surrounding the canyons, wild horses raced forth. They were all beautiful and free, tearing across the countryside, unencumbered by being beasts of burden for men or dinner for dragons.

"Horses?" Annwyl scratched her head. "I have a horse."

"Wait," Morfyd said, stepping next to Keita, "this won't work."

"Have you even tried, Princess Doubt?"

"Only Mother can summon them, and she told me she wouldn't."

"Why do you wait for her?"

"She's our mother and queen of these lands. Should I go against her?"

"Have you not learned it's easier to ask for forgiveness than permission?"

"That's how you and Gwenvael survive. I can't live like that. Besides, if you summon them and you piss them off, Keita, they'll tear these humans to bits."

"On that note . . ." Dagmar turned to leave, but Keita caught her arm.

"Leave it to me."

Keita released Dagmar and stepped to the very top of the ridge. She'd hoped she could get Morfyd to do this. As heir to their mother's Magickal power if not her throne, she would most likely have an easier time of it. But Keita had learned a long time ago to wait for no one, especially her easily frightened sister.

Breathing in a huge amount of air, Keita threw her head back and opened her mouth. A line of flame exploded out of her and charred the tops of some trees, fire filling the sky above. When she felt her point had been made, Keita cut off the flame and returned her gaze to the horses. And, from amidst the shiny and moving horseflesh, they appeared, splitting off from the herd they ran with and charging toward the five females.

"Holy—" Annwyl began.

"—shit," Talaith finished.

"Let me speak." Keita moved them all back from the ridge and decided more specific directions were needed. "Actually, Talaith, feel free to connect with them as witch. Morfyd, if you won't help, at least don't complain. Dagmar, if you feel you can help, please do. Annwyl . . . say *nothing*."

"How come I don't—"

"Nothing."

"But I'm—"

"Absolutely *nothing*!" Keita snarled. When Annwyl pouted but no longer argued, Keita looked back at those who raced toward them. The centaurs. One of the few beings dragons showed only respect to and never dreamed of hunting for food or amusement. They came over the ridge and drew to a restless halt about twenty feet away.

Keita gave a small bow of her head. "My ladies. My lords."

"You are dragon, but you are not the queen," a male told her. "And you dare summon us?"

"Told you," Morfyd whispered.

"Shut up!" Keita snapped back

"Perhaps you were not warned that we are not to be fooled with, lizard," the centaur continued.

"My gracious lord, please," Keita said, ignoring the insult. "If you'd only give me a minute to explain—"

"Keita?" An older female moved out of the small herd and

walked up to the group, hooves lightly tapping the ground as she moved. "By the gods . . . it is you."

"Bríghid?" Keita grinned, relief flooding through her. "Oh, Bríghid!"

The female opened her arms and leaned down a bit, allowing Keita to run right into them.

"I don't believe it," Bríghid said, stroking Keita's hair and kissing her forehead. "Look how you've grown."

"The last we heard about you," Keita said, "you'd moved down to the Alsandair borders."

"I gave my heart to the wrong centaur, so I returned to my herd." She pushed Keita back and took her face in her hands. "Gods, Keita. You're actually more beautiful. How is that possible?"

"Excellent bloodline."

Bríghid laughed. "That's my Keita." She looked at the group again. "Morfyd?"

"Hello, Bríghid."

Bríghid held her hand out for Morfyd, and Keita's sister took it. The pair embraced before Bríghid said, "My girls. How beautiful you both are." She kissed them both on the top of their heads. "I've heard such wonderful things about both of you. I've always been so proud."

Keita, knowing it would annoy her sister, added a smirk to highlight Bríghid's words. Morfyd bared a fang, and instantly Bríghid grew tense.

"Still fighting?" And the warning was in her voice. As it had always been.

"No, ma'am," they immediately said.

"Good. Now." Bríghid stepped back, studied them both. "Neither of you are your mother, nor have you replaced her on the throne. So what has you risking my annoyance and the annoyance of my herd?"

Since Bríghid's "annoyance" was often more vicious than her rage, Keita quickly explained, "You know I would not have risked this beautiful hide of mine had I not desperately needed your assistance."

"You?" Brighid asked. "Or her?"

When Brighid's gaze locked on Annwyl, the queen's hand immediately moved to her sword, but Dagmar slapped Annwyl's hand away, eliciting a whined "Ow!" from the brave, deadly queen.

"This is Fearghus's mate."

"She who bore the twins," Brighid went on. "The twins who should not exist."

"But they do. And, although they are human in body, they are dragon in spirit."

Brighid snorted. "The humans can't handle them, eh?"

"The nannies run away."

"Can't their mother care for them?"

Annwyl, always easily insulted, stepped forward, but Dagmar jumped in front of her. "The queen, of course, does what she can. But she has a kingdom to run. A kingdom to keep safe. You and your herd, as you call it, are free to run through these lands as you like, my lady, because Annwyl is queen and has no desire to enslave you. Would you prefer someone else take her place who may not be as . . . open minded? I believe that hunting your kind was a favorite sport of her father's at one time."

Eyes narrowing, Brighid pushed Keita and Morfyd aside and walked forward, hooves now stomping on the ground, until she stood before Dagmar and Annwyl. Leaning in, she brought her face close to Dagmar's and asked, "Do you know what I am, human?"

Keita watched her brother's mate closely. For such a tiny thing, she showed no fear. Instead, she leaned around a bit and said, "Based on the large horse's ass attached to you"— Dagmar moved back, her gaze fixed on Brighid's—"I'm going to go with centaur."

Bríghid, straightening up, folded her arms over her bare chest. "And who are you?"

Years from now, they'd never know why they did it, but before Dagmar could say a word, their small group recited as one, "She's Dagmar Reinholdt. Thirteenth Offspring of The Reinholdt, Only Daughter of The Reinholdt, Chief Battle Lord of Dark Plains, Adviser to Queen Annwyl, Human Liaison to the Southland Dragon Elders, and mate to Prince Gwenvael the Handsome."

"She's also known as The Beast," Talaith tossed in for good measure.

And it was The Beast who turned on them. "Was that *really* necessary?"

It was only a glimpse, but Keita saw the brief smile on Bríghid's face. The centaur quickly hid it and said, "At three thousand and eight winters, I am much too old to be running around, chasing *somewhat* human children."

Keita remembered well how stubborn Bríghid could be. Especially once she'd made up her mind. If she put her hoof down now, there would be no going back. Desperate, she quickly looked to her sister, and Morfyd said, "Of course you deserve your time to relax, Bríghid."

Wondering how her sister could be so stupid, Keita lifted her hands and mouthed, *What are you doing*?

Morfyd mouthed back, *Shut up!* She placed her hand on Bríghid's hip, where her human form met her horse form. "But perhaps you have someone you can recommend. Someone Fearghus will trust as he would trust you. Someone who—"

"I'll do it." Bríghid's body tensed as a young female separated from the herd. "I'll do it."

"Princess Keita, Princess Morfyd, Queen Annwyl . . . this is my daughter, Eadburga. We call her Ebba for short. She's my fifth oldest and—"

"I'll do it."

"And apparently quite eager to leave the herd." Bríghid leaned over and said low in her daughter's ear, "Although I hope you're leaving for the right reasons."

"I am."

Bríghid straightened up. "You commit to this, Ebba, you are to stay and help raise the children until they are of age. For humans that's at least their eighteenth winter. My commitment to the Dragon Queen was much longer, but I made it and stuck by it. You agree to this, you swear to the same as I'll not have you bring shame to this herd by flitting off."

"I have nowhere to flit to." Ebba's tail flicked nervously against her back. "Let me do this, Mum. We both know I'm ready."

"Perhaps you are." Bríghid kissed her daughter's brow and nuzzled her jaw. She stepped back and, after clearing her throat, said, "Let's see this queen."

Keita motioned to Dagmar to move, but she shook her head. *Damn difficult humans!*

Keita reached over and yanked Dagmar out of the way. Bríghid motioned to Annwyl with a crook of her finger, and the queen approached. Bríghid examined Annwyl for several long moments, her expression getting darker and darker the more she looked.

"What's wrong?" Keita asked.

Bríghid stared at Annwyl and asked, "Do I know you?"

Dagmar whispered against Keita's ear, "By all ancient reason, she killed one of them once, didn't she?"

Ragnar walked in to the Great Hall. Although none of the royals were up, his brother and cousin were already at the dining table eating.

"Where have you been?" Vigholf asked once Ragnar sat down and reached for bread.

"Out."

"What's wrong, brother? Did Her Majesty leave you all to your lonesome last night?"

In answer, Ragnar grabbed the back of Vigholf's head and slammed it into the table.

Curses and blood oaths followed, but Ragnar ignored them, instead choosing to dig in to the bowl of hot porridge placed in front of him by a servant.

"I thought you'd want to know," Meinhard said to Ragnar.

"Know what?"

"Heard some of those Cadwaladrs talking outside earlier this morning—they know about Keita and Esyld. I didn't know what they were talking about until one of their females cornered me, and asked about our trip here through Outer-plains."

"And?"

"I told her everything—mostly. Figured that's what you'd want. But you should have warned us beforehand."

"You're right," Ragnar admitted. "Sorry."

Meinhard watched him for a time, until Ragnar demanded, "What?"

"So when you going to tell her?"

"Tell who what?"

"Keita. Tell her that she's yours?"

"If I really want her to be mine?" Ragnar sighed. "Never."

When Bríghid combed her fingers through the left side of Annwyl's hair, Keita thought she'd have to shift, grab the human queen, and make a desperate run for it.

"When I met you," Bríghid remarked, "this wasn't here."

Annwyl shrugged, her gaze focused on something far past Bríghid's arm. "My brother had shaved it off the night before."

"Aye." Bríghid released Annwyl's hair but gripped her chin, lifting her face. "It was you."

"That was a long time ago, mistress."

Bríghid smiled. It was that warm, indulgent smile she usually reserved for the royal hatchlings of dragon queens. "That only makes it more meaningful. Not a lot of . . . what were you then? Eleven?"

"Twelve."

"Right. Twelve. Well, not a lot of twelve-year-olds would risk their father's wrath by releasing a stranger from his dungeon. Your father knew he'd caught himself a centaur, but you didn't, did you? I had only two legs by the time you found me, and you thought I was human. Why would you risk that for some female in your father's dungeon?"

"You were naked and alone in a dungeon. I knew I couldn't leave you there."

"How did you know that? You were only twelve."

Annwyl's far-off gaze spoke volumes. "I *knew* I couldn't leave you there."

Bríghid nodded. "If she hadn't released me," she explained to the others, "they would have tried to use me for hunting." Releasing Annwyl's chin, Bríghid moved back and held her hand out. Her daughter placed her hand in her mother's, and Bríghid said, "Queen Annwyl, I present my daughter Eadburga. She would be honored to raise the twins of the one who once rescued a lone woman in a dungeon."

Annwyl cleared her throat. At first, Keita thought maybe Annwyl was embarrassed by such praise, but another part of her wondered if Annwyl's father had found out what she'd done. If she had suffered for her betrayal. Quite a few of the scars that covered Annwyl's body were not from her battles against men with swords.

"Talaith's daughter, too," Annwyl added. "If that's all right with you? The three of them don't like to be separated."

Ebba nodded. "That's fine with me."

"Then go." Bríghid released her daughter's hand. "With my blessing and my heart."

　　Ebba hugged her mother, and the small group of humans, dragons, and one centaur stood on the ridge as Bríghid and her herd returned to the canyon. When they were gone, Ebba faced them and, sounding much like her mother, said, "Let's get started then."

Chapter Thirty-One

Ragnar heard gasps, and someone dropped plates on the floor. Then he heard his brother and cousin growl in appreciation.

"Now that's a fine-looking woman," Meinhard muttered around his fourth serving of porridge.

Curious, Ragnar looked over his shoulder. His breath caught, and he immediately rose from his chair. He reached back and grabbed his brother and cousin, forcing them both to their knees. He went down on one, too, his head bowed out of respect but also necessity. He'd be able to look at her over time, but for now, her Magick shone too brightly, blinding him.

"Uh . . . cousin?" Meinhard whispered. "A little much for a naked woman, isn't it?"

"She's not a naked woman, you idiot."

"Anyone else smell horse?" Vigholf asked, earning himself a punch to the head.

"Horde dragons," the naked female said. "How interesting this place is."

A soft hand reached out and stroked Ragnar's head. He felt Magick flow through him that was as old as time, as powerful as the ocean. "Don't worry, Lord Ragnar," she said. "It won't be easy, but it'll be worth it."

And, she said in his head, *you are nothing like your father. So you can let that fear go.*

She took her hand away, and he immediately felt the loss of her power. She touched Meinhard's chin and Vigholf's head, where he'd had a very nice lump growing. "The honor of you three astounds me. You've chosen your allies well, Queen Annwyl."

"Just Annwyl."

"Whatever you choose to be called, you are still queen." With that, she headed toward the stairs. "I'll see the children alone." Then she was up the steps and gone.

A dirty bare foot tapped in front of him now, and Ragnar slowly raised his head. Keita had her arms crossed over her chest, her lips pursed. "I think you still have some drool hanging from your lips there, warlord."

"She's a centaur."

"I know."

"But she's a centaur."

"And I am a dragoness."

"But *she's* a centaur."

"Perhaps I should just slap the drool from your mouth."

"Or we can eat!" Annwyl grabbed Keita's arm and pulled her to the table.

"That wasn't subtle, cousin," Meinhard chastised as the three got to their feet.

"But *she's* a centaur."

"We know!" the entire room yelled at him, so he decided to let it go.

Ebba opened the door and stepped into the room. A babe stood on wobbly legs in her crib, her tiny hands holding on to the bars.

"Hello, beautiful," Ebba said as she reached for the child and lifted her up out of the crib.

"Her name's Rhianwen."

"I know. And you're Iseabail." She smiled at Rhianwen's sister, who stood in the doorway, keeping an eye out for trouble. "But you call her Rhi."

"How did you know that?"

"I know lots of things."

Iseabail stepped farther into the room. "You're the new nanny."

"I am."

"And you're kind of naked."

She laughed. "I'm that too." She shifted back to her natural form and heard the girl gasp, felt her swell of excitement and curiosity, her eagerness to know more, to know everything about Ebba's kind. And, more importantly—more *impressively*—her immediate acceptance of something that was vastly different from herself.

"Oh, by the gods! You're a centaur!"

Ebba laughed. "I am."

"Oh . . . no, no, no." Ebba didn't even have to turn around to know that poor Izzy was now making a mad dash across the room, trying to stop the twins who'd eased from their hiding place and crawled onto the closest side table so they could leap from it to Ebba's back. The girl with her sword drawn, aimed right for Ebba's neck.

Amused more than she had been in an age, Ebba clicked her tongue against her teeth. She heard Izzy slide to a stop, and Ebba looked over her shoulder at the two toddlers hanging from midair behind her.

Nuzzling the affectionate babe in her arms, the two of them understanding each other more than any would ever know, even these twins, Ebba slowly turned toward the siblings, making sure not to knock anything over with her horse's hindquarters.

"So," she said, "this is them? The infamous twins of the Blood Queen."

She smirked at them, and the boy, Talan, burst into pathetic fake tears. A skill she could only imagine his Uncle Gwenvael had taught him, based on what her mother had always said about "the hatchling I loved and loathed in equal parts." While the girl, Talwyn, snarled and snapped like she had a mouth full of fangs rather than baby teeth and kept stabbing her tiny wooden sword in Ebba's direction.

"I'm sorry," Izzy said. "I've been told they're like that with, uh, new people."

"That's all right. No need to apologize. They were only protecting your sister, and I'd be awfully miserable if they were like everyone else's children."

"They're definitely not that."

"No. They're definitely not."

Leaning in, Ebba waved one finger in the girl's face before plucking the sword from her. "Now let me make this clear, little ones. There will be none of this sort of thing from now on. No silent attacks, no screaming attacks, no assaults of any kind. While you're under my care you will learn to read and write and the proper care of those you'll one day lead. We will be very good friends, and you will learn to adore me, for I fear your other options will not be as amenable to you." She walked around the bed, and suddenly the children were falling and screaming.

Izzy again dashed across the floor, her arms outstretched to catch the babes, but Ebba had no intention of letting them actually hit the floor. At least not until they were much sturdier.

Izzy's hands slid under her cousins, but the toddlers hovered inches over them. And Ebba kept them there.

Shifting back to human, she sat on the edge of one of the small beds, adjusting Rhi so she was cradled in the crook of her arm, and said to Izzy, "I think this position will suit me well. Don't you?"

Her grin wide and quite beautiful, Izzy nodded. "Oh, yes, I think this position is *perfect* for you."

Keita watched her baby brother closely. He'd come down to first meal and, without his usual greeting, sat at the full table and stared at the food sitting in front of him. He didn't eat. He didn't talk. He didn't do anything but stare at his food.

Éibhear's reaction was so strange that Keita even stopped glaring at Ragnar over his reaction to Ebba. Considering she didn't understand what this strange, new, and quite unpleasant feeling was, the fact that her brother could distract her from it said much.

First, thinking her brothers were behind Éibhear's mood, Keita looked to them. But, as usual, they were oblivious. Then she looked to Morfyd, who watched their brother as Keita did. When Keita looked around the table, it was her sisters—those by blood and those by mating—who saw the difference in Éibhear the Blue. And, to her surprise, the Northlanders.

Ragnar caught her attention and motioned to Éibhear. She could only shrug, unsure of what was wrong or what she could do to fix it. Keita would admit it, she liked to fix things. Especially when it involved her baby brother. Yet she'd never seen him like this. Not once in almost a century.

"Morning, all!" Izzy said, tearing down the stairs. She stopped at the table long enough to grab a loaf of bread, glancing around. "Anyone seen my puppy?"

"If you got him from my kennel, brat, he's not your anything," Dagmar reminded their niece.

"Oops," Izzy laughed. Then she gushed. "I love the new nanny! She's a centaur!"

Keita ignored the pointed look she received from Ragnar.

"All right. I'm off to run up Flower Hill with Branwen."

Keita frowned and briefly re-focused her attention on her young niece. "Whatever for?"

"Have you seen that hill?" she demanded. "Go up that thing a few times a day, I'll have legs like iron."

"You already have legs like iron."

"All right. Steel then. Steel's harder than iron, I think."

"Come on, ya fat sow," Branwen called from outside. "Move that shiftless ass!"

"*Fat?*" Izzy screamed back. Then she took off running, and Keita heard her cousin squeal in a very non dragonesslike manner before, Keita was sure, running for her life.

Giving a little giggle, Keita began to eat again, only to stop when she saw that her brother's gaze was locked on the door through which Izzy had run out.

Now, of course, it was all making more sense. Had Izzy teased him? Insulted him? What had Mistress Brat done *now* to Lord Sensitive?

As if in answer, and without a word, Éibhear pushed back from the table, stood, and walked out.

By now, her dim-witted elder brothers had caught on that something was amiss, and as one group all at the table stood and silently followed. Izzy and Branwen had run off to the left toward Flower Hill. Éibhear, however, turned right. Together, and from a distance, the group followed her brother as he walked out the east exit and down the worn path leading to the lakes.

His pace was steady and calm, his body relaxed. But something was terribly wrong, and they all knew it. But it seemed no one knew what to do about it.

They followed him over the small hills and past several small lakes and a stream until he reached the big lake where most of the Cadwaladr Clan made their temporary and occasional home.

"Éibhear! Wonderful morning to you!" Ghleanna greeted him. She and Addolgar must have arrived that morning or the night before. They looked tired but happy to see their kin. But Ghleanna's cheerful greeting received nothing more than a nod from Éibhear while he walked right by her. She blinked in surprise and watched her nephew pass all his kin, each stopping what he or she was doing to watch him.

He continued on, passing uncles, aunts, cousins, distant cousins, those related only by mating—he ignored them all. Until he reached Celyn.

"Ho, cousin!" Celyn called out, looking quite chipper this morning, and Keita cringed because she had the distinct feeling she knew why. "What brings you down to—"

Éibhear had him by the throat, lifting Celyn off his big feet. Gasping in horror, Morfyd reached for her brother, but Keita caught her left arm and Briec caught her right, holding her back. Good thing, too. For Éibhear pulled his arm back and shot-putted Celyn into the closest tree.

Keita cringed, hearing something break, but since Celyn managed to get back to his feet, she didn't worry it was his head.

Celyn twisted his neck, the bones cracking. "Wanna do this now, cousin? You sure?"

Éibhear glanced at the ground, picked up one of the training shields that Keita's kin used when in their dragon form and chucked it at Celyn with such force, it shoved her cousin's human body through the tree he'd been standing next to.

"Guess he's sure then," Fearghus muttered.

Annwyl knew none of the dragons would get in the middle of this. The Cadwaladrs wouldn't because this was how they handled things. And Fearghus's siblings wouldn't because they knew this had to do with Izzy.

Did any of them, but especially Éibhear, really expect that girl to stay a virgin forever? They couldn't compare Izzy to Annwyl. True, Fearghus had been her one and her only, but that came more down to twenty-three years under her father's protection and two years of her troops' fear of her. Had Fearghus made her wait worth it? Absolutely. Did that mean she would have waited if offered the chance with someone she truly liked before she'd met him? Probably not.

And Éibhear had made it perfectly clear he "didn't think of Izzy like that."

Perhaps not, but something told her that a beating from Izzy's father wouldn't be this bad and Briec was a mean bastard when it came to his women.

No. It looked like she'd have to do something about this on her own.

Still, as insane as Annwyl knew the world thought her, she wasn't about to jump between two battling dragons. She might be insane, but she wasn't stupid. True, both dragons seemed to be staying human for this fight, but that could change in a moment. And unless she was willing to fight to the death, she preferred strict rules of engagement when fighting her dragon kin. Otherwise she risked hurting something that even Morfyd couldn't repair. And life staring out a window and drooling held no appeal to her. So Annwyl turned and ran the other way.

She hard-charged past the gates of her home, into the forest, past Dagmar's little house, and straight through until she hit the western fields. She kept going until she saw Flower Hill. She charged toward it and up. Izzy was right about this hill, too. Annwyl ran it every day, several times, until her legs were screaming in pain. But then every night Fearghus ran his hands over them, growled a little, and muttered something like, "Your legs drive me wild."

Thank the gods for dragon males. She was relatively certain there were few human males who'd feel the same about their women.

"Oy!" She dashed past the females and stopped.

"Annwyl!" Izzy cheered. "Come to join us?"

"I think you forgot to tell me something."

"I did?"

"About Celyn?"

Scowling, Izzy looked at Branwen.

"It wasn't me!"

"It wasn't Branwen," Annwyl confirmed. "It was Éibhear."

Izzy's eyes grew wide. "Wha-what? But he doesn't know."

"He's telling everyone right now—"

"*What?*"

"—by beating the life from his cousin."

"Oh, gods." Izzy's hand went to her stomach. "Oh, gods!"

"Don't just stand there!" Annwyl ordered. "Move!"

"How long have you known?" Briec asked his mate while keeping an eye on the damage his brother was doing to Celyn. Although Celyn had finally gotten back to his feet and was now putting up a fight.

"Since I saw them together when he arrived. They didn't do anything," she added. "But a mother knows."

"And you said nothing to her?"

"Say what to her? I had her when I was sixteen. She's nineteen, and as long as she's careful—"

"You could have told me."

Talaith smirked. "A beating is one thing, Lord Arrogance. Your family will forgive Éibhear that. Especially since the only ones who don't seem to know how he feels about my eldest daughter are Éibhear and Izzy. But a dead Celyn is something they'd never forgive you for."

And gods-dammit if she wasn't right.

"I had no idea," Ragnar admitted.

"Nor I." Vigholf leaned back against a tree trunk, his arms crossed over his chest. "Who knew the boy had it in him?"

"I knew." And the brothers looked over at their cousin. "I knew it was waiting there to be released."

Blood slashed across Meinhard's face, and he wiped it off

with the back of his hand. "He's got a rage in him, that one. He just don't know it yet."

"He knows it now."

"Nah. He has all sorts of excuses for this. But whatever set him off is only part of it."

"Why didn't we set him off earlier?" Vigholf asked. "We could have used *this* royal in a few battles to do more than clear trees."

"Who would have taken that beating? Which of our kin would you have saddled with being beaten by Éibhear the Chivalrous? It's better this way. A Southlander gets him started, and now, if he comes back with us, we can start to really hone that rage until he's like a living, breathing weapon we can unleash at our whim."

Ragnar tipped his head to his brother. "Told you the armies should report to Meinhard."

"And report they shall."

"You named him the Chivalrous?" Dagmar asked from behind them, and all three males winced.

"Dagmar—"

"That was rather petty of you." To those who did not know her, those words probably didn't sound nearly as harsh as they actually were.

Her mate's gaze moved back and forth among the Northland group. "What's wrong with chivalrous?"

"You get a name like that in the north, it just means you're weak. Too nice to fight." Dagmar shook her head. "And he has no idea, does he?"

"If it helps"— Ragnar watched Éibhear slam his cousin to the ground face first and hold him down with one hand, while twisting his arm around to his back until something broke— "I doubt he'll be keeping that name much longer."

Cursing, and with a broken arm, the cousin got Éibhear off him by slamming the back of his head into the Blue's face. Then he faced him and got in a few good punches to Éibhear's head, too, with his sound arm. But those hits only seemed to piss Éibhear off more. The blue dragon head-butted his cousin so hard that the sound cracked across the lake and everyone in earshot flinched. Then the royal caught hold of his cousin's throat with one hand and began to pummel him in the face with the other. What impressed Ragnar the most was that both managed to stay human during the whole thing. That was a skill even Ragnar didn't think he had. His ability to stay human often hinged on whether he felt like it or not.

He looked over and saw Keita watching. She cringed at every blow, winced at every hit. Although she wouldn't get involved, she still didn't like it.

Ragnar motioned to his brother and cousin. "We should stop this."

"Why?" Vigholf asked. "Even their kin aren't getting in the middle of it."

"I know. That's why we should stop it. We have no emotional stake in this."

"No," Meinhard said. "But I'm guessing she does."

Iseabail pushed past everyone in her way and briefly watched Éibhear and Celyn. At this point, the cousin's face was nothing more than a bloody mess, but still Éibhear held him steady in one hand while he continued to hit his cousin over and over again. Not exactly chivalrous, now was it?

Then again, Ragnar had the feeling the cousin had stopped putting up a fight simply because Izzy was standing there.

Snarling, Izzy stomped over to them, yanking her arms from kin who tried to stop her. As she neared the two battling Fire Breathers, she grabbed up another training shield in both her hands.

"Gods," Vigholf said in awe, and Ragnar had to silently agree with him. A training shield might not be made of solid steel, but it was made for dragons who trained every day to be warriors. He remembered his first one and how tired his forearms got from holding it those first few months of training.

And yet here was this human—a female, no less—who swung that shield like she'd been born wielding one, somehow ignoring the fact that the shield was several inches taller than she and probably weighed the same. She swung it and slammed Éibhear's side, knocking him off his feet and right into a few of his kin who stood nearby. For the first time, Ragnar realized exactly how little chance his father had had when he'd faced and died at the hands of this girl and her witch mother, Talaith.

Yet it was a tribute to the hardheadedness of these fire-breathing royals that Éibhear did nothing but rub the side of his head and scowl at Izzy as if she were one of the dark gods herself.

"You stupid bastard!" Izzy accused, throwing the shield down and making the ground shake just enough to have every dragon marveling at her.

"*Did you even think about who you were fucking?*" the Blue thundered at her.

"Oh, I thought about it," she replied, venom dripping from every word. "I thought about it and *enjoyed* every second of it."

"Damn," Vigholf muttered at Izzy's words. "You know that one had to hurt."

Izzy reached down and, with the help of her cousin Branwen, pulled the battered cousin to his feet. With one arm around Izzy's shoulders and the other held close to his body, Branwen pressing into him to give leverage, the dragon let them walk him back to the fortress. He was weak, losing a lot of blood, but he made sure to look back over his shoulder one last time so that he could give his cousin a blood-filled smile.

Seeing that smile for what it was—lusty leering and "I won!" triumph—the Blue was on his feet again, but Meinhard moved faster and slammed him back to the ground.

"It's over, lad," Meinhard told him in that way that always earned the respect of his young trainees. "Anything else now will just get that girl to hurt you worse than she already has. And your ego won't come back from that."

Morfyd slipped past them, crouching in front of her brother. "Oh, Éibhear."

"I'm all right, Morfyd." Éibhear got to his feet, and his sister stood with him, her gaze troubled as she examined him.

She caught hold of his hand. "Come with me." She dragged him off, ignoring his protests, and Ragnar went to Keita.

"You all right?" he asked her.

"I wasn't the one getting beaten into the dirt."

"No. Nor was it your precious baby brother getting beaten into the dirt either. Not really."

"I tried to warn you. You shouldn't underestimate him."

"I think I shouldn't underestimate any of you." And without much thought, he used his thumb to wipe away a few drops of blood that had splashed along her cheek. Her lashes lowered, and her skin grew heated. That was all it took for her.

Then again, it took even less for him.

Still, with all that went on between them without a word spoken, neither could ignore the silence that had developed around them.

The attention of both royal and low-born was on them, Ragnar unable to read the expressions and deciding it was probably best not to.

Ragnar dropped his hand away. "I'll see what I can do for your cousin. I'm pretty good help after a brawl."

The princess nodded and said nothing else, so he followed after Izzy and tried to ignore all the eyes that were on him.

"A Lightning?" Ghleanna demanded. "Have you gone round the bend?"

Keita rolled her eyes. "When have you ever cared what I do?"

"Your father will care. And your mother will bloody care."

"Well, that'll keep me up nights."

Ghleanna grabbed hold of Keita's arm and yanked her a few feet away from their kin. Her grip was brutal and her anger palpable. Normally, Keita would try to ease her aunt's concerns, telling her what she wanted to hear. But not this time.

"What are you playing at?"

"I don't know what you're—"

Her aunt's fingers tightened, making Keita's eyes water. "Don't play your games with me, little miss. This is bad enough, but now I hear about you and—"

Ghleanna cut herself off, and Keita snapped, "Me and who?"

"I can't believe you're that stupid."

Keita tried to pry Ghleanna's fingers from her arm. "I don't know what you're talking about, and I'd like it if you'd let me go now."

Her aunt's eyes, black like Bercelak's, narrowed; her lips thinned. Ghleanna had little patience for those who didn't listen to her and jump at her commands. But Keita didn't jump at anyone's commands.

"Let her go, Ghleanna." Fearghus stood next to them now.

"We're just talking."

"You can talk later." Fearghus took Keita's other arm and pulled her away from their aunt. "You should come to the castle tonight and see the babes."

Fearghus led Keita off.

"I don't know what's going on," Fearghus said when they were halfway between the lake and the castle. "But whatever it is, little sister, I hope you know what you're doing."

"Don't I always?"

Fearghus stopped. "I'm not joking. I've got enough shit to worry about without worrying you're about to end up on the wrong side of the Cadwaladrs. Especially if what I'm hearing about you and Esyld is true."

"You need to trust me, Fearghus," she said, unable to outright lie to her eldest brother about something so important.

"I do trust you, Keita. That's what has me worried. You're not usually this . . . obvious. And the strength and speed with which this rumor has spread has the earmarks of Dagmar Reinholdt all over it. Yet I know she likes you. So then why would she say anything that could put you in such trouble?"

"Give me a little time. Please."

"I will." He leaned down and kissed her cheek. "But in the meantime, watch your back."

Izzy took the bowl from Branwen. It was filled with bloody water and would be the fourth one she'd replaced in the last thirty minutes. She walked out into the hall, relieved to see a servant rushing toward her with fresh water and clean cloth.

She started to exchange the bowls with the servant when her mother walked up. "Peg, take that in to Lord Ragnar." She opened the door and let the servant go in, then took the bowl Izzy still held. She placed it on the floor to one side of the door and took Izzy's hand.

"Come on." Izzy let her mother drag her to a room a few doors away. It was one of the guest rooms, reserved for nobles and kin.

Talaith closed the door and faced her. Izzy had prepared herself for this. She knew her mum would take Éibhear's side on this. She knew she'd be appalled that Izzy hadn't been keeping her virginity intact for the "right male," as she'd told Izzy to do a short time before she'd gone off with the troops. Yet it didn't matter. Izzy had made her choice quite a few months back, and now she'd stand tall and would not feel ashamed about what she did or what just happened. She wouldn't. No matter how pissed off her mother might be.

"Are you all right?" her mother asked.

Izzy jerked a little in surprise at the question but caught

herself in time. She went for casual disdain, as she liked to call it. "It wasn't me that got hit, was it?"

Her mother stepped closer, and Izzy waited for it. The accusations, the recriminations. She waited for all of it.

"I'm not asking about anyone but you, Iseabail." Talaith reached up and pressed the palm of her hand against Izzy's cheek. "Are *you* all right?"

Izzy blinked several times, trying to hold back the tears she suddenly felt burning behind her eyes. Tears that at one time she could show no one else but her mother. She'd thought that closeness was gone, thought she was too old for all that "boo-hooing" as Ghleanna called it. But with her mother not judging her, just worried about her, and the pair alone in this boring room, she couldn't hold those tears back.

"How could he do that, Mum?" she sobbed out. "In front of everybody? Gods." She covered her face with her hands. "Even Dad."

Her mother pulled Izzy into her arms, bringing them both down to their knees so Izzy didn't have to bend over to have her good sob, and Talaith didn't have to spend all her time on her toes.

"And what he said to me!"

"I know, luv. I know. That was hurtful and mean." Talaith rubbed Izzy's back and let her cry. "And I don't care how angry he was, just a gods-damn shitty thing to do."

Knowing her mother understood, and knowing she took her side made all the difference to Izzy. She clung to her mother, her hands gripping the back of her shirt as she cried on her shoulder. She had no idea how long she was going for, but it lasted a good bit. Yet her mum never once complained.

When Izzy finally cried herself out, they sat on the floor, Talaith holding her hands tight in her own.

"Don't be disappointed in me, Mum."

"Why would I be?"

"For, ya know"—she turned her face into her shoulder and wiped her remaining tears since her mum held her hands— "not waiting."

"Not waiting for what?" When Izzy only gazed at her, "Oh . . . oh! Right. Waiting. Well, I didn't exactly wait either, did I? And Celyn is very handsome. Just like your father was when we . . ." Talaith's remark faded out, and her eyes grew wide. Immediately Izzy knew what had her mother worried.

"Don't worry, Mum. I . . . I take precautions." Her mother's wide eyes narrowed, and Izzy insisted, "I do. Honestly." Although, except for the twins and Rhi, there'd been no other word yet about other dragon-human babes, Izzy had no desire to risk that what had happened to Annwyl and her mum. To Izzy that was simply too great a chance to take. "You know how much this all means to me, and I'm not at the point where I can do both. A child and making morning formation with my unit."

"But you will be there. One day."

"That's my plan. Then I can decide about having little Izzys running around."

Talaith smiled. "As long as you have a plan."

"I always have a plan."

"Good." Her mother squeezed her hands. "And do you love him, Izzy?"

Outraged she'd even ask, Izzy instantly replied, "After what he did to Celyn? Not anymore!"

Talaith cleared her throat, glanced around the room, cleared her throat again, and finally admitted, "I, uh . . . meant Celyn."

"Oh." Mother and daughter stared at each other a long moment before Izzy admitted, "This is awkward."

Then they both exploded in a fit of giggles that felt really inappropriate at the moment, but also very necessary.

* * *

Ren eased around the corner, waited until the soldiers had passed him. He'd arrived in the Quintilian Province more than a day ago. He'd been astounded by the beauty of the buildings, the artwork, the women. The heat made him miserable, but he loved the country.

Still, with the beautiful, came the ugly. The slaves, the cruelty, the mistreatment. And at the heart of it all were the Irons who ruled. Although dragon symbols reigned throughout each home, each business, and in all government buildings, the Irons mostly went around as human. But everyone knew who they were. Then again, they were hard to miss.

In some ways the dynamics between dragon and human Sovereigns reminded him of the relationship between his kind and the humans of the East, except for one major difference. There was no fear among the Eastland humans. Instead they celebrated the existence of the dragons because they wanted to, not because they were afraid not to.

With the area clear, Ren crossed from one side of the cavern to the other, then slid through solid rock to go from one side of the mountain wall to the other. One of many skills bestowed upon his kind that he enjoyed taking full advantage of, and one of the reasons Rhiannon had sent him on this mission.

As soon as he made it through, Ren stopped and gazed out over the land in front of him. The land currently filled, it seemed, from one end to the other with troops. Legions and legions of troops. A good number of them Irons, thousands and thousands of them human. They trained under the hot suns, readying for battle.

Readying for war.

Ren fought the urge to panic and worked hard to focus on what he was doing here. Gathering information and bringing it back to the Southland queens. A task he'd do to the best of his ability.

Turning away from the overwhelming sight before him, Ren eased his body through the mountain and back into the cavern.

Chapter Thirty-Two

Keita crouched by her baby brother, watching while Morfyd cleaned the blood off his hand. It seemed he'd broken his knuckles on Celyn's face and Morfyd wanted to make sure to heal them correctly and ensure that they didn't get infected.

"I need to make a poultice," Morfyd said, moving over to some plants nearby to search out ingredients.

Keita gently lifted her brother's hand and held it between her own. "Are you all right?" she asked.

"Aye, sister," he said, sounding worn after his explosion of anger. "Ease yourself."

"Oh. I will." Then she slammed her hands against his broken knuckles, enjoying the scream of pain her brother unleashed.

"What the hells are you doing?" Morfyd demanded.

"You!" Keita said, pointing at Éibhear. "How dare you do what you did to Izzy! In front of her parents, no less!"

"*I was trying to protect her!*"

"No, you weren't, you lying sack of shit!"

"Keita!"

Now she spun on her sister. "And you!"

"What did I do?"

"Babying him! As if he deserves it!"

"Oh, I'm so sorry I'm not acting the way Keita the Viper thinks I should. I'm sorry I'm not performing to your specifications!"

Keita shoved her sister, and Morfyd shoved her back. They nearly had each other's hair when Éibhear got between them. "Stop it! What's wrong with you?"

Pulling away from the pair, Keita stalked off. She was too angry even to think straight.

She felt for Izzy, and that was the truth of the matter. Why? Because she'd been there before. Some male calling her out in front of everyone because he couldn't have her for one reason or another. Well, mostly one reason. That Keita didn't want him. And although not the same exact situation, she still knew how her niece felt. Mortified was how she felt. And who could blame her?

Keita had thought she'd raised Éibhear better than that. Obviously she was wrong! For once.

And what was even stranger to her? That the only thing she wanted to do at the moment to make herself feel better was not go shopping, destroy a town, or steal something from her mother's treasure. She wanted to do none of that. Instead, all she wanted to do was see Ragnar the Cunning. See him. Talk to him. Let him make her feel better.

A desire, she had to admit, she found a tad appalling!

Ragnar and Vigholf took the young dragon out to the east fields. They placed him down in the center and walked away. Once a good distance back, they pulled off their clothes and shifted.

"All right, lad," Ragnar called out. "Shift, if you can."

It took a bit, but flames burst and the young dragon was back in his natural form.

Ragnar returned to his side, checked the broken bones in

his face, his broken arm, his broken ribs. Honestly, it was a good thing Izzy came along when she had.

Ragnar had hoped he'd be able to heal the young dragon while he'd still been in his human form, so the lad could stay in a soft bed with all those females coming in and out of the room to check on him and soothe him like their favorite wounded pet. But Ragnar simply didn't have the level of understanding of human bones that he did for his own. He waited as long as he could for Morfyd to return, knowing her skill in healing far outstripped his own, but by mid-afternoon, he decided he could wait no longer.

"What do you need from me?" Vigholf asked Ragnar.

"Something to eat. A cow should do."

"All right. I'll be back."

Ragnar leaned in. "Can you hear me, Celyn?"

The Fire Breather nodded.

"This shouldn't take too long, but it'll hurt. A lot. Understand?"

"Do it," he whispered.

"I can do something that will hurt less, but you'd take longer to heal. You'd be bedridden for a few days, though."

Celyn forced his eyes open, gazed at Ragnar. "Do it."

Ragnar went down on his knees and raised his front claws over Celyn. He closed his eyes and let the power stored in the ground beneath him rise up through his body. When he had what he needed, he unleashed that power through his claws and into the Fire Breather's body.

Celyn growled in pain, fangs clenched together, while his bones locked back into place and knitted themselves whole.

Although some would probably take the less painful but longer healing route, Ragnar knew why this one wouldn't— Iseabail. Celyn wasn't about to let his cousin have any time alone with her. Not if he could help it anyway.

Ragnar had seen it before. The fight between kin over a female. Something that rarely ended well.

After fixing the last bone, Ragnar checked to make sure he hadn't missed anything that could lead to hemorrhaging later. Once he felt confident about that, he lowered his claws, and his body dropped back. He'd have hit the ground if his brother wasn't there to catch him.

Panting, he nodded at his kin. "Thanks."

"Here. Something for you to eat."

Vigholf helped Ragnar to the still thrashing cow, letting him be the one to finish it off by wrapping his maw around its neck and breaking it. Then Ragnar fed until he felt his strength return.

By the time he offered the remainder of his meal to his brother, Celyn was sitting up. A lot of blood still covered his body and Ragnar was sure he'd be sore for days, but he was alert.

"Thank you," Celyn said with a nod.

"You're welcome."

The young dragon got to his feet but stumbled a bit.

"I better help him back." Vigholf walked off with Celyn, and Ragnar stayed behind picking cow flesh out of his teeth.

He'd just dislodged a good-sized rib bone when Keita walked toward him. She'd changed into another gown, her hair tied into a loose ponytail down her back, and still no shoes. What did she have against shoes?

"Hungry?" he asked, offering her what was left of the carcass.

"No, thank you. How's Celyn?"

"Better. I fixed his bones, and stopped the bleeding. How's your brother?"

"Playing the self-righteous Lord of Gloom by one of the lakes with Morfyd as his adoring nursemaid."

Ragnar shifted to his human form. "You sound angry with him."

"I am. Very angry. And I'm angry at Celyn. Playing this game with poor Izzy caught in the middle of it."

"'Poor Izzy' can hold her own."

"I guess."

She was pacing, tense. "What's wrong, Keita?"

"Nothing."

"Then why do you seem fit to crawl the walls?"

"I don't know. I just feel that . . ."

"Something's coming? Coming to destroy all you love?"

Keita stopped pacing and faced Ragnar. "Actually, I was going to say I just feel like I wouldn't be happy until I saw you, and I had no idea what any of that meant."

"Uh . . . oh."

"But I sense the 'something's coming to destroy all you love' should be a bit more of my concern right now, wouldn't you say?"

"Well . . ."

She placed her hands on her hips. "Do not fuck me about, warlord. What haven't you told me?"

"It's something Vigholf told me about your human queen. It has been bothering me since."

"Gods, who did she try to kill now?"

"No, no. Nothing like that. It's just . . . she's been having dreams."

Keita's arms slowly lowered to her sides. "What kind of dreams?"

"Of brutal warriors riding on demon horses that are coming for her children."

Keita paced away from him again, her gaze on the ground. "Human warriors?"

"Humans, yes. But witches. If I'm guessing right, she's dreaming of the Kyvich. Warrior witches from the Ice Lands."

Keita stopped pacing, her back to him.

"Ragnar . . . do their horses have horns?"

* * *

Annwyl had canceled her training today, and she was glad she had too. There was simply too much going on for her to be able to concentrate. And not being focused meant more damage than she was in the mood to tolerate at the moment.

She walked in to the Great Hall, coming in the back way, and found Talaith at the dining table. She had food in front of her, but seemed to be picking more than eating.

"How's it going?" Annwyl asked, dropping into the chair beside her friend.

"It could be worse, I suppose. I wish it were better."

"What has you worried? Other than the obvious, I mean."

Talaith shoved her plate back. "I worry that Izzy's going to make stupid decisions just to irritate that idiot I adore like my own son."

"It is frustrating when you love them but still want to smash their faces in, isn't it?"

"They're too young for all this."

"I can send her to another troop. She can deal with the raiders on the coast."

Talaith scrunched up her face. "That kind of makes it her fault, doesn't it? She adores her unit, but we'll be sending her away because of this . . . this . . ."

"Centaur shit?"

"Exactly. By the way," she said, abruptly changing subjects, "I adore Ebba."

"Adore," Annwyl agreed. She raised her hand. "Listen. She's keeping them quiet, but you don't have that sense of dread that we'll be hearing her horrified screams at any moment."

"It's wonderful."

"Uh-oh."

Talaith cringed. "What?"

Annwyl motioned to the open Great Hall doors, through which Éibhear and Morfyd were walking.

Talaith tapped her fingers against the table. "I shouldn't get involved."

"No. You shouldn't."

"It's none of my business."

"No. It's not."

After three seconds, Talaith slammed her hands against the table. "I can't let it go!"

Annwyl rubbed her nose to keep from laughing, watching as Talaith rounded the table, heading for a wide-eyed and completely panicking Éibhear, while Morfyd stepped in front of her brother, ready to defend him.

"I'm so mad at you right now, I don't have words."

"Celyn is taking advantage of her," he argued.

"That's none of your business, Éibhear."

"Look, I'm sorry if I offended you, Talaith—"

"Me? You need to say that to Izzy."

"—but she was lying to everyone!"

"Again that's none of your business."

Annwyl saw Izzy charge down the hallway and take the stairs, probably having heard Éibhear's voice. She'd just hit the last step when Annwyl met her and caught hold of her arm. "Why don't we go for a walk?" Annwyl offered/ordered.

"You!" Izzy screamed over her shoulder while Annwyl led her out the back way. "Are a self-righteous prat!"

"I was thinking of you, you dozy sow!"

"*Sow?*"

Annwyl yanked her niece out the door and kept going, confident that if she stopped even for a moment, Izzy would run right back inside and rip every blue hair from Éibhear's giant head.

* * *

Ragnar watched Keita closely. "You've dreamed about them too?"

"Once . . . maybe twice." She scratched her throat. "I didn't think much of it because I'm not much for having prophetic dreams." She stepped closer. "How bad is this?"

"The Kyvich?" He gave a little laugh, but they both winced at the sound of it. "I've never seen them in battle, but I've heard that a warlord or monarch losing a war can change his fate should the Kyvich take up his cause. Half a Kyvich legion—and their legions have far less than a normal army's legion—can lay a city to waste. They walk the path of the warrior and the witch perfectly. They kill without thought or remorse, and have been known to break the souls of men who annoy them, until they turn them into their own personal battle dogs, I guess you'd call them. Unleashing the poor sods during battle to wear the enemy down a bit, feeling nothing when the men are killed."

"And what else?" She tightened the arms she had folded over her chest. "There's something you're not telling me. What is it?"

"There are few Kyvich born into their ranks. They . . ."

"Say it."

"They take girls from their mothers. Usually before they're old enough to walk. Often their mothers hand them over rather than risk the rest of their children or their entire village. Not that I blame the mothers for their reluctance. The training of the Kyvich is brutal and . . . ruthless. And starts by the time the girls are five or six winters."

"And Talwyn would be perfect for them, wouldn't she?"

"From what you told me. Also, right now, Talwyn has no loyalty to any god because of her age and her parents. But if she becomes a Kyvich, the war gods, at the very least, would ensure she'd be working for them through her allegiance to the Kyvich." He took a breath. "Keita, if I'd known you'd dreamed about them as well—"

"We can't worry now about what we should have done,

Ragnar." And all that royal training came to the fore, Keita showing no panic or fear. She simply said, "We have to warn Annwyl and Fearghus."

"I agree." Ragnar headed across the field back toward the castle. "I think this is what Annwyl has been training for without even realizing it."

"Any idea when they'll get here?"

They entered the forest that surrounded the fortress walls. "Not sure. I've heard their skills and gifts are immense. That they can move quickly and go for thousands of leagues undetected. Truthfully, for all we know—they could fly."

"Well, at least most of the family is here to protect—"

Ragnar stopped and looked over his shoulder. "Keita?"

He walked back to where he'd last heard her voice. "Keita?"

"Lord Ragnar?" a voice asked.

He turned and looked at Éibhear, who came stalking into the woods. "Have you seen my sister? Keita?"

"Didn't you see her?"

Éibhear gazed at him. "Sorry?"

"Didn't you see Keita? She was right here."

Éibhear shook his head. "No, sir."

Ragnar didn't understand. "But she was just here."

Ragnar heard her voice in his head. It was faint, but it was definitely Keita's.

Up.

He looked up and then pushed Éibhear back toward the castle. "Go. Get your brothers, your sister." He pointed at the royal standing there looking confused. "Go! Now! Tell them to follow my scent!" Then Ragnar shifted and took to the air.

"I say we should have let Éibhear kill the bastard."

Talaith rubbed her eyes with the tips of her fingers. She adored her mate, truly she did. But there simply was no grey area for him. There was only black, white, and annoying.

"Killing him seems a little harsh," she reminded Briec. "It's not like he forced Izzy to do anything."

"All I know is Celyn can't stay here," Fearghus insisted. "Don't want him here. Eating our food. Using our clean water so his oozing wounds can heal."

"You're all being ridiculous," Morfyd said. "We can't throw him out."

Gwenvael, the only one sitting down, tossed his feet up on the table. "I've been thrown out for less, don't see why he shouldn't be."

Dagmar raised a finger. "If you have nothing of use to add to this conversation, Defiler, then quiet."

"It's not like we're telling him to leave the Southlands completely," Fearghus argued, probably thinking he was being quite generous.

"*I* think he should leave the Southlands completely." Briec pointed at the two Northlanders feeding at the other end of the table. "He can go back to that shit-hole of a territory with those two idiots."

Talaith winced and mouthed to their now-scowling guests, *Sorry*.

Éibhear ran into the hall.

"You should have killed him," Briec said again before his brother could utter a word.

"What's wrong?" Fearghus asked.

"I don't know, really."

"What do you mean you don't know?"

"Lord Ragnar told me to come and get you."

Gwenvael's feet hit the floor. "Why?"

"I don't know. I was looking for Keita and, you know"— he shrugged—"figured if what everyone was saying was true, he'd know where she was, but then he asked *me* if I'd seen Keita. The way he was acting—it was like she'd vanished right in front of him."

Talaith shook her head. "This can't be good."

"Everyone calm down," Morfyd cut in. "She probably ran off because she couldn't stand the sight of him anymore. You know how she is."

"Perhaps we shouldn't assume that our baby sister simply vanished during a conversation merely to get away from him." Fearghus pointed at Gwenvael. "Go check behind the guard houses. Briec, check the—"

"Wait. Wait," Morfyd said with an annoyed sigh. "Give me a moment to check for her."

Morfyd closed her eyes, and Talaith watched the tendrils of Magick that surrounded the dragoness at all times lift away from her body and stretch out in all directions. It was a beautiful and amazing thing to witness, and a shame only a few could actually see it.

"Will this take long?" Gwenvael asked. "I'm already bored."

"I say we rip the scabs off our cousin . . . to pass the time," Briec suggested.

Morfyd's eyes snapped open, and she looked around the room. "Oh, gods."

Talaith slipped off the table where she'd been sitting. "What is it?"

"Elestren."

A moment of stunned silence followed, all of them staring at each other. Then they were running for the Great Hall doors.

Not wanting to slow them down, Talaith and Dagmar followed, even though they had no intention of going anywhere.

Briec stopped by the Northlanders, sizing them up before he asked, "You'll watch out for them, until we return?"

Vigholf—Talaith could only tell the Lightning apart from his cousin because of his short hair—nodded once. Briec glanced back at Talaith and then bolted out the door.

Meinhard—he had the longer hair and the slightly bigger head—looked up and asked, "Think we can we get more food while we're watching out for you?"

Chapter Thirty-Three

Keita landed hard, her shoulder shoved out of place, two of her talons breaking. Groaning, she rolled onto her back, but the rope around her throat, made out of extra-strong steel, tightened and yanked her to her knees.

"Come, come, cousin. I thought you were tougher than this."

Keita had shifted to dragon as soon as her cousin looped the rope around her neck and yanked her off the ground like a sack of grain. Elestren hadn't taken her far, but she was in a cave she didn't recognize. It was well lit with torches and multiple pit fires. Something told Keita this was a meeting place. But meeting for what, she probably didn't want to know.

Elestren grabbed Keita by the hair, snatching her head back. "Did you think you could betray your queen and there would be no repercussions from us, princess?"

When Keita didn't answer her question, Elestren shoved her forward again. Keita's head bounced against the floor, and for a few brief minutes, everything went black.

When she woke again, more dragons had arrived. Two Elders and several of the Queen's Royal Guard. Keita noticed that her father was not among them.

"She's the queen's daughter, Elestren," Elder Teithi was in the midst of arguing.

"And a traitor. She protected Esyld and met with those two idiots we know for a fact are trying to remove the queen from the throne." Elestren walked around Keita. "I'm not saying she should die. But we can't allow her to be roaming free, working against us."

"So what do you suggest?"

"We take her to the desert borders. My cousins will keep her busy at the salt mines until this is straightened out."

Damn. Now she understood where she was. The meeting place of the Royal Guard Council. They chose those who earned a place among her mother's guard—and judged those who broke the guard's rules. In theory, the Council should only be judging members of the royal guard, not a royal. But Keita sensed that a real trial was the last thing her cousin would allow at the moment.

"You mean hold her captive."

"If it keeps our queen safe . . ."

"He blames me," Izzy said, when she knew she could speak without blubbering.

"Of course he blames you. That's what they do. As sweet as our Éibhear is, he's still his father's son. He's still male."

"I should have hit him harder with that shield."

Chuckling, Annwyl dropped to the ground in the middle of the field, and began sharpening her sword with a stone. "I'm still amazed you could pick that bloody shield up."

"It was just a practice shield."

"For *dragons*, Izzy. A practice shield for dragons."

Izzy shrugged, gazing across the field and into the surrounding woods. She sat down beside Annwyl, relieved to be out of the fortress, at least for a little while. Away from Éibhear *and* Celyn.

"It'll be all right, Izzy."

"It will never be all right. Those two will make up, and I'll be relegated to the whore who got between cousins."

"You think Celyn will walk away from you that easily?" Annwyl grasped Izzy's chin, tugging until Izzy had to look at her. "Or is that what you're hoping?"

Frustrated, Izzy shook off her aunt's hand. "Everyone acts like Celyn is supposed to Claim me as his own now."

"Is that what you want?"

"No."

"So it's what you want from Éibhear."

Izzy gave a snort of disgust. "I want nothing more than to see the back of him."

"Is that so?"

"He judged me like he had a right. Like he has some say in my life."

"You don't want Celyn. You don't want Éibhear. What do you want, Izzy the Dangerous?"

Now she looked at her queen without fear or shame, and admitted the truth. "I want to be your squire."

"I have a squire," Annwyl said flatly. "He's fat now."

Shocked, Izzy giggled. "Annwyl!"

"He is. Wonderful with horses, though. My Violence loves him." She glanced at the enormous black beast calmly grazing on the grass several feet from them. "But my squire's fat, and that's because I don't go anywhere. I don't do anything. If you become my squire, Izzy, all your talent will go to waste. I won't have that, luv. Not for you."

"So you won't being going to face the Sovereigns in the west?" Izzy asked, having heard her parents talking the night before.

Annwyl shrugged, pulling her knees up so she could wrap her arms around her legs. "I'll send legions to meet Thracius head on."

"Is that what *you* want?"

"At the moment that's all I can have, Izzy."

The horse pawed the ground, shook his head.

Annwyl gave a little laugh. "As you can see, my Violence doesn't like the sound of that at all."

Eyes on Violence, Izzy frowned, not sure Annwyl's words were the horse's concern at all.

"Izzy."

Her queen's voice was soft when she said her name, so soft Izzy might have missed it if she weren't right next to her. But Izzy heard the fear and slowly looked away from Violence.

They'd come out of the trees, but Izzy had heard no sound. They moved like death. And yet there were so many of them, Izzy couldn't even count the number. Izzy had never seen anything like them before.

Animal skins and leather barely covered hard, muscular bodies that had seen many battles. And they all bore many tattoos. No tattoo the same. Some of them wore them on their arms, their thighs, their chests, but absolutely all of them had tattoos on their faces. Black, tribal markings disturbed only when facial wounds had left scars.

Most were on foot, but a good forty were mounted, with large doglike creatures beside each one.

What they rode were like horses, but Izzy had never seen any so wide, their oversized muscles rippling as they stood restlessly, swinging their heads to the ground so their horns could dig in to the dirt. Izzy had the feeling the digging was their way of sharpening those horns. And their eyes were blood red. The doglike animals also had horns, but their horns curled inward like the rams Izzy liked to chase on the Western Mountains. Unlike the large dogs Dagmar bred and raised, though, these things were bigger. Some looked close to three hundred pounds, all of it hard muscle and flesh. Like something coughed up from the underworld.

Yet none of that disturbed Izzy as much as what were being held back by thick chain and collar. While the dogs had no leash and the horses had no saddles, these things were controlled by the thick metal collars around their throats and the chains being held by their captors. These had no horns, no otherworldly eyes, no bulging, overdeveloped muscles—and that was because they were men. Human men frothing at the mouth, more than eager to kill. Men who'd lost their minds and humanity long, long ago.

Slowly, Annwyl got to her feet, her gaze locked not on the entire legion before her but on the one who rode at the head. A woman. A witch. Izzy might not be one like her mother and sister, but she could spot one. She could spot them all.

"Izzy," Annwyl said again, her voice now stronger. "Go."

"Leave you to fight alone?"

"No. Get me help."

The witch leader lifted her hand, palm up, middle and fore-finger out. Izzy waited for her to unleash a spell with that hand, but all she did was swipe her fingers to the left. The collars on the men were jerked by the females who held them and the metal unlocked and dropped. Unleashed, the men howled in their madness and charged.

"*Izzy, go!*" Annwyl screamed, lifting one of her blades.

And, as her commander ordered, Izzy shot off toward home.

"Are you going to keep pacing?" Dagmar asked Talaith. "You're making me dizzy."

"How can you be so calm?"

Busy writing a list, Dagmar replied, "I choose not to fret. Fretting doesn't help."

"She doesn't understand, you know." And Dagmar slowly raised her head to look across the table at the god who sat there, her feet brazenly resting on the wood. Her arm had grown back. "Not everyone's like you."

"Why are you here?"

The war goddess pouted. "That's not very welcoming."

"Who are you talking to?" Talaith asked.

Dagmar sighed. "A god."

And that's when Talaith threw up her hands and shouted, "Well, that's not good!"

"Do you really think her brothers will allow you to get away with this?" Elder Siarl asked.

"I'll talk to Morfyd. She'll understand. And I'll deal with any repercussions."

"Then why have you even bothered to summon us?"

"I will present what I have found to the Council, and you will judge her accordingly. Then punishment will commence."

"Punishment? In the salt mines?"

"For betraying our queen."

"I don't like it," Elder Teithi argued.

"It's for the best."

"No, cousin," Keita finally managed to say. "It's for your ego." She dragged herself to her claws. It wasn't easy. She hurt everywhere.

"What I do, I do for my queen."

"What you do," Keita snarled back, "you do for yourself. Don't blame the queen for you being such a self-righteous cunt."

The fist slammed into the side of Keita's snout, sending her crashing to the ground.

"Elestren! Stop this!"

"Perhaps the snobby slit would like to challenge me." Elestren kicked her, sending Keita's dragon body flipping up and over. "Come on, princess! Pick up a sword and fight me! Prove your innocence by killing your challenger."

"Elestren, I'm telling you right now to stop this!" Elder Siarl ordered.

"I'm giving her a chance to walk away from this." Elestren

unsheathed her sword, flipped it so that she held it by the blade. "Take it, princess. Prove me wrong. Let the gods decide our fate."

Coughing, Keita slowly pushed her body up. When she saw her cousin's body relax, Keita picked up a handful of dirt and flung it at Elestren's still-useful eye.

Dropping the sword, Elestren backed up, screeching as she tried to wipe out the dirt. Keita scrambled up, put her front claws together, talons interlocking, and swung at Elestren's face. She hit her hard, Elestren's entire head jerking to one side. But she was still standing and, it seemed, relatively unfazed by the hit that had Keita's claws throbbing.

Slowly, Elestren faced Keita.

"Oh . . . shit," Keita muttered seconds before her cousin swung her own fist, sending Keita flying back and into the cave wall. She hit it hard and then hit the ground a little harder.

"Elestren! No!"

But her cousin ignored Elder Siarl's demand, grabbing hold of Keita by her hair and flipping her over. She slammed her knee down on Keita's chest and raised the sword she retrieved over Keita's head.

"Sorry, cousin," she said, although they both knew she didn't mean it.

The screaming men charged forward, and Annwyl readied her weapon, pulling it up so the handle was by her shoulder and the blade a little lower. When the first few were close enough, she swung the blade in an arc. She cut several in half, took the arms of others. A handful shot by her and went after Izzy. Although she wanted to follow, to protect her niece, she knew she had to let Izzy prove her worth. She couldn't and wouldn't turn away from this fight. Not when she'd been dreaming about it for so long now.

This had been what she'd been waiting for, and Annwyl had no intention of walking away.

More men charged her, and Annwyl went to work.

Izzy jumped over tree stumps and dashed around boulders. She could hear the men coming up behind her, slavering for her blood. Begging for it. She didn't turn around; she didn't look at them. She couldn't afford to. The forest could be tricky. And although she was armed, she couldn't stand and fight now. Not when Annwyl needed help. Not when those protecting the twins—and, more importantly, her sister— needed to be warned.

Keita brought her claws up, hoping to somehow block the blade before it entered her chest, but a flash of light had her gasping and Elestren yelping and stumbling away from her. Keita turned over and watched with her mouth open as Morfyd landed in front of her.

Elestren blinked in confusion. "Morfyd?"

"You bitch." Morfyd raised her claws and unleashed bright white flames that sent Elestren flying back. "*My sister!*" Morfyd bellowed, advancing on Elestren. "*You do this to my sister!*"

Elestren got to her feet, snarling. "You'd protect this lying, betraying *bitch*?"

"She's my *sister*!"

Elestren raised her blade to attack, and Morfyd opened her mouth and unleashed a line of flame that snaked across the cavern, wrapped around the blade, and yanked it from Elestren's stunned grasp.

Those who'd been with Elestren ran for the exit, but they met Briec and Gwenvael, who didn't seem to be in any mood to let them leave.

Elestren held her claws up. A sign of surrender. A move rarely made by a Cadwaladr, but one that clearly signaled the fight was over.

Ragnar landed beside Keita, dropping to one knee.

"Gods, Keita."

"Help me up."

She held up her claw, and he took it. Fearghus landed on the other side of her and grabbed her other claw. Together they helped her stand.

Keita watched as Morfyd raised her claw and chanted, pulling her talons in until she made a fist. Elestren went down screaming as if something inside her was being torn apart.

Éibhear grabbed Morfyd's shoulders, tried to pull her back, to stop her. But with a flick of her wrist, she sent their oversized baby brother spinning across the cavern, Ragnar and Fearghus quickly pulling Keita out of the way.

Talaith looked away from Dagmar and the god she couldn't see. It felt like her chest was being squeezed, and the last time she'd felt that, her Izzy had been in trouble. She moved from the table, her gaze shooting up to the top of the hallway stairs. The centaur stood there, watching her, Ebba's serene, but direct expression telling Talaith all she needed to know.

She was up on the long table and over it in seconds, running out the Great Hall front doors.

Talaith saw the two Lightnings coming from around the building.

"Vigholf!" she yelled. "Meinhard!"

They both stopped and watched her dash by and out the side exit. She was near the forest that would take her into the west field.

"Mum!"

She saw her daughter running toward her—saw what was

behind her. Nearly on her. Men that were no longer men. And that meant only one thing.

Kyvich.

"Don't stop!" Talaith yelled at her. "Go!"

Mother and daughter charged past each other, Talaith pulling out the blade she always kept tied to her thigh. She cut the throat of one mad bastard, leaped onto a nearby boulder, and shoved off with one foot, slashing her blade across the throat of another. When she landed on the ground, she kept running, trusting her daughter could take care of herself.

Izzy did as her mother ordered and kept running. She ran until she cleared the trees, and that's when the first one slammed into her from behind, flipping them both over.

He caught her by the hair, yanking her head to the side and wrapping his mouth around the side of her neck. Teeth dug in and bit down. She screamed out, her hand reaching for the blade she kept tucked into her boot. She had her fingers on the handle when the man was pulled away from her, his brains dashed when a Lightning in human form slammed him to the ground.

Izzy released her knife and got to her feet.

"Izzy!" She looked up as Meinhard tossed an ax to her. She caught it, spun, and hacked through the crazed male closest to her. She stopped, swung the blade up, and tore through another from his bowels to his neck. Then she hefted the ax and ran back into the forest.

She saw her cousin and screamed, "Get the kin. Get them all! Meinhard! Vigholf! Follow me!"

Morfyd crouched in front of the keening warrior at her feet. "Did you really think you'd get away with this?" she asked. "Did you really think I'd let you do this to my sister?"

She heard someone calling to her, someone yelling at her to stop, but she couldn't. Not after seeing what Elestren had done to Keita. How she'd hurt her. How she'd been moments from killing her.

"Tell me, cousin, what does it feel like?" she asked in a whisper. "What does it feel like when I turn the blood in your veins to shards of glass?" Morfyd squeezed her fist, making the shards inside her cousin bigger. "Does it make you want to scream? The way you tried to make my sister scream?" She caught Elestren's green hair and yanked her head up, bellowing in her face, "*Does it hurt?*"

She watched the human queen tear through enemy men that her sisters, trained in the art, had broken and tormented until they became nothing more than attack beasts. The loyal dog at her side, however, was her companion and partner. She protected him as she protected herself and her horse. But these men were of no concern to her and allowed her to wear down the Blood Queen of Dark Plains.

A head flipped past, and Storm picked it up in his fangs, shaking it before offering it to her horse, Death-bringer, so they could play tug. They loved playing tug together.

"Ásta," her second command, Bryndís, called to her. "A Nolwenn."

Surprised, because they'd had no warning, Ásta watched the Nolwenn witch charge into the field. She had a blade and nothing else.

Ásta growled a little, Death-bringer pawing the ground restlessly beneath her.

"Hulda," Ásta said softly. "Kill it."

Hulda grinned and tightened her legs, her horse knowing exactly what to do.

Nolwenns were the bane of the Kyvich. The why of that

fact had been lost to memory a millennia ago, but the hatred remained.

The queen had nearly finished with the males, an outcome Ásta cared little about.

"Unleash the second wave," she said, her voice never going above a very soft call.

Bryndís lifted her arm. "Second wave!" she cried out. "Forward!"

Kyvich who had not yet earned their seats screamed and charged forward on foot, their weapons at the ready.

Annwyl had yanked her sword from the body at her feet when she heard the call. She turned and watched the women charging her. About twenty, but unlike the bodies littering this field, these females weren't crazed, uncontrollable, broken humans. They were like her. Well-trained and only as crazy as necessary to get the job done.

The first who reached her ducked the fist aimed for her face and went up and under until she was behind Annwyl, slamming her fist into Annwyl's kidney.

Screaming in pain and rage, Annwyl turned and swung her sword. Their swords met, slamming into each other with such force, the power of it radiated down Annwyl's arm. Another blade swung at her, and Annwyl leaned back, catching hold of the hand attached to that sword. She held the two females, teeth clenched, muscles straining.

More came for her, and she waited until the last second before she lifted her legs, kicking the one in front of her. Her legs swung back down, and Annwyl dropped to the ground, her legs spread wide, her hand still gripping the sword arm of one woman and her own blade keeping the blade of another at bay.

She yanked the arm she held and twisted, breaking it in several places. The woman dropped to one knee, and Annwyl used her elbow to shatter the bones of the right side of her face.

The woman fell back, screaming but not dead. Annwyl pulled a blade she had tucked into the back of her leggings and shoved it into the lower belly of the other female. That one dropped, her blade still in her hand and blood pouring out of her wound.

Annwyl had no doubt she'd be back on her feet in seconds; the other one with the shattered face was already halfway up.

Rolling to her feet, Annwyl raised her blade again, but a large hand from behind her caught hold and twisted. Annwyl went with it, not wanting her wrist to be broken. She dropped the blade she held and turned her body in the same direction that her arm was twisted. She fell to her knees and came around until she faced her opponent. She took her free hand, balled it into a fist, and rammed the bitch in the groin until she heard bone break.

Teeth gritted, the woman dropped to her knees, and Annwyl head-butted her.

She pulled her arm away and stood, shaking off the pain.

Izzy charged straight for her, so she stepped to the side. Izzy flew past, colliding into three females who'd been coming up behind Annwyl.

The two Northland dragons flew in, landing hard in front of Annwyl, their backs to her. Vigholf unleashed bolts of lightning at the witch's leader.

Smiling, the cold, tattooed bitch raised her hand, and the lightning strikes broke into pieces, dropping to the ground. Stunned, the dragons could only stare, and the woman sniffed in disgust and flicked her hand. As if shoved apart by gods, the two dragons flew into the surrounding forest, mowing down trees and creating a new path for those who needed to get through.

Annwyl realized then she didn't stand a chance.

Of course . . . that had never mattered before.

* * *

"What have you done?" Dagmar demanded of the god.

"Why do you assume I've—"

Dagmar slammed her fist against the table, truly feeling like her father at that moment—he'd be proud.

Eir eyed her coldly. "Perhaps, human, you forget who I am."

"Woman, I don't give a battle-fuck who you are. Tell me what you did."

Dagmar heard panting right by her ear and turned in time to get an enthusiastic lick across the face. Then she understood. Eir had done nothing.

"Nannulf," she said to the wolf-god who adored her. "Can you show me what you've done?"

Nannulf charged for the door, and Dagmar followed.

The last thing she heard from Eir that day, "I'll expect an apology, you rude cow!"

Ásta knew when the queen realized she didn't stand a chance. When she knew she'd die this day. As would the two females fighting by her side. She knew they'd all die and there was nothing she could do about it.

Yet the human queen retrieved her sword and went back to work. Fighting those still considered novices by the Kyvich Elders.

"Fire Breathers," Bryndís warned her calmly. She knew how Ásta hated to be yelled at. What was the point? When they started to panic in battle, all would be lost.

"Shield," Ásta ordered.

Bryndís nodded at their left-flank unit. As one, the women raised their left hands, and the Fire Breathers leading the charge were the first who slammed into that shield created by the Kyvich. Snouts breaking, blood spurting, they flipped back and crashed into the ones behind them.

Ásta again focused on the defeated queen—who didn't fight as if defeated.

Realizing that the rage all the siblings had in one form or another had hold of her sister, Keita pulled away from Ragnar and her brother, and ran-limped her way across the cavern until she crouched beside her sister.

"No, Morfyd. Let her go."

Elestren began to cough up blood. And Keita was horrified to see there were pieces of glass in it.

"Please!" Keita gripped her sister's face between her claws, forced her to look her in the eyes. "Stop it." She shook her. "Please, Morfyd, let her go. For me, let her go!"

Morfyd unclenched her claw, and Elestren's head slammed back to the ground. Morfyd's gaze roamed around the cavern as if she didn't know where she was.

Panting, Keita pressed her snout next to her sister's. "Breathe," she whispered to her. "Just breathe."

Morfyd swallowed. "I'm . . . I'm all right. I'm all right."

Keita leaned back, searched her sister's eyes. The rage was gone, and the Morfyd that Keita knew was back.

Talaith threw a ball of flame at the horse charging toward her. It reared up, and its rider swung off, landing on her feet. She raised both her hands, pulled them back to garner energy from the land around her, then shoved them forward. The power of the blow slammed into Talaith, and she flew back.

She knew she headed for the trees. That the probability of her slamming head or neck first into some hearty oak was quite high.

She called up a charm she'd been working on, thought it, used it, and power Talaith had never known flooded through her, rampaging into her system. Talaith stopped her body's uncontrollable movement, suspending herself in midair. Then she rose up, her body hovering over land as if she had wings. The Kyvich stared up at her, enraged, and screamed.

Talaith screamed back and raced down to meet her. She collided into the witch, their bodies smashing to the ground and tearing across it from the momentum. By the time they rolled to a stop, they were in a pit of their own making and swinging at each other with nothing but their fists and the age-old hatred of their people.

They'd gotten her lovely ax away from her, but instead of using the many weapons they had on them to finish her off, they fought her with bare hands. That was fine by Izzy. She always did love a good bare-knuckle brawl.

She ducked a punch to the face, but not the punch to her lower back. It dropped her to her knees, but she put her hands down on the ground and brought her leg back, kicking someone in the chest. She rolled forward and up, ducked another punch to her head, and retaliated with a punch to a shoulder. Bone shattered on impact and the female's body jerked back, but the witch used the momentum to turn in the opposite way, the back of her fist slamming into Izzy's face. The blow sent Izzy flipping into someone else who caught hold of her by the throat and took Izzy to the ground.

Izzy swung at the hands that held her down, kicked out at the legs near her. But the one holding the blade over her chest . . . Izzy couldn't avoid her.

She didn't call for her mother or for Annwyl. They had their own fights, and she'd die knowing she had done what she could to protect her queen.

They slammed her arms down, held her legs pinned to the ground.

"Do it, bitch!" Izzy screamed, blood spitting on those who held her. "Do it!"

"As ya like." The witch raised the blade above Izzy's chest, and even though Izzy wanted to cringe and look away, she didn't.

The blade swung down, and Izzy pulled her right arm one more time, taking the witch who held her by surprise and yanking her over Izzy's chest. She was determined to take at least one of these crazed bitches with her.

"Fuck!" the startled witch cried out.

"Hold, Kyvich!" someone else called out, and the blade stopped inches from the witch's back. She let out a breath and dropped on Izzy.

"Fuck me," she whispered, and Izzy couldn't agree more.

Ragnar watched as Morfyd helped her sister up, but he took Keita in his arms and nodded at Morfyd. "I've got her."

Morfyd nodded, patted his arm.

Ragnar smiled down at Keita. "You do manage to find piles of shit to fall into everywhere you go, don't you?"

Keita laughed at that. "Some might say."

"What do you want us to do with this lot?" Briec asked, still blocking the exit with Gwenvael.

"We can't let them go," Keita said and when her brothers smiled and reached for their swords, "No, no! We can't kill them either!"

"Dammit." Briec shoved his sword back in its sheath, and Gwenvael seemed to pout.

Keita looked at Fearghus. "We need Ghleanna. She can take care of this lot. Because it's time I told all of you the truth about what's been going on."

"What are you thinking?" Ragnar asked.

Reaching up, she wiped the blood from her snout. "I'm thinking we've run out of time."

Ragnar gently kissed her. "I think you're right."

* * *

Blood covering her; her knuckles torn, battered, and broken; her nose shattered; at least one shoulder no longer in its socket; both eyes swollen along with her lips and chin; and nearly every inch of her bruised, Annwyl watched the witches who'd been fighting her back away. They kept backing up until seven of the mounted witches rode past them, the one that she'd pegged as leader in the middle.

Dressed in animal skins and with jewelry made of silver, steel, and animal parts, they truly looked like Ice Land barbarians.

Annwyl looked down and saw her sword. She reached for it, almost lost her balance, but stopped herself. She lifted the sword with both hands, planted her feet firmly, and raised the sword higher, ignoring the screaming pain coming from her damaged shoulder.

The witches pulled their horses to a stop and dismounted. They stayed at least three paces behind the one who led them, stopping completely when she was only a few feet from Annwyl.

They stood and watched her until Annwyl screamed, "Come on then! Let's finish this! *Come on!*"

The leader's head tilted to the side. "You can't win," she said, her voice soft, calm.

"I'll kill you, though, cunt. I'll make sure to kill you. So come on. Finish it."

The witch glanced up at the sky. "Your dragon kin are coming. I can hear the flap of their wings. Don't you want to wait?"

"I wait for no one." Annwyl tightened her grip, dug her feet in deeper. "Raise your weapon. Come for me. We end this now."

The leader reached for the sword tied to her back. A long sword covered in runes. The other six—three standing on each side of their leader—pulled their weapons as well. Two long swords, one short sword, one warhammer, two axes, each covered in runes, each held by females who knew how to use them.

With her sword raised, the female walked toward her.

"Annwyl!" she heard Fearghus bellow as he approached.

Annwyl smiled, for she already knew no matter what happened here, she'd meet Fearghus on the other side when his time came. They wouldn't be apart forever.

Standing right before Annwyl, the witch raised her sword high, point down, and Annwyl pulled her weapon back a little farther, aiming right for the witch's chest.

The witch's sword unleashed, Annwyl watched it closely. Watched for the right time to strike, watched for the moment when she'd have her chance to—

The sword slammed into the ground in front of Annwyl, and the witch looked first to the left, then the right.

Each witch with her slammed her weapon into the ground, blade or hammer end first. Then they dropped to their knees before Annwyl.

When they were all on their knees, their leader looked back at the legion of warrior witches behind her. As one, those witches dropped to their knees while their horses lowered their heads and their dogs lay down in the dirt.

Unsure what the fuck was happening, Annwyl kept her sword raised. "What is this?" she demanded.

"We're here for your children."

"And you'll not get them."

The witch smiled at her. "We're not here to take them. We're here to protect them, while you lead your legions against the Sovereigns." The witch pulled out a blade and cut her palm, stepped forward, and dragged her hand down Annwyl's face. "Our life and blood for you, Queen Annwyl. I give you my sword."

"My sword for you," another said.

"My hammer for you!" another yelled out.

"My ax for you!" another screamed.

Then the entire legion was screaming, committing their weapons, lives, and souls to Annwyl and to her children.

Not knowing what the hell to do, Annwyl looked around her. As the witch had said, her dragon kin dropped from the sky, surrounding them, but it was the warlord's small daughter she searched out. She was the one Annwyl knew would have the answers. Dagmar stood there among all those enormous dragons, Canute on one side of her and the cutest little puppy on the other. The puppy Izzy couldn't stop playing with.

Dagmar flicked her eyes toward the castle, and Annwyl took a step back, then another. She lowered her sword, turned, and without a single word, walked off.

Fearghus watched as his mate turned her back on a legion of warriors cheering and screaming.

Izzy, who he'd thought for sure was dead, picked herself up from the ground and walked backward away from them, her weapon retrieved and raised. Her mother did the same thing on the opposite side of the field. They walked away from the warriors they'd been fighting until they were a good distance away; then they turned and followed Annwyl.

"Go with her, Fearghus," Dagmar whispered to him. "Go."

He did, not bothering to keep an eye on the witches because he knew his kin would.

"We make camp here!" one of the witches yelled over the din. "Burn the bodies, a sacrifice to our gods and Queen Annwyl!"

They reached the side entrance to the castle, and Fearghus went up and over while Annwyl, Izzy, and Talaith took the door.

Annwyl was on the stairs when her legs gave way and she dropped.

Fearghus, stepping past Izzy and Talaith, caught his mate in his arms before she hit the ground. He lifted her up and smiled when she opened her eyes.

"Can't trust you alone for five minutes, can I, wench?"

Annwyl grinned, showing bloody teeth but at least all those teeth were there. "They started it, knight," she teased back.

Chapter Thirty-Four

Ren of the Chosen Dynasty ran across the rocky ground, Sovereign troops right on his naked ass. He'd been moving in and out of this territory undetected for two days, but the eldest daughter of Overlord Thracius, the one they called Vateria—and who frightened Ren as no dragoness ever had before—had seen him and sent her father's guards after him.

Knowing he'd only get one chance at this, he charged up a hill, pulling Magick from any living thing near him. Trees, water, grass, anything. As he made it to the top, he unleashed the Magick that would open a doorway. A skill gifted to his people from the gods who watched over them. Ren could travel hundreds of miles with the doorways he was able to open. His father could travel to other worlds. However, it usually took him weeks or even months to carefully calibrate where he'd end up once he went through a doorway. Too bad he didn't have that kind of time.

Ren knew the troops were right behind him, hands and claws reaching for him, and he hoped that the doorway he'd just opened would take him to where he needed to go—and not into something much worse.

Praying for the best, Ren dove in headfirst, slamming the doorway shut behind him, and leaving the rest to his gods.

* * *

They heard the horrified and panicked screams from the courtyard below.

"Mum's here," Gwenvael said with his feet in Dagmar's lap and Izzy running a brush through his hair for his nightly three hundred strokes. She was the only one among them willing to do it without complaint.

Keita didn't know how all her siblings, their mates, their offspring, Ragnar, his brother, his cousin, Dagmar's dog, Annwyl's dogs, and in a few seconds, her parents had all ended up in Fearghus's and Annwyl's bedroom—but here they were.

Ragnar, more used to warriors than "dainty little princesses" as Gwenvael kept calling Keita when she complained about the Northlander's rough hands, helped Annwyl get her shoulder back in its socket while Morfyd healed Keita's damaged ribs and tended to the lacerations that could lead to unattractive scars if not carefully handled.

The door burst open, and Rhiannon came into the room, her arms spread wide. "My little ones!" she exclaimed.

Only to receive muttered, "Mum. Mother. Mumsy." The last being from Keita *and* Gwenvael.

Her arms dropped to her sides. "Is that all I get?"

"I'm eating," Briec explained around a mouthful of food.

Rhiannon walked all the way inside the room, and her mate followed behind her. As soon as Bercelak saw his youngest daughter's face, though, Keita scrambled up out of her chair and caught hold of her father's arm.

"Don't, Daddy."

"When I'm done there won't be anything left of that green bitch for my brother to put on the pyre."

"Ghleanna's handling it," she told him.

"I don't care."

Realizing her father was moments from walking out the

door and that no one was even trying to stop him, Keita slapped one hand to her bruised side and cried out in pain.

Instantly, her father's arms went around her. "Keita? Are you all right?"

She managed a few tears. "It hurts a bit. Take me to the chair, Daddy."

"Of course." He helped her inside, Keita kicking the door closed with her foot. "My brave, sweet girl," he said. "Isn't she amazing, Rhiannon? Facing that bitch Elestren all by herself."

Rhiannon had picked up her youngest granddaughter, and was rubbing their noses together. "I don't think she had much choice, my love."

"She knew she was at risk, but she was brave to protect this family and your throne."

Keita saw Morfyd roll her eyes and sneer. When her father turned his back to make sure he brushed off the chair before placing Keita's delicate and perfect ass in it, Keita yanked Morfyd's hair. Morfyd slapped at her hands, and Keita slapped back. They were in a mini-brawl before Brastias barked, "Pack it in!"

"You promised me," Rhiannon reminded Keita, "that you'd let me know as soon as you were contacted."

"I lied," Keita admitted.

"Then I guess you shouldn't be shocked you got your royal ass kicked." Her mother pointed at the window. "And why are there scantily clad warrior women with tattoos on their faces lurking in your courtyard?"

"They're the Kyvich," Dagmar explained. "Sent by the gods you insist on worshipping to protect the babes. But, of course, Annwyl had to fight nearly to the death before they'd take the job. They are Ice Landers, you know. That's their way."

"I hate the Kyvich," Talaith complained from her spot on the floor, tucked comfortably between her mate's widespread legs.

"You keep saying that," Briec pointed out, "but you haven't explained why."

"Because the Nolwenns hate the Kyvich." When everyone only stared at her, "I shouldn't have to explain myself! I just don't want them here."

"Well, suck it up," Annwyl said. "I didn't decimate wave after wave of barbarian, murdering scum in tiny little outfits so you can claim, 'I just don't like them,'" Annwyl finished in a high-pitched imitation that Talaith didn't seem to much appreciate.

Making sure Keita was in the chair and comfortable—Elestren seemingly forgotten at the moment—Bercelak asked Annwyl, "Were they the ones you'd been dreaming about?"

"Aye. It was them. Down to the horses and those bloody dogs."

"I love those dogs," Dagmar whispered to Gwenvael. "Think they'll lend me a breeding pair?"

Bercelak studied Annwyl. "And how did you do then?"

Annwyl's answer was a warm smile that had Bercelak grinning back at her in return, and giving her a proud nod.

That's when Fearghus stood up, his finger pointing between the two. "What was that?"

Annwyl quickly looked down at the floor, and their father shrugged. "What was what?"

"That look between you two."

"And how did he know she'd been having dreams about violent warrior witches?" Gwenvael asked, ever the instigator, and earning himself a swat to the head from Izzy, who wielded a brush much like she wielded her sword. "Ow!"

"Be nice!"

"You?" Fearghus demanded of Annwyl. "You and my . . . *father?*"

"I can explain."

"*How can you explain this?*"

"Maybe we should all calm down?" Morfyd begged.

"Annwyl, answer me!"

"All right, fine!" Annwyl bellowed back at her mate. "You

want the truth? I've been training with your father every day
for the last year! There! Now you have the bloody truth!"

Keita looked past Annwyl's brawny shoulders to Ragnar.
She loved the adorably confused expression he wore at the
moment. His brother and cousin equally lost. Finally he
looked at her and mouthed, *Training?*

Keita quickly pressed her fingers to her lips to hold in the
laughter.

"You've been training with him all this time," her eldest
brother demanded of his mate, "*and you never told me?*"

"Because I knew you'd get upset!"

Keita tugged on her sister's sleeve. "Can this day get
stranger?" she asked.

Morfyd raised a finger. "It's about to get stranger in three
seconds."

"How do you—"

Keita abruptly stopped talking, the air in the room briefly
sucked out then rushing back in as Ren of the Chosen Dynasty's naked body sprawled in the middle of the floor.

Gwenvael tapped his niece's arm. "That Ren always knows
how to make an entrance."

Ragnar did not, never would, and wasn't sure he ever
wanted to understand the Southland royals. That being said,
he'd come to find them damn amusing, as had his brother
and cousin.

Meinhard helped up the Eastlander and handed him some
leggings, blocking the view from Izzy, who was trying to see
around him for a better look—much to Éibhear's growing
annoyance.

"What news do you have, Ren?" Gwenvael asked while
Ren pulled the leggings on.

Meinhard stepped back, and the now-dressed Ren placed
his hands on his hips. "It's as we feared. Thracius readies his

Dragonwarriors and his human soldiers for a two-pronged attack on Dark Plains. Bringing his Dragonwarriors down through the Northlands." Ren focused on Ragnar. "With the help of your cousin Styrbjörn."

"I'm not surprised it's him," Meinhard remarked.

"It's a little thing," Ragnar said, moving to Keita's side.

Vigholf crossed his arms over his chest. "I'll enjoy opening him up from bowel to throat."

"And he'll be sending Laudaricus through the Western Mountains?" Annwyl asked.

Ren nodded. "From what I saw, Annwyl, that human has hundreds of legions at his command. But before any of that happens, Thracius hopes to get Keita on the throne."

Keita's sudden burst of laughter startled everyone in the room, and she quickly covered her mouth. "Sorry."

Ragnar leaned down a bit and studied her. "What are you thinking?"

"According to everyone, I don't think."

He straightened up, understanding her far too well these days. "You can bloody well forget that idea!"

Keita looked around the room as if seeing it for the first time. "I'm sorry. I wasn't aware I'd entered a new plane of existence where I take someone's orders *other than my own*!"

"Yell at me all you want, princess, you're not doing it."

"You *are* calling me prince-ass!"

"She's not doing what?" Briec asked.

Keita raised her hands to calm everyone, but Ragnar would not be calm about this and let her wiggle her way through.

"It's actually quite perfect," she reasoned.

"You've lost your bloody mind."

"Elestren has already done the work for me," Keita explained. "My face is battered and bruised, I have these awful lacerations that may take entire *weeks* to heal, and bruises around my ribs. It's perfect!"

"It's insane." And to Ragnar's shock, that came from Ren. "You can't really be considering going into Quintilian Province."

"If I go there now, looking like this, Thracius will gladly take me in."

"Then what?"

"Then I'll take care of it."

"I'm sure you will. But then you'll be trapped in the Provinces with his very pissed-off kin."

"I've been in worse situations."

"No, you haven't, Keita." Holding her sleeping grandchild, Queen Rhiannon walked around to face her daughter. "I know what the Sovereigns can do, and I've already lost a father to them—I'll not lose a daughter."

"Mum—"

"No." And her voice was calm, severely controlled. The teasing, the humor, the nicknames all gone in this moment. "You may protect the throne, daughter, but I *rule*. You will *not* go into the Provinces."

Frustrated, but most likely realizing there was no way around her mother for the moment, Keita relaxed back in her chair.

"Any chance you found out," Ragnar asked Ren, "what or who Styrbjörn escorted to the Southland borders from his territories?"

"I did, actually," Ren said. "And it was something rather surprising, although not nearly as surprising as what I discovered right after that."

"Which was?" Ragnar asked.

Ren glanced around the room. "Esyld. I think I found Esyld." And, with sorrowful eyes, he looked at Keita. "And she's not in the Provinces."

Keita frowned. "Then where the hells is she?"

Chapter Thirty-Five

The gate to Castle Moor slowly opened, and Athol watched Keita the Viper limp toward him.

He didn't trust her, but he was curious to see why she was back. She came alone this time, no strange dragon monks following her.

"My Lady Keita."

She raised her head, pulling back her hood, and Athol gasped before he could stop himself.

"My gods, Keita."

She fell into his arms then, clinging to him. "My own family did this to me, Athol. Even now they look for me. Can I stay here? Just for a little while?"

"Of course." He helped her in, motioned to his guards to close the gates. "You'll be safe here, my lady. I promise."

Elder Gillivray caught up with Elder Lailoken. They were both in human form and were heading toward a paid carriage that would take them the rest of the way to the Outerplains. From there, they'd get another transport to Quintilian Provinces.

Together they'd left Dark Plains nearly two days ago,

fleeing when word had spread about the attack on Princess Keita. She'd also disappeared, the princess's Northland lover and his kin sent packing, and the queen in a rage few had seen before. So, for their own safety, worried that the Cadwaladrs would turn their attacks on them, the pair had headed off.

Overlord Thracius had guaranteed their safety, and they would take him up on it.

They hurried around a corner but froze, the light flooding from the open back door of a pub glinting off a battle ax resting on broad shoulders.

"My lords."

"Who in all the hells are you?"

"Name's Vigholf. The bloke behind ya is me cousin, Meinhard." And the one behind them was bigger than the one in front. "Lord Bercelak asked us to do a favor."

"And we love doing favors."

"I'm surprised Ren's not with you."

Keita took the cup of tea Athol's assistant handed her, but she didn't drink from it, simply held it in a shaking hand.

"I don't know where he is. Things have become so awful."

"And Gwenvael?" The siblings had never been to his castle at the same time, but Athol knew they were related. He also knew what they were. He knew what everything was that entered his domain.

"Angry with me. They're all angry with me. They think I betrayed my mother."

Athol sat back. "Did you?"

"Of course not. I'd never take such a risk. You know well how she feels about me as it is."

"True." She stared into her cup, and Athol asked, "Why did you come here before?"

"I was looking for my aunt. I'd heard my mother was searching for her and . . ."

"You wanted to make sure she was safe."

Keita suddenly placed her cup of tea on the side table, allowing her to begin wringing her hands. "You need to understand . . . I would never hurt Esyld. I simply needed to ensure that she'd say nothing to my mother that could create problems for me." She licked her lips. "I just would have sent her someplace safe, where my mother couldn't find her." Keita winced, touched the wounds on her beautiful face gingerly. "Now *I* need to find someplace safe."

"There's no one who can help you?"

"The two Elders who were my allies in my mother's court have gone missing."

"You mean Gillivray and Lailoken?"

Keita's head snapped up, her eyes wide in panic. "Gods!" she nearly screamed, jumping up, her chair falling backward and crashing to the floor. "You're working with my mother!"

"No, no." Athol quickly stood and caught her hands. "I promise you I'm not. Ease yourself."

"Then how did you know about—"

"It's all right. I promise."

Athol closed his eyes, a voice calling to him. *Bring her to me, Athol.*

Putting his arm around Keita's shoulders, he said, "Come, Keita. I want you to meet someone."

Athol took her through a door in the back of his private rooms that led to a staircase. With his assistant behind him, he escorted Keita to the fourth floor—and to another set of rooms that she'd never been to during her time at Castle Moor.

"Where are you taking me?" she asked.

"These are my private chambers for special guests."

"I am in no mood for any of that, Athol," Keita said, trying to pull away.

"Of course you're not. That's not what's here."

He led her through several rooms until he reached glass

doors in the very back. He knocked once and opened them, stepping inside.

"Keita, it is my pleasure to introduce you to your mother's cousin and Overlord Thracius's wife—Lady Franseza."

Keita had heard about Franseza. She, like many who'd feared Rhiannon's reign, had fled when Keita's mother took power. But no one had any idea Franseza had joined forces with Thracius and become his wife. Then again, no one had really cared about Franseza at the time.

"My mother's cousin?" she asked, making sure to sound appropriately confused.

"Hello, my dear."

Franseza was dressed in the Quintilian fashion of a long, sleeveless tunic draped around her human frame, gold bangles on her wrists, gold earrings dangling from her ears, and a thick gold necklace around her throat. "I have waited so long to meet you, dearest cousin."

"Meet me? Why?"

"We can discuss all that later." Franseza held her arms out. "Come. Let me get a better look at you."

Keita stepped forward, moving around a large bed. But she stopped, her gaze catching sight of the naked female lying on the floor, a thick collar around her neck, and the chain attached to it locking her to the bed.

"Esyld!" Keita ran to her aunt, carefully turning her over, and cradling her in her arms. "What have you done to her?"

Franseza cringed dramatically. "That was horrible of me, wasn't it?" And the beauty of that statement was that it was said without even a trace of sarcasm. "I know. I know. On the surface it looks terrible, but she simply wouldn't cooperate."

Esyld's eyes opened, and when she saw Keita's face, she grabbed hold of her niece's fur cape. "I said nothing," she told Keita, hysterical. "I swear, Keita. I told her nothing!"

"Shh-shh. It's all right, Esyld."

"I don't think she realized that was part of the problem.

Not telling me things. If she'd only told me things, I wouldn't have had to hurt her so. That was hard for me, you know? We are first cousins after all."

Keita felt sick just hearing the female's voice, but nothing had her more worried than the fact that her aunt was cold to the touch. She was a She-dragon of Dark Plains. She was made of fire. The last thing Esyld should ever feel was cold.

Hands clasped together, steepled forefingers pressed under her chin, Franseza asked, "Now, Keita, how would you like to one day rule the land of Dark Plains?"

"Rule? Dark Plains?" Keita had to work hard to keep the game up when she felt her aunt dying in her arms. But she knew this scenario for the test—and warning—that it was.

"I know it sounds impossible, my dear, but I promise you it's not. You just have to trust me."

Desperate, her aunt clung to her tighter, shaking her head. "Keita, please."

"It's all right, Esyld. Really." She kissed her aunt's forehead and carefully lowered her back to the floor. She petted Esyld's cheek once, deciding then it was time to end this game. So Keita closed her eyes and sent out one thought: *It's time, Ragnar.*

She stood and faced Franseza.

The She-dragon's smile grew wider. "Are you about to challenge *me*, Keita the Viper? Don't be foolish."

"I'm never that." Keita pointed at the plate of fresh fruit on the table beside Franseza. "Isn't the fruit here delicious? I've always enjoyed it myself."

"Yes. It's very tasty. And so juicy, I've been picking some every day."

"From the tree that hangs over Athol's gate, yes?"

Athol took a step forward. "Keita?"

Keita giggled. "All right. I can't lie . . . much. Honestly though, Franseza, I've been watching you for days. Every morning you'd come out, pick your fruit, and nibble on it throughout the day, between fresh cow carcasses that are delivered. And the servants don't touch the fruit anymore because you already had a servant girl whipped who did. That is just like the Irons, isn't it? Claiming everything as your own."

"You little—"

"It wasn't too bitter, was it? What I used? I do try to be so careful about taste and all."

Her breath growing short, her hand on her stomach, Franseza asked, "Do you think I'm alone here, that I have no one to protect me?"

"I know you're not alone." Keita tossed her hair. "You know, the poison would be much less effective if you were dragoness. Too bad about Athol's spell keeping you in human form."

The Iron looked at Athol, but he only shook his head. "I can't. If you can shift, so can she. And anyone else she has with her."

"Too bad for you, eh, cousin?" Keita asked, unable to stop her smile.

"Kill her, Athol," Franseza ordered, dropping to her knees.

Keita snorted, swiped a dismissive hand through the air. "He can barely move after what he's been drinking." Keita glanced back at Athol. "Did I mention your assistant *hates* you? Plus . . . he wants this place. All I had to do was promise him we'd fix the walls we're about to destroy and he happily slipped that Banallan root right into your wine." Keita clapped her hands together. "Isn't this fun?"

The building around them rumbled, and the wall behind Franseza ripped away.

Athol stretched his arm out, terrifically weakened Magick flickering back and forth between his hands before he crashed to the floor. Ragnar and Ren made their way into the room through the space they'd created where that wall used to be.

Knowing that once they were *inside* Athol's palace, their

Magicks would be greatly diminished, they'd decided to tear the building apart from the other side of the gate first and left Morfyd outside to work on the next part of Keita's plan.

With Ragnar and Ren managing Athol, Keita walked toward Franseza.

"So sorry there's no one to rescue you," Keita said, using the same tone Franseza had when discussing what she'd done to Esyld. "The guards who'd been with you are busy getting gutted by my brothers."

"All you're doing," Franseza gasped out, "is bringing war to your weak queens, war that will tear this territory apart."

"Perhaps," Keita said. "And I must admit, I was fighting so hard to stop this war—even ready to come to your territory to try to work something out." She crouched down and looked into Franseza's bloating face as the poison took hold inside her human form. "But then I was told my aunt had been captured. And my friend, Ren, told me he sensed she was in some pain. After that, cousin, there was no going back. Not for anyone. Not for you."

Keita stood again. "Although it has been said that sometimes war just can't be avoided." She smiled, making sure to use her prettiest one. "But don't you worry, cousin. With the help of my friends and kin, I have come up with the loveliest idea to get everything started just right!"

The crowd roared as the two gladiators circled each other. It was the last day of the games, and now Vateria, eldest daughter of Overlord Thracius, was officially bored beyond anything she could remember. In fact, when she felt that slight earthquake under her feet, she hoped it might get bigger and open a chasm to swallow up all these boring beings tainting her and her father's world. Anything to end the tedium.

Then she heard the gasps and saw her noble father lean forward in his chair. She focused again on the battle, but the gladiators had stumbled back. Not from each other's blows, but from whatever had suddenly formed in the middle of the field.

A mystical doorway. She'd heard of this kind of Magick but had never met anyone who could actually perform it.

It was a small dragoness in human form who stepped out. A Southlander, from the look of her. She gazed up at the now-silent crowd until her eyes locked on Vateria's father.

"Overlord Thracius," she called out. "A gift from my queen, in honor of her father, my grandfather."

Then she tossed something away from her, and it rolled and bumped along, until it came to an abrupt stop on the field.

Vateria's father shot to his feet, but by then what had been thrown had changed from human to dragoness. Vateria recognized her mother even from this height.

Thracius gripped the railing, his gaze moving back to the Southlander.

"And this is a little something from me."

She reached back into that doorway and yanked three males out. Two old dragons and an elf.

"If it's war you want, Overlord," the Southlander shouted up to him, "then war you shall have!"

Then she was gone. Leaving Vateria's raging father, who'd just lost his mate, and three quaking foreigners in the middle of his gladiator ring.

Well, if nothing else, *everything* had just gotten a lot more interesting.

Annwyl waited in the war room, her rear resting against the table filled with maps and correspondence from her commanders, her arms crossed in front of her chest. Behind her stood Dagmar and Talaith.

Brastias opened the door and let in the two women.

"General Ásta and her second in command, Bryndís," he

announced. Once they were inside, he closed the door and came to stand close by Annwyl, big arms folded over his chest, his steady gaze on the ones who'd challenged his queen.

The second in command, Bryndís, dropped to one knee, her ax slamming into the floor, her head bowed. Ásta, however, merely bowed her head. But she kept it bowed, waiting for Annwyl to acknowledge her.

Before she did, Annwyl motioned Dagmar over and whispered in her ear, "Why can't I get this kind of bowing and scraping from you lot?"

"Because you'd force us to kill you in your sleep if you tried," her battle chief whispered back; then she winked.

Annwyl grinned, but cut it short, getting a good scowl in place before focusing her attention on the two women.

"So you're here"—Ásta raised her head as Annwyl spoke—"to protect my twins."

"That is the task we've been given. That is the task we'll carry out."

"And what if I tell you I don't need you? What if I tell you to go?"

"Then we'll go. Our orders are to follow your orders. That is what we'll do."

Annwyl briefly glanced back at a practically snarling Talaith, and asked, "We have a Nolwenn babe here as well. Will she be safe around you?"

"We have never harmed a Nolwenn not of age. We will not start now. We are not here to cause any harm, Queen Annwyl. Or take your children. You have met us in direct combat and have earned our respect. We will carry out our orders to the best of our abilities. We will protect your children with our lives. Our very souls if need be."

"Why?"

"Because you are all that stands between a world of many leaders, many cultures, many gods—and a dictator. War calls for you, Queen Annwyl. You must answer."

Before Annwyl could reply, a knock came at the back door to the room and Ebba entered. She walked on two legs and wore a dress, coming to Annwyl's side, and whispering in her ear, "You wanted me to tell you when I was putting the babes down for the night."

"Thank you," Annwyl replied, but then she saw the witch, Ásta, watching the centaur and smirking. The other, Bryndís, was still down on one knee, head bowed. "This is Ebba," Annwyl told the witch. "The babes' nanny."

The two females sized each other up until the witch said, "A centaur. We once hunted your kind for sport."

Ebba smiled. "And we used to devour your kind as snacks. Don't cross me, Kyvich, or I'll leave nothing for your sisters to mourn but what I pick out from between my teeth." Then, with a nod to Annwyl, Ebba walked out.

Annwyl again leaned down to Dagmar and whispered in her ear, "Adore. Her."

Rhiannon watched from her throne as her offspring approached, her sister held in Gwenvael's arms. Beside her was what remained of the Elders. Those who'd been involved with Elestren were among them, safe. They'd been pulled into the She-dragon's need for vengeance without realizing it, and Rhiannon wouldn't hold that against them . . . this time.

"Is it done?" Rhiannon asked once her offspring stood before her.

"It is done," her eldest son answered for them all.

"Good." She slipped off the dais and moved closer to Gwenvael. She brushed the hair from her sister's battered and torn face. Now she remembered why she'd always hated Franseza since they were hatchlings—the bitch was mean. "Hello, sister."

Esyld's eyes opened, and widened a bit more when she

saw Rhiannon staring down at her. "I-I told them nothing, sister. I swear. I never betrayed—"

"Hush, now. It's over. I know what you've sacrificed." Gods, did she know. The Northlander had touched Esyld's hand, and what he saw, he sent to Rhiannon. Esyld's Quintilian lover who'd tried to warn her, to protect her, only to get his throat cut in front of her; the beatings; the torture. Ragnar had shown Rhiannon all of it. She hadn't asked him to, but she understood why he'd done it. So that there would be no question about Esyld's loyalty, and there wasn't any question. Esyld was and would continue to be loyal—to Keita. It had been Keita Esyld wanted to protect. It was Keita she'd suffered for, afraid of what would happen to her niece should Franseza get to her. And that was how it should be. "You're safe, sister. You're home."

Rhiannon motioned to her guards. "Take her to the healers."

Esyld was carefully removed from Gwenvael's arms and taken out of the meeting chamber.

"We are sorry for what you suffered, Princess Keita," one of the Elders said. Rhiannon didn't bother to see which one.

"And Elestren has been removed from her position among my royal guard."

"Elestren should be removed from this world," Briec said.

"No." Keita glanced at her brother, shook her head. "I won't allow it."

"Why do you protect her, Keita?"

"She thought I betrayed the queen—she was doing her job. Perhaps a little overenthusiastically. Besides, she's *family*." Rhiannon sensed her daughter had been forced to have this conversation with her brothers quite a lot since they'd left for Castle Moor.

"The decision's been made," Rhiannon said, returning to her throne. "Ghleanna will decide Elestren's fate." She sat down and glanced to the Elders. They all nodded, and Rhiannon focused on her children. "Now, there's one last thing. . . ."

* * *

Together, Keita and her siblings, Ragnar and his kin, walked through the courtyard and up to the Great Hall steps. It had been a long flight home, and all of them were exhausted, looking forward to getting some food and some sleep.

But they stopped at the very bottom of the steps and waited. They waited for Annwyl the Bloody. She sat in the middle of the stairs, watching them all. Behind her stood Dagmar, Talaith, and Brastias.

"Annwyl?"

Annwyl looked her mate in the eyes. After a time, she spoke. "We proceed with the celebration feast for the children as planned. Then, once all is ready, I'll be leading my legions to the Western Mountains and into war against the Sovereigns."

Fearghus let out a breath. "And I'll be leading Queen Rhiannon's troops into the Northlands to fight against the Irons."

The mated pair stared at each other a long moment until Annwyl stood and said, "Then, my love, we best get ready."

Chapter Thirty-Six

Celyn waited for Izzy by the small lake they liked to go to together. It was growing late, and the first day of the three-day feast to celebrate the twins' birthday would be starting soon. His mother expected him to attend, and the way she was feeling about him right now, he was loath to miss it. But he needed to see Izzy alone.

"Celyn!" She charged through the trees and into his open arms. "You won't believe it!" she gushed, arms and legs tightening around him.

"I won't believe what?"

She dropped to the ground and held his hands. "I'm going with Annwyl into the west. I'm going to be her squire!" She bounced up and down on her toes. "Mother's absolutely *livid*!" She laughed and hugged him again. "I'm out of formation and fighting by Annwyl's side!"

He forced himself to smile. "That's wonderful."

"And Brannie will be coming with us. Your mum doesn't want to split us up. She says we work well together. Isn't that amazing?"

"Amazing."

Izzy frowned a little. "What's wrong?"

"Izzy . . ." He decided just to break it to her. "I'm being sent with Queen Rhiannon's troops into the Northlands."

Izzy's eyes grew wide, and then she hugged him. "You lucky bastard!"

"What?"

She pulled away and grinned at him. "You'll be fighting alongside Lightnings! Meinhard and Vigholf and Ragnar. Me and Brannie have been training with them every morning the last few days, and they're brilliant! I think they're part of the reason Annwyl's made me her squire. You're going to learn so much. I'm so jealous!" She punched his shoulder.

He gawked at her, and she frowned. "What's wrong?"

"Aren't you going to miss me at all?"

"Of course! I'll miss you terribly." But then she clapped her hands together and squealed, "But I'm going to be Annwyl's squire!"

Gwenvael sat in the chair, his foot tapping.

"So," Dagmar said from behind him, her voice very calm, very controlled, "you'll all escort Esyld back to Outerplains when you leave?"

"Aye," he replied, clenching his hands. "She still smiles, but I think she grows weary of my mother. Any longer and I'm afraid she'll crack from the pressure."

"Are you sure she's strong enough to return?"

"Morfyd said she will be by the time we leave. But she is still healing."

"I know she is, but I'm sure she's ready to return to her home and try to find a way past what she's been through."

"You'll be sure to have someone keep an eye on her, won't you?"

"Already taken care of," she said, her hand on his shoulder. Her soft, reassuring hand. "And remember I love you very much, Gwenvael."

"I know you do." He waited, teeth gritted. And he lasted right up until he felt Dagmar pick up that first lock of his precious, precious hair!

"I can't!" he said, jumping out of the chair and scrambling across the room.

Dagmar tapped those viperous scissors against her leg. He knew those scissors were out to get him. He could *feel* it.

"You cannot go into the Northlands *and* battle with all that hair." He noticed that her voice was no longer calm and controlled. "It's unseemly."

"Will you not miss my hair at all?"

"I'll miss you more, but the hair needs to go. Now get in this blasted chair!"

"I can't do it. It's my hair. It loves me for who I am."

"You act as if I plan to shave you bald. I only plan to cut up to the middle of your back or so."

Gwenvael gasped, horrified! "You might as well shave me bald!"

Dagmar threw down the scissors, and Canute slipped under the bed in the face of his mistress's rarely seen rage.

"Just let me get through the feast," he said, bartering. "Three more days not only for me, but for *you* to luxuriate in my hair."

Dagmar crossed her arms over her chest. "My father was right, you know. . . . You *are* completely insane."

Briec sat on the bed, his elbow resting on his knee, his chin in his palm, and watched his lady love rage.

"Who does she think she is? Making my daughter her squire?"

"Perhaps she thinks she's queen."

"Shut up!" She paced in front of him, looking wonderfully yummy in a dark blue gown he'd had made for her. "And that simpering idiot—"

"You should just call her Izzy."

"—is running around *announcing* it to everyone like it's a good thing. 'I'm going to be Annwyl's squire. I'm going to face death on a daily basis with this crazed monarch.'"

"I don't remember our Izzy's voice being so high before."

"Shut up!"

Izzy charged down the hallway toward her bedroom. She needed to get dressed; the guests were already arriving for the feast. She turned a corner and ran head first into that slab of brick that someone had the nerve to call a chest.

She fell back, her ass hitting the floor. And while rubbing her forehead, which seemed to have taken the worst of the impact, she scowled up at the big idiot in her way.

"Are you all right?" he asked, trying to sound so concerned.

"I'm fine." He reached for her, and she slapped his hands away. "I don't need your help, thank you very much."

"Are you going to keep acting like this?"

"Yes." Izzy stood. "You're a prat. I knew you were a prat—I just didn't realize the extent of your pratiness!"

"Fine. Be that way."

Éibhear walked around her, and Izzy tossed out, "And nice move getting Celyn sent to your brother's troops."

He stopped and faced her. "What are you talking about?"

"Like you didn't know."

"Celyn's going to be in the Northlands? With *me*? Well, I'm going to end that centaur shit right now."

She caught his arm before he could search out Fearghus. "Or you could stop this shit between you. I don't need you watching out for me, Éibhear. I don't need you beating up my lovers—"

"*Never* use that word to me again."

"—or deciding who I can fuck and who I can't."

"We're not having this conversation."

"He's your cousin," she reminded him.

"*And you fucked him!*" Éibhear bellowed in her face.

Izzy was calm when she replied, "I did. More than once. And you're not going to make me feel bad about that. But he's your cousin. Don't ruin what you have with your kin over something you can't control. Which is namely me."

She headed to her room, slamming the door behind her.

And Branwen didn't even look up from the book she was reading when she gleefully stated, "I swear, you two have the *best* arguments."

Fearghus dashed across the room and yanked the small eating knife from his daughter's hand, his son falling back on the bed laughing hysterically, as Annwyl finished turning around to show off the new gown Keita had chosen for her.

"It's not bad, is it?"

"No." Fearghus shook his head, probably more times than was actually necessary. "Not bad at all."

"Are you all right? You look like you're sweating."

"Just seeing you in that dress has my blood surging."

Annwyl scowled, her gaze locking with her daughter's. "Did she just *snort*?"

"No." Fearghus placed his hand over his daughter's giggling face and pushed her back to the bed next to her brother. "She probably just has a little sniffle."

"You are such a bad liar. How did you ever convince me that you and the knight were two separate beings?"

"Probably because you never let me finish a sent—"

"It's insane to even imagine it now—you're *such* a bad liar."

Keita, who hadn't quite managed to get any clothes on for this evening's dinner, removed herself from Ragnar's cock and clambered across the bed until she faced him.

"What did you just say?" she demanded.

Covered in sweat and, well, covered in her, Ragnar lifted his head. "I said you should accompany us all to the Northlands as a Battle Maid."

"Is that like a tent whore?"

"*No.*" He closed his eyes, took a deep breath. Let it out. "It is an honored position among my people."

"You sure this isn't just a way for you to get me back to the Northlands and keep me busy with your cock when you're not out fighting the Irons, so that I'll eventually stay with you forever?"

Ragnar gazed at her, blinked once. "Of course not. Whatever gave you that idea?"

She pointed a finger at him. "Because I'll give myself to no male. I don't mind having a regular lover, but I'll not become my mother. Chained to some male who adores me beyond all reason."

"Because what female would want that?"

"Is that sarcasm?"

"What gave you that idea?" He motioned to his still hard, and deliciously thick cock. "Now would you mind getting back over here and finishing?"

"As long as we understand each other. I'll come as your Battle Slag—"

"Battle *Maid.*"

"—but I'll make no commitment beyond that. And I won't be the winning prize of any Honours, my wings will *never* be threatened, and you won't even *think* about scarring up my perfect, *perfect* body with flames or lightning or whatever it is your kind uses to brand your victims."

"Mates."

"Whatever."

"I guess that's fair enough."

"I will not be Claimed, warlord. By you or anyone else."

"Fine."

Feeling confident she'd gotten her point across, Keita crawled back across the bed and on top of Ragnar. She caught hold of his cock and positioned it underneath her, allowing her pussy to slowly slide down until she'd taken him fully inside her once more.

Keita groaned, still shocked at how much she always enjoyed the feeling of Ragnar the Cunning sliding inside her.

Ragnar caught the back of her neck, big fingers massaging the muscles there. "But remember that while you are with me, princess—"

"I still hear prince-*ass*. . . ."

"—you'll have no other cock inside you. No other male's claws or hands on you. That seems a fair trade, don't you think?"

"Fair enough," she gasped, already rocking her hips against him. "Fair enough."

Dagmar headed toward the stairs. She wore another dress picked out by her sister-in-law Keita that looked as good as the first she'd given her. Apparently the royal intended to get Dagmar "an entire new wardrobe of pretty things!" A thought that horrified Dagmar a bit, mostly because she knew Keita had no intention of actually *buying* that new wardrobe, so she feared for any caravans that might be traveling through the area in the next few days.

Halting her steps, Dagmar glanced down at Canute. She raised her brow at the dog, knowing they both had sensed it, and went back down the hallway until she stood in front of her niece's room. Without knocking, she walked inside and caught her niece quickly hiding something behind her back.

"Give it," Dagmar ordered, her hand out.

"But—"

"Iseabail, Daughter of Talaith and Briec, *give. It.*"

"He cheers me up."

"Don't give me that face, Queen's Squire." And she saw her niece purse her lips, trying to stop the smile she got anytime someone called her that.

"Can't I keep him until we leave?"

"Trust me, Izzy. You can't keep him at all. Now give him over."

Sighing, she pulled the puppy from behind her back and placed him in Dagmar's hand.

"I like dogs," Izzy said.

"Izzy, you like everything." Dagmar kissed her forehead and headed out of the room. "Get dressed. Dinner soon."

Dagmar took the puppy down the stairs and out the back way of the Great Hall before she tossed him to the ground. "Stop pretending you're a puppy, Nannulf!"

The wolf-god landed on his giant paws and grinned at Dagmar, his tongue hanging out. If he had a human form, she had no doubt he'd be laughing at her. "And leave my niece alone," she warned him. He opened his mouth, and she quickly added, "And no barking!" The fortress walls couldn't stand the damage that would cause.

Nannulf pouted, tail hanging low, until Dagmar petted his head. Then he slathered her face with his tongue; spun around, hitting Dagmar with his tail and almost knocking her on her ass; and took off running.

"Who are you talking to, Dagmar?" Morfyd asked as the Dragonwitch came up behind her.

"A god," Dagmar said simply.

Turning right around, Morfyd marched back inside, muttering, "Show-off," as she did.

Éibhear walked up to his sister and tugged on the sleeve of her gown. She faced him, one brow raised, her lips pursed in disapproval, before he'd managed to say a word.

"Don't still be mad at me, Keita," he said. "I can't stand when you're mad at me."

"Did you apologize to Izzy?"

"No." He folded his arms over his chest, knowing he was pouting but not caring. "And I'm not going to. She's crazed! Won't listen to reason."

"*She* won't listen to reason?"

"You know, you were *my* sister before you were *her* aunt. Does that mean nothing in this family?"

"Of course it doesn't." Keita walked away from him, and Éibhear stared down at the floor. This was intolerable. He had his brothers constantly telling him, "You should have killed Celyn when you had the chance, you idiot," and Morfyd petting him and telling him, "It'll be all right, luv. Don't you worry now." All expected reactions, but he didn't realize until this moment how much he needed the full balance of his kin's reactions, including Keita's direct but fair advice. So having her simply angry at him without talking to him or telling him how she thought he should handle things was too much. Especially since Keita was the only one of his siblings who didn't treat him like he was stupid or made of spun glass.

Éibhear heard something scrape the floor, and he lifted his head, watching Keita drag a big chair over to him.

"Isn't that Annwyl's throne?" he asked, looking around for someone to be concerned.

"I'm just borrowing it." Keita placed the throne in front of Éibhear and stepped onto the padded seat. Now that they were at eye level, she placed her hands on his shoulders. "You do know I love you, don't you, little brother?"

"I guess. But it would be nice to hear it."

Keita smiled, and Éibhear felt relief at the sight of it. "It may take some time—you are ridiculously stubborn like the rest of this family—but I know you'll make this right one day. Until then"—she wrapped her arms around his neck and hugged him tight—"remember that my love and loyalty always belong to you."

"Aw. Thanks, Keita."

She pulled back and pointed a finger at him. "But when you are rude, little brother, I will not hesitate calling you a prat!"

That part Éibhear already knew.

"Oy, you dizzy cow!" Annwyl yelled from across the hall. "What the battle-fuck are you doing with my throne?"

Ragnar stared at his kin, his mouth slightly open.

"What's that look for?" Vigholf asked. "You said to do it."

"Even gave a suggestion," Meinhard tossed in.

"I thought you two were joking. Have you both lost your bloody minds?"

"We were trying to be nice," his brother argued.

"And when that crazed human monarch cuts off the rest of your hair, I don't want to hear any more—"

"Who did it?" Annwyl demanded from behind him.

Ragnar faced her, "My lady—"

"Who? I want to know whose idea this was"—she held up the training mace, battle ax, warhammer, and shield, perfectly sized for a two-year-old girl with both human and dragon blood—"and I want to know now!"

Vigholf and Meinhard raised their hands, and the queen's eyes filled with tears. "This is so sweet! Thank you. Thank you both!" She hugged them, arms going wide to reach around their chests.

That's when Ragnar let Annwyl know, "It was I who suggested the shield."

Keita slid in next to her sister and the duke of something or other and his boring human mate, the duchess of something else or other, and announced, "I'm going to the north to be a Battle Whore!"

"Maid!" Morfyd yelped. "She's going to be a Battle *Maid*." Morfyd forced a smile. "Will you excuse us?"

Morfyd grabbed Keita's arm and dragged her across the Great Hall. "Is there something wrong with you?" she said, pushing her away once they arrived on the other side of the room. "Something that's contagious?"

"Why are you yelling?"

"Battle Whore?"

"Whore. Maid. What's the difference?"

"You purposely embarrass me!"

"It is a skill, but you make it so easy."

Lips tight, Morfyd shoved Keita, and Keita shoved her back. There was a pause and then they both threw their drinks down and lunged for the other, but Dagmar stepped between them, her yummy-looking dog right by her side.

"I will *not* have this again."

"She started it!" they both accused.

"I don't want to hear it. This feast is to celebrate the birth and lives of your niece and nephew, and the least you two can do is have a little respect for their mother, who's had to make the hardest decision any female can make. How hard do you think this night is for her? And you two fighting like cats?"

Realizing the tiny barbarian was right, Keita looked at her sister and said, "Sorry."

"Aye," Morfyd replied. "Me too."

"Thank you." Dagmar began to walk away but was blocked by the human queen and her new squire's seething mother.

"Are you *trying* to get my daughter killed?"

"Yes!" Annwyl said, spinning around to face Talaith. "That's what I want. To get my niece killed. That's my whole fucking goal!"

"Mum!" Izzy charged up, her giggling baby sister in her

arms, her well-armed twin cousins hanging from around her neck. "You promised me you wouldn't do this!"

"Stay out of this, Izzy. I'm talking to your betraying *whore of an aunt*!"

Dagmar glanced back at Keita and Morfyd. "I won't discuss it," she said simply. "I just won't."

She walked off and a few seconds later, snapped, "Canute!"

The dog pressing into Keita's leg looked up at her with big brown eyes.

"You'd better go," Keita whispered.

And, sighing, he walked off after his mistress. The arguing sisters-in-law and Izzy had also moved to another spot so they could give *all* the guests in the Great Hall a clear view of their hysterical yelling.

"I don't know about you," Keita said when Briec had to rush over to help Izzy separate her mum and the human queen of all the Southlands from a rousing yelling match and slap fight, "but I'm having a most entertaining night."

Morfyd signaled to one of the servants for more wine. "Surprisingly, sister, and perhaps for the first time in the history of all dragons—I must agree with you."

"She's mine, you know."

Ragnar let out a heavy sigh. "I'm not sure The Beast would use that particular term, but all right."

"I'm just making it clear where we all stand, Liar Monk," Gwenvael explained. "So you'll understand why I'll have to kill you if you try anything."

"You still haven't figured out I love your sister?"

"This isn't about Keita. This is about me."

"I thought it was about Dagmar."

"In relation to *me*."

Unable to stand any more of this, Ragnar leaned in and whispered into the Ruiner's ear, "I've heard you're getting your hair cut. All those long, golden tresses falling helplessly to the floor . . ."

Gwenvael lunged away from him. "*Bastard!*"

Keita quickly stepped aside—the two mugs of ale she'd been carrying over nearly tragic victims to a Gold's idiocy—and let her brother pass.

"What was that about?" she asked, handing him one of the mugs.

Ragnar stared into it. "Is this your father's brew?"

"Don't be weak, warlord. Swill it!"

"Perhaps later." He placed the mug on the table behind him.

"Well?" she asked, grinning.

"Well what?"

"Did my brothers come over here and threaten you yet? Tell you if you try to take their adorable baby sister as your own, they would beat you within an inch of your life?"

"Uh . . . no."

Her brows lowered. "What do you mean no?"

"I mean no. They haven't said a word. Wait. That's not right." Her face lit up. "The two eldest said, 'Move!' and I said, 'Piss off!' That was about it."

She stamped her bare foot, and he knew at some point he'd have to find out why she refused to wear shoes. "Does this family not love me at all? Do I mean nothing to anyone?"

"I—"

"Don't say it!"

Ragnar laughed, pulling Keita into his arms.

"They threaten Brastias all the time," she whined. "Why not you?"

"Because they know you don't need their protection. You take care of yourself just fine."

She sniffed. "That was actually very good."

"I thought so."

Smiling, Keita placed her ale on the table and put her arms around Ragnar's neck. "Tell me, warlord, this Battle Slag—"

"Maid."

"—position. Does it make me queen of the Northlands?"

"No."

"Is there a throne?"

"No."

"Shopping trips? A gold carriage? An entire troop of handsome warriors to protect me at all times?"

"That would be 'no' three times in a row."

"Then what is the purpose of a Battle Trollop?"

"Maid. And, basically, you'll get to braid my hair before I fly off into battle."

Keita stared up at him. "You're joking."

"And unbraid it when I return."

"Yes, because after more than a century of being a Protector of the Throne, I so look forward to braiding your hair for the next six or seven centuries."

"I was desperate," he admitted. "My cock was hard, you were wet, and I needed to come up with an excuse that would get you to travel with me. I was almost positive telling you that I love you and want you to meet my mother would not do the job."

"And you would have been right." Instead of running off once faced with the truth, she asked, "But what am I going to do while you're out battling Irons? Besides sitting around looking beautiful and shaming all those pathetic Northland females?"

"Help me destroy those who would betray me and my kin?"

Keita stepped away from him. "You'd willingly put me into danger? Willingly risk my life to further your own gains?"

He shrugged, unable to lie to her. "If it got me what I wanted."

"Gods," Keita said on a shaky breath, moving back into his arms and hugging him tight. "It's like you want me to fuck you right here."

Ragnar held her close. "Well, if you really want your brothers to beat me within an inch of my life . . . *that* would be the way."

Epilogue

It seemed that all of Dark Plains was silent this early morning, the suns barely awake themselves as the Blood Queen came out on the steps, dressed in full battle gear. Her mate, already shifted to dragon and in his battle armor, waited for her with his kin. Their last night together had been far too short, but, by the gods, it had been memorable. And would hopefully help them both get through the time they'd be separated from one another.

She stopped and looked back at her offspring. She crouched down and held her arms open. Her children tore away from their nanny and charged over to their mother, wrapping their arms around her, hugging her tight. She kissed them both and picked them up, handing them back to their keeper.

She leaned in and whispered, "Even a hint of trouble, Ebba—"

"And I'll take all the children and be gone, my Queen. Have no worries."

The Blood Queen stepped back and looked at those she called her sisters. The assassin witch, the scheming warlord. They'd all had their sobbing good-byes nearly an hour ago, in private. They'd have no more here for an audience.

The queen winked at her toddler niece, the little girl waving good-bye to her.

Turning, she went down the steps and met her mate. The Dragon Prince of Dark Plains pressed his head carefully against her, the pair long ago beyond words. She kissed his snout, and walked away from him to her waiting horse. Her eldest niece, now her squire, held out her helm. The queen put it on, tossing off her shoulder the long mane of purple hair that came from the crown of her helm, winking at the Northlander all that hair had once belonged to. He smiled in return and briefly bowed his head in respect. She put her foot in the stirrup and mounted her horse.

Once settled, she took one last glance around. General Brastias would ride to her left, his second in command, Danelin, to her right. Dragon Princess Morfyd had again taken up her role as Battle Mage to Queen Annwyl and waited patiently to leave with the human troops. Her brothers, along with their youngest sister and the three Horde dragons who'd accompanied Princess Keita's return into the Southlands, would be traveling into the north to face their enemies near the Ice Land borders.

Manning the inside and outside of the Garbhán Isle gates and the sides of the Great Hall steps were the Kyvich warrior witches. Their leader bowed her head to the queen, the black tribal tattoos on her face unable to make her look as frighteningly fierce as that one female truly was.

The Blood Queen felt confident that she could do no more to ensure her children's safety while she was gone—except win this war. Losing had never been an option for her during any battle, but there was even more truth to that now. She'd feel no regret, no guilt, no sorrow for what she'd have to do to win.

And Annwyl the Bloody, Queen of Dark Plains, knew that when this was all over, when the last shield had been cleaved, the last commander eviscerated, the last body burned, either her head would be on a spike in the ruling Quintilian Provinces—or the Blood Queen would have truly earned her name and her reputation.

Did you miss the first three books in
G.A. Aiken's fabulous dragon series?
The magic beings with
DRAGON ACTUALLY . . .

DRAGON ACTUALLY

It's not always easy being a female warrior with a nickname like Annwyl the Bloody. Men tend to either cower in fear—a lot—or else salute. It's true that Annwyl has a knack for decapitating legions of her ruthless brother's soldiers without pausing for breath. But just once it would be nice to be able to really talk to a man, the way she can talk to Fearghus the Destroyer.

Too bad that Fearghus is a dragon, of the large, scaly, and deadly type. With him, Annwyl feels safe—a far cry from the feelings aroused by the hard-bodied, arrogant knight Fearghus has arranged to help train her for battle. With her days spent fighting a man who fills her with fierce, heady desire, and her nights spent in the company of a magical creature who could smite a village just by exhaling, Annwyl is sure life couldn't get any stranger. She's wrong . . .

[And just wait until you meet the rest of the family . . .]

ABOUT A DRAGON

For Nolwenn witch Talaith, a bad day begins with being dragged from bed by an angry mob intent on her crispy end and culminates in rescue by—wait for it—a silver-maned dragon. Existence as a hated outcast is nothing new for a woman with such powerful secrets. The dragon, though? A tad unusual. This one has a human form to die for, and knows it. According to dragon law, Talaith is now his property, for pleasure . . . or otherwise. But if Lord Arrogance thinks she's the kind of damsel to acquiesce without a word, he's in for a surprise . . .

Is the woman never silent? Briec the Mighty knew the moment he laid eyes on Talaith that she would be his, but he'd counted on tongue-lashings of an altogether different sort. It's embarrassing, really, that it isn't this outspoken female's Magicks that have the realm's greatest dragon in her thrall. No, Briec has been spellbound by something altogether different—and if he doesn't tread carefully, what he doesn't know about human women could well be the undoing of his entire race . . .

WHAT A DRAGON
SHOULD KNOW

Only for those I love would I traipse into the merciless Northlands to risk life, limb, and my exquisite beauty. But do they appreciate it? Do they say, "Gwenvael the Handsome, you are the best among us—the most loved of all dragons"? No! For centuries my family has refused to acknowledge my magnificence as well as my innate humility. Yet for them, and because I am so chivalrous, I will brave the worst this land has to offer.

So here I stand, waiting to broker an alliance with the one the Northlanders call The Beast. A being so fearful, the greatest warriors will only whisper its name. Yet, I, Gwenvael, will courageously face down this terrifying . . . woman? It turns out The Beast, a.k.a. Dagmar Reinholdt, is a woman—one with steel-gray eyes and a shocking disregard for my good looks. Beneath her plain robes and prim spectacles lies a sensual creature waiting to be unleashed. Who better than a dragon to thaw out that icy demeanor?

And who better than a beast to finally tame a mighty dragon's heart?